THE FIRST DAYS

THE FIRST DAYS

· AS THE WORLD DIES ·

Rhiannon Frater

A TOM DOHERTY ASSOCIATES BOOK · NEW YORK

THE FIRST DAYS: AS THE WORLD DIES

Copyright © 2008, 2011 by Rhiannon Frater

All rights reserved.

A Tor Book
Published by Tom Doherty Associates, LLC
175 Fifth Avenue
New York, NY 10010

www.tor-forge.com

Tor® is a registered trademark of Tom Doherty Associates, LLC.

Library of Congress Cataloging-in-Publication Data

Frater, Rhiannon.
 The first days : as the world dies / Rhiannon Frater.—1st ed.
 p. cm.
 "A Tom Doherty Associates book."
 ISBN 978-0-7653-3126-7
 1. Zombies—Fiction. I. Title.
 PS3606.R4255F57 2011
 813'.6—dc22

 2011011563

First Tor Edition: July 2011

Printed in the United States of America

0 9 8 7 6 5 4 3 2 1

Dedicated to my mother, with much love and affection

ACKNOWLEDGMENTS

Special thanks to Michelle, Connie, and Kody for being the first to take a stab at making this story better than the original.

Eternal thanks to Melissa, my editor, who pushed me even further in making sure it's the best story possible.

Heartfelt thanks and appreciation to Dr. Pus of the Library of the Living Dead Podcast, who spread the word about the original version of this story to the zombie fans.

A special acknowledgment to Corey, my loving husband. Without you, honey, I would have never had the courage to do this.

Somewhere in Texas

· CHAPTER ONE ·

1.
Tiny Fingers

So small.

So very, very small.

The fingers pressed under the front door of her home were so very small. She could not stop staring at those baby fingers straining frantically to reach her as she stood shivering on the porch. The cool morning air lightly puffed out her pink nightgown as her own pale fingers clutched the thin bathrobe closed at her throat. Texas weather could change so fast, and this early March morning was crisp.

I knew we needed weather stripping, she thought vaguely.

The gap under the front door was far too large. These new modern homes looked so fancy, but were actually not very well built. If they had bought the nice Victorian she wanted, there wouldn't be a gap under the front door. A gap large enough for that little hand to slide underneath.

The tiny fingers clawed under the edge of the door.

The banging from inside the house had become a steady staccato. It had a rhythm now, as did the grunts and groans. The sounds terrified her. But what was truly horrible were those tiny, desperate fingers.

Her voice caught in her throat when blood began to trickle out from beneath the door. Of course the blood would eventually flow out. There was so much. It had been everywhere when

she stood in the doorway of Benjamin's bedroom. The walls had been splashed red.

She covered her mouth with her hand. Another wave of chills flowed over her as her knees knocked together.

The rhythm changed to a new beat as a second set of fists banged against the door.

Through the lead glass of the door, she could see the dim outline of her husband's body. It was distorted by the thick smears of blood on the inside of the panes. She stared long enough to make out Lloyd's misshapen hands battering against the glass before her gaze was inexorably drawn down to those tiny fingers scrabbling so frenziedly toward her.

She really should have insisted on Lloyd putting in weather stripping.

An angry howl from the other side of the door made her jump, and her thick raven hair fell into her face. With trembling hands, she pushed back her tresses. Her gaze did not waver from those tiny fingers.

The pool of blood was slowly spreading toward her bare feet.

She should move.

But where?

The tiny fingers were now raw, with tips of bone showing. Yet they still sought her out.

There was a loud *thunk* to her left, and her attention shot over to the window. Mikey stood there, hissing as he beat on the window with clenched fists. His torn lips were drawn back in a grimace as his dead eyes latched on to her hungrily.

"Why, Mikey, why?" Her voice was a plaintive whisper.

Why had her twelve-year-old son rushed back to try to fight his father? Why hadn't he run when she screamed at him to follow her?

Clutching her head, she swayed slightly. She felt something cold touch her toe and looked down to see blood welling around her foot. Stepping back, she returned her focus to the fingers

pressed under the front door. The tips of the tiny fingers were skinless.

"Benjamin, please stop," she whispered.

He always followed her everywhere. Every time she went to the bathroom, the persistent three-year-old would be on her heels. She could never relax and just go. She would have to talk to him as he lay outside the bathroom, one eye pressed against the crack, his tiny, chubby fingers pressed under the door.

Was one eye pressed against the crack under the front door now?

How had he managed to get downstairs? There was so little left of him. Lloyd always was a big eater. . . .

She almost vomitted as both hands flew up to cover her mouth. Gagging, she stepped away from the door. Her body was shaking violently. She heard a clattering sound now, painfully loud. Covering her ears with her hands, she took another step back.

Why wouldn't it just all stop?

The rattling noise was louder and her jaw hurt.

Oh, her teeth were chattering.

She closed her eyes, swaying.

Those tiny fingers . . . those tiny fingers . . .

Glass shattered and growls filled the cool morning air. Her eyes snapped open to see Mikey trying to shove his way through the broken window.

"No, no, no . . ." She stumbled backwards down the front steps and fell when her bare foot slipped on the slick dew-drenched grass.

The glass shards ripped away Mikey's flesh as he scrambled through the window, but the twelve-year-old didn't seem to notice. He kept pushing forward, growling and snarling.

It was then that she screamed. Screamed louder than she ever thought possible. Screamed as she should have when she found Lloyd hunched over Benjamin, eating away her baby's tender flesh. Screamed as she should have when Lloyd pursued her and

Mikey down the stairs. Screamed as she should have when Mikey turned back to try to defend her. Screamed as she should have when the front door slammed behind her and she realized she was alone.

She screamed until her voice died in her throat.

And still Mikey grunted and hissed as he slowly dragged his torn body through the shattered window. Lloyd, blood drenched and crazed, came up behind Mikey and fastened his vicious gaze on her. Determined, he crawled over his son, breaking the remaining glass out of the window frame.

Slowly, she stood. Her gaze strayed to the door.

Tiny fingers still searched for her.

She pressed her hands against her face as she watched Lloyd and Mikey wiggle and jerk their way through the narrow window.

"Get in the truck now!"

She blinked.

"Get in the truck now!"

She turned slowly. An old, battered white truck sat on her perfectly manicured lawn. The engine was hot and grumbling.

Where had it come from?

"In! Now!"

She raised her eyes to see a tall, slim, blond woman in a business suit and hunting jacket standing next to the truck with a shotgun in one hand.

"Get in now!"

Looking back, she saw Mikey slip from the window, wet, bloody, and battered. For a moment, she remembered how he looked when he had just been born. Her shriveled-up little monkey boy.

After struggling to his feet, Mikey leaped forward.

It was time to leave her family. The money she had carefully squirreled away to provide for her and the kids in a new life would have to stay hidden in the closet. The suitcase she had packed for when they finally ran away to the women's shelter would have to remain in its hiding place in the attic.

Lloyd had destroyed what remained of their life together.

It was time to go.

Wrenching the passenger door open, she looked back to see Mikey hurtling toward her. She jumped in and slammed the door shut just as he impacted with the side of the truck. His battered, chewed-up face pressed against the glass as he bared his teeth and his growls ripped at her ears.

"Mikey," she whispered. She pressed her hand against the glass, blocking his gruesome face from her view.

She looked away.

The blond woman slammed her door shut and shifted gears. The truck roared into reverse as Lloyd rushed toward them, hissing loudly.

The blond shifted again and the pickup truck rolled forward and accelerated down the quiet suburban street just as the sun rose over the tops of the houses.

She dared to look back, dared to see what followed. Falling behind were Lloyd and Mikey: her husband and her son. And they were not alone. Others, bloodied and crazed, were racing out of houses, screaming in either terror or hunger.

She tore her gaze away from the things running behind her.

And the tiny fingers she knew were still pressed under the door.

2.

Together

The battered pickup swerved around a corner and nearly side-swiped an SUV that was stopped dead in the middle of the road. Forced to slow down, the driver slammed the flat of her hand against the steering wheel, cursing under her breath.

The blond woman's green eyes glanced into the parked vehicle. She immediately wished she hadn't. A man sat in the driver seat, staring straight ahead. His eyes were wide, unblinking, his mouth moving in words that were too easy to make out.

"Stop, please, stop."

Despite his plea, the female passenger hunched over him, covered in blood and gore, continued to pull ropes of intestine up to her greedy mouth. As the truck passed by, the woman looked up and hissed, slamming her hand against the SUV's windshield.

The driver mashed her foot down on the accelerator, and the truck lurched ahead. She stole a glance at the pale, fragile creature beside her. The woman she had rescued sat silently with one hand pressed against the bloody smear on the passenger-side window.

"Hey," the driver said, reaching over and tapping the stranger's knee. "Hey."

The woman slowly turned her head, and the driver saw that her eyes were glassy and distant.

Great, she was in shock.

"Hey, my name is Katie. I need your help, okay?"

"The man," the woman said in response.

Katie turned her attention to the road just in time to see a man trying to wave them down. He was drenched in blood and sobbing violently. She started to slow the truck, but two small children suddenly leaped onto the man, their baby teeth ripping into his throat.

"Just go," the passenger said in a dead voice. "Just go."

Katie drew in a shivering breath. "Yeah. You're right."

She drove on, leaving the man wailing as blood spurted into the air and the children rode him to the ground. Katie swallowed hard as she forced her gaze from the rearview mirror and concentrated on maneuvering through the suburban hell they were caught in.

The rescued woman drew her pale pink bathrobe tighter around her shivering body and stared straight ahead. Her eyes were as dark as her black hair.

Katie slowed down just a tad to a quick but more reasonable pace. The street they were on appeared to be peaceful. She needed

to get her thoughts together. She forced herself to take several deep breaths. She had to keep calm. She knew that much.

"Listen, I need you to take my cell phone and call the first number in the speed dial. Nine-one-one is not working right now, but hopefully we can get through to the police department. I can't pay attention to driving and call."

She had to swerve again, this time to avoid a pack of rabid humans racing toward them from a side street. Chaos was spreading quickly. The pack tried to pursue the truck for a few seconds, but was drawn off by another car tearing out of a garage in an attempt to escape.

The dark-haired woman nodded as she took the phone from Katie. She flipped it open and stared at the tiny screen. On it was a picture of a lovely woman with short-cropped brown hair and amber eyes.

"She's pretty," the woman whispered.

Katie choked back a sob and fought the hot tears suddenly stinging her eyes. "Yes, she is." She brushed her mouth with her hand and tried not to cry. She couldn't think of Lydia right now. She just couldn't. She had to find her way out of this hellish neighborhood and to safety.

The woman worked easily through the menu and dialed.

Even Katie could hear the busy signal.

"Keep trying, okay?"

"Okay."

Katie drove past a school bus. It was empty and the open door was smeared with blood. The rest of the block looked calm, but she knew it was not. Whatever was happening in the rest of the city was happening here. They had to be very careful. Katie had seen too many horrors this morning to think they could be safe.

"I'm Jenni. With an *I*, not a *Y*. I like it spelled that way," the woman said softly.

Katie smiled despite everything. "Hi, Jenni with an *I*. I'd say I'm happy to meet you, but under the circum—"

"The little boy, that was my son, Mikey. His dad . . . he . . . my husband . . . Lloyd . . . did something to him. To him and Benji . . ."

Katie shuddered slightly at the harsh, brutal memory of seeing Jenni pursued by the ravaged little boy and his blood-splattered father.

"I'm so sorry." It was all Katie could think of to say.

"It's still busy," Jenni said.

"Please, keep trying."

Jenni nodded as she pushed the button again.

Katie spun the steering wheel, and the pickup headed around a corner, barely avoiding two cars. She saw frightened families inside and whispered a silent prayer for them. She was hopelessly lost, not sure how to get out of the neighborhood. She and Lydia lived miles from this new, modern, cookie-cutter suburb. Lydia had designed their custom-built home. It was tucked into a hillside overlooking the lake and the city. It should have been safe there. It should have been, but the terror of this morning had reached even their quiet street.

Her feet were aching in her high heels and she wished she had found shoes in the truck. The old man's hunting coat was comforting, warm, and smelled of fresh tobacco. It reminded her of her grandfather.

How had this happened? What did it mean? One minute, she had been sitting in her brand-new convertible, top down despite the cool morning, enjoying a cup of coffee and readying herself for a long day at her job as a prosecutor. The next, she had been fighting off a man who had reached across the passenger seat, grabbed the jacket of her Ann Taylor suit, and tried to drag her out of the car. She had slipped out of her jacket, grabbed her briefcase, and smashed it into her attacker. She'd struck him so hard, she heard his skull crack.

She'd leaped from the car, ready to fight . . . and then saw that his throat was torn out and that a long train of intestines

trailed behind him. But none of that stopped him from trying to climb over the car to get to her.

To her growing horror, she saw more mutilated people rushing straight for her through the early rush hour traffic that always snarled up the narrow road leading down into the city. She had turned and started to run blindly, past honking cars, vehicles with music so loud, her teeth throbbed, and SUVs packed with children going to school. All of them seemed oblivious of the danger quickly running toward them.

"Hey, missy!"

An old man stood outside his white truck, waving at her, a shotgun clutched in his hand. "Get in my truck! We'll off-road it! Hurry!"

She hadn't needed to look behind her to know she was pursued. She heard the slap of their feet against the pavement.

Katie had almost been to the truck when suddenly the old man was grabbed from behind. A woman bit into his throat and viciously dragged him down to the ground. Katie almost stopped, but the old man had waved her on.

"Get in the truck! Take the gun! Get out of here! Go! Go!" He fought with the woman that had assaulted him, but his blood was already a fountain against the pavement and he faded fast.

Pausing for the barest of moments, she had grabbed the shotgun from his quivering hand and jumped into the pickup on the driver's side. After slamming the door shut, she reached for the ignition, only to realize the engine was already on.

The old man's gurgling voice had shouted, "Go! Go! Go!"

She obeyed: shifted gears and went. In the rearview mirror, as she drove down the shoulder and past the stopped cars that honked at her, she had seen the small pack of mutilated humans reach the old man and dive onto him.

"Don't turn here!"

Kate shook herself out of her memories and slammed on the

brakes. "Shit!" It was a cul-de-sac. She quickly started to turn around when she saw a nightmarish vision. Around fifteen of the *things* erupted into the street and raced toward the pickup, cutting off their escape route.

Her hands tightened on the steering wheel as she quickly pulled the white vehicle around to face their pursuers.

"Just do it," Jenni said softly beside her. "They're not real anymore."

Katie aimed right for the center of the throng, floored the gas pedal, and braced herself. The deer guard caught the first few and flung them away from the vehicle. One skinny teenager bounced onto the hood and clung there, beating at the windshield with one hand.

Katie slammed on the brake. Momentum carried him away, and his hand, barely fastened to his arm by strands of tendon and skin, snapped off, still gripping the edge of the truck's hood.

"Oh, God," she whispered.

"It's okay," Jenni assured her in a distracted tone. "Really."

Katie hit the accelerator and moments later they bumped over the youth's body. Maybe it was just her imagination, but she could have sworn she heard a mushy popping sound as the wheels passed over the *thing*.

"What is happening? What the hell is this?" Katie shook her head, her blond hair falling across her brow.

"The end," Jenni sighed. "It's the end."

3.
As the City Falls

As the white truck hurtled down suburban streets that were quickly falling into bloody bedlam, it was obvious that whatever was happening was spreading at an accelerated pace. Gunshots rang through the morning air. People's screams rose in a

cacophony. Cars careened crazily through the streets. At times, only Katie's quick reflexes saved them from an accident.

Beside her, Jenni hit the Redial button once more. Katie couldn't bear to look at the phone and see Lydia's beautiful face smiling out at her.

If this wasn't the end, it sure looked like it. It had to be terrorists. Some sort of weapon that made people crazy. PCP, something. Katie rubbed her mouth with her fingers. That had to be it.

Since Jenni's proclamation of the end, they had both been silent. It was too much to absorb.

Too much to comprehend.

They just had to keep moving.

They had to keep going.

But where?

If only her dad would answer his cell phone. Of course, he was probably going nuts trying to reach her. She could see him now, in the midst of the chaos, being the strong police chief of legend. Big Bruce was certainly doing his best to get this insanity under control. Tears threatened to fall as she thought of his strong, craggy face under his military buzz cut. It was a soothing thought in this moment.

"I got him!" Jenni exclaimed, switching the phone to speaker.

Suddenly, Bruce's voice filled the truck cab. "Hello? Katie?"

"Daddy!"

"Katie, are you and Lydia okay?"

Katie shook her head and whispered, "No, no. I'm fine, but Lydia, she didn't make it. She . . . Daddy . . . she . . ."

"I'm sorry, Katie-baby. I'm sorry."

She could tell by his voice that he truly was. Despite his misgivings about her lifestyle, he had come to accept and be quite close to Lydia. Though her mother remained blissfully in denial until her death, her father had tried hard to understand. His painful, sometimes embarrassing questions had only shown her how much he was trying. And when he had shown up at her wedding dressed

in his military uniform, beaming and near tears, to walk her down the aisle, she knew that he loved her even if he didn't understand her completely.

Now they shared a moment of silence over the woman Katie had loved.

"I'm sorry, honey," he said again. "But you can't let it affect you right now, understand?"

"Yes, I know. I'm trying to keep a cool head."

"Good girl." A tinge of pride crept into his tone. "Listen, Katie, whatever the hell this is, it's all over the city. You need to get down to the police department. We're barricaded in, and you'll be safe here. We got the National Guard on its way."

"Okay, Daddy. We'll be there as soon as we can."

"Katie, be careful." His voice was rich with emotion.

"I'm armed, Daddy. I have a good vehicle."

"Not that little—"

"No, no. A truck. I'm in a truck."

"How—? Never mind . . ."

Katie continued to drive, trying not to let her emotions overwhelm her. "Daddy, what are they?"

"I don't know. I don't know. The damn Russkies are behind it, I know. We never could trust them. Everyone else is saying terrorists, but I'm telling you, Katie, the Soviet Union never really died."

She couldn't help but laugh a little. He was such a Cold Warrior. She could hear many voices behind him, demanding, questioning. Without a doubt, her dear old dad was at the center of the storm.

"Katie, I gotta go. I love you. Get here as soon as you can. Be careful."

"Okay, Daddy. Okay. Love you."

Jenni snapped the phone shut, the image of Lydia vanishing from view, and smiled weakly.

Katie drew in a deep breath, trying to refocus herself. She needed to get them to safety and not think about what these

things were. Of what her beloved had become. She couldn't think of how she had pulled up to their beautiful home to see Lydia and their neighbors tearing at the mailman. She couldn't think of how Lydia had rushed toward her, not to kiss her and hold her and make the world better, but to kill.

"I know what they are," Jenni informed Katie. She was intently staring at her feet, especially her bloodstained toe.

"Yeah?"

"Zombies."

Katie laughed bitterly; then her voice died away as they crested a hill. Before them lay the city. It was smoldering. From their high position, Katie could see clearly that the city had been overrun. The things were everywhere. Chaos swirled through the streets.

The phone rang.

Katie snatched it from Jenni and pressed it against her ear.

"Katie?"

"Daddy?"

"Katie, don't come here! Don't come here! I just got word in. It's not safe. The National Guard was overrun. Don't come, Katie! Run! Get the hell out of the city! Keep safe, baby, keep safe."

Her father's anguished voice filled her with despair, and she rested her forehead against the steering wheel. "Daddy . . ." Tears brimmed in her eyes as she struggled for words. All she truly wanted in that moment was to feel his arms around her and know that she was safe. Either he hung up or the service went out, for suddenly there was nothing on the line.

Katie looked up as a car sped past, heading for downtown. In a few seconds, only blocks away, it was overrun by a horde of those *things*.

"We need to go now," Jenni's faint, singsong voice said. Katie looked at her and saw that Jenni's eyes were glassy. She thought her own probably looked the same. Katie turned the wheel and they headed back up the road.

"Turn here," Jenni said.

Katie obeyed automatically. Tears streamed down her face.

Jenni pointed again. "Turn here."

Katie sped down a back road that sliced behind the suburbs nestled into the hills.

"This will take us far away from the city," Jenni sighed, then reached down and cleaned her toe with the edge of her bathrobe. "Away from the zombies."

Katie whispered, "There's no such thing."

"Then what are they?" Jenni's voice held a hint of emotion. "Some bum bit Lloyd last night when he was coming home from work. This morning, he ate my baby!" Abruptly, her voice was on the edge of hysteria.

Lydia racing toward her, bloody hands stretched out, her chest torn open . . .

Katie drew in a sharp breath.

"If they're not zombies, what are they?" Jenni's voice was shrill.

Katie grabbed Jenni's cold, clammy hand with her own. "Zombies, okay, Jenni. They are zombies. And you're right: This is the end."

Jenni nodded and rested her head against the passenger seat. "I know. . . ." She closed her eyes and slept.

4.
Into the Hills

Jenni woke to the steady hum of the road. She opened her eyes slowly. Her nightmares released her and she sighed with relief. Her dreams were even worse than this new, horrible reality. In her sleep, she had curled up, resting against the passenger door. Now, raising her head, she saw the dried blood her son had smeared on the window when he tried in vain to reach her.

Not for hugs and kisses, but for far worse.

Beyond the swath of gore, the world was speeding by. Hills,

large and small, were covered in trees decked out in colorful spring blossoms. Time for Easter and Easter baskets. She would fill them with candies and toys, and the kids would scramble around the backyard, looking for colorful eggs.

No, no. That wouldn't happen now.

Lloyd had taken away her kids. Stolen them away. Just as she had known he would. Maybe he had been a zombie when he attacked them, but Jenni knew he had only finished the cycle he began when they'd married. She had been seventeen, and his looks, money, and success had blinded her. He was older and wiser. She hadn't truly loved him, but she had believed that one day, she would. When he spoke of his first failed marriage, she had vowed that she would never let him down. She would be the perfect wife, the perfect companion, and he would never say a negative word about her.

But no matter how hard she tried, she had failed. At first, his weapons were words—fierce lashings of scorn and anger. Then it was the back of his hand and, eventually, his fists. Nothing she had done was enough, though she'd done everything he asked of her.

Toward the end, she knew in her heart that either she would die at his hand or he would kill the children. She should have run away sooner and not waited. But then again, how was she to know he'd turn into a zombie?

"I always fail," she sighed.

"What?"

Jenni directed her gaze slowly to the woman beside her.

The driver of the truck was very pretty, with golden hair that fell just to her shoulders in tousled curls. She had a strong yet feminine face with catlike eyes and a sensuous mouth. Jenni was sure that the driver had been the sort of girl who was homecoming queen, head cheerleader, and student council president all rolled into one. The smart, pretty girl who was actually nice. Jenni felt comforted by this. She understood these girls. They lead; you follow. It was that simple.

Her name was Katie. That was right, Katie.

"I was dreaming," Jenni answered finally.

Katie flicked her gaze toward her for a second, then returned it to the road. "You didn't miss anything. After the last traffic light on the edge of the neighborhood, it was smooth sailing. We're about an hour out of the city."

"No one comes this way anymore. Not since the toll road was built. I like it out here. It's peaceful." Jenni didn't feel so cold anymore. She still felt awfully numb, but it was a pleasant sort of numb.

"I'm not sure where we're going," Katie said after a beat. "I'm just driving."

Jenni looked at the phone resting on Katie's lap. "Did you talk to your dad again?"

Katie shook her head, pressing her lips tightly together. "No. There's no signal." She motioned to the radio. "And that doesn't work."

Jenni nodded, understanding. They were alone, detached from the rest of the world. Since this was how she often felt, it was almost comforting.

Besides, she was sure Katie would figure things out. She looked strong and very capable.

"We'll need gas soon," Katie said. "Know if there are any stations out this way?"

"Yeah, there are. One is coming up soon, about two hills over." Jenni slid her fingers through her hair and sat up. "Maybe those things aren't out here."

"That's what I'm hoping for."

Jenni laughed a little, her voice sounding odd to her ears. "You know, this isn't supposed to happen. The zombocalypse isn't supposed to be real."

Katie exhaled slowly. "Maybe it's some sort of terrorist weapon. Something like that."

"No," Jenni said firmly. "It's zombies."

Katie cast a thoughtful look in her direction. "I agree they look like zombies."

"They are zombies," Jenni stressed again. Katie had to accept this as truth.

The blond woman stared straight ahead as she drove. It took several long seconds before she said, "Zombies, or whatever they are, definitely shouldn't exist in a rational, ordered world. It suddenly feels like we're living in a horror movie."

"A Romero movie," Jenni agreed, then frowned. "They aren't supposed to be so fast. They're supposed to be slow. Very slow." Running down the stairs, trying to evade Lloyd, had been terrifying. There had been no time to think, just run. It was sheer luck that he didn't seem to know how to open the door and had just banged against it.

"Why do you say that?"

"In the original movies, they were slow. Lloyd always watched those movies. I was afraid, but he made me watch." Jenni chewed on her bottom lip. "If the movies are right, we can't let them bite us." She looked over at Katie warily. "You're not bitten, are you?"

Katie looked at her for a long, frightening moment. "No! Are you?"

Jenni sighed, relieved. "No. I'm not."

But she almost had been. Lloyd had almost grabbed her; then Mikey had turned back and yelled, "Leave Mom alone!" She covered her face with one hand. She tried hard not to remember the horrible fear she had felt as she screamed at her son to run and raced out the front door.

How it slammed behind her, she didn't know. Maybe she closed it. Maybe Mikey did. Maybe when Lloyd had grabbed her son, he had shoved it shut. But the front door had slammed, and she had been alone.

"How did you find me?"

"I got lost in your neighborhood, trying to get off the highway.

I heard you screaming, then saw you in your front yard," was Katie's answer.

That easy. That simple. That tiny difference between life and death. Jenni studied her reflection in the smudged side mirror. Her eyes looked too big, too wide. Her face was very pale.

"I think I'm in shock," she decided.

"Aren't we all," Katie responded in a harsh, bitter voice. Her tone softened as she hastily said, "It was hard to see my wife like that. But your children—" She reached out and gripped Jenni's hand tenderly. "—I can't imagine how it feels to lose your children."

Jenni clung to Katie, grateful for the kindness. She really didn't care about Lloyd being dead . . . undead. . . . The children. That was harder. Much harder. They had been so sweet and innocent, and for them to die . . . She didn't want to think about it, and quickly closed off that train of thought.

She wanted to ask Katie about her wife, the beautiful woman in the photo on the phone, but she was afraid to ask. Afraid that Katie might think she was being judgmental and withdraw her comforting hand.

"Shit!" Katie jerked her hand away from Jenni and yanked the steering wheel hard to the left. As she slammed on the brakes, both women were thrust forward, then caught painfully by their seat belts.

A car was idling on the right shoulder of the road. Near it stood a man covered in blood. He looked in their direction in a daze; then it was as if something snapped inside him and he flung out his hands and rushed toward the truck.

Katie quickly shifted gears, and the pickup leaped forward. The man's hand slapped hard against the side of the truck and they could hear his nails scrapping the metal as they escaped.

Jenni whirled around in her seat to look out the back window. The man was running after them, pumping his arms and screeching. "How fast are we going?"

"Thirty," Katie responded. "He's keeping up."

The man howled as his legs suddenly spread askew and he tumbled hard to the pavement.

Katie braked sharply and looked back.

"Why did you stop?"

"I want to see if what I'm thinking is true."

Jenni watched as the man staggered to his feet, looked around, saw the truck, and slowly hobbled toward them. "Now, that is the way they are supposed to be!" Jenni grinned at Katie triumphantly.

"He blew out his knees!" Katie laughed. "I thought that was what happened, but I wanted to make sure. They aren't super-human. They can still be hurt."

They both screamed as a mouth filled with sharp teeth suddenly appeared in the back window.

"Shit!" Jenni screamed.

"Oh, my god! It's a dog," Katie said with relief.

A German shepherd was staring at them, appearing a little dazed.

Katie flung open the door to get a better look at the bed of the truck. A veterinarian's temporary cardboard carrier was strapped with bungee cords to the big silver toolbox under the back window. A corner of the carrier had been chewed open and the young German shepherd stood on wobbly legs before her.

Jenni leaned out the driver's side. "Uh, zombie—"

Katie looked up to see the man still shambling toward them.

Jenni picked up the shotgun from the floor of the truck and handed it to Katie. "Just shoot him in the head. That's how it works in the movies."

Katie blinked at her, then looked at the man. "I can't." She handed the gun back and reached out to the dog. "Come here, puppy, come here."

The dog padded slowly over to her and she lifted his heavy body out of the bed of the pickup. Holding him tightly, she slid him into the cab, then reached back to snag the vet paperwork taped to the carrier.

Meanwhile, Jenni solemnly got out of the truck, released the safety, pumped the shotgun, and waited. The zombified man was moaning, reaching out to her. For a moment, he looked remarkably like Lloyd.

She fired.

The headless corpse hit the pavement.

"What the hell did you just do?" Katie looked utterly shocked.

Jenni shrugged. "We have to kill them."

Katie opened her mouth to say something, then closed it. Silently, she climbed into the cab and shut the door.

Jenni climbed in as well, slipping the safety back on the shotgun.

"We don't kill," Katie said at last in a low voice. She appeared shaken. "We can't kill them."

"You ran over the runners back in town."

"I panicked. I . . ." Katie faltered.

Jenni sighed sadly. She needed Katie to be strong. She needed her to be the strong one. She hadn't minded shooting the zombie, and she would kill them in the future, but Katie needed to lead. Jenni couldn't bear the thought of having to figure everything out.

Katie stroked the dog's fur as she looked at Jenni for a long moment. "We'll talk about this later. We need gas now." Katie read over the vet's paperwork swiftly while she scratched behind the dog's ears. "As for Jack, here—well, we need to keep him up here. Poor baby just had surgery. Good thing he was knocked out during most of our escape." She nuzzled the dog and kissed him.

"Jack?" Jenni smiled. "I like that name." She wrapped her arms around the dog and pulled him onto her lap.

"That's what his vet papers say. Jack Horton. His human daddy was the Reverend Horton. That is the man who saved my life. Jack and the reverend lived out of the city near the lake."

"It's a good name."

Katie smiled slightly. "Okay, gas station next. Gas, food, sup-

plies, and we keep going until we figure out where the hell we are going? Sound good?"

"Yeah," Jenni answered. Snuggling the dog tight, she exhaled with relief.

Katie was back in control.

It would be okay.

· CHAPTER TWO ·

1.

In the Shadow of the Dying World

Katie was pleased when she saw the gas station sign up ahead. The needle on the gas gauge was dipping dangerously under empty. Despite the lack of any zombies on the road, she did not want to get stuck walking anywhere.

Beside her, Jenni was busy lavishing attention on the German shepherd. Katie was having a tough time understanding Jenni. The first time she had seen her, Jenni seemed to be in a daze. Now she appeared more alive, more animated. It was weirder somehow than her trancelike state.

But who was she to judge? What was normal when the world was dissolving around you and reality suddenly looked like a Dalí painting?

Pulling into the gas station, Katie leaned forward over the steering wheel to study the scene before her. There were no cars parked on the concrete apron or beside the gas pumps. The place looked utterly deserted.

"If we're lucky, the pumps are still on. I'll use my credit card," she said.

Jenni looked up, rubbing her lips against the dog's ear. "If there is a gas can in this truck, you should fill it up, too."

"This is Texas, and this is a truck. Of course it has a gas can. And if we can get into the store, we should load up on food."

Katie slowly released the brake and let the pickup glide up to

a pump. Looking around once more, she turned off the engine. She reached down and picked up the shotgun.

"Here is the plan: I'm going to pump the gas. You're going to keep watch and hold the shotgun. You see any of those things, you tell me immediately." Katie handed Jenni the shotgun, studying her intently. Though she looked frail in her pink nightgown and robe and bare feet, now that Jenni wasn't looking like a zombie herself, Katie could see she was quite pretty, with deep, alert eyes.

"Okay. I can do that. But we should leave Jack in the truck. He's still really groggy," Jenni responded.

"Agreed. Now, listen, we don't take any risks. We don't shoot anything unless we have to. That box at your feet—those are the only shotgun shells we have."

"Oh," Jenni said, and frowned. "We need more."

"I know, but a convenience store is not the place to find them. So no fancy shooting, okay?"

"Gotcha," Jenni answered, and slid out of the truck.

After leaping out of the truck herself, Katie quickly slid her small wallet out of her trouser pocket. In this moment, she was so glad she despised purses; otherwise, the wallet would have been far away in her old car. Swiping her credit card, she watched the digital display anxiously.

It flashed AUTHORIZING over and over again.

"You have to come in and swipe it here. That scanner isn't working," said a disembodied young male voice.

Both Katie and Jenni started, and Jenni whirled around, shotgun ready.

"You have to come in and swipe the card," the voice persisted.

Katie realized the speaker on a column next to her was hissing. For a moment, she could not believe what she was hearing. The world was falling apart, Lydia was dead, and some teenager was still working his shift at the gas station?

"I'll be right in," Katie said, and looked at Jenni. "He must not know what's going on."

Jenni just blinked at her.

Mystified, Katie strode speedily across the parking lot and into the convenience store. The dimly lit interior threw off her vision for a moment; then she saw a tall, scraggly-looking teen-age boy and a short Hispanic girl standing behind the counter.

"The reader outside broke and you have to swipe inside," the boy explained again.

"You don't know, do you?" Katie arched an eyebrow, and the gas station attendant looked at her warily. The Hispanic girl gasped and stepped back from the counter.

Katie ducked away from the door before realizing Jenni had come in, holding the shotgun.

"Look, please don't hold us up! We don't have that much money!" The boy held up his hands, his eyes huge.

"We're not holding you up. You really don't know what is going on, do you?" Katie walked swiftly to the counter.

"Uh, no." The boy was trying to look calm and brave, but he was sweating profusely.

The girl, behind him, was holding on to his arm so tight that Katie could see blood pooling under her nails.

"The city has gone insane. It's burning! People are dead and . . . and . . ." Should she tell him that the dead apparently were getting up and eating everyone?

"Zombies. It's zombies," Jenni said.

Katie rolled her eyes and exhaled slowly. "What she said."

"Yeah, right," the boy said sarcastically.

"I don't know if they are really zombies, but there is something going on that has people attacking other people like maniacs," Katie explained.

"Kinda like you two?"

"No. With their bare hands." Katie watched the look of disbelief on the boy's face grow deeper. "Look, swipe my card. We need gas to get the fuck out of here."

The boy frowned. "You're really not good with this robbery stuff, are you? You're not supposed to pay."

"Just swipe the damn card already!" Katie waved it in his face.

"We should get lots of food. And some more gas canisters," Jenni said behind her.

The boy took the card and looked at them with growing unease. "You guys are on the run, aren't you?"

"Yes, like I told you. The city has gone insane—"

"With zombies," Jenni added helpfully.

Katie didn't think the teenage girl could get any paler.

There was a screech of tires outside, and they all turned to see two cars pull up. Both were fully loaded with people. Men with guns leaped out and ran into the store.

"Papa!" The girl looked relieved and ran toward one of the men. A flurry of Spanish followed, and suddenly the girl looked like a ghost. "I'm leaving! My grandma ate my aunt!"

And she was gone, running with her family out to their cars.

Katie looked at the boy, whose mouth was hanging open.

From behind her, Jenni said, "Told you."

"I don't believe you," the boy said in a small voice.

"Then you are going to die," Katie said firmly, and grabbed her card from him.

The day grew warmer as the sun rose steadily over the hills. The breeze brushing back her blond hair was warm and not very soothing. It felt grainy and harsh.

Katie sighed and kept looking around as the pump slowly clunked away, filling up the old truck's tank. Jack sat behind the steering wheel, watching her. She wondered how much he'd seen that morning as he lay in his crate in the back of the truck.

The dog let out a light woof and she got the impression he was telling her, *So far, so good.*

The pump clicked off and she quickly screwed the cap back onto the gas tank.

Inside the convenience store, her new companion was rushing around filling plastic bags while the boy dutifully scanned

every item, charging them to her credit card. Meanwhile, Katie held the shotgun in one hand and kept a keen eye on the terrain around her. Save for a small red hatchback tucked into the hedges next to the gas station, the white truck was the only vehicle around.

In this moment of relative calm, Katie found herself struggling to feel real. The world felt real. The gas station seemed real, with its pumps and store and the teenage boy behind the counter.

But it wasn't real. It couldn't be if zombies walked the earth.

Katie moved across the parking lot, sweeping her gaze back and forth, at times walking backwards, shotgun at the ready, extra shells jiggling in her pocket. Shoving the door open with her elbow, she entered the convenience store.

Jenni paused midstride, and Katie saw that she had found some flip-flops somewhere "Do you want coffee? I didn't get my coffee this morning."

"Yeah. Black."

Jenni nodded and ran to the dispenser.

"Look, if you are not holding me up, you better put that away because my manager will be here soon," the teenager whined.

Katie considered punching the boy.

There were at least ten filled plastic bags of supplies piled near the door. Katie was surprised to see that one of them held dog food. Jenni was thinking of everything.

Jenni rushed up. "Give me the keys. I'm going to back the truck up."

"Okay. Take the shotgun." Katie handed it over and whispered, "I need to go to the ladies' room."

"I already went. Stuff some toilet paper in your jacket pocket. I could only grab half a roll. It's really way too expensive to buy here." Jenni was out the door. She rushed across the parking lot, her bathrobe flowing behind her and the shotgun held firmly in her hands.

Katie looked at the clerk. "Don't you have a radio or a TV somewhere around here?"

"It's against the regulations. Our owner is a man of principles, and he believes that we should not inflict our modern music and bad news on our customers, but greet them with a smile and a friendly conversation."

"You had to memorize that, huh?"

The boy blinked blankly. "Yeah. Look, lady, zombies don't exist. I think you're criminals on the run. And Lucy is always flaking and running away from work. I'm not going to leave my shift and get fired."

Katie shook her head with exasperation, her hands resting on her hips. "You're going to end up dead if you keep acting like a good little drone. The world is over. Finished. It's all different now. You better stop following and start acting." With that, she escaped into the bathroom.

After a few minutes, she washed her hands in lukewarm water and gazed at her face in the spotted and scuffed mirror. The lighting did her no favors. She looked washed out and drawn, older and tired. Just about how she felt, now that she thought about it. Reaching for the door, she heard raised voices and felt her body quiver anxiously. Her stomach fluttered and she hesitated.

What if those things were outside and all she had were two pockets full of toilet paper and damp hands to defend herself?

She realized the voices were arguing, not screaming, and heaved open the door.

A man in an expensive silk suit, minus the coat and plus a coffee stain on his shirt and tie, was standing at the front of the store, shouting at Jenni. She stood quietly, head down. Katie saw that the shotgun was hidden in the folds of Jenni's bathrobe.

". . . and I don't need a mental case ruining my morning. I have a very important meeting at eleven A.M. in the city, and I don't need to deal with retarded country hicks."

"Is there a problem here?" Katie strode up to the man, hands on her hips, head tilted to one side, and gave him her most direct look.

The man was in his early to mid-thirties, dark hair, blue eyes, clean shaven in that almost too clean look. He was holding his phone in one hand and a cup of coffee in the other.

"Yes, I can barely get into the store because of some hick truck pulled up to the door. I get inside and this retard spills coffee on me, and now I have a blond bitch giving me lip."

Katie motioned to his phone. "Does that work?"

He blinked, obviously not expecting that response. "No, because we are in Hicksville and there is no signal."

Katie slightly nodded. "Or the world has gone to hell and the city is in ruins. Doesn't anyone listen to their radio anymore?"

"Look, bitch, I make six figures. I don't have time for radio or TV. I work constantly. My time is money. I am money. I have a meeting in one hour in the city, and I'm running late thanks to your stupid friend here and that damn truck."

"Well, buddy, hate to tell you this, but the world is over. The city is in ruins and you aren't going to make that meeting and you're not going to get a signal. Your six figures means nothing now."

The businessman moved forward and towered over her, clearly trying to intimidate her.

Katie looked up at him, her eyes cool, her jaw set.

"I don't deal with crazy people. And no one talks to me like that," he hissed.

"She does." There was an audible *cha-chung!* as Jenni raised the shotgun and cocked it. Her eyes were dangerous.

The businessman stumbled backwards. "You people are crazy."

"If you go into the city, you're the crazy one. You'll die. Something has gone wrong. People have gone insane and are killing each other. We barely escaped."

The man shook his head at Katie's words and backed up to

the door. His eyes were wide and unbelieving. "You're crazy, psycho redneck bitches!"

Katie looked at Jenni, and they both started laughing.

That was enough. The businessman darted out, narrowly avoiding the back of the pickup, and ran to his Mercedes. Katie noticed he held on to his coffee, and that made her laugh all the more.

"You really need to put that gun away or I will call the police!" The teenager finished bagging the latest batch of food and supplies and slid it across the counter.

Katie arched an eyebrow. "Will you, really?"

The boy ducked his head and mumbled.

"Thought so."

She grabbed several bags and headed out the door. They needed to load up the truck and leave as soon as possible. She felt too exposed and too vulnerable. Jack gazed at her solemnly through the back window and let out a tiny woof.

"We're hurrying," she assured him.

Jenni slung some bags into the truck bed and ran back into the store. Katie followed and grabbed more bags. A few more trips and their stockpile looked pretty healthy. Jenni huffed past her, lugging several gallons of water, and Katie walked back into the store as her gaze flicked briefly toward the road.

Still empty.

"You need to sign your receipt."

Would he never stop being annoying? Katie walked over and signed the receipt. It had to be at least three feet long.

"I will never pay this. The bill will never arrive. You need to understand this," she said firmly. "I'm trying to save your life."

"Look, I just want you to leave before my manager gets here, okay?"

There was a loud squealing noise outside, and Jack began to bark fiercely. Katie whirled around to see a car nearly clip the truck and slam into the side of the building. The walls shuddered, and the glass windows cracked.

From the steaming wreckage, a young woman wearing the same color smock as the irritating cashier stumbled out, gripping an older man about the waist. He was barely on his feet, and it took all her strength to carry him. He was covered in blood.

"Mr. Carver! Rachel!" The boy ran past Katie and out the door to meet them.

Jenni looked at Katie, and their eyes met. Jack's barking was frantic.

The women dashed for the truck.

Behind them there was a scream of agonizing pain; then the boy shouted, "Mr. Carver! Mr. Carver! Get off her!"

Katie slammed her door shut and started the engine. Jenni was still standing outside the truck, watching, transfixed as Mr. Carver took another large bite out of Rachel's spurting throat.

"Run!" Katie shouted at the boy as loud as she could, hoping he could hear her over the dog's barking.

The boy finally listened to her and ran for his car, fumbling in his pocket, probably trying to find his keys.

Mr. Carver now had Rachel down on the ground and was biting at her savagely as her body convulsed.

Jenni slid into the cab, shut the door, locked it, and looked at Katie. "We need to go now."

Katie shifted gears and drove. She glanced into the rearview mirror to see a bloodied, resurrected Rachel and Mr. Carver pursuing the boy, whose name tag she had never noticed. Apparently unable to get into his car, he was running away from the gas station, into the valley behind the building.

"You did tell him," Jenni said as Katie turned onto the highway.

"Yeah, I did."

"Coffee?" Jenni motioned to the cup holder fastened to the dashboard. Two cups of steaming coffee sat there.

"Yeah, sounds good."

They drove on.

2.
A Taste of the Dead World

Sometimes the world changes and you don't even notice. One day slips into the next, and the world subtly transforms around you. A new building goes up. A tree is cut down. Your neighbors move out. The potholes in your street are repaired. A newly elected official takes office. You gain five pounds. Your friend loses ten.

And then there are stark changes that upturn your world and leave you in shock, breathless, and lost.

Like hearing chewing noises and your baby screaming.

Or how at eight thirty this morning, you didn't even know your traveling companion and now, at nearly eleven, you're both eating beef jerky and doughnuts with a stiff chaser of cold coffee.

"I think if we keep to back roads, we'll be safer," Katie said to Jenni.

Jenni peered down at the battered map she had found in the glove compartment. "Okay, I think I can figure it out." She felt good when Katie made choices. It gave her a role to play again. Mother and wife were gone, but she could be Katie's helper.

Katie sat in the driver's seat, one arm propped on the edge of the door and her head resting on her hand. The dog they had discovered in the back of the truck slept halfway on her lap. Jenni could tell that Katie was struggling not to let her emotions get the best of her. A few times, Katie had touched the cell phone beside her and Jenni could see the internal struggle not to flip the phone open to look at the photo.

Jenni sighed. She didn't even have photos. She had nothing. Nothing at all.

Except for Katie, the dog, the truck, and the winding road.

Since leaving the gas station, they'd seen a few other vehicles,

usually speeding toward the city, the panicked people inside barely glancing at them as they flashed by. In one small town, they had seen no signs of life at all. At one point, they saw a farmhouse on a hill, being boarded up by distant figures.

They felt very alone.

"We can't drive forever. We'll have to stop eventually and get more gas. More supplies." Katie sighed.

Jenni pursed her lips and carefully ran her finger along the lines on the map. Slowly, her eyes strayed up to the state park. She shivered slightly, her head swimming. . . .

How could she be such a bad mother?

Jason, her stepson, was up there, camping out with the rest of his freshman high school class. Far away from the city, from his dead father and half brothers . . .

How could she have forgotten him?

Tiny fingers straining under the front door rose menacingly in her mind and she felt herself shudder. Her stomach coiled and she reached out to brace herself against the dashboard.

"Hey, are you okay?" Katie's gentle hand stroked her hair. "Jenni?"

Jenni looked up at her, shaken. "I . . . uh . . . forgot my son."

Katie flicked her gaze toward Jenni, then back at the road. "No, hon, we couldn't bring him . . . he . . ." Her voice faltered.

Jenni shook her head. "No, not Mikey . . . not him. Jason. My stepson . . . I forgot about him until just now . . . how could I . . . I'm . . ."

Her zombified husband was right. She was a bad mother. Incompetent. Stupid.

Katie continued to stroke her hair while trying to keep her eyes on the winding road. "It's okay. It's okay. This whole day is fucked up."

Jenni felt tears rolling down her cheeks. "I just . . . forgot him. He just came to live with us last year. But I shouldn't have forgotten him."

Katie slowly pulled over, drew Jenni into her arms, and gave her a firm hug. "It's okay. Calm down . . . shhh . . . shhh . . ."

Jenni clung to her and whispered, "I try so hard."

"It's okay. It's okay. Maybe he got out of the house," Katie said softly.

"He wasn't in the house! He's here! Here!" Jenni thrust the map at Katie, one finger jabbing at the state park. "He's here! Safe. The zombies can't be out there! He's safe and he needs me and I forgot about him!"

"Okay, okay. Jenni, listen to me. Listen to me," Katie said firmly.

The dog whined a little and licked Jenni's face, trying to soothe her.

Jenni tried to concentrate on Katie's face and voice. It was so hard. All she could hear was her husband's voice berating her for being such a stupid whore and a terrible mother.

"This day and everything about it is awful. We're both in shock. We're both scared out of our minds. We're not thinking straight and that's okay. We just need to survive right now. We need to make it through today and be safe. If we can do that, we can get our heads together and start to figure out exactly what we are going to do. But for now, we live in this moment and make our way to the next."

Jenni sniffled and nodded. "What about Jason? I can't leave him there."

That would be her last great failure. He was all that remained. Maybe he wasn't her son by blood, but she was obligated to take care of him and love him.

Katie looked at the map for a long moment. "I think we can go get him. Maybe even stay there if it's clear of the infestation. Honestly, we need to stay away from any area with too many people. A lot of people will not know what is going on, and that will endanger us." Katie faltered for a moment. "Hell, I don't know what is going on."

"Zombies," Jenni reminded her helpfully.

"Okay, zombies, but why? How? If your movies are right and the bite is how it spreads, then keeping away from major populated areas is our best bet. Less chance of infection. So going and finding your stepson and seeing what the situation is out at the park may be our best option for now."

Jenni threw her arms around Katie and hugged her tight. "Thank you, thank you. I have to make it up to him!"

She had to let Jason know that she loved him and that she would be a good mother to him. She would learn to do better and be better. That was all there was to it.

Katie drew back, squeezed her hand tightly, and gave her a tender smile. "We'll be okay. It will be okay. We just need to keep it together. Okay?"

Jenni nodded, reassured. Katie was right. They had to keep it together. And survive. And go get Jason. She wrapped her arms around the dog, and he nestled against her body.

Katie shifted gears, and the white truck started down the road once more. "Jenni, I know you're scared. I am, too, but right now, we can't fall apart, okay? When we find a safe place, we can both mourn." Katie reached out to pat her hand, gracing her with another smile.

Jenni took a deep breath and nodded. "I can be strong until we're all safe."

"Good." Katie returned her gaze to the road.

Jenni shuffled the dog and the map and settled down once more. She had a job to do, and she had to do it well. It was obvious to her now that Katie had been sent to her. Katie was strong and she was going to get them through. It would be okay.

"What the hell?" Katie murmured.

As the truck slowed, Jenni saw a convoy of army vehicles heading their way. The first few trucks went past; then a jeep pulled to the side, and a soldier in the passenger seat waved for the white pickup to stop.

Jenni felt a flutter of excitement. Maybe this was how they would find safety. The army would take them to a place free of

the zombies. The men looked strong and capable with their large weapons and thick armor. They could rescue Jason.

A tall black man walked toward the truck and motioned to them to get out. Two other men leaped out the back of the jeep and followed him.

Katie didn't look very happy as she turned to Jack. "Stay down, boy. Don't bark. Be calm. Lie down on the floor."

The dog tilted his head, and his gaze followed her motions to the floor of the cab. Obediently, he got down.

"If they're anything like cops, they'll shoot him if they feel threatened," Katie said.

"They wouldn't!" Jenni was shocked.

"Just answer them truthfully and calmly. This is a different world, Jenni. We don't know how it works yet."

Jenni felt a pang of fear as she got out of the truck.

Katie stood next to the cab, as relaxed as possible as the very tall, broad-shouldered soldier approached. At his gesture, Jenni joined Katie and they stood side by side, a former prosecutor in her suit, high heels, and a hunting jacket and a housewife in flip-flops, nightgown, and bathrobe.

"Are you two together?" His voice was deep and strong and had a soothing quality about it.

Jenni bobbed her head as Katie answered, "Yes."

"Did you come from the city?"

"Yes," they chorused.

"Either one of you bit?"

"No," Katie answered, and Jenni nervously whispered, "No."

Without warning, he began to run his hands over their limbs, squeezing to see their response.

Jenni started to protest, but Katie gave her a look that silenced her. The man's hands skimmed over her sides and down over her limbs, searching for wounds. She could see sweat glistening in his dark hair and beading on his neck. Dirt and dried blood stained his uniform. His hazel eyes were bloodshot and weary. Despite the discomfort of his search, she unexpectedly

felt sorry for him. He had been fighting the zombies and understood that the world was dying, which probably meant if he found a bite on either one of them, he would take dire measures.

Jenni was all too aware of the two soldiers standing nearby, guns ready. *They'll shoot us if we are bitten*, she thought.

She endured the rough, large hands on her body until he finished his search.

"No sign of wounds!" the soldier called out. The other armed men visibly relaxed.

"Head to the town of Madison. There's a FEMA rescue center there. It'll be secure." He looked into the cab to see Jack staring at him intently from the driver's seat. With a small smile, he reached in and patted the dog's head.

Katie made a show of looking at his name badge, then said, "Yes, Lieutenant Reynolds."

He dipped his chin to them briefly and walked back to his vehicle. The other soldiers were already inside.

As the jeep sped past them to rejoin the convoy, Katie sighed. "They're heading into the city," she murmured.

"Are we going to Madison?"

Katie shook her head. "No. I think we're better off on our own."

Jenni silently agreed, her black hair whipping around her face. The wind was blowing hot and fierce.

Katie stood with her hands on her hips and shook her head still. "Yeah. We're better off depending on ourselves. We're heading out to get your stepson. Then we'll figure out what's next. I don't like the idea of us being all herded into one spot with only FEMA to protect us. We need to find more ammo and another gun."

"Yeah, I agree. It's up to us to save Jason." It was clear that the soldiers had more on their minds than rescuing people from the zombies. They had many more battles to fight. It would be up to Katie and her to save Jason and make it to safety.

Once back in the truck, they started down the road again.

They had a plan now, and Jenni felt comforted. The world seemed a little more bearable now.

A few miles down the road, they saw two vehicles pulled over onto the shoulder. Bodies, young and old, were strewn about both cars, riddled by bullets. A few had obviously run for it, but hadn't made it to safety. As the white pickup passed, Jenni recognized the girl from the convenience store, still in her gas station smock. Half her head had been blown away.

Katie didn't say a word as she turned onto an even narrower back road.

"I guess," Jenni said after a moment, "one of them was bitten."

· CHAPTER THREE ·

1.
The Truth of Things Yet to Come

Katie was tired of the sun blazing through the windshield and the steady hum of the road. It was nearly one o'clock in the afternoon, and they had been slowly winding deeper into the Texas wilds. Some of the roads were so narrow that two cars passing would have to hug the shoulder and slow down considerably. The thick line of juniper trees hugging the road made the drive claustrophobic. Herds of cows, peach groves, and empty fields were all they saw for miles. Occasionally, there was a house in the distance, and as they sped along, the women observed families working diligently to reinforce their homes. Out in the country, people were apparently barricading themselves in as the heavily populated cities probably went to hell.

"What do you think is going on?" Jenni's voice sounded raw.

To save gas, they had finally turned off the air conditioner and opened the windows. Warm air blew through the cab, and dust caught in their noses and throats.

"Where?" Katie asked.

"Out there? Austin, Houston, Fort Worth . . ."

"It was spreading so fast . . . Maybe the army can get a handle on it, I don't know. Yesterday, there was a commuter plane crash in Chicago that they were blaming on someone going crazy and attacking the pilots. There was a race riot in Philadelphia. But now I have to wonder."

"I didn't see the news. The kids were watching Disney movies when Lloyd got back. Some bum bit him on the hand when Lloyd rolled down the window to give him some coins." Jenni laughed. "He was such an asshole to his family, but always generous to everyone else."

"He used to hurt you, didn't he?" Katie spoke gently, but she knew her words would sting.

"Better me than the boys," Jenni admitted. "Did you see the news this morning? Was it bad?"

"Lydia and I had a strict policy of keeping our mornings as peaceful as possible. It made the rest of the day easier if we could relax, drink coffee, have breakfast, watch the sun come up. . . ." Katie faltered as the tranquil memories of the morning came back to her.

Lydia had been wearing a long, dark dress with stylish ethnic jewelry around her neck and wrists. Her short, spunky hairdo looked retro and cute. It had been a lovely morning. Katie could still remember how cool and soft Lydia's hand had been in hers when they kissed one last time before the world fell into chaos.

Jenni's hand on her wrist brought her out of her reverie and she could feel tears on her cheeks. "Maybe if we had paid attention to the news," Katie said with a slight sob in her voice.

"There is a lot of bad stuff in the world. Sometimes it's just better to shut it out."

Katie tried to pull herself together. She had to concentrate on the here and now and get them to a safe place. Where that was, she wasn't sure, but they had to keep moving.

As the truck sped around a curve in the road, an old station wagon came into view. A middle-aged man, wiry and sunburned, stood next to it, waving desperately. Katie automatically slowed down, and Jenni gripped her arm.

"Maybe we shouldn't stop," Jenni said fearfully.

Katie deliberated her words, then shook her head. "If we can save someone, we should." She stopped the truck and listened to the hot engine tick and rumble.

The man walked briskly over and gripped the edge of the window frame with unsteady hands. "Good thing you gals came along. My wife isn't doing so good. We broke down about two hours ago."

"What's wrong with your wife?" Katie asked, though she suspected the answer.

"Got some crazy shit going down on the highway. People grabbing other people out of cars and doing all sorts of just—" He shook his head. "I can't even explain it. It was just insane. Wife had her window down, and some little kid bit her arm. I didn't think it was that bad, but she's not doing too well right now. I was heading back home, avoiding the highway, when we broke down. I think she needs a doctor."

Katie exhaled sympathetically. The man had a very earnest face and kind eyes. His skin was weathered from the Texan sun, and beads of sweat trailed down his long nose. For an instant, she just wanted to hug him and comfort him. He didn't understand. Not yet.

The passenger door creaked open, and Jenni slipped out. Jack started to follow, but she shut the door on him and he woofed at her.

"Lady, we need your help bad," the man said, obviously unnerved by Katie's silence.

"There isn't any help for her," Katie said finally. "Anyone bit is . . . doomed."

"What the hell are you talking about?"

"You know how people were attacking each other on the highway? It's that way in the city, too. People get bit, then they get sick and attack other people." She wasn't sure how he would take to the zombie theory.

A flutter of pink caught her eye. Jenni was staring into the station wagon. As Katie watched, Jenni took a step back, looked at Katie, and shook her head sadly. The warm Texas wind blew hard against the truck, rocking it, and sent bits of dry grass and leaves spinning across the road as Jenni hurried back.

The man was silent for a long time. He was obviously thinking hard. "Then we gotta get her to the hospital before it's too late."

"She's almost gone," Jenni said as she stepped up next to the man. "She's real bad, Katie. I think maybe we should . . ." She motioned toward the shotgun.

"Mister, I know you love your wife. Trust me, I know how you feel, but you need to come with us and leave her. She's not going to be the woman you love in just a short while," Katie explained. Impulsively, she laid her hand over his. "Please, come with us."

Jack let out a sharp bark followed by a growl.

All three humans turned toward the station wagon. A woman with long blond hair was struggling out the open passenger window. Her gray skin and opaque eyes said it all. She was dead and hungry.

"Shit!" Jenni and Katie both hollered .

"Honey?"

"Get in the truck!" Katie flung her door open, and Jenni crawled in over her. The man hesitated as his wife hit the road hard, landing on her face.

"Please, get in the truck!" Katie screamed at him.

He looked at her in confusion, then back at his wife, who was struggling to get to her feet. "Lady, you're both fucking nuts," he decided, and headed toward his wife.

Katie slammed the door shut. "Shit!"

"Run her over," Jenni ordered. "Just flatten her ass and save him."

The man was moving toward his newly zombified wife. She was obviously disoriented by her fall to the ground and was staring off in the opposite direction. He called her name and she whirled around, snarling.

"Stupid," Jenni hissed.

Katie reversed slightly, shifted gears, and floored the truck. "He loves her," she answered.

The zombie ran at her husband, her face an ugly, twisted version of its former self. Katie swerved around the man and rammed the truck into the female zombie, sending her flying. The creature tumbled wildly, limbs flailing. Katie shoved her foot down on the brake, and both women stared at the fallen woman through the windshield.

Jack gave a sharp little bark.

"You fucking bitches!" The man slammed his fist into the side of the truck bed and scrambled toward the door on the driver's side.

Katie ducked away as he tried to grab her through the open window. Jack jumped on top of Katie's back, barking fiercely at the man.

"You killed her! You killed her!"

Katie was trying to get out from under the dog, when Jenni climbed over her and shrieked, "She's already dead! She's dead, and you need to get in the truck before she eats your ass!"

"You're crazy! You killed her! You killed her!" The sobbing man lashed out, trying to grab hold of Jenni.

Jenni shoved the man away from the window. "Get off me!"

The man and Jenni screamed at each other as Katie let her foot up off the brake and tapped the accelerator. The truck rushed forward and Jenni fell back into her seat with a grunt. Katie braked again, grabbed the steering wheel, and pulled herself up. Jack scooted back, but kept barking.

"She's up!" Jenni yelled .

Shoving her blond curls out of her face, Katie looked down the road at the undead creature crawling slowly toward them. Its torn body struggled to move, and the expression on its battered face was inhuman.

"Honey, honey!" The man ran toward the zombie.

"Fuck," Katie groaned in resignation.

"Run the bitch over and let him live," Jenni said.

"He won't come with us if I do that," Katie countered.

"Save his damn life and then let him find his own way," Jenni replied.

The man was getting closer to the zombified woman.

"Katie, do it."

With a weary sigh, Katie shifted gears, and the pickup rumbled as it surged forward. As they passed the heartbroken husband, he realized what they were doing and threw himself at the truck. He missed, falling to the pavement. Jack growled at the crawling zombie just before the truck's front left wheel rolled over it. When they bumped over the woman's body, the horrified howl of the man they were trying to save filled the air.

Jenni leaned out her window and screamed at him, "She would have eaten you!"

Katie continued driving, not looking back. Jenni fell backward into the cab and stared ahead while the dog twisted around to look out the window. Katie tried hard not to look into the mirrors. It was difficult enough hearing the man screaming in agony over the decimated body of his former wife.

"We were just trying to help," Jenni muttered, sulking.

"I know," Katie answered, and ran her fingers through her hair slowly. She massaged the tender knots on the top of her head with her fingertips and tried to relax. Her whole body was tense and painful. She had just run over a woman and reduced her to road kill. And yet, she had no regrets. In this new world, violence was the way to redemption.

If only she could have released Lydia . . .

Jenni looked grumpy as she propped her feet up on the dashboard. "He could have listened to us. We could have helped him."

"Not everyone understands what is going on," Katie said after a beat. "I'm still adapting."

Sighing, Jenni pulled the dog close to her.

2.
Keep Moving Until You Stop

Keep moving, Katie. Keep moving, her father's voice whispered in her mind.

Had he really said those words?

She sighed and shifted in her seat. The air-conditioning was blowing full blast, making it nice and cool in the cab despite the sun blazing through the windshield. It was too hot to drive without running it anymore, despite the drain on the gas tank. Damn erratic weather had it cold in the mornings, roasting by noon, and cool in the evenings. Right now, it was at full broil. Four o'clock in the afternoon was the hottest part of the day.

They had stopped for a short time to take a bathroom break and eat some of the food they had gathered at the gas station. Jack seemed to enjoy watering all the trees nearby while Jenni kept a close watch on him. Their four-legged companion showed no interest in darting away and kept close to the truck.

Now Jack and Jenni had dozed off, Jenni curled up under the hunting jacket with the young German shepherd, no more than an overgrown puppy, beside her. Jenni's head slightly rested on Katie's thigh, and her black hair fell around her pale face. She and the dog were both snoring.

The sound soothed Katie's nerves for some strange reason.

She had finally kicked off her shoes. Her sleeveless silk tank and navy blue trousers seemed brutally out of place in her new existence. She would need to find better clothes soon. Where, was the question. For miles, she'd seen nothing more than farmland and forest and occasionally a house set back from the road.

Once they'd passed a farm where workers were patrolling the grounds with guns. One of them had waved at them, perhaps asking them to slow down, but Katie's gut clenched at a glimpse of one man's heavily bandaged arm, and they sped by.

They weren't the only paranoid ones. They had to go around a very small town that had set up roadblocks guarded by armed men. A huge makeshift sign had read NO OUT OF TOWNERS ALLOWED. It made sense. There was no assurance that the city folk weren't bringing the infection with them.

Ahead of the truck were more hills and more trees. It felt peaceful and surreal. Usually at this time of the day, Katie was either in court or buried under stacks of paperwork. Lunch— usually takeout—would be long gone, and she and Lydia would be texting back and forth as the day went on.

Instead . . .

She looked down at Jenni and sighed.

Jenni unnerved her. Jenni was a battered wife—the faint bruising on her legs and one arm confirmed it. And as Lydia had often pointed out, Katie wanted to save the world and everyone in it. Already Katie felt very protective toward Jenni. She would do everything she could to take care of her.

That thought gave her the will to move on and not give in to despair.

Above the trees, an enormous billboard suddenly rose up.

TOOMBS HUNTING STORE—STOP BEFORE YOU SHOOT!

Katie laughed. Country people were one of a kind. She reached down and gently stroked Jenni's hair. Exhaustion was pulling on her eyes and limbs. She longed for a nap, but she couldn't let herself rest until they found a safe place for the night. The heat was making her drowsy, and she didn't blame Jenni for catching some sleep. The stress of the day had been overwhelming at times, and she had a feeling this was Jenni's way of coping. Checking out into the world of dreams seemed like a great way to escape the present chaos of reality.

"We're gonna be okay," she promised the sleeping woman.

The truck crested a hill. Below was a town of sorts—six buildings lined the road, four on the left, two on the right. Behind the buildings were fields and trees and a smattering of houses and trailers.

A huge sign stood on top of the two-story building on the right.

TOOMBS HUNTING STORE—GUNS, SUPPLIES, LICENSES AND MORE! STOP BEFORE YOU SHOOT!

"Wonder if they have a zombie hunting license?" Katie murmured as she slowly drove into the town.

The hunting store looked to be at least 150 years old, with thick stone walls and heavy iron bars over the windows. Framed by a pair of painted deer antlers, TOOMBS was painted in yellow letters across the big iron front door. The building looked like an old-time jail.

Letting the truck idle in the middle of the street, Katie looked around before returning her gaze to the hunting store. The town was eerily quiet and devoid of any visible people. Unexpectedly, a shot rang out. Katie jumped in her seat. Jenni woke with a scream while Jack sprang to his feet and started barking.

Katie had been so startled by the gunshot that for a second she wasn't sure what was going on. Then she saw a small child lying on the ground right beside the truck, a neat hole blown through its head. Its torso and right arm were a mangled mess, the flesh ripped from the bones.

"Shit," she said.

"Are you bit?" A male voice rang out through what sounded like a bullhorn.

White-faced, Jenni held tightly to the growling dog.

Katie leaned over and rolled down the passenger-side window low enough to yell, "We're not bit! We're looking for some help! Some guns! Supplies!"

"Get out of the car slowly and show us," the voice responded.

"Don't!" Jenni grabbed Katie's arm. "They might hurt you."

"They shot the zombie. I think they're okay."

Jenni's hand shook as she withdrew it. She looked at Katie fearfully.

"It's okay," Katie said again. She whispered to Jack, "Stay," and slipped out of the truck.

Holding out her bare arms, shotgun in one hand, she slowly turned around. She caught a flash of color and looked up to see two elderly people on top of the gun shop. The man was holding the bullhorn; the woman had the gun.

"And the other one."

"Jenni, get out. Leave the dog inside," Katie said firmly.

An apprehensive expression on her face, Jenni slowly slid out of the truck and took off her bathrobe. Her arms were bruised, but it was clear she had no blood on her.

The elderly couple consulted each other, and the old man disappeared from view.

"You better get back in the truck until he unlocks the door," the old woman said through the bullhorn, her voice tinged with an accent. Then she set it down and picked up a rifle.

Both refugees climbed back into the truck. Katie pulled the pickup as close as she could to the shop.

"They could hurt us," Jenni said softly.

"They would have already if they wanted to," Katie answered truthfully.

Two more shots rang out, and Katie looked over in time to see two people fall dead just outside an old-fashioned grocery store. There were more zombies trapped inside, jostling about as they tried to get to the tasty morsels on the street. Most of the undead were pressed up against the windows, clawing at the glass. The two dead ones had stumbled through the rotating door to their doom.

The big metal door to the hunting store opened, revealing an old man with thinning silver hair, dressed in jeans and a plaid shirt. Turning off the truck, grabbing the keys, and snagging Jack's collar all in one deft movement, Katie exited the cab and hurried into the shop. Jenni followed, looking flushed.

"Name's Ralph. Wife is up top. Her name is Nerit," he said as he bolted the door behind them. He was a slight man with keen blue eyes.

"I'm Katie, this is Jenni, the dog is Jack," Katie said.

"Nice to meet ya," Ralph said. He petted Jack, who gave him a big goofy doggy grin.

"Thanks for letting us in. We're pretty desperate for more weapons. We didn't have much ammunition to begin with," Katie explained.

"Got plenty here," Ralph said, and motioned about the shop.

"I can pay," Katie offered.

"Money means nothing now, missy. We'll do business later. Come meet the missus and relax. We're safe in here."

Looking around, Katie saw rack upon rack of rifles and cases full of guns. The back of the store was full of all sorts of camping gear.

Ralph started up the stairs. Realizing they were staying awhile, Katie followed. Her hand gripped her weapon a little less securely as she felt the tension in her body ease. Jenni slipped her hand into Katie's as they climbed.

"Are you sure this is okay?" Jenni asked.

Katie cast a reassuring smile over her shoulder. "About as okay as anything is going to be today."

When they came out onto the roof, the absolute beauty of the hills around them struck Katie. Endless, rolling green hills, lush and beautiful spread out around them.

A thin woman with long, yellowish white hair stood near the edge of the roof, rifle in hand. Nearby were a large tent, some chairs, and a small table. The older woman leaned over the table and crossed out three items on a list written on a notepad.

"That's the rest of the Greens," she informed her husband.

Katie gradually grasped that the scenery was dotted with dead bodies: fallen halfway into bushes, next to cars, and in the doorways of nearby houses.

"Out-of-towner came here, bitten. Went into the store. Now they're all dead. Some got out and went home. Infected their families. Got seventy in the town. We've shot twenty dead. Not accounting for tourists," the old man informed them, hands tucked into his pants.

"You're both okay, though," Katie said.

"Yeah. Store's closed today. It's my birthday." Ralph shrugged.

Nerit smiled at her spouse before narrowing her eyes at something down the road and raising her rifle. She shot, turned, and crossed off another item—and Katie realized the list was made up of the names of everyone in town.

"Last of the Millers," Nerit said in a rich accent.

"Nerit is from Israel. She was a sniper in the Israeli army. Married her two years ago. Glad I did. Dead-on shot."

Nerit gave Ralph a slight smile. "That better not be the only reason you're glad you married me, old man."

Ralph chuckled. "One of many reasons, honey."

Katie laughed and looked at Jenni. She was glad to see the other woman was actually smiling. Jack sauntered over to an old hunting dog lying nearby.

"That's Tucker. He won't mind the pup. He's too old." Ralph shook his head sadly. "Damn shame to happen on my birthday. Damn zombies."

"Car coming, Ralph," Nerit said.

They all drew close to the edge and saw a very fine silver car pull up. A man climbed out and looked around frantically. He was completely oblivious of the hungry zombies in the store behind him.

He spotted the people on the roof and started waving. "Hello!"

"Shit, it's the guy from the gas station," Katie said to Jenni.

Jenni narrowed her eyes. It was obvious she remembered the man who had been such an ass earlier in the day.

"Six-figure guy," Jenni murmured.

"Yeah," Katie said. "Wonder how he made it out here."

"Hello! I'm looking for Madison! The radio says there's a rescue center there!" Six-Figure Guy kept waving at them, stirring up the zombies even more.

Ralph raised the bullhorn. "Are you bit?"

Katie noticed then that the man's forearm was heavily

bandaged. She looked at Jenni. The dark-haired woman was staring at the newest arrival with a blank expression.

The guy looked at his arm. "I have lots of money! I can pay you for your help! I need to get to Madison and get medical attention."

"Are you bit, son? If you are, my wife here can help you out," Ralph replied.

"Well . . ." The man hesitated, then nodded. "Yeah, but it's slight. I'm sure—"

The crack of the rifle made Katie flinch.

The man stood with a shocked look on his face for a second, then fell forward. Nerit had shot him through the forehead.

"He wasn't turned. We just can't do that," Katie protested.

Nerit regarded Katie with an expression that was set with determination. "Yes, we can."

"And you're going to have to," Ralph added. "If you're going to survive."

Katie stood, eyes blinking rapidly, and shook her head. "Oh, God." It was one thing to kill the ones who had already turned, but innocents who were infected? Could she do that?

"Anyone who is bit is going to become one of those things. Gotta shoot them and put them down. Only way." Ralph stood somberly, with his hands tucked into his jeans pockets. "Only way to keep safe and keep their numbers down."

Katie remembered Lydia and shivered.

"Now, come on downstairs for a bit to eat. Sun is about to start down, and we don't want to have empty stomachs," Nerit said, walking past them with her rifle.

"She cooks real good. First we eat, then look at guns, maybe shoot a little, then sleep."

Jenni sighed contentedly, obviously relaxing. "I'm so happy we are here. It feels good to be around real people, not dead ones or stupid ones. We saw a few of those on the road."

"I'm sure you did," Nerit said sadly.

Ralph smiled at Jenni and put a gentle arm around her shoulders. "Glad to have company. Glad to help you two out."

Jenni, Nerit, and Ralph headed downstairs, leaving Katie standing on the roof in quiet contemplation. She looked at Jack, who returned her gaze. If she had a choice, to die quickly or turn into one of those things, which would she prefer? Letting out a soft sigh, she rubbed her forehead.

"Jack, has the world gone crazy and everyone in it?"

Jack slightly whined.

"Thought so."

Together they followed the others down the stairs.

3.
The World Ends

Below, Katie saw that Nerit and Jenni had veered off into an old-fashioned kitchen while Ralph continued down the hall to a comfortable living room. If not for the enormous flat-screen TV, it would have looked like the Norman Rockwell version of the perfect grandparents' home. The big TV was on and scenes of violence were playing silently; in a corner of the screen, big green lettering read MUTE.

"Got tired of watching. Too much talk, too little information," Ralph told her with the shrug of his bony shoulders.

Katie stood mesmerized at the scenes of mayhem. Dutifully recorded by the media, visions of destruction and violence played out on the screen. A reporter came into view obviously standing high above street level, out of the range of the violence. It looked like New York City. Throngs of bloodied, crazed people were running down the street, attacking cars, buildings, and the people within. The army was firing at will into the crowd.

"This morning, the authorities called it race riots. When the

crisis hit more cities, they called it mob violence. Early this afternoon, they started calling them 'the infected.'"

Ralph sat in a comfortable, overstuffed chair while Katie sank down slowly on a flowered sofa with big crocheted doilies decorating the back and armrests. Jack sat at her feet and yawned.

"I haven't seen any of this," she admitted. "I was attacked during the early-morning rush hour. A man tried to rescue me, but they got him. Jack belongs—belonged—to him. On Jack's vet papers, it says his owner was the Reverend William Horton. He saved my life."

Ralph tilted his head toward her sympathetically, regarding her. "And you saved the girl with you."

"Yes." Katie's gaze remained fixed on the screen, which was now showing a map of the United States, highlighting where the violence was occurring. "I had driven home to check on my . . . spouse." She hesitated, not sure if she wanted to come out of the closet to this old-timer. "It was too late."

"They got him," the old man said softly.

Lydia rushing toward her, screaming, her chest torn open . . .

Katie wiped away a tear. "Yes."

Ralph shook his head. "It's gone crazy. The whole world."

The reporter was now interviewing a man in a doctor's white coat.

". . . and for anyone to suggest that this is anything other than a viral infection that causes psychotic behavior is ludicrous. We are not living in the Dark Ages," the doctor said firmly.

"Because of the nature of the severe wounds on the attackers, people are claiming they are actually the reanimated dead," the reporter pointed out.

"Preposterous! We live in a modern era of medicine and science, not superstition. If we do not treat this as a medical crisis immediately, we are doomed. Those who have been bitten and are infected must immediately report to the nearest hospital for treatment."

"Most of the hospitals are now overrun with what the CDC is calling reanimated corpses," the reporter said.

"The CDC has fallen prey to the hysteria of a population overwhelmed by the mass infection of an Ebola-like virus. . . ."

Ralph muted the TV. " 'Bout one o'clock, they said not to go to the hospitals anymore. Then the CDC came on and said it was a bunch of dead people getting up. Called them reanimated corpses. Found it funny. Nobody wants to say *zombie*."

Katie smiled slightly, remembering her own reluctance to embrace that word. When had that changed? She wasn't sure. But it was clear to her now that the dead had returned.

Mesmerized, she watched reporters around the world trying to broadcast only to be run down and torn apart. She watched anchormen and -women break down crying as more and more reports flowed in. Maps were flashed on the screen showing where blackouts were occurring. TV helicopters hovered over masses of the reanimated dead as they ran through the streets howling, chasing anyone still alive. Scenes of fires burning, armies firing, bombs exploding . . .

"It's the end," the old man said.

Katie rubbed her face and glanced at him. "You think so."

"Too many of them now," Ralph answered grimly.

Katie wiped away another tear and looked back at the screen. A reporter was sobbing as he read a list of overrun shelters to be avoided. Ralph flipped a channel to show Chicago on fire. More maps showing the infection. Their part of Texas, Katie noted, was free of any of the major markers. That figured, since they were in a sparsely populated area. The cities and larger towns were death traps. She was relieved; she had made the right choice to run into the hills.

A hand tenderly took hers as Jenni sat down next to her. Katie smiled slightly and squeezed Jenni's shaky hand.

"The president is being evacuated from the White House to Camp David and will soon release a statement to the nation," the local anchorwoman said, her lips trembling. "We are about

to abandon our station to go to a shelter. Anyone who is still watching this, stay where you are, be happy if you are with your family. Don't go into the cities. Don't risk it. Don't listen to what anyone on the news is saying. We don't know anything. No one does. Just fight to live until you don't want to go on anymore. My family is dead. I just got the word. Do you understand?" She was crying openly now, and her co-anchor reached out to calm her. "I don't want to die like that. I don't want to be one of those things! It's all over!"

The camera started to swing away from her, but it wasn't fast enough to keep viewers from seeing the anchorwoman lift a gun to her chin. The sharp retort and blood splatter hitting the co-anchor were vivid evidence of her suicide.

Jenni sobbed as Ralph switched off the TV.

"She had some good advice. They don't know nothing. I got more information watching zombie movies on the late-night picture show," he decided.

Katie shakily stood up. Nerit came to hold Jenni and whisper to her soothingly. Jenni continued to sob loudly. Jack whined and tried to soothe her with little doggy kisses. Katie moved on stiff, numb legs across the living room and pushed back a heavy brocade curtain at the window.

The sun was setting behind the hills. Below her, in the street, stood a man, bloody and mutilated, looking left, then right, over and over again. She knew if he looked up and saw her, he would start that horrible shriek.

Katie let the curtain fall back into place. Standing before the window, she felt herself let go of the old world and embrace the new. She would survive this. She would go on. That was all there was to it. She wouldn't give up without a fight. She would do whatever it took to survive.

Turning to Ralph, she said, "When's dinner?"

· CHAPTER FOUR ·

1.
Purgatory

Jenni was bored.

Her finger clenched.

The head with the long blond hair burst, and the body tumbled forward.

"Dwayne Emory," Ralph said behind her.

Nerit crossed another name off the list.

They all stood on the roof of the hunting store once more. The evening sky spread out above them, a lush panorama of cold stars and velvet darkness. The zombies of the small town spread out on the dirty street below in a shambling mess of dead flesh and lost hopes.

"See if you can get the one over the corner?" Ralph suggested, pointing.

Jenni aimed again, her finger squeezed, and another head popped like an overripe tomato.

The evening had started off well enough. A delicious dinner with good conversation followed by cheesecake made her feel better than she had all day.

Afterwards, they had trudged downstairs into the shop at Katie's insistence.

Nerit had found a skirt and T-shirt for Jenni to wear, and she felt more comfortable. She had thrown the bathrobe and nightgown away with disgust, never wanting to see them again. The

color pink would forever haunt her. She wanted to forget about this morning and those tiny fingers . . . those tiny fingers. . . .

Ralph had shown them around his spacious store, explaining the history of the well-fortified building. Originally, it had been the town jail, before the great fire that wiped out most of Main Street, and then it had been the town bank. Finally, when the town had mostly died out, it became a hunting store.

"Hunters come here for all seasons. Make a good living off of them. And the Internet," Ralph said as he showed them a state-of-the-art computer. "I sell hunting and camping gear online. Works well. Makes money." The little offices in the back doubled as the city hall and post office. Ralph was the mayor and Nerit, the postmistress.

The building was jammed with everything a small town could need. Jenni found it all very boring. Katie, though, was absolutely riveted by everything Ralph explained to her. They had talked about all sorts of things that Jenni didn't understand or care about. Small-town politics, law enforcement, gun laws . . .

Jenni had wandered to the front door and watched two women slowly eat away at Six-Figures Guy. One of them looked up at her, snarled, and ran for the window. Jenni didn't flinch when the woman ran straight into the heavy metal bars and busted her face open. The zombie tried to wedge a hand through the bars, and Jenni watched the woman's torn fingers scratch futilely at the window.

So much like those tiny fingers . . .

"More are getting out of that store. Gonna have to put them down tonight or we'll have issues in the morning," Ralph stated behind her.

Then had come the most tedious part of the night. Two hours of Ralph going over the variety of guns they had to choose from. They went through a slew of guns until they found at least two they were comfortable with. Finally, they had trudged back up to the roof and gotten a lesson on loading and reloading the guns.

Finally, they had started shooting zombies. That was much better.

Jenni had enjoyed shooting the woman who had rushed the window. Now she stood next to Katie, the night wind buffeting her dark hair, aiming at yet another zombie as it staggered out of the darkness and into the light pooling below the streetlamps. Tilting her head slightly, she studied his labored swagger, his profuse beer belly. His wife-beater shirt was stained with blood and gore.

She shot him in the knee.

He went down, growling, clawing at the ground. Over and over again, he tried to get up, only to have his leg give way beneath him. Finally, he looked up and saw her. Shrieking, he reached up hungrily.

Jenni narrowed her eyes and fired.

The bullet punched neatly through his head.

"Nerit and I have been talking, and we know you said you just want supplies, but we want you to consider staying here. Once we clean out the town, it will be safer than the world out there."

Jenni turned swiftly. "We can't!"

Katie flicked the safety on her rifle and reached out to calm Jenni with a gentle touch on her arm. "We need to get her stepson. He's stranded out at a camp in the state park."

Ralph scratched his chin. "When you get him, then what?"

Katie glanced at Jenni, then back at Ralph. "Honestly, we haven't talked about it."

Jenni hung back a little behind Katie. She really liked the old people, but wasn't sure this was the place for them. She liked Katie being in charge, and she wasn't sure about changing that dynamic. Yes, they had spent only maybe ten hours together in the car, but in that time, she had grown to trust Katie. Suddenly, she just wanted to be in the truck, with Katie and Jack, and far away from here.

"Well, you're welcome to come back here. Nerit and I could

use the company. The town is gone," Ralph said; then his keen gaze caught sight of something below. He took steady aim and fired. "Gunshots are bringing them out. Might as well clean up as many as we can."

Nerit inclined her head in agreement and took up a position at the back of the building.

After an hour of firing, it was clear that whatever could walk their way had done so. Whatever remained of the town was likely locked away in houses or cars. The street was littered with bodies: young, old—male and female. A few dogs wandered over to sniff at the bodies before darting away, whimpering.

Jenni's ears hurt from gunfire and zombie shrieks despite the earplugs she wore, and she felt rather moody as they were shown into the guest bedroom.

"Hope you don't mind sharing," Ralph said.

"It's fine," Katie assured him.

"Bathroom is through that door. Laid out big T-shirts for you gals to wear. See you in the morning," he said, and shut the door.

Jenni sat on the bed and exhaled slowly. She watched as Katie tossed aside the hunting jacket she had worn on and off since she rescued Jenni. Katie sat on the bed beside Jenni, kicked off her high heels, and sighed.

"You want to shower first?" she asked.

"Katie, are we coming back here?"

Katie sighed again, her hands resting on her knees. "Maybe. It seems about safe as it's going to get."

Jenni nodded, letting her hair fall into her face. "I just . . ." Jack nosed her hand and she started to pet him slowly. "I just . . . just . . ."

"It's too much right now. I know. Too many changes." Katie put a gentle arm around Jenni's shoulders and leaned over to kiss her cheek. "Too much to deal with . . ."

"I felt safe in the truck," Jenni whispered. "I know that sounds stupid, but I felt safe with you driving and Jack on my

lap. But here . . . we have to shoot things and be behind bars and it feels . . ."

"Like a prison?"

"Like I'm back home, not able to go out when Lloyd isn't with me. Having to . . ." Jenni faltered. It was hard to explain that today had been the most "free" day of her life in more than a decade. She clung to Katie and wept. Wept out of guilt because she felt free and because that freedom existed only because Lloyd was gone and so were her babies.

Katie held her tightly, her fingers lightly stroking her hair. It took Jenni a second to realize Katie was crying, too.

"It's okay. We're safe and we need to remember that," Katie said soothingly. "Tomorrow, we'll do what we have to do. And the day after that. And the day after that."

Jenni clung to Katie. "Okay . . . okay . . . I trust you." And she did. With all her heart.

Later, when Jenni came out of the shower, pink and clean, hair glistening, Katie combed her hair and dried it with a towel before helping her into bed. For the moment, Jenni felt utterly safe and content. Tears still flowed, and her sobs came in soft hiccups, but she felt comforted by Katie's presence.

"It's okay to cry now," Katie murmured.

Jenni covered her face with her hands and wept.

For her dead children, for the dead world, and for her new-found freedom . . .

2.
The Moment

The water sluiced off Katie's body as she sat at the bottom of the old-fashioned tub—complete with clawed feet. Her forehead rested on her knees. With her hands flat on the tops of her feet, she sat sobbing softly. How long she had sat there, she wasn't sure, but the water was growing cold. Soon after climbing

into the shower, she had been overcome with grief. Sobs had racked her body with such viciousness that every muscle ached.

She missed Lydia so much, it was a palpable pain.

All it had taken to start the torrent of tears was the thought, *I missed my jog.* And the deluge had started. Every night, she and Lydia would jog through their neighborhood and up into the hills before coming home to a nice bath, a simple dinner, and maybe a few hours of TV. Afterwards, they would curl up together and fall asleep to the soothing sound of each other's breathing.

It had been bliss.

But now . . .

All she could hear was the damn moaning outside. Most likely, more of those *things* were showing up outside the building.

The water was growing colder.

Katie turned off the flow and struggled to her feet. She'd gotten stiff, squatting there at the bottom of the tub, and she stumbled getting out. Landing hard on the mat, she started to cry all over again. This time, her grief was mingled with rage. She kicked the door to the cabinet under the sink to vent her feelings. Wiping her tears away angrily with her cold fingers, she snorted and sniffled, her nose running wildly.

Why . . . why . . . why . . . goddamnit . . . why? . . .

A hand on her damp hair made her raise her head. Jenni's face swam before her, pale and concerned. Jack sat at her side, yawning and looking bleary eyed.

"I just can't," Katie sobbed.

Jenni stroked her face. "Can't what?"

"Let her be dead in my heart," she answered.

Katie refused to remember Lydia shrieking and charging at her, her chest torn open and her heart gone. Instead, she made herself see Lydia as she had been just thirty minutes before: smiling, happy, kissing her good-bye, a cup of coffee clutched in one hand.

Jenni wrapped her arms around Katie and held her tenderly.

Her black hair was soft and soothing on Katie's cold skin, and Katie leaned into her. They sat that way for a long time, until Katie's sobs finally subsided.

Awkwardness set in and Jenni sat back, her brow furrowed, looking anxious and confused. Katie rubbed her face, feeling flushed and tired. Nothing in this new world felt right.

Jenni tried to kiss her, very awkwardly and tentatively. Katie caught hold of her immediately and held her back. "Don't."

"I just want to make you feel—," Jenni mumbled, her face reddening.

"Don't. I'm not your husband. I don't need sex to comfort me." Katie held Jenni firmly. She realized in that instant that part of her had been waiting for this. Subconsciously, she had recognized that Jenni was looking for security in this new world. And that would mean fitting Katie into a role Jenni understood. Jenni was used to a strong male figure, one she could calm with sex, follow obediently, and maybe fear a little.

Jenni lowered her eyes, and tears fell. "I don't know . . . I just wanted . . ."

Katie smiled and forced Jenni to look her in the eyes. "It's okay. I understand. But this is not who you are. Right?"

Jenni nodded, embarrassed. "I thought I could learn—"

"This is not who we are," Katie said firmly, stroking Jenni's hair.

Jenni looked at her, eyes wide, trying to understand. "I just want to be useful. For you to need me."

"But I do, Jenni. We are bonded by all that happened today. For better or for worse, we have a bond. You and me." Katie took Jenni's hands firmly in her own and held them tightly. "My dad told me a lot about his war buddies. They loved each other and they shared a bond no one really understood, because they were not part of it. I think I understand that now."

Jenni sat down cross-legged, her hair falling over one shoulder. Jack immediately set his head on Jenni's knee. "I don't know how to . . . I don't have any female friends or

know any . . . lesbians. . . ." Jenni rubbed her nose with the palm of her hand. "I don't know how to act."

Katie smiled and kissed one of Jenni's hands. "That's okay. Hell, for both of us to be utterly insane right now is okay. But I just need you as my friend. I need you to be whoever you are, Jenni. Okay?"

"Okay." Jenni seemed relieved even as her shoulders slumped.

Katie forced herself to stand and pulled on the T-shirt and shorts Jenni had left in the bathroom for her. Her business clothes were wadded up in the trash bin along with her high heels. She knew she would never wear them again, and in a way, that was a relief.

"I wish it would stop," Jenni whispered.

Katie raised her head, realizing she had been mentally blocking out the sound of the moans. "Yeah, me, too."

"Well," Jenni said with a wry smile, "at least we live in Texas, where people actually own guns and hunt."

"Well," Katie echoed with a grin of her own, "at least we're in a hunting shop and not a mall."

Jenni giggled as she stood, stretching her long legs. "Yeah. Or a farmhouse. Do you know how to fly a helicopter?"

Katie laughed. "You are a die-hard fan of Romero!"

"Are you?"

"Romero all the way." Katie walked out into the bedroom and crawled onto the bed.

Jenni climbed in after her, looking much more relaxed now. "I had hoped if this ever happened, they at least wouldn't run like they do in the new movies." Jenni pouted.

Outside, the moaning continued; it had become almost a lulling sound as it ebbed and flowed over and over again. Jack crawled into the bed between them and nestled down.

Snuggling on either side of the dog, the women were both lost in thought. The tension that had been brewing between them had dissipated. They now knew where they both stood, and it was good.

Without fear, without reservation, without being afraid of being misunderstood, Katie reached across the dog and took Jenni's hand. Jenni squeezed it tenderly.

"Tomorrow, we'll get your stepson," Katie assured her.

"And kill more zombies," Jenni added.

Katie half laughed, her eyes still feeling horribly large and swollen. "Yeah, and kill zombies."

"But avoid farmhouses and malls and helicopters."

"And find ourselves a handsome black man to play the main lead in our story," Katie added.

They both started to laugh, and it felt amazingly good.

Outside, the zombies gathered and moaned.

3.
The Midnight Hour

Jenni's heart pounded almost as fiercely as her footfalls as she rushed down the stairs with Mikey beside her. Her fingers slid along the banister while she struggled not to fall headlong down the stairs. Mikey's hand was slippery in hers and she tugged him along when she reached the bottom of the staircase and headed for the front door.

She felt Lloyd grab her long hair and yank her backwards.

"Don't touch my mom!" Mikey's hand slipped from hers, and her little boy launched himself at his father.

"No," Jenni whispered, and her eyes snapped open. Her heart was beating so hard in her chest, it hurt. She struggled to catch her breath.

Katie was sleeping with her arms wrapped around the German shepherd. The dog eyed Jenni drowsily and she rubbed his brow.

"I'm okay," she lied.

He licked her arm lightly before laying his head back on his paws. She was sure he was tired, too, after their long day. Plus,

he had started the day with surgery and endured their crazed escape from the city in a drugged stupor.

Still feeling shaken, Jenni slid from the bed and stood in the darkened room, listening to the moans of the dead outside. Lloyd always used to make her watch zombie movies because he knew they scared her. Scaring her had been something he enjoyed. Every time they watched a zombie film, he'd do things to upset her, like pretend to be a zombie. His moaning always made her scurry away from him. She hated it. Zombies terrified her.

And then this morning . . .

Don't think about it, she told herself.

She ran her fingers through her hair, combing it back from her face, and walked to the door. Careful not to make too much noise, she turned the handle and slipped into the hallway. She saw a dim light in the living room, where the TV was still on but muted. An ashen-looking anchorman from one of the major networks was talking to several people, including a minister. Ralph was asleep in his lounge chair with a quilt laid over him. A rifle lay on the floor next to him.

"He couldn't sleep," Nerit said quietly from behind Jenni.

Jenni turned around. The older woman was dressed in a nightgown and holding a cup of tea. "I had nightmares."

"Me, too," Nerit said with a weary smile. "Would you like some tea and cheesecake?"

"That would be awesome."

In the kitchen, Jenni settled into a stiff-backed chair as Nerit put on a fresh pot of tea.

"You know, zombies always scared me," Jenni said after a quiet moment.

"I never thought much about them or any movie monsters," Nerit replied honestly. "I always thought the monsters of the real world were much more terrifying."

"Serial killers and all that?"

"All that." Nerit's expression was shadowed with pain, her gaze flicking to the wall near the table.

Following Nerit's gaze, Jenni drew close to the old black-and-white photos hung in gilded frames. Some were of farmers and cattlemen, probably Ralph's ancestors. But some had a distinctly old-world look about them. In one photo, there were Stars of David sewn onto the coats of the family posing outside a shop.

"Oh," Jenni said, understanding. "Oh."

Nerit nodded as she cut two slices of the Italian-style cheesecake. "I used to fear the real monsters and had very little patience for fantasy. But Ralph likes the monster movies. He said they're a safe kind of scary."

"Not anymore," Jenni decided grumpily.

"No, not anymore," Nerit agreed, and set down the dessert plates before taking a seat.

"My children died this morning," Jenni said, gazing at Nerit. She half expected the older woman to accuse her of being incompetent, but Nerit only responded with, "I'm sorry."

"My husband got bit last night. A bum, he said." Jenni stabbed at the piece of cheesecake with her fork.

"Ralph discovered what was going on at the grocery store. We had stayed in bed late to celebrate his birthday. He was going across the road to grab the paper when he saw the attacks inside." Nerit cut her piece of cake into small sections and played with one tiny slice with her fork. "I didn't believe him at first. People eating each other. It sounds so ludicrous."

Jenni set down her fork and stared at her plate. "Lloyd liked to sleep on the sofa. He said I move around too much in my sleep and that he couldn't get a decent night's rest. I would hear the TV on all night. If he had been in our room . . .

"Benji's room is the first one off the stairs. I think that's why Lloyd went in there first. . . ." She covered her face with her hands and tried so hard not to think of what she had seen. It was a blur, actually, just a swift image of Lloyd stuffing something thick and fleshy into his mouth and Benji's little body looking wrong and all that blood staining the floor. Her mind

fought between adding in details and wiping the image out altogether.

Nerit's fingers were soft and dry as she drew Jenni's hand down from her face. Gently, she held Jenni's hand in her own and said, "There was nothing you could do."

Jenni forced back a sob and wiped away her tears. She wasn't sure if that was the truth, and she didn't want to think about it anymore. Already, yesterday morning felt so far away, and the world already felt very different. Mikey, Benji, and even Lloyd felt like shadows to her.

"When you saw them inside the store, what did you do?"

"At first, we were going to go in and try to rescue people. But the . . . zombies—" Nerit slightly laughed at the word. "—the zombies rushed toward the door, and we realized very quickly that we couldn't go inside. We ran back here and locked ourselves in. At first, we thought the people were infected with some strange virus, like the news said, but one of them came up behind the hunting store, and he was chewed down to the bone. There was no way in heaven he could be that badly damaged and walking. He saw us through the window and beat on it. We decided to head back upstairs and figure out exactly what was going on. That is when we saw our neighbors forcing themselves into people's homes and attacking them. We took some out from a distance, but . . ." Nerit shook her head. "We've been killing our neighbors all day. We had no choice."

Jenni took another bite of cheesecake and let the rich flavor distract her for a few precious seconds. Then she said, "Does it bother you to kill them?"

Nerit stood up, stretched, and headed toward the teakettle, which had begun to whistle. "The real question is, Do we have a choice?"

"It doesn't bother me to kill them," Jenni confessed. "Not at all."

The older woman poured hot water into a cup and set it down in front of Jenni. "It doesn't bother me either."

The hot water was letting off a small plume of steam, and Jenni waved her hand through it. It felt good against her skin. The cold spring night was pressing against the windows and she could feel a chill in her bones. The warmth from the hot water was a soothing sensation. Dumping too much sugar into the tea, Jenni tried hard not to think too deeply about anything other than rescuing Jason in the morning.

Nerit sipped some tea and eyed Jenni thoughtfully. "It's a good thing, you know."

"What is?" Katie padded into the room appearing bleary eyed. Jack was at her heels, yawning and investigating for the nearest food bowl.

"Being able to kill them," Nerit answered.

Spotting the teakettle, Katie headed over to it.

"Couldn't sleep?" Jenni dumped in more sugar for good measure.

"Nightmares," Katie confessed. "But I guess we better get used to them."

"Get used to all of it," Jenni agreed. Her friend looked pale and tired. They both needed to rest, but the sound of the zombies was dragging on all of them.

"You don't think it will be stopped, do you?" Katie slipped into a chair, a mug in her hand.

Nerit shook her head and reached out for a pack of cigarettes sitting on the table. "No. It's too late. They didn't do what they needed to do in the beginning."

"Which was?" Katie shoved her blond curls out of her face.

"Kill everyone bitten," Jenni answered. She leaned her head on Katie's shoulder and sighed softly. "Everyone bitten should have been killed right away. Lloyd was bitten. The emergency room gave him some shots and told him to make a follow-up appointment with his doctor."

Nerit lit a cigarette and exhaled slowly. She leaned over and flipped on an air filter next to the table to suck up the second-hand smoke. "The authorities told all the wounded to go to

the hospitals and rescue centers. They accelerated the infection rate."

"They still don't get it." Ralph walked into the kitchen, rubbing his eyes. Clad in pajamas and an old robe, he looked frail. "Anyone saying *zombies* or *end of the world* is getting mocked. Got the CDC taking back some of what they said and still telling people to go to rescue centers. Got major cities burning all over the States, and they still can't figure it out."

"What does the president say?" Katie drank her tea without any sugar; Jenni winced at the thought.

"Nothing since he was evacuated to Camp David," Ralph answered.

"And the vice president?" Katie poured herself more tea, tilting her head toward Ralph.

"In East Texas on a hunting trip," Ralph answered, and sat next to Nerit. "News is all confusing now, full of half truths and bullshit. Got one guy on last night saying it's a strain of Ebola."

Jenni rolled her eyes. Katie snagged her plate and dragged the uneaten cheesecake over to her. Jenni didn't mind. She couldn't eat, now that she was thinking of all they had endured. All they would endure. She laid her head down on her folded arms on the table. Ralph reached out and patted her head lightly. It comforted her.

"It really is the end," Katie decided.

They all knew it, but hearing the words again helped it sink in. To accept it was to be empowered. Jenni understood that and she knew the people at the table understood it, too. To survive meant to kill and to fight.

· CHAPTER FIVE ·

1.
Into the Breach

The hammering on the back windows was annoying, but Katie tried to block out the sound. The number of undead outside the building had grown during the night, and they were insistently banging on the windows. There had been some discussion about trying to thin out the new horde of undead, but they all recognized time was of the essence if they were going to have a chance at saving Jenni's stepson. Ralph was confident that the heavy bars over the windows and the reinforced doors would keep the zombies out. The sound wore on the survivors' nerves, but they tried to ignore the undead as they brainstormed for a good plan to save Jason.

Ralph spread out a map on a table in the office downstairs. Nerit leaned against the wall nearby with her hands tucked into her jeans pockets. Her yellowish white hair was pinned up on top of her head, and her dark green eyes looked sharp and intense.

Jenni, perched on a folding chair, was clad head to toe in hunting gear: camouflage pants and jacket, a T-shirt that read I AIM TO SHOOT, and heavy Doc Martens. Her black hair was in a ponytail; she looked very young and delicate. Katie noted that today there was a difference in the way she held herself. After they had returned to bed after their midnight snack, Katie had trouble falling asleep, but Jenni seemed to have found some peace within herself and had slept soundly.

Katie drew near to Ralph and crossed her arms over her breasts. Like Jenni, she was wearing camo pants, plus a black tank top and the reverend's hunting jacket. The scents that clung to the fabric—the warm smell of tobacco and the faint smell of her savior's aftershave—gave her a sense of security as well. It was as though the old man was still watching over her. She sipped from a cup of coffee and tucked a blond curl behind one ear as she studied the map.

"Truck you came in is not going to cut it. This ain't the old world, where a low tank means a trip to the gas station. Electricity is still up here. Grid hasn't gone down—yet. TV is static except for the emergency broadcasting network. Bunch of horseshit regurgitation like yesterday. Not worth much. But we can't take it on face value that any of the gas stations between here and the camp are up and working. Gotta plan for the opposite."

"Gotcha. So we're limited to what we can carry in canisters and what is in the tank," Katie said.

"Right. Now, the truck yer in, well, it got you here, but probably not much further without a refuel."

"We are dangerously low on fuel," Katie admitted, "though we have at least five gallons of extra gas in those red canisters in the back of our pickup."

"My truck has a half tank of gas, and we can move your gas cans into it. Also, my truck has a bigger cab. You can fit your young one and any other survivor back there, along with Jack. Gun rack is perfect for your weapons. Also got a CB in there that can keep you in touch with us. Keep to Channel Twenty-three." Ralph pointed at their location. "Here's Hillsboro. This is the state park. Mapped out the most fuel-efficient way for you to get there. You can do a round trip sticking to the route, but any detour might stick you out yonder with just the reserve fuel."

Katie agreed and glanced at Jenni. Jenni's eyes were huge and desperate. Katie knew instantly what she was thinking. "We're still going," she promised her, and Jenni relaxed.

"Keep to the route. Don't veer off. I mean it. There's a major highway near that park. If any infected people made it that far, you could have zombies on the roads." Ralph stood staring at the map, rubbing his chin, and looking deadly serious.

"I understand," Katie assured him. "We'll grab Jason and head back."

"Don't hesitate to run those things over," Nerit said from her corner. "Don't hesitate to shoot them."

Jenni giggled a little and Katie smirked. "I don't think that will be a problem. Not anymore" She wanted to survive and unlike yesterday, she understood to so meant she had to kill both the undead and the infected.

"Okay, then take the map, gear up. Take what you can in three backpacks. If you get caught out there, you'll need supplies," Ralph said. His eyes were so sharp and thoughtful, Katie couldn't look at him. His expression reminded her too much of her father.

"MREs, ammo," Katie ticked off.

"Flashlight, knives . . ." Ralph faltered. "I should go with you."

"No, no. You belong here with Nerit."

A loud crash made everyone jump. Jenni ran across the room and whipped back the curtains, revealing an massive zombie slamming his body into the bars across the window. Though huge chunks of his flesh had been torn away, there was still a lot of him to hurl against the building. The empty cavity of his torso behind the sheets of shredded flesh made Katie turn away.

"You fucking stop that!" Jenni shouted at the zombie, and slammed her hand against the glass.

The zombie growled and crashed into the bars again.

Something about him drove Jenni over the edge. She turned and raced up the stairs. Katie followed, her boots thudding against the wood steps. Jack charged past her, barking, excited.

When Katie hit the second floor, she saw no sign of Jenni, but the door to the back patio was open. After running to the

doorway, she saw Jenni standing near the rail, gun raised, Jack at her heels, barking away.

"Hey, fuckface!" Jenni's voice was full of hatred.

The zombie turned slowly, saw her up on the balcony, opened his mouth to shriek, and rushed forward. As soon as he was clear of the window, Jenni put a nice little hole through his right eye. The enormous zombie pitched forward onto two female zombies who had turned to see Jenni, effectively trapping both of them under his immense girth.

Katie stood next to Jenni, a little shocked by Jenni's sudden violent streak. Jenni turned and saw at her, then shrugged. "He looked like my dad," she explained, then calmly walked back into the building.

Katie hesitated before following. She'd been questioning Jenni's sanity for a while now, but then again, they were all slightly insane now, weren't they? She watched the two female zombies trying to wiggle out from under the huge dead man and smiled slightly. Turning on her heel, she followed Jenni into the store.

She was surprised to find Jenni standing near the top of the stairs, apparently waiting for her. From her expression, Katie could see that she was struggling internally.

"We should have gone last night," Jenni grumbled.

"In the dark? With those things?" Katie lifted an eyebrow. "Would you really want to do that?"

Jenni shook her head. "I'm just worried about Jason."

"I know, but we have to take care of ourselves, too, you know."

"I know, Katie." Jenni sighed. "But we really need to get out of here and go save him."

Packing was quick. Ralph, being an old pro, knew what they needed. Nerit gave them a cooler full of sandwiches and drinks. She seemed pensive, but she smiled supportively whenever her gaze rested on them.

Katie was busy double-checking the small bag holding

their ammo when Nerit came up and laid Katie's phone on the table.

"I found this up on the roof. I thought you might want it," she said in her warm, richly accented voice.

Katie glanced at it and hesitated. "There isn't any service anymore."

Nerit flipped the phone open to show Lydia's lovely, smiling face. "For her."

Katie looked at the older woman sharply; her hand closed the phone. Anxiety coursed through her.

"She was beautiful. And she loved you. I can see it in her face," Nerit said tenderly.

Katie's eyes filled with tears. "She was my life, but she's not here now, and I'm just trying to live minute to minute. Lydia was always so damn strong and calm. I'm trying so hard to be like her."

Nerit looked past her to Jenni. The other woman was rearranging one of the backpacks with a very dire expression on her face. "You're doing a good job being strong and calm. And you like to take care of people. I can see that in you. Now you are going to take care of Jenni. And her son. I can see it in your eyes. It's what you do."

"Well, I can't say you're wrong," Katie admitted.

Nerit took Katie's hand in her old, leathery ones and pressed it between her palms. "You are a good person, Katie. Come back safe. I think I want to know you better and make you family."

Katie flung her arms around Nerit in a tight hug. "Thank you. Thank you for everything you've done for us."

" 'Nuf of that. Sun is climbing. If you are going to round-trip it today, gotta start now," Ralph said from behind them. "I thinned out the zombies a bit in the back for you, Nerit."

Nerit let go of Katie. "I'll take care of the rest." She headed toward the stairs, snagging her sniper rifle off the counter on the way.

Katie stuffed the bag of ammo in her backpack, shrugged it on, grabbed the cooler, and followed Ralph.

"Nerit will toss the decoy in five minutes. You head out the back door. She'll cover you from up top, and I'll cover you from the door. Keep your eyes sharp and head straight for the truck."

Katie and Jenni looked at each other and in that gaze, steadied each other. They both wore heavy backpacks and each held a weapon. Katie had slung the cooler's long strap over her shoulder. Jenni carried an extra backpack that she would drop if she had to. Katie gripped the truck keys firmly.

A few minutes later, a lot of noise erupted in the front of the building. A man's voice talking loudly about the zombie infestation quickly drew the attention of the undead milling behind the store. As they headed around the side of the building, Ralph shouted, "Now!"

Katie threw open the door and ran. Ralph's red truck was parked under a small carport about fifteen feet from the back door, but it seemed an eternity away. She could hear Jenni right behind her, and Jack bringing up the rear.

Shots erupted almost immediately. Out of the corner of her eye, Katie saw something drop.

A man came running around the truck, screeching with his hands thrown out to grab her. Katie raised her gun and fired, almost point-blank. The zombie's head exploded in a volcano of gore, and he went down. More gunfire told her Ralph and Nerit were covering them.

She kept pressing the button to unlock the truck as she ran, and finally she heard the singsong sound of the alarm flicking off and the click of the doors unlocking. Jenni reached the truck first and opened the passenger door.

"Jack, in," Jenni ordered. She threw her packs into the backseat before scrambling inside.

Katie reached the truck and started to open the door when she felt someone grab her foot. Looking down, she saw a baby grappling with her boot.

"Shit!" She pitched the cooler into the truck while trying to shake the baby off. There was no way it could bite through her boot with its tiny teeth, but it was hissing and trying to crawl up her leg.

"They're coming back, Katie! Just go!" Ralph shouted. She heard the door slam shut.

Katie shook free of the mutilated baby, which looked like it was maybe eleven months old, and slammed her foot down on its head. Using it as a step, she slid backpack first into the truck.

Three zombies were closing in fast on her side, and she raised her gun and fired. The first one went down, the second spun around as the shot took it in the shoulder, but the third was on her.

At the last second, she frantically raised her gore-splattered foot and slammed it into the thing's chest. Its hands scrabbled at her leg, but it didn't seem smart enough to bend down and bite it. Its eyes were on her face, its hands straining for her. Its face was so mangled, she wasn't sure if it was a man or a woman.

Over her shoulder, Jenni's hand appeared, holding her gun. Katie twisted to the side as Jenni rammed the gun into the thing's face and fired. Katie's ears went numb.

Blood splattered everywhere. Katie jerked her legs all the way in and Jenni reached out and slammed the door.

Katie shrugged off her backpack and tossed it into the back-seat where Jack was already perched, growling and barking out the back window at the swiftly approaching zombies.

More shots sounded, and Jenni looked anxiously out the passenger-side window. "I think the radio-in-the-dummy ruse is over." She hit the button to lock the doors.

"There are more out there than we expected," Katie said.

Katie's fingers were shaking so violently, she could barely get the key into the ignition, but she finally managed to slide it in and twist. The engine roared to life and she quickly reversed.

She could feel as well as hear the *thunk* of several bodies

hitting the back end of the truck. She shifted and aimed for two others who were blocking their way. They bounced off the deer guard in a graceful arc.

Jenni laughed and clapped her hands. "Nailed 'em!"

Moving swiftly down the gravel drive that cut behind the hunting store, the truck sent several zombies hurtling into the building or down a steep embankment behind the store.

Katie turned the truck onto the main road and floored it. "Get Ralph on the CB, Jenni."

Jenni fumbled with the buttons before managing to turn on the CB radio.

"You girls safe?" a voice crackled.

Jenni grabbed the handheld CB transceiver off its holder and pushed the button. "Roger that! We are safe and en route to rescue point!"

Katie smothered a laugh that was born of both amusement and a little hysteria.

"We're a little more infested than we thought. I think some of the bed-and-breakfast folks had a large crowd in town. We'll try to clean them up as much as we can before you get back to-night," Ralph answered. There was a long pause. "Katie, you didn't get bit, did ya? That guy was right on ya."

Jenni's eyes widened as she looked at Katie nervously.

"I'm fine. Tell him I'm fine." Except for the ringing in her ears, that was.

Jenni sighed with relief. "She's okay. We're both okay."

"Good. Now, you girls take care out there. Come back safe."

"Roger that. Over and out." Jenni carefully put the CB trans-ceiver back on its hook and fastened her seat belt.

Katie once more marveled at how well Jenni was doing. From dazed survivor to gun-toting mama, but then again, she had a feeling this might have been the most living Jenni had ever done.

"We're gonna do this and come back," Jenni said firmly.

"Yes, we are," she agreed with determination.

But deep down inside, she had a horrible feeling things were not going to go quite as they hoped.

2.
Hell Has Highways

The drone of the road was steady and unwavering as the truck roared over the slowly warming asphalt. The sun was climbing and would soon be an unmerciful torment of heat and light. Jack lay snoozing in the backseat with his nose tucked beneath his front paws, all doggy contentment and cuteness.

Jenni smiled at him and looked back toward the road. Ralph's truck was a lot more luxurious than the white pickup they'd escaped from the city in. It was much bigger and sat higher off the ground; the seats were leather and very comfortable. They had listened to the emergency broadcasting radio network for a short time, but as Ralph had said, it was just bullshit. Jenni found it amusing that she understood more of what was going on than officials in high places because of her steady diet of zombie flicks, thanks to her asshole of a husband.

Glancing at Katie, she was relieved to see her companion looking cool and in control. They had used wet wipes Jenni found in the glove compartment to clean up the blood and gore from the zombie she had killed. The very sporty men's sunglasses Katie was wearing made her look like a cop, Jenni thought, and she giggled. Katie peered at Jenni over the tops of the sunglasses and slowly stuck out her tongue.

It was a huge relief to know exactly how things were supposed to be now. Yesterday—oh, God, it was just yesterday!—Jenni had spent the morning swinging between sheer panic and a trancelike state. By afternoon, she had felt safe in Katie's presence and confident that her new friend would protect her and

help her survive. Jenni was comfortable with a heroine in the hero's role. Her mistake had been in thinking that just because Katie was a lesbian, she was merely a man in a woman's skin.

But last night, seeing Katie naked and overwhelmed with grief, Jenni had realized that Katie was all woman. She had been a damn fool trying to comfort her like she was a man. Jenni blushed at the memory of her awkward attempt to kiss Katie. She hadn't felt any attraction to Katie, but Jenni was accustomed to putting aside her needs and her desires for the men in her life. First her father, then her brother, then her husband. She had shut up, put up, and dealt with whatever they wanted from her.

But Katie . . .

Jenni smiled at her affectionately.

Katie caught her look out of the corner of her eye and gave her a quick glance. "What?"

Jenni kept smiling goofily.

Katie just kind of laughed and turned her gaze back to the road. "You try kissing me again——"

Jenni laughed. "Noooooooooo!" She snuggled down in the seat and pulled the map onto her lap. "We're looking for the handsome, black leading man, remember? I'll kiss him."

Katie grinned, but quickly sobered as they passed a sign for a town. "Checkersville. What do Ralph's notes say?"

Jenni, also serious now, studied the map. "It's got a small population. It's Emorton we need to worry about. It's a lot bigger."

Katie let out a long breath. "We're two miles out. Get ready."

Jenni dutifully drew her gun and snapped off the safety.

They hit the small town at seventy miles per hour. Checkersville was four blocks long with a traffic light bisecting it. The town appeared completely deserted. At the end of the first block, Katie expertly swung the truck around a car stalled in the middle of the intersection.

"So far, so good," Jenni said with relief.

"Don't curse it," Katie chided her as they started down the second half of the street.

A man broke free of a building ahead of them, running fast, and screaming, "Stop! Stop!"

Hearing human speech was so startling that it took a second for the women to react. The truck sailed past the man before Jenni yelled and Katie shoved down on the brakes, saying, "Get ready to open the door, Jenni."

Jack raised his head blearily. The man ran toward the truck, sobbing and clutching one of his arms. It was a mangled mess.

"Go," Jenni ordered in a strangled tone.

"What?"

"He's infected."

Katie looked into the rearview mirror, saw the man's arm, and banged her fists against the steering wheel. "Fuckfuckfuck-fuckfuck."

The man drew nearer the truck, waving his good arm and looking relieved. Behind him, three battered running figures appeared.

"Just go," Jenni sighed.

Katie glanced into the rearview mirror as Jack started bark at the approaching zombies. "Sorry," she whispered as truck moved forward. More zombies shuffled into view.

"No!" the man shouted. His voice was full of disbelief, despair, and terror. "No! Don't leave me here!"

Jenni considered shooting him, but hitting him in the head or anywhere vital enough to kill him instantly seemed just impossible, given the truck's speed. She tried not to look behind her, but her eyes strayed to the side mirror. She winced when the man was caught by the zombies and dragged down. Her hand lashed out and grabbed Katie's. Katie held it firmly and they both sat in silence while the town vanished behind them.

After a few miles, Katie withdrew her hand and put it back

on the wheel as they drew near Emorton. Jenni consulted the marked-up map. "Ralph advised that we go down this side road. It will help us avoid the main part of town. FM 1342."

Katie gave a quick nod. "Okay. Got it."

Jenni looked at Katie again and thought of Katie's words last night. They did share a bond. She felt it. She felt comfortable now with the warmth in her heart when she watched Katie. She had a new friend, a sister . . . a comrade. She could love Katie and not be afraid of being used or hurt.

Katie turned onto the farm road. As the town grew closer, the women became more tense, aware that larger towns were death traps. Jack softly woofed from the backseat, and Jenni turned to see that the dog was staring straight ahead with a very serious look on his face.

Three large buildings loomed ahead. Emorton Elementary, Junior High, and High School, all in a row. The parking lot was crammed with cars. High fences and locked gates surrounded the school buildings except for one section. Two cars evidently had rammed into the fence and toppled it. The crashed cars were abandoned and their doors were open. Jenni could see that the car doors were smeared with blood.

"Not good," Katie said grimly.

"The school must have been the rescue center." She studied the buildings as they passed. Blood and bits of bodies were littered across the courtyard in front of one of the buildings. The doors to what appeared to be the gym were wide open.

"Katie, floor it!"

Two zombies raced out of the gym toward the truck, and it was as if a dam had broken. A torrent of moaning, screeching zombies poured out of the building, a mix of adults and children, sprinting toward them. Slower, more mangled corpses lurched out behind the first wave, intent on joining in the feast.

"There's a fuckload of zombies coming our way!" Jenni cried out.

Jack barked angrily at the approaching mob and looked at

Katie worriedly, as if wondering why she wasn't hurrying away.

Katie was driving as fast as possible along the road as it curved around the schools; on the other side of the road was farmland and no easy escape. The truck swiftly approached a knot of cars that had crashed into one another.

"They're gonna cut us off!" Jenni was horrified at how shrill and terrified she sounded. But then again, she was terrified.

The first of the zombies scrambled past the wrecked cars and onto the road. They immediately charged the truck.

"We're meals on wheels," Jenni said with a bitter laugh.

"Chewy center is what it's all about," Katie said gloomily.

The truck plowed through the first zombies, but more were spilling out of the gap in the fence. As the truck barreled through them, Jenni saw yet another turn in the road—and more zombies coming through another broken section of the fence.

Ahead of them, a ragged line of cars clogged the road. People had obviously abandoned them in haste, probably dashing for the school. Now those same people were probably running for the truck.

"Damn stupid people!" Katie braked sharply.

"Just go!" Jenni yelled . To the right, the fence hugged the roadway; to the left, there was a slight shoulder and an embankment. If they didn't keep going, they were dead.

The zombies reached the truck and slammed their fists against metal and glass. Katie reversed, shoving her foot hard down the accelerator, looking very satisfied as the truck bounced over a few zombie bodies. She aimed the truck for the narrow path to the side of the blockade of cars.

"We might tip," she said through gritted teeth.

"Go down! Off road through the field," Jenni said urgently, trying not to look at the zombies banging on her window. "Before they break in!"

Katie didn't say a word, just expertly dodged one crashed car and started down the embankment. The truck tilted scarily to

one side and Jenni found herself clinging to the door handle to keep from falling into Katie. Some of the zombies were still banging on the windows.

The pickup reached the field, and the wheels plowed through the sun-hardened earth. Luckily, it was just a field of wildflowers and the truck was a 4x4. The zombies kept following. Some even clung to the edges of the truck bed. In the mirror, Jenni could see more zombies surging from the school.

Katie aimed the truck for the road on the other side of the field. "How are we doing?"

"We got stowaways and lots more trying to catch up.

There was a tremendous jolt as the truck struggled up the slope and back onto the road. Jenni saw two zombies fly off the back of the truck and onto the asphalt. One had managed to get into the truck bed and was staggering toward the back window. Jack was barking wildly.

"Stop!"

Katie obeyed immediately.

The zombie pitched forward and hit the back of the cab. It fell back into the bed, out of sight.

Jenni flung the door open, jumped out, and raised her gun. The zombie grabbed hold of the side of the truck and hauled itself up, straight into Jenni's line of fire.

"Pop," Jenni said. She pulled the trigger, and the zombie's head did pop, like an enormous blister. The thing tumbled over the edge of the truck onto the road.

"Get in!" Katie was struggling to keep Jack in the truck's cab.

Jenni could see the two zombies who had fallen off, closing fast. Not far behind them was an enormous crowd of the undead from the schools.

After jumping into the truck, she slammed the door shut. Jack licked her face with relief. Katie drove on at top speed, her gaze flicking toward the gas gauge.

"How far?"

"An hour, but just back roads from this point out," Jenni answered, trying to get the map turned the right way.

"We're close."

"He's alive, Katie. Jason is alive. I know it." She did not add that she needed to save him to make up for her failures as a mother. Katie wouldn't understand.

"We'll save him," Katie assured her. "We will."

Jenni believed her.

· CHAPTER SIX ·

1.
Frayed Edges

Katie was still unsteady from the episode at the schools. Leaving that poor man behind was bad enough, but seeing the torrent of zombified families coming out of the school buildings had left her feeling sick to the very pit of her stomach.

Maybe they were being foolish for thinking Jason was still alive. Hell, it was sheer luck that she and Jenni were both alive. Right place at the right time. She didn't want to dwell on it too much, but what if she hadn't slipped free of her coat when that horrible undead thing had tried to drag her from her car? What if Jenni's zombified son had made it out the window just a little faster?

Up to this point, luck had a lot to do with the fact they were still alive. Now it would be keeping their wits about them in situations like the one they had just experienced that would dictate if they survived or not.

So far, so good.

Katie glanced at Jenni, who was staring straight ahead. Her lips were pressed firmly together and her brow was knotted. Jenni was desperate to rescue her stepson, Jason. Even if he wasn't Jenni's flesh and blood, Jason was all she had left, the only living connection to her past. To her previous life.

Katie was envious of that. There was nothing, absolutely nothing, left of her former life except for a picture of her wife in

a cell phone. Soon the battery would run out. She didn't have a charger—and there was no way of knowing how long there would be power.

She looked at the gas gauge again. It was dropping faster than she liked. She hadn't told Jenni yet, but they had blown one valuable part of their plan when they escaped from the hunting store. The extra jugs of gas were still sitting in the back of the beat-up white truck. In their panic to get safely on the road, they had forgotten to load them into Ralph's truck.

Now, what was in the tank was all there was. Pure and simple . . . and terrifying. The needle was dropping far faster than she hoped.

"We're close," Jenni uttered in a frightened voice. She was pale as a ghost.

The trees were growing taller and more numerous. They had turned onto a logging trail, where they'd seen large patches of freshly hewed stumps, but so far, no undead. They were a mere five miles from the interstate and had to consider this entire area a danger zone.

"Katie," Jenni said in a hushed tone, "I'm scared."

Katie took her hand and gave it a reassuring squeeze. "Just keep breathing."

Finally a sign appeared directing them to the back entrance to the camp. Jenni drew out the shotgun and laid it next to her.

Katie could feel her chest tightening and stomach fluttering. *Please, God, please, let Jason be alive.*

Dry red dirt flew up in a cloud as they drove along the winding unpaved road. It hadn't rained in a month, and the earth was cracked. At last, they could see the cabins used for youth camps through the trees. There was no sign of anyone.

Jenni was close to hyperventilating and her hands fluttered around her face.

"Jenni, calm down. Breathe. Jason needs you to be calm," Katie said firmly.

Jenni gulped air, trying to steady her nerves. "Yes . . . yes . . . yes . . ."

The whitewashed mess hall—the main meeting space for the campers—came into view, and Katie slowed the truck to a stop. From where the truck sat idling, they could see the long road to the front entrance to the camp. One lone van sat in the gravel parking lot.

The scream of the zombie girl as she hit Jenni's window made both women jump. The girl, her face a mask of blood, guts, and a gaping mouth with no tongue, slammed her hands against the window.

"They're here," Jenni whimpered.

Jack barked furiously at the zombie.

Katie reversed sharply, making sure not to end up in a tree. The zombie girl stood right in front of them, confused for a moment at their sudden disappearance. Then she realized where they were and charged. Katie stomped on the gas pedal, and the truck roared forward. When they hit the girl, her head hit the deer guard, and blood, bits of brain, and grayish fluid spewed across the hood.

Katie felt sickened, yet satisfied at the same time.

Jenni sobbed, wringing her hands.

"Jenni, calm down!" Katie ordered, but she feared that Jason was gone. Gone, like the rest of the world.

The mess hall shutters were all down and smeared with blood. Definitely not a good sign. The door cracked open and someone stepped out onto the front step, shading his eyes to see who was in the truck.

"Jason!"

Jenni was out of the truck and running before Katie could even try to grab her. Jenni's gun remained on her seat. Jack bounded out of the truck at her heels. Katie cursed, reached over and yanked Jenni's door shut, tucked Jenni's gun into her waistband, grabbed the shotgun and the keys, shoved her door open, and raced after them in an astonishingly short amount of time.

Jenni had almost reached the figure when she cried out in anguish, "You're not Jason!"

Katie was right behind Jenni, shotgun cocked and ready in her hands. A zombie came screeching around the corner, hands out, and Katie didn't hesitate to blast him in the face.

The boy on the doorstep grabbed Jenni and pulled her inside.

2.
Unraveled

"Jenni!" Katie screamed, terrified, aiming the shotgun at the shadowy figure.

Jack ran into the building, growling.

"Get in," the boy called out.

Human! She barely kept from pressing the trigger. Katie jumped through the doorway and the door slammed shut. Instantly, there was banging on the door. Oh, God! There had been zombies right behind her and she hadn't seen them, she had been so panicked.

Jenni stood nearby, sobbing, with her hands over her face.

Katie clutched her arm. "Don't do that again! We can't afford to screw up!"

Jenni looked at her, stricken, and Katie grabbed her, holding her close. "I'm sorry, I'm sorry. I thought . . . I thought . . ."

Katie became aware that they were standing in a hallway that led to a kitchen. At the end of it stood a tall, good-looking boy with masses of straight brown hair that fell into his eyes. An expression of shock fell over his face as he recognized Jenni.

"Jenni?"

"Jason?" Jenni's voice rose to a scary pitch. She ran into the boy's arms. He was almost as tall as she was. "Jason! Oh, Jason."

"Jenni, where's Dad? And the kids?"

Katie glanced at the other boy standing near the door. His

pale blue eyes were swollen and his freckled cheeks were stained with tears. Running both his hands through his blond hair, he stared at her with such sorrow, it made her wince.

"Hi, I'm Katie. We're here for Jason."

"I'm Brian." His voice was raw with fear as his eyes darted toward the kitchen and the loud crashing noises coming from that direction.

"What is that?" Katie asked, trying to identify the steady thumping.

"The other zombies. In the mess hall," Brian said simply, pointing at another set of doors. "They won't hold for long."

The doors were vibrating under the heavy onslaught from the other side. Kitchen equipment was piled in front of the doors, but Katie knew the boy was right. The barricade wouldn't withstand the zombie bombardment for much longer.

"Jenni? Jenni? Where are Dad and the boys?" Jason asked again. "Please, answer me, Jenni."

Jenni was bawling so hard that she couldn't answer the handsome teenager who was cuddling her close. All she could do was shake her head no. Jason's face crumpled as he fell against her and started to weep.

Katie collected herself, forced her fear down, and regarded Brian. "What's the situation here?"

His gaze remaining on the shuddering doors, Brian answered, "All day yesterday, people were showing up to pick up kids. Me, my sister Vicky, Jason, and a few other kids ended up here all alone last night after the counselors bailed. They just left, saying our families would get us. Around midnight, a family showed up to get one of the other kids. The mom had a bite from one of those zombie things. We didn't know that. We thought the mother was just asleep. We were all sleeping in the mess hall . . . you know . . . to stay together and safe. When we woke up, she was eating one of the girls—the one you creamed outside. Jason hit the zombie over the head with a chair and kept hitting her

until she was really dead. We ditched the girl out the door before she could . . . come back."

Katie winced. Behind her, Jenni and Jason were crying together, holding each other, mourning. She cast a wary glance toward the shaking doors.

"We didn't know that others had gotten bit in the scuffle. Jason, Vicky, and I had come in here to get some food when the screams started. We looked in and saw this guy—he was a football player before—attacking people. We just slammed the doors shut and bolted them. But—" Brian showed Katie his hand. "—I got bit."

Katie looked sharply at the boy, then at Jason.

"He's fine. We were going to try to escape when my family got here. But . . . the girl outside . . . she bit my dad. He's over there with my mom. He dropped his car keys somewhere outside. I . . . didn't . . . We couldn't leave. . . ." The boy's miserable eyes looked at Katie again. "I know we're dead. I know the bite is what makes you a zombie. Please, take my mom and sister, okay?"

Katie looked at the doors behind her that were being systematically tackled over and over again, trying to organize her thoughts into an escape plan. Jack sat in front of the door, growling low in his throat.

"We need to leave now," she asserted.

"Kill me and my dad first," Brian urged her.

Katie regarded the boy with compassion, but also reluctance. She hated the idea of ending his life, but wasn't it at an end anyway?

"Please, I don't want to be . . . that." Brian looked at the doors to the mess hall, his lips quivering .

Unable to gaze at his face, Katie walked into the kitchen. In one corner, she saw a man and a woman locked in a tight embrace. Sitting on the floor near them was a young girl around ten with the same coloring and features as Brian.

The woman looked up at Katie with glassy eyes and said, "Who are you?"

"I'm Katie. I'm here with my friend Jenni to rescue Jason."

"Oh," the woman said, her chin trembling. "You need to help us, too."

Katie walked over and studied the man. He definitely didn't have much time left. The man was sweating hard and his face looked grayish-green. He had multiple bites on his neck and shoulder. Blood was streaming down his chest. He was fading faster than his son, who just had one little bite.

The dying man looked at Katie's gun, then at his wife. "Take my wife and daughter with you. Do me and the boy a favor," he said in a breathless voice, gesturing at the gun. "You better go soon."

Katie hesitated, feeling numb and overwhelmed, but nodded. "I will." Ralph was right. In this world, she was going to have to learn to kill both the infected and the walking dead. She laid down the shotgun on the counter and drew Jenni's gun.

"I'm not leaving them! I'm not leaving them," the woman shrieked. She was the classic soccer mom—blond, short, bob haircut; slightly pudgy; dressed in jeans and a T-shirt.

Katie ignored her and walked over to the big stainless steel sinks. If her memory of the outside of the mess hall was correct, she ought to be able to see the outside door through the high window over the sinks. Hoisting herself up, she peered out. To her relief, just one zombie was banging on the outside door. But that didn't mean there weren't more out there.

After jumping down, she strode over to Jason and Jenni. "Listen. Now." Her voice was so authoritative that to her own ears, she sounded like her father. "We're leaving. I need both of you to stop crying right fucking now!"

They both blinked rapidly. Jason immediately understood and rubbed his tears away. Jenni reluctantly let go of her stepson and stood beside him, shivering.

"Brian is bit. So is his dad. The mother and sister are fine.

Those who are not bitten are leaving now before the zombie football player busts through those doors." Katie turned to look at the man, who was looking more and more dead with every passing second. "Sir, I'll take your wife and Vicky."

The young girl didn't seem to notice that Katie was even there, staring at her father with huge tears rolling down her cheeks.

Brian's father nodded, his fingers pressed tight to his bleeding throat. "Finish me. And my son. Don't let us . . . don't let us . . ."

Katie gave a short nod of her head. "I won't."

Brian hoisted Vicky to her feet and drew her to their parents. The man kissed his wife and daughter, and his son threw his arms around both his parents. The family clung together as Katie approached.

She felt sick. She felt shaken. She felt anger. She felt sadness. Brian's father looked kind, despite his terrible pallor, and he looked up at her with eyes the color of his son's. The thought of killing him made her stomach quiver, but she didn't want this self-sacrificing man to die like the man back in that town. As Lydia had.

"Vicky, Wendy, go with them. Get to safety," the man urged, pushing them away.

Brian grabbed hold of his mom by the waist with one arm and dragged Vicky back by her shoulder.

"No, Simon, no!" his wife cried out.

Simon gave Katie a nod, closing his eyes.

Katie fired a single shot.

Blood spray didn't affect her anymore, she realized dully.

Brian looked up at her, crying, covered in fresh blood, then also nodded . . . ready.

In that instant, the mother launched herself at Katie, screaming, "*Murderer!*" and slashing at her with a knife she must have been holding. Katie had no time to dodge, but Brian tackled his mother, driving her into Vicky. The girl let out a sharp cry as they all three tumbled to the floor.

"Shit!" Katie uttered, her eyes wide, watching mother and son struggle on the floor.

Vicky rolled away, the knife buried in her chest. The little girl let out a soft, shuddering sigh as she died. Wendy rose, screaming, and charged at Katie again. Brian crawled over to his sister, crying out in despair.

Jenni stepped forward and smacked the mother upside the head with a frying pan, sending the crazed woman sprawling. Wendy immediately tried to get to her feet, but her son grabbed on to her, holding her down.

"Go!" Brian shouted.

Wordlessly, Katie handed the revolver to Jenni, picked up her shotgun, and headed for the exit. Without hesitating, she whipped open the door and shot the zombie outside in the head before it could react. She ran for the truck while reloading the shotgun, with Jack, Jenni, and Jason close behind.

Brian's mother came out of the building behind them, still screaming incoherently. Howls rose in the forest. It was obvious that there were zombies out there and that they'd heard the woman and were now alerted of their escape.

"Fucking bitch!" Jenni shouted in anger.

"Just run!" As Katie ran, she could see figures emerging from the woods, moving fast. It would be close. Down to seconds.

She automatically hit the unlock button on the keyless remote, and the truck whistled in response. Ripping the driver's-side door open, she turned to cover those behind her with the shotgun. Knowing the drill, Jack hurtled into the cab. Jenni raced around the truck, Jason in tow, heading for the passenger side. As they disappeared, two sharp cracks of Jenni's revolver let Katie know the zombies were getting closer.

Wendy was almost on top of her, screaming wordlessly. She wasn't infected, but her mind was gone. Her son had followed her out of the building, one hand clutching the knife his mother had accidentally killed his sister with.

"Mom! Mom," he cried out.

Behind him, in the doorway, appeared a large, looming zombie. Katie could see others milling behind him.

Football Zombie guy—and his entourage—had arrived.

The first blast of Katie's shotgun took out the crazed mother.

Brian recoiled, stopped, and stared at Katie. Then, obviously resigned, he leaned forward, his hands on his knees.

Feeling numb and tired, but determined to do as the boy had asked, Katie fired. The boy fell back just as the football player zombie hit him.

Katie leaped into the truck, slamming the door. Jason sat with Jenni crammed between him and the passenger door. A zombie was banging on the passenger-side window.

"That went well," Katie said sardonically as she turned the key. She made a sharp U-turn and sped down the dirt road away from the camp.

3.
Return to Hell's Highways

The next few minutes were rough. Jason slid between the front seats onto the back bench, where he found himself with a lap full of dog. Jenni turned around in her seat, held his hands, and recounted her story in a tremulous voice.

It hurt Katie to hear Jenni's account . . . and she'd lived through much of it with her. Jason's sniffles told her how much his stepmother's words devastated him.

At times, Jenni's voice vanished into anguished sobs of despair, and Katie would reach out, eyes still on the road, to touch her shoulder.

Jason whispered, "No, no, no," as his stepmother spoke, but Katie could hear the beginning of acceptance in his voice. His family was gone and he had probably known that this was most

likely what had happened since the outbreak reached his camp. He seemed so young, no older than fifteen, and he would have to grow old quickly to survive.

When Jenni told how Katie had rescued her, Jason's hand—a boy's hand still—touched Katie's shoulder, and he whispered, "Thank you."

It took all Katie's willpower not to cry.

Finally, Jenni told Jason about the hunting store, about Ralph and his Israeli wife who used to be a sniper.

"And the hunting store is safe?"

"As safe as this world gets now," Katie answered. "Which reminds me, I need to check in."

Soon, Ralph's voice filled the cab.

"Yeah, we cleared out most of the town. Awful mess, though, all those bodies. I'll have to figure a way to get them away from the store so the stench won't be so bad. Turns out Bill, our deputy sheriff, was holed up down the road at the Parker place. He managed to get here on foot. Mighty brave of him. He wasn't bit. So he's safe. We'll put him and yer boy up in the living room on cots."

"That's good news. You don't know how badly we want to get back." Katie couldn't help but smile at the thought of reaching the store.

"How's the gas?"

"Honestly, we're coming in on fumes. We . . . ah . . . forgot the backup canisters."

"Noticed. Well, stay yer course. Stay steady. You should make it back okay if you do. We'll be on the lookout for you."

"Thanks, Ralph. We'll see you soon," Katie said, and handed the CB transceiver to Jenni, who promptly secured it back to the dashboard.

Glancing into her rearview mirror, Katie saw Jason rubbing his eyes and nose. Jack was pressed up against him, whimpering softly, licking at his face. That brought a small smile to the boy's face and he hugged the dog snugly.

"Listen, both of you. We need to keep our heads together the rest of this trip. We can't lose it now."

Jenni looked at Katie plaintively. "I know. I know. I blew it."

"We just got lucky. But it could have gone down so much worse. You even left your gun behind."

Jenni took a breath and let it out gradually . She ran her hands over her bedraggled ponytail. "I . . . I just wanted him to be alive."

"And I am," Jason said. "But I don't want to lose my only family member. My only mom."

Jenni looked at him and clasped his hand over the back of her seat firmly. "I won't lose it again. I'll be strong."

Katie pushed her sunglasses up on her nose, appearing grim. "We can't let our emotions rule us. We just can't. We have to keep calm."

She could see out of her peripheral vision that both of them were nodding. A little of the tightness in her belly lessened, but her hands still felt shaky despite her firm grip on the steering wheel.

Glancing at the fuel gauge, she exhaled slowly. It was going to be tight.

No deviations.

No detours.

Straight on.

To safety.

To their new home.

The truck crested a hill and for a second, Katie couldn't draw breath.

"Fuck," Jason blurted out.

"No," Jenni whispered in horror.

"Gawddammit!"

Katie slammed on the brakes.

Running full speed toward them was an enormous crowd of zombies. It had to be the zombies they'd first seen in Emorton—children, old people, young people, adults, all bloodied and all

chewed up, all screaming, moaning, screeching as they flowed along the narrow farm road and spilled into the trees.

Jenni started to moan. "No, no, no."

Katie pounded her fist on the steering wheel. "They fucking followed us. They fucking followed us!"

"What are we going to do?" Jason asked, his voice edged with panic.

Jack barked.

Katie grabbed the CB mic. "Ralph, Nerit . . . we have a situation."

"What's wrong?" Nerit's voice said coolly, but tinged with worry.

"There was a shitload of zombies in Emorton. They pursued us when we went through the town. Evidently, they kept running after us, and right now, they're about a mile away and closing fast. They fill the fucking road all the way into the trees."

"Can you gun it and get through them?" Ralph's voice asked.

Katie looked at Jenni and Jason. They both looked afraid, they both looked desperate, but they all knew the truth.

"No. We can't. Too many." Katie rubbed the back of her hand over her lips and tried to swallow. Her mouth was so dry. "We have to . . . we have to turn around."

"Katie . . ." Ralph's voice was soft.

"Sorry, Ralph—" Her voice caught. "—we wanted to make it back."

"Turn around. Go to FM 1226. Keep out of their sight. They'll keep going straight on, hopefully. Take FM 1226 to CR 1113. That'll bring you back here," another voice said.

Probably the deputy.

There was some discussion over on the other end.

". . . not enough gas . . ."

". . . drive out to them . . ."

". . . risky in Ashley Oaks . . ."

"We're doing it," Katie said, then handed off the mouthpiece to Jenni.

The zombies were closing fast. She could see they were desperate to get to the truck, roll it, break it apart, and eat what was within. A few in the front stumbled, fell, and were crushed beneath the onslaught of those behind.

Katie swung the truck around, aimed it back in the direction they had come from, and floored it.

"Pray for us," Jenni said into the mic.

"Just keep moving . . . until you can't no more. We'll come get you," Ralph said.

Katie's eyes flicked to the rearview mirror and the zombie horde cresting the hill behind them. She pushed harder on the gas pedal.

They had to keep calm. They had to keep strong. They had to survive.

It was as easy as that.

· CHAPTER SEVEN ·

1.
By the Pricking of Their Thumbs . . .

Jenni furrowed her brow and traced the farm road they were on with her finger. They were speeding away from the road that led to Emorton. Jason leaned over and pointed to a little dot on the map marked ASHLEY OAKS. Jenni frowned some more, then glanced over at the boy. She could see his eyes narrowing as he concentrated.

"That adds approximately ten miles to our trip." He glanced at the gas gauge. "Possibly doable."

Jenni smiled slightly. Jason was good with figures, and she trusted him. "Ralph will come get us."

"We need to not be too far out when we hit empty," Katie said. "We really don't know what the situation is out here. We're hoping for a low number of zombies, but Emorton taught us a fairly bitter lesson."

Jenni could feel the heat of the sun pressing down on her and she glanced toward it. It was lower in the sky as the day wound to a close. They were running out of time. "What does it look like?" Katie asked.

Jason took the map and studied it. "No towns except the one Ralph talked about. At least not between us and Ashley Oaks."

Jenni barely glanced at the occasional house or trailer along the road. Most of them looked boarded up. No cars anywhere.

The world was as good as dead now, it seemed, at least here in rural Texas.

She was trying hard not to panic. Not to feel overwhelmed. She gripped Jason's hand tightly. They had saved Jason. She had done her duty, and that gave her a strange sense of calm. But now they had to stay alive. Otherwise, their rescue of Jason would be pointless. Yesterday, on her own doorstep, Jenni had almost given up. Almost given in, but not now. No, not now.

The truck roared as it turned down the narrow country road Ralph had directed them to. Katie's knuckles were white as she gripped the steering wheel.

They all felt it, Jenni knew. They were running out of time.

"I'm starving, Mom."

"There's food in the bags next to you," Jenni answered. She glanced out the window, toward the hills and the fields covered in spring flowers. It was such a pretty day.

Behind her, Jason rummaged through the backpacks they had brought with them from the gun store. The tearing of cellophane sounded behind her, and Jason wordlessly handed her a Danish. She took it and began to eat ravenously. The day was slipping by fast and they had forgotten to eat. Jason handed a pastry to Katie, and they all ate in eerie silence.

If the zombies catch us and tear us open, will they enjoy the sugary goodness inside, Jenni wondered grimly.

The vision of all those zombies running toward them was too horrible to think about, yet she couldn't help but do so. What if they figured out, somehow, from some instinct, that the truck had pulled onto this road?

"I gotta pee," Jenni said abruptly. The urgent need had hit her suddenly. She was a little surprised when Jason and Katie both said, "Me, too."

"Looks clear," Katie added.

Katie stopped in the middle of the narrow road, lifted the

shotgun off the console, and looked at Jenni. "You first. Take your gun. I'll cover."

Jenni grumbled as she released her seat belt. "This is fucking annoying. Not being able to go without an armed guard."

Jason cleared his throat and said, "What about me? I gotta go like right now."

"I'll cover for you, too. Jenni can cover for me."

Jason looked at her warily.

Katie gave him a reassuring smile. "I'm a lesbian. It's okay. I'm not interested in your boy parts. I won't look."

"Really?" Jason's eyes somewhat lit up. "I saw a movie with lesbians once."

"I'm sure you did." Katie rolled her eyes and flung her door open. She slid out, muttering something about all men being alike.

Jenni found it uncomfortable to squat in the tall grass and summer wildflowers and try to pee while Katie hovered over her with the safety off on the shotgun. She tried hard to concentrate on the far horizon, staring across the wide valley of farmland.

Suddenly she realized she could see the country road they had been on before—and see the crowd of zombies, still racing along. If one of them should look over and see the bright red truck perched high on the hill across the valley . . .

She yanked up her pants. "Katie," she whispered, and pointed.

Katie looked, studied, and realized what the dark swarm of antlike creatures on the far road was. "Fuck." She motioned to Jason, who was standing nearby, trying to pee. "Empty your bladder now. We're outta here."

Jason glanced up and saw what had the women so spooked. "That sucks."

Meanwhile, Jack decorated all four tires with a nice yellow stream and left a tidy little brown package behind the truck in the middle of the road. He followed Jason back into the truck, giving Jenni a doggy grin that told her of his satisfaction.

"Hoping a zombie steps in it, huh," Jenni said with a little smile as she climbed into the truck.

She could have sworn Jack's smile got bigger.

Casting a wary glance at the distant zombie throng, Jenni whispered a silent prayer. Katie shifted into gear and they sped off with only a thin line of trees and a valley of farmland separating them from certain death.

"What if one of them looks this way?" Jason asked, his voice sounding a little higher than usual.

He's terrified, Jenni thought. And she had to admit she was, too.

"Pray that they don't," Katie answered.

Much to their relief, the road swerved and put the zombie throng behind them instead of alongside.

Jenni couldn't help but turn around in her seat and stare out the back window. Jack and Jason did the same. The dog gave a light woof; Jenni couldn't decide if it was comforting or not.

"This cannot get any worse!" Katie half yelled. Jenni felt the truck slow and spun around to look out the front window.

A narrow bridge lay before them, completely blocked by a large, overturned farm truck and its bulky haul of hay bales. Inside the overturned truck cab, two zombies were flailing against the glass, having spotted the pickup full of potential meals. The driver was badly mauled and was probably not much a threat due to the fact that it was completely missing one arm and half the other. The female zombie with only a throat wound visible was a bit feistier.

"Bet he was trying to save her and she ate him," Jason said.

Jenni kept blinking, trying to force what she was seeing to change, but it was all too clear. There was no way across the bridge.

Next to her, Katie was rhythmically banging her head against the pale white knuckles of her hands, saying, "Fuckfuckfuckfuckfuckfuck."

"We have to go back," Jenni said softly.

"Fuckfuckfuckfuckfuckfuck."

"Maybe we could wait until the zombie army passes the intersection back there, then hightail it back to the gun store," Jason suggested.

"Fuckfuckfuckfuckfuckfuck."

Jenni looked behind the truck, then ahead. There was no choice.

"Fuckfuckfuckfuckfuckfuck. Fuckaduck," Katie said with finality, and sat up. "Okay, do we sit here and wait for—?"

The female zombie had finally managed to locate an opening in the bashed-up cab and was squirming out.

"That answers that," Katie decided.

"Woof," Jack said. He was staring at the back window. Jason turned to see what the dog was looking at and said, "Uh . . . we have zombies. . . ."

Jenni whipped around to see three old women—well, what had once been three old women—still clad in flowered summer dresses, running toward them. Behind them were what looked like two field-workers.

"I think we picked up . . . um . . . a zombie parade," Jason said mildly. "Probably from some of the farmhouses back there."

"Fuckfuckfuckfuckfuck," Katie said again as she started to turn the truck around on the narrow road. Her careful maneuvering took long enough that by the time the truck was pointed away from the bridge, the scary old women zombies were banging on the windows.

Jenni flipped off the safety on her gun and tried to steady her nerves as the female zombie from the wreck finished worming her way out, stood up, and started for the truck.

"Go!" she shouted.

The truck roared down the road, effectively taking out two of the farmworkers.

"Tell Ralph," Katie said.

Jenni reached for the CB.

Ralph's voice was somber when he responded after hearing

of their situation. "Take FM 1995. You'll end up in a town named Ashley Oaks. They're doing a lot of construction there, fixing up the place. Renovations of the downtown. Get there and see if you can hole up with a group of survivors there. I've found some chatter on Channel Nine few minutes ago. Tune in to that channel. Trucker made it to Ashley Oaks and he put out the word there is survivors there. I was hoping you were going to make it home, but you better try for them. They're closer."

Jenni looked at Katie hopefully, and Katie nodded. "Ralph, we're gonna try for it. That's a big ol' ten-four, big buddy!"

Jason winced at his stepmother's words, and Jenni playfully wrinkled her nose at him.

"You watched way too much *Smokey and the Bandit*, Mom."

"Jason, get the map," Katie said. "Check out Ashley Oaks."

Jason immediately grabbed the map and studied it, measuring with his fingers, looking at the gas gauge, and calculating in his head. "It'll be really tight."

"As usual," Katie sighed.

Jenni looked worriedly at Katie, then grabbed the CB. "Uh, Ralph? Please tell me . . . the survivors in Ashley Oaks . . . they're not in a mall . . . right?"

Katie's laughter rang out. Jenni just pouted at her.

"Why don't you just ask if their leader is a black man?" Katie said with a grin.

"Nope and nope," Ralph said. From the sound of his voice, Jenni could tell he was both amused and worried. "I'm guessin' they're downtown somewhere. Probably near the renovations. Keep us informed. I'm worried sick."

"Ten-four. Can and will do. Over and out," Jenni said, trying to sound like she wasn't scared out of her mind. But every time she looked at the gas gauge, she feared that they were going to be stranded and have to fight their way to safety on foot.

She looked across the valley at the dark cloud of dead flesh moving across the distant road. The sign announcing the junction with their new destination flashed by as the pickup rushed

down the road. Jenni hoped they'd make the turn before the zombies noticed them.

Katie turned the truck onto FM 1995, which sloped up a hill. It was a long, steady climb, and Jenni couldn't help but turn and stare out the back window. Between the shaggy brown hair of her stepson and the back of the German shepherd's head, she saw a handful of zombies. Probably the stragglers from the big group.

The red truck crested the tall hill, and Jenni looked ahead to see the entire valley and the hills beyond, painfully beautiful, serene, and majestic. And then they were descending the other side.

Jason turned around, white-faced. "Mom, did you see?"

"What?" Jenni asked.

"Didn't you see?"

"No."

"Maybe ten or twenty zombies started running across the field toward this road."

Jenni rested her forehead on the back of her seat and sighed.

From beside her came a steady string of *fuckfuckfuckfuck-fuck*.

2.
Salvation This Way Comes

Katie couldn't stop cursing, nor did she want to. This was getting ridiculous. She just couldn't believe how downhill their plan had gone. But every time she started to curse herself for leaving the safety of Ralph's hunting store, she would catch a glimpse of the kid with the shaggy brown hair in the backseat. She knew it had been worth the risk.

Katie had felt helpless after saving Jenni. Yeah, they had survived, but she had failed too many. Lydia, the kid at the convenience store, the family at the camp . . . how many others had

she bypassed without notice? Lydia always teased her that she wanted to save the world, and she was right. Katie wished she could save the world, but knew in her heart that she couldn't. All she could truly do was keep the people and the dog she had rescued alive and safe.

Now they were heading at eighty miles per hour toward a possible camp of survivors while a throng of zombies jogged along behind them in an unrelenting pursuit of flesh. Her flesh. And Jason's. And Jenni's.

She glanced at the dog, who looked back at her questioningly. If the zombies wanted Jack or not had yet to be seen, but they wouldn't get him if she had her way. Jack went back to chewing on some jerky Jason had given him, eyeing Katie suspiciously.

Slowly, their destination appeared, shimmering out on the horizon before resolving into more detailed images.

Katie could clearly see the downtown area partially ringed by tall redbrick buildings that seemed out of place in the flatness of the rest of the town. The farm road they were traveling on would lead them straight into the center of town.

Where were the survivors?

Time to find out.

Katie grabbed the CB and flipped it to Channel 9. "Survivors in Ashley Oaks, this is the bright red truck heading your way. We're a party of three with a dog companion."

"Bright Red Truck, what direction are you heading in from? FM 1995 or Route 6?" It was a woman's voice. Calm. Reassuring.

"Ashley Oaks, we're coming in from the west on FM 1995. We're running low on fuel and have company bringing up the rear. They are probably a few miles back, but they don't seem to get tired."

"We understand. Keep on course and when you reach the wall, get out of the truck and we'll lift you over."

"Wall?" Jenni and Jason said at the same time.

"We don't understand," Katie said with some confusion.

"You will. Just be ready." The woman's voice cut out.

As they barreled down the road, Katie felt the truck give a little shudder. The needle on the gas gauge now sat below the line.

"This is going to be close," Jenni exclaimed.

"As usual," Katie responded.

The tall red buildings, very early 1900s retro in style, loomed larger. The rest of the town zoomed past—a smattering of rundown houses, boarded-up buildings from the 1970s, empty car lots, and abandoned gas stations. Katie estimated that the center of town was maybe four blocks away now. It looked a little intimidating. They could now see that three of the tall buildings hovered over what looked like a construction site. Several large trucks appeared to ring it. On one end, a yellow machine was perched on the bed of an enormous truck that was filled with dirt. The construction vehicle had a long mechanical arm with a large scoop.

"Where are the zombies?" Jason asked worriedly. "This town has to have some."

The truck sputtered once and died.

They were a block from their destination.

Katie immediately grabbed the CB mic, but before she could speak, it cackled and a voice said, "We have a distraction going. Run for the corner where we are signaling."

"Corner? Corner?" Jenni looked scattered and afraid.

"Stay calm, Jenni!" Katie spotted a man standing next to the big yellow machine she thought was called an excavator and waving a Texas flag. "There! Follow me!" She grabbed her shotgun, her backpack, and the bag of ammo and leaped out of the truck with Jack right behind her. Jenni followed, struggling with her backpack. Jason hopped out, backpack on.

"Run," Katie ordered.

They ran.

Katie was in good shape—she and Lydia had gone running every day—but she wasn't used to running with so much weight.

She felt slow and vulnerable, grateful for the comforting heft of the shotgun in her hand. She and her companions raced past empty stores with faded FOR LEASE signs on their ruined doors, past blood splatters on the sidewalk. They ran past empty cars with open doors that told of other people's terror. They ran across an old redbrick street and aimed for the large yellow arm of the piece of the excavator, which was being extended down toward them.

"Get in, get in!" a man yelled.

Katie's legs felt rubbery after all her time in the truck. Jenni and Jason were huffing behind her.

"Hurry!"

Her lungs hurt, her back hurt, everything hurt, but she ran.

The large scoop of the machine crunched onto the road. Encrusted with dirt, its jagged teeth were somehow welcoming. They ran for it with the screeches of the undead ringing in their ears.

The same man's voice boomed out. "Get into it!"

Katie reached the excavator and whirled about . The zombies were coming around the corner. Jenni lost her footing and tumbled forward, but managed to fall into the clawed scoop. Jason jumped in after her. Katie grabbed the dog and heaved him in.

The large scoop had already begun to lift with a steady, mechanical whine.

The zombies were close, and Katie considered firing, but realized she didn't have time. She half fell, half jumped into the machine, landing on top of Jenni and the others, half-in, half-out of the scoop.

The world shifted as they rose, and Katie felt sickeningly exposed. She was shivering so violently, she was sure she was going to vomit. The moans of the dead surrounded them when a hand, grisly and bloodied, grabbed one of the dirt-encrusted teeth of the excavator. The scoop arm was barely a few feet above the heads of the crazed zombies.

The zombie tried to get a better hold while its other hand

fumbled at Katie's foot. Katie was too terrified to move for fear of rolling off the others and into the crowd below. She could only stare in fear at the scrabbling hand.

Jack solved the problem. He grabbed the groping zombie hand in his teeth and shook his head savagely. The thing lost its grip and fell. The machine lifted faster and higher and swung about. Katie felt herself slipping, and Jason and Jenni grabbed on to her. Then the world tilted again and they were being lowered.

Katie lost her balance and slid painfully over the teeth of the contraption. Instead of plunging into the undead, she landed on soft soil.

A man's hand came down, took hers gently, and helped her to her feet. "You, okay?" he asked.

Looking up, Katie smiled as she took in his appearance. He was taller than she was and sturdily built, with curly brown hair and the nicest hazel eyes she'd ever seen. He radiated gentle power and kindness. His height and build spoke of a man used to hard work. He seemed oddly familiar to her, and she instantly felt camaraderie with him.

"Yeah." She nodded and looked at his hand, which was still clutching hers as he guided her from the excavator. His fingers were caked with dirt and bits of cement. "That was scary."

"Only way to get people over the wall," he answered. "It's not very comfortable, but it's the only way for now. I'm Travis."

"Katie," she answered, awkwardly drawing her hand away. Instinctively, she knew Travis was behind the rapid building of this fortress. She was good at reading people, and he had a vibe similar to her father. One of those quietly strong men who inspired people to great things.

Jenni stood next to her, staring at the handsome man. "Hi, I'm Jenni and this is my son, Jason."

Travis greeted them both with a warm handshake. With a smile, he kneeled down to pet Jack. "I saw what you did. You're a good pup, defending your mama."

Jack gave him a doggy grin in response and licked his hand.

Travis stood again. "Welcome to our little fort. Glad you made it here okay. Ralph let us know what is going on. You are okay, right?"

"We're fine. None of us is hurt." Katie looked around curiously. "Is it safe here?"

They were in a large enclosed area filled with people working hard to construct a wall around the site.

"Without a doubt. We don't have anyone infected with whatever is causing this."

"So you know about the bite," Katie said with relief.

"Sadly, we do."

"So are you in charge?" Jenni blurted out.

Travis laughed, shaking his head. "No, no. I'm just a guy working on a construction site. Mayor Reyes is running the show. Juan, the foreman, and I have been giving him some suggestions along the way, but he is the elected official in charge and also the emergency coordinator for the town."

"Ah, I see. The wall is impressive. The whole setup is great," Katie remarked.

Katie looked past Travis, turning her head to take in her surroundings. She stood at the edge of a spacious construction site that was flanked on two sides by enormous buildings. One was at least ten stories tall and sprawled across one whole side of the site. It was an old-fashioned hotel made out of the red bricks that seemed a signature of the town. The second building was flush against the far side of the hotel and took up most of the rear of the construction area. It, too, was made out of red bricks, but had been whitewashed at some point long ago and painted with an old Coca-Cola advertisement that was now a faded reminder of another era. An old metal sign was raised over the building and read ASHLEY OAKS PICAYUNE NEWS MESSENGER. Storage containers and construction equipment and vehicles were parked along the edge of the truck line near the old newspaper building.

A narrow, three-story city hall sat across from the newspaper

building at the midpoint of the block. Its windows were covered in fancy ironwork and appeared newly refurbished. A beautiful mural adorned the side of the building with an idealized portrayal of the downtown under the words ASHLEY OAKS CITY HALL: HOME OF FRIENDLY PEOPLE. FOUNDED 1867.

Only two borders of the site were open to the quaint Texas town, and those were cut off with a hurricane fence that had been put in place for construction. Beyond the fence was a ring of construction trucks. Piles of dirt and bags of cement filled the formerly empty spaces beneath the trucks and between the cabs and their loads, forming a secondary wall. There was a third wall made of concrete bricks being constructed within the hurricane fence, running from building to building. Already it connected the city hall to the hotel. The construction workers who had been on the renovation job when the zombies first appeared now seemed to be striving to create a fort the size of a city block within their worksite.

Katie was staggered by what she saw. The mobile office trailer for the site had apparently been turned into residences—an elderly woman and younger man holding a child emerged from it to gaze at the newcomers. There was a lunch wagon parked in one corner, serving food. A majority of the survivors appeared to be the construction workers, but there were a few women and children sitting around in the shade watching the new arrivals with interest.

"It's not a mall," Jenni sighed with relief.

Kate realized, much to her surprise, that she felt safe. "This is amazing! You did all of this since yesterday?"

Travis nodded. "Yep. We really didn't have much of a choice. Give me a moment, and I'll show you around." He turned toward the man who had been running the excavator. "Hey, Juan!"

"He's not black," Katie joked under her breath to Jenni as Travis walked over to Juan to share a word with him.

"But I'll kiss him anyway," Jenni said dreamily.

Katie lifted an eyebrow at her.

"Well, you won't!"

Kate smiled and shook her head slightly.

Travis glanced over at them, and Kate had to look away. She felt unnerved by his gaze. Something had happened when she first looked at him. New knowledge had sprung strong and sure into her mind: This was now home. And Travis was going to play a very important role in her future. All her life, Katie had always trusted her instincts about people. She formed quick and firm attachments. It had taken her all of one minute to fall in love with Lydia. She already felt completely attached to Jenni and Jason. They were her new family. Her gut told her that Travis was also important in this new world.

She looked back and saw him staring at her.

He knows, too, she thought.

The wheels of destiny had turned, and a new reality was being spun into existence.

She looked at Jenni. She could tell that the younger woman was in crush city.

Jason, meanwhile, was kneeling next to Jack, keeping the excited pet from dashing off. The teenager gazed around at the equipment and the people hard at work. "This is really cool, Mom."

"Yeah," Jenni agreed, relief in her voice. "Really, really cool."

Travis smiled at Kate and she smiled back.

We're going to fight this war together, Kate thought. *You and me, Travis. We're important, and now that we're both here, things are going to happen. Do you feel it?*

And by his gaze, she knew he felt it, too.

1.
The New World

Jenni let her backpack fall to the ground with a *thunk* and shook out her hair to get all the caked mud out of it. They were all pretty dirty from being transported over the wall. There was a flair to the movement, a bit of feminine guile in her smile.

Katie grinned to herself. Jenni was trying to get Travis's attention.

He walked back toward them, dirty, tired, but smiling. "Okay, sorry, things are a little crazy right now. Your arrival really surprised us. We had a truck driver come in a few hours ago, but by now, honestly, we weren't too sure anyone was left out there alive."

"It's really bad out there. I can't believe how fast this whole thing spiraled out of control." Katie tucked her hair behind her ears and looked around the site again. "Are y'all in touch with FEMA or any other agencies?"

Travis set his hands on his belt and shook his head. "Phones are down. The Walmart truck driver said he saw lines down a few miles from here. Cell phones are dead in the water. We still have cable Internet, but that is spotty as sites go down. We've been listening to the emergency broadcast, but nothing makes sense. They don't seem to have a clue in hell what's going on."

"Zombies," Jenni said firmly. "It's zombies."

Travis glanced at her, grinning. "Yeah, zombies."

Katie looked again at the newly constructed cinder block wall. She couldn't help but be curious about her surroundings. To finally feel safe and secure behind high walls was a real blessing as far as she was concerned. Being on the road had seriously frayed her nerves, and it felt good to be in an actual community of survivors. "So you did start the wall right away."

"About one o'clock yesterday," Travis said. "We should have the rest up soon."

"Were you building all night?"

"Yep. Had to. We're short on people since a lot of my crew took off for home. Can't blame them, really; with all the badness going down, people want to be with their families," Travis answered sympathetically .

Katie shivered as she remembered Lydia.

Travis took hold of her shoulder and rubbed it lightly. "You okay?"

She knew her eyes were glistening. "Just . . . We've all lost family."

"Yeah." There was a wealth of grief in the word Travis uttered. "My parents . . ."

"Jenni lost everyone but her stepson. I lost . . ." She faltered.

Travis's eyes were so warm, so compassionate. "You lost your husband."

Katie hesitated. Then, knowing that something was fast developing between her and Travis—some kind of bond . . . It was best to be honest.

"My wife."

Travis's gaze dropped for an instant, but his hand did not. He rubbed her arm tenderly, then said, "I'm sorry. She had to be real special to be with you."

Even if his words were just his Texan manners, they touched her. They unleashed something deep within her and she covered her mouth, tears springing from her eyes and running down her face. Their gazes met—strong, understanding—and he put his other hand on her other shoulder.

"It's so hard to not have her here . . . ," Katie gasped.

"But she'd want you to survive," Travis assured her.

"I know, but it doesn't make it any easier," Katie admitted.

Katie had been so focused on Travis that she was startled when Jenni wrapped one arm around her waist and leaned against her, offering comfort. Travis let go and stepped back to let the friends have a moment.

"I'm so sorry, Katie," Jenni whispered. "I wish she was here, too."

"I'm glad we're here together."

Katie observed that Jenni looked confused by the intense emotions of the last few minutes, and she could guess why. To Jenni, things between men and women were black-and-white—Katie had seen that in Jenni's behavior. It was all sex and power with Jenni. Travis and Katie clicking on some subliminal level had to be throwing her. She gently tucked a tendril of Jenni's dark hair back from her friend's face and smiled tenderly at her. Jenni returned her smile and Katie felt the pain inside lessen.

Katie looked down at her feet to regain her composure. Finally, she peered up at Travis again. "Thank you for being so kind. I do appreciate it."

"We've all lost people. It's going to rough for all of us to move on. We're all going to have to help each other." Travis shrugged slightly. "We'll do what we have to."

"Hey, Travis," a tall Hispanic man said as he joined them. He appeared in his late twenties and had long, curly hair flowing out from beneath his cowboy hat. His dark hair had glints of red, and his eyes were dark green. He was tall and deeply tanned and had the lean-muscled build of someone who did a lot of hard physical labor.

"Jenni, Katie, Jason, this is Juan. He's the foreman," Travis said by way of introduction.

"Nice to meet ya," Juan said in his thick Texan accent. "That zombie maid is at it again, Travis." He pointed, drawing their attention to a window high above them.

"That's the old hotel," Travis explained. "The renovation was just finished recently and they were getting set to open soon."

"How do you know she's a maid?" Katie wondered.

"How do you know she's a zombie?" Jenni added, squinting, trying to see where Juan was pointing.

"Only staff was in the building, so we're assuming she's a maid," Travis answered. "And she has beat her head against that window hard enough to smear it with blood, which seems like a zombie thing to do."

The first three floors had no windows, but farther up, glass caught the rays of the setting sun, glimmering purple and pink. Near the top floor, the shape of a woman battered herself against a window.

"Oh, wow," Jason said, transfixed. "She is really messing herself up good."

"She breaks out of that window, she's coming straight down," Juan observed. "Right straight down on us.

"Maybe she'll land on her damn head," Jenni mused. "I'd like to see her head bust open."

"Feeling a little hostile there, Mom?" Jason arched an eyebrow under his thick fringe of bangs.

"I kinda hate zombies." Jenni shrugged.

Juan looked toward her, his arms folded over his muscled chest. "They do bring out the hate, don't they?"

"Oh, yeah," Jenni muttered.

Katie narrowed her eyes as she observed the scene above her. "That window is cracked."

"She's been working on it since sometime last night. Bet she went to hide up there after being ripped up." Travis shook his head. "Poor thing."

Jenni stepped closer to Travis. "What if there are more up there?"

"Then it'll be raining zombies," Juan said with a chuckle. "And I hope they all bust their damn heads open when they land."

At that moment, the maid finally broke the tempered glass

just enough to get her hand through. While those below watched in horror, she worked at the opening with her fingers until she pushed herself all the way out. It was a long, almost graceful fall, with her blond hair streaming behind her and her pink bloodstained dress billowing up around her waist. She landed feet first on the hard-packed soil a few feet away. Every bone in her legs shattered as she crumpled to the ground. Unable to get up, she systematically crawled toward the spectators.

Juan sighed. Snatching up a shovel, he started to walk toward her.

Katie cocked her shotgun.

"No. No guns. The sound will bring more zombies," Travis said.

"Good point."

Katie tried to look away from the scene taking place before her, but couldn't. A few people gasped, and a woman hurried her child away as Juan drew near the growling zombie.

"Get it done," Travis called out.

Juan nonchalantly drove the shovel through the head of the zombified maid, and the drama was over.

"We need to build a catapult and just toss them over," Juan muttered as he motioned to another man to dispose of the body. "Ditch it over the wall."

Travis chuckled grimly. "We just may."

Jenni grinned. "Use them as cannonballs against the rest of the damn zombies."

Juan regarded Jenni appreciatively. "Now, that would be fun."

Jenni hovered near Katie's side, blushing slightly. Jason was right behind her, holding on to her arm and Jack's collar.

"I'm kinda hungry, Mom," Jason whispered to Jenni.

"Got anything to eat around here?" Katie asked, overhearing.

"As a matter of fact, there was supposed to be a fund-raiser last night for the local volunteer fire department. There's so

much food up in the community dining hall, you're gonna feel like you're in heaven," Travis answered.

"Thank God," Jenni said with relief.

"So we're staying?" Jason asked. "We're not heading back to the hunting store?"

Katie looked at him and then at Jenni. Jenni smiled at her, her gaze flicking to Travis, then back to Katie. It was obvious that Jenni was enamored of Travis. That didn't really surprise Katie. Jenni seemed inclined to look for a strong male figure to protect her. They had joked about finding a Romero-type hero, but Katie could tell that Jenni really did crave one. Katie suspected Travis was now firmly assigned to that role in Jenni's mind.

"Yeah, we're staying," Katie decided. "At least for now."

"Good. Because we need you here. I feel it," Travis said. He put one arm around Jenni and the other around Jason. "Now, let's get you fed."

Katie didn't think Jenni could get any redder or any more giddy. She followed the little group toward the city hall, glancing back once to see the dead zombie being loaded onto the arm of the excavator to be dumped back among her own kind.

"Besides," Katie mused. "How the hell would we get out of here?"

2.
Through a Door Softly

Jenni felt special, walking with Travis's arm around her shoulders. His voice was like fine leather against her skin, and she felt herself blushing even hotter. She hoped Travis didn't notice. She most definitely hoped Jason didn't. Behind her, Katie walked briskly, holding her shotgun in one hand and her backpack in the other.

"Wait, Travis! I almost forgot. There are zombies following

us here. We told the person on the CB. It'll probably take a little while for them to get here," Katie said urgently.

"Crap. Okay. We can deal with that," Travis answered, releasing his hold on Jenni and Jason. He turned and signaled to Juan.

Juan tucked his thumbs into his work belt, sauntered over, and looked at Travis expectantly.

"There are more zombies on the way. Get the harnesses ready," Travis said. "I'm heading in to get them fed, then talk to Mayor Reyes about the incoming zombies. We might as well prepare."

"They finally bust out of the damn school?" Juan asked.

"Nope. This is a different group. They followed our new friends," Travis answered.

"Great. It's not like we don't have enough of them out there as it is." Juan groused. "Are you sure? Where'd you pick 'em up?" He stared at Katie pointedly.

"Emorton was overrun. It looked like the whole town was turned. They aren't too messed up, so they're fast," Katie answered.

Juan shook his head. "We lost a man keeping them off the perimeter before."

"We've learned from our mistakes. We need to keep them thinned out or we'll get overrun." Travis patted Juan's shoulder. "We can handle it."

"You better get the mayor on board," Juan urged. "You know how he likes to be included in the planning."

"What are you going to do?" Katie asked. "What are the harnesses?"

"We're going to secure some men with safety lines. When the zombies come up against the outer perimeter, we stand above them on the trucks and stab down through their skulls with spears we made and shovels, jumble up their brains. We took out around a dozen that way before we lost a man the last time. But we didn't have the safety lines the first time out," Travis said, his voice tinged with sorrow.

Juan looked up at the darkening sky. "Good thing we got the lights set up. And if the grid goes down, we're on backup power. . . ." He exhaled with exasperation. "This is a fucked-up situation."

"Just get some men ready and hooked up."

"It's like we're dangling bait in front of the zombies, Travis," Juan protested gruffly.

"They're gonna come anyway," Travis answered. "First sign of trouble, we yank our people back."

"Yeah, yeah. Shit." Juan sighed heavily. "Okay. I'm on it."

The men's conversation made Jenni feel anxious and she could tell by the look on his face that Jason was unnerved. Katie, in contrast, seemed comforted, and Jenni realized it was because Katie felt that at last someone had a working plan of action.

Travis clapped Juan on the shoulder. "Keep me informed."

"You got it, Travis," Juan replied in a resigned tone and walked off.

Travis turned to finish escorting the newcomers into city hall, but instead of resuming his comforting embrace, he lightly touched Katie's arm. "I want to hear about what's up with you. How did you end up here?" He opened the door for them.

"Sure, but let's eat first." Katie gave him a slight smile. "We're seriously hungry."

Jenni hung back for a second to watch Juan order several men away from the construction of the wall, then followed Katie and Travis inside. She felt moody all of a sudden and wasn't sure why. She trudged up the stairs behind the others, struggling not to spiral into a bad mood. The first whiff of fried chicken helped push her dark thoughts away as her stomach grumbled with anticipation.

As Travis had promised, there was more than enough food in the community dining room, which was on the second floor of city hall. There were a few people piling food onto their plates and they took the time to smile at the newcomers. Jenni returned

their smiles while checking out the potluck dishes. All the best of Texan fare was laid out on several tables. Someone had recently heated up some of the food, judging by the fragrant steam that rose off the chicken, fajitas, enchiladas, and macaroni and cheese. There was plenty of cold potato salad and variety of pasta salads. Jenni and Jason almost ran to the table and started loading up plates.

"I'm dying of hunger," Jenni declared.

"You and me both, Mom," Jason agreed, feeding Jack a little bit of chicken skin. "And Jack, too."

"Y'all help yourselves," an older woman with dark hair streaked with silver said as she set out a steaming pile of tortillas. "And welcome to Ashley Oaks."

"Thank you. It's good to be here," Jenni said, plucking one of the tortillas up with the tips of her fingers.

"If you need anything, let us know. Peggy is the city secretary, and she'll make sure you're settled in. I'm Rosie."

"Nice to meet you," Jenni said, trying to shake hands and balance her plate at the same time. She nudged Jason, hoping he would get the hint and greet the woman, and he extended a greasy hand. "Jason!"

"Eating, Mom," he said defensively, chewing on some fried chicken.

"It's okay. I have a son, too," Rosie said with a wink. "They're always eating at his age." The kindly woman returned to arranging the food as a few construction workers appeared, sweaty and dirty, looking for dinner.

Katie hung back, talking animatedly to Travis, her shotgun still in her hand. Feeling disgruntled again, Jenni tried to adjust to their environment and not feel resentful of the burgeoning friendship between Katie and Travis. She sat down at a long folding table, like those she'd seen at social functions in church while she was growing up, with a plate full of down-home cooking. Beside Jenni, Jason was already halfway through his plateful of chicken, and a warm weight on her foot told her

Jack had taken up station under the table, where he probably could find all sorts of good scraps.

Katie and Travis were talking swiftly, voices melding seamlessly as Katie finally filled a plate with warm food. When they'd first arrived, Jenni had been convinced that Katie and Travis knew each other from before. There had been a look of recognition in Travis's eyes when he took Katie's hand to help her to her feet. But neither one of them said, *Oh, hey it's you!* or anything remotely like that.

So maybe they had just met.

But it felt as if some sort of invisible box had sprung up around them, locking everyone else out.

Jenni did not like that.

She definitely liked Travis. He had such a strong presence and sweet eyes. And she had already caught him giving her that special look men have for women they find attractive. She knew Katie was no threat in that regard, even though Katie had the kind of looks men gravitated to. Katie was gay. Pure and simple.

But Katie was her new best friend. Her sister. She was uncomfortable with Katie drawing close to anyone else. Travis just appearing and clicking with Katie was making Jenni a little nuts. She felt unbalanced and kept trying to get Katie to at least look at her. She felt needy, selfish, and a little embarrassed. It was foolish to feel this way. After all, Katie had risked her life to help Jenni save Jason, and she'd promised to look after Jenni and her son.

Jenni stabbed at her congealing potato salad and glanced at Katie again. Katie made her feel safe. She needed to feel safe.

"So the first priority is the wall," Katie was saying as she sat down at the table.

"Exactly," Travis replied. "Then we'll secure the two buildings that border us so we can inhabit them as well."

"Walling off all the ground floor windows would be a start," Katie suggested.

Travis nodded. "And we have the bricks for it. Since the service

entrance is on the side of the hotel and there is no entrance on the side that faces us, we'll have to bust through a wall." Travis was drawing on a piece of paper, more doodling than anything, but clearly enthralled by Katie's input.

"You'll have to clear the building," Katie said. "Do you have guns?"

"Our only surviving police officer still has his weapon. We used our tools to kill off any zombies that attacked while we were constructing the outer perimeter. A solid blow to the head and they go down."

"We could get more guns," Jenni said softly.

They both looked at her and she blushed.

"You mean back at Ralph's?" Katie asked.

Travis frowned a little. "My family moved to Houston from England when I was a toddler. They were very anti-gun and we've done all right so far with our shovels. But . . ."

Katie laid her revolver on the table in front of him. "Soon this will be the answer. It's fast and more efficient if you've got good aim."

Jenni rolled up some chicken inside a tortilla as she bobbed her head in agreement with Katie. "Well, yeah, I mean, I know you said that thing about the gunfire drawing the zombies, but one day, they are just gonna show up. And they're gonna make it real hard on us."

Travis sighed, leaning back in his chair. "So your friend Ralph has weapons? He just told us he was the mayor of a small town."

"He is, but he also owns a pretty big hunting and camping store," Jenni answered.

Travis rubbed his chin thoughtfully.

"It wouldn't hurt to talk to him. Besides, I just realized we need to let him know we're okay." Katie looked at Jenni and winced.

"Ralph must be worried sick," Jenni said. She felt a little better now that she was part of the conversation.

Katie turned to Travis. "I know you're in charge here—"

"The mayor —"

"I know you're in charge here," Katie repeated, "and I'd like to suggest that maybe you should arrange with Ralph to pick up some weapons. If you can clear out the lot of the zombies out there right now, maybe we can head over to Ralph's."

Travis looked at Katie, his gaze steady and thoughtful. "Yeah, you got a good idea there. We got about twenty of those things out there now, not counting the ones you said were coming."

"Then we can't waste time," Katie suggested.

Travis exhaled slowly. "Yeah. I think it's time to go talk to the mayor and get hold of your friend."

Katie had barely eaten anything, but she stood up as Travis did.

Jenni pushed her plate away quickly and got to her feet, saying. "I'll come with you."

"I'm still hungry," Jason said firmly, shoving some fajitas in his mouth.

Jack seemed to agree with this declaration as he licked his chops.

Jenni said, "Keep the dog with you," and hurried around the table to follow close behind Katie and Travis, desperate to be included.

Downstairs, they entered a large room that was sectioned off into cubicles. The city secretary and a little boy who was probably her son were setting up a bed behind her desk. The woman and little boy looked remarkably alike, from their coloring to the tense expressions on their faces. The little boy shrank behind his mother, regarding Jenni suspiciously.

Jenni felt a lump rise up in her throat and she struggled not to think about her dead children.

"You the new girls, huh?" the woman said as she folded a blanket. "I'm Peggy. The city secretary." Her brown hair was a little mussed up and her face looked weary, but her eyes were bright and curious as she regarded them.

Jenni thrust her hand out, trying to push back her nervousness. "I'm Jenni. My friend is Katie."

"Good to meet you," Katie said with a smile.

"Peggy has been keeping up with the emergency response center," Travis said. "She's been invaluable."

"I don't know about that. The phones going down have been a real kick in our balls," Peggy groused. "Lie down, sugar," she said to her son, but he only whined and held on to her tighter.

"We're going to talk to the mayor for a few. He's in his office, right?" Travis motioned to a door nearby.

"He hasn't budged from his computer all night. It's the most work I've ever seen him do." Peggy shrugged. "Not much to see out there anymore. I'm sure Manny would love the company. Tobias has been sulking around and not much help."

"Tobias is the city manager," Travis explained quickly.

Jenni stared at the little boy at Peggy's side, her eyes beginning to burn with unshed tears. Her fingers trembled as she thought about her own little ones. Katie took her hand and squeezed it, and Jenni looked at her gratefully.

"C'mon," Travis said, noticing Jenni's discomfort. "Let's talk to the mayor." After striding over to the door to the mayor's office, he rapped once then opened it.

"As communication with Europe has ceased, there is no word on how far the plague has spread. The CDC, still operating in a slowly burning Atlanta, continues to issue guidelines for destroying the reanimates—," a voice said from inside the office.

It took Jenni a second to realize it was a broadcast.

Travis waved them inside. Jenni and Katie scooted into the small office. The mayor sat behind his desk, listening to the emergency broadcasting channel.

The mayor saw them and turned off the radio. "Travis, who are our new friends?"

"Jenni and Katie, this is Mayor Manny Reyes. Mr. Mayor, this is Katie and Jenni. Jenni's son and his dog are still enjoying supper."

"Very good to meet you, ladies," Mayor Reyes said warmly, standing and extending his hand in greeting. He was an older man with broad shoulders and a beer gut poking out over his belt buckle. His dark hair was skimmed back from his receding hairline, and he had an open, friendly face.

"It's good to meet you, Mr. Mayor," Katie answered, shaking his hand.

Jenni shyly shook his hand, studying his face. His smile was pleasant, so she relaxed a little.

"Not much on the radio, huh?" Travis asked.

"The broadcast is on a loop now. Not a good sign, is it?" The mayor settled in his chair, the springs creaking as he tipped back, his hands folded on his stomach.

Travis shook his head and took a seat in a nearby chair. "What about the CB and ham radio?"

"Lots of truckers still out there, trying to find safe places, but some are running out of gas and some have gone off the air. There are not as many out there as there were." The mayor sighed. "And I haven't heard a thing from the county emergency coordinator. E-mails are bouncing, and with the phones down . . ." He shrugged. "We're on our own. How is the wall coming along?"

"I think we'll have the area fully enclosed by the new wall by morning if we keep working all night. But another batch of zombies is headed our way. Zombies followed Katie and Jenni here. Maybe around twenty. I have Juan organizing some men to kill as many as they can. We'll use safety lines this time."

The mayor let out a long breath as he ran a hand over his balding head. "And we have those zombies down at the rescue center at the school. If they get out—"

"Which brings me to something. That man, Ralph Toombs, who told us the girls were en route? He owns a hunting store." Travis spoke earnestly and with respect, but Jenni could tell he was subtly trying to steer the mayor in the direction he wanted him to go.

The mayor took in this information, then said, "I have an idea. We could send someone to get some guns once we thin the zombies around the wall."

Travis hesitated, then said, "That sounds like a good idea. I can try to get ahold of Ralph tonight and maybe send out someone in the morning."

"See what you can figure out and let me know," the mayor replied.

Travis nodded. "I'll get right on it."

The mayor slowly turned and brought up the CNN homepage on his computer. "Still the same as last night. No updates."

Travis stood. "We may not get any more, you know."

The mayor stared at the screen, then carefully typed in another URL. "The government won't let us be in an information blackout for long."

"If the government's still out there," Jenni said darkly, unable to hold her tongue.

Katie bobbed her head in agreement.

The mayor stared at the women, and Jenni shifted uncomfortably on her feet. "You have a point, but we can hope."

"That may be all we have," Travis said grimly. "I'll keep you updated."

"Thanks, Travis. Nice to meet you, ladies."

"Nice to meet you, Mr. Mayor," Katie said, and Jenni waved at him as they followed Travis out of the office.

Peggy and her son were out of sight, the lights off in her area of the main office. Jenni guessed they were lying down for the night. Travis led them to a side room, where a very young man in a police uniform sat in front of a ramshackle assortment of communication equipment. He looked pale beneath his tan, and his thin blond hair was matted with sweat. Jenni thought he didn't look much older than Jason. He was a good-looking kid with lovely blue eyes that looked a little lost.

"Hey, Curtis!" Travis said, walking over to him. He quickly introduced Katie and Jenni to him.

"Nice to meet you, ladies."

"How's it going?" Travis asked.

The police officer shook his head and said in soft voice, "It's getting quieter out there."

Travis laid a hand on the younger man's shoulder and squeezed lightly. "Have you spoken to that man, Ralph Toombs?"

"He asked about the women. I told them they arrived safely."

"Good. Think you could get him back on the line?"

"Yeah. Give me a sec." Curtis turned back to the equipment and fussed with it.

Jenni stood close to Katie. It felt good to be inside city hall. Safer, somehow. But she still felt off balance. Katie looked at her, smiled, and tenderly swept some loose locks of Jenni's black hair back from her face.

"You okay?"

Jenni immediately warmed under the attention. "Yeah. Just nervous."

Katie kissed her cheek lightly and slid her arm around Jenni's waist. "Yeah. Me, too."

As Curtis turned to his equipment, they could all hear the moans and screeches of the dead rising outside, mingled with shouts of alarm.

The zombies had arrived at the perimeter.

1.
The Night of the Dead

"You two stay here," Travis said, and hurried out the door.

Curtis looked at the two women, then lowered his head solemnly. He seemed worn down, tired, and overwhelmed. Katie remembered that Travis said that the local police force had been wiped out; Curtis was likely the only survivor. She had an inkling that Travis had asked him to oversee the communications center to keep him feeling useful . Curtis looked no older than twenty-one, and Katie bet he hadn't been on the job long.

Jenni grabbed her hand. Her dark eyes were bright with excitement and fear. "If we go upstairs, we could probably see out the window."

Feeling restless and not wanting to be out of the loop, but also not in the way by trailing after Travis, Katie followed Jenni out of the room and up the stairs. They darted past the dining room and down the hall.

Already other people, workers and their families, were rushing down the corridor to see the battle. A small crowd clustered around the windows, which overlooked the street. Managing to push their way into a good position to see out one of the windows, Katie and Jenni looked down at the men getting into position to fight the zombies. Ladders had been used to scale the new wall and get up onto the trucks. The harness lines glinted

in the radiance from the huge lights set up around the perimeter. A series of pulleys and long ropes attached to the crane arm allowed the construction workers behind the line of trucks to hoist the men up away from trouble if necessary. There were three workers to each line. The volunteers up on the backs of the trucks carried shovels and homemade spears with what looked like trowels attached to the ends. Below the armed survivors was a group holding reserve weapons.

Moaning loudly, some of them screeching, thirty or so zombies clustered under the men, beating the sides of the trucks, eager for the flesh of those above.

Katie's heart jumped a little as she caught sight of Travis running up one of the ladders, still fastening his harness, his shovel under his arm. Of course he would be part of this. He was not the sort of man to send others to do something he wouldn't do himself.

As if his appearance on top of the truck was a sign, all the men squatted down and rammed their weapons down as hard as they could into the heads of the dead below. Katie could see the shovels busting open zombie heads and trowel-ended spears being driven through the eye sockets of upturned faces. When a zombie managed to grab a weapon, the living man immediately let go and was handed a new one. Katie wondered if the person who was lost in the earlier battle had fought with a zombie for his weapon. In this new world, you had to learn fast to survive.

In a few minutes, the construction workers took out at least ten zombies, but the truly dead remained standing and pressed up against the trucks due to the constant push of the undead behind them. The men had to reach farther out to strike the living undead. One man lost his footing and swung out over the crowd. Juan shouted, and immediately his towline was drawn up and back. Zombies tried to grab his feet, but the man was pulled to safety.

"Shit," someone said nearby, and Katie couldn't agree more.

Her eyes continuously strayed to Travis. His height and long arms gave him a greater reach than many of the other fighters as he drove his shovel down with a strange, staccato rhythm.

"He is kicking so much ass," Jason said from behind her as he joined them at the window, standing on his toes to see over their shoulders.

Jack managed to wedge himself between Katie and Jenni to get a view of the action below. He let out a series of low, disapproving growls.

Travis yelled something, and all the other men backed away from the edge of the barrier. The great mechanical arm of the excavator came swinging over their heads; the scoop was loaded with what looked like big sandbags. Travis gestured, guiding the driver of the machine to just the perfect spot, then made a downward stroke with his arm. The driver released the load of heavy bags right into the center of the remaining zombies. Most were effectively crushed.

Out of the original throng of thirty zombies, maybe five were still staggering about, tripping over their dead comrades. They were too far away from the perimeter to kill with the spears, and Katie knew the townspeople wouldn't risk shooting at them and possibly drawing more zombies.

Travis motioned again and the defenders retreated down their ladders, moved the ladders over to the wall, then scrambled up and over, into the construction site. Once the ladders were hauled back in and everyone was safe, cheers erupted throughout the complex.

Katie turned to Jenni and saw that her face was very flushed and excited.

"He's amazing!" Jenni giggled, hugging Katie.

Katie returned the embrace and said, "Yep, he is."

At that moment, Travis looked up at the window. His gaze met Katie's and he smiled.

2.
Another Moment

It had to be the best peach cobbler Katie had ever eaten in her life. Even cold and with no ice cream to top it off, it was the food of the gods. She shoveled another bite into her mouth, savoring the sweetness on her tongue.

For the time being, she was alone in the dining room. Jenni and Jason were off walking Jack and spending some quality mother–son time together. Until this moment, Katie hadn't realized how much she needed a chance to finally relax and let go of the terror and stress of the last two days. Now the quiet around her was soothing. It was growing late and those not working on the wall were turning in for the night.

Feeling like a glutton, she stood up and served herself another piece of cobbler, snagging a bottle of water on the way back to her seat. The night pressed against the tall windows lining one wall of the spacious room. She had never been afraid of the dark before, but she felt haunted by the darkness hovering outside the glass. Ignoring her fear, she took another bite.

"Mind if I join you?" Travis slid into the seat across from her, clutching a cup of steaming coffee in one hand.

Katie broke the sugary crust of her cobbler with her spoon, staring at the glistening peaches beneath it. She wasn't sure she wanted company, but didn't want to be rude, so she said, "Not at all. Taking a break?"

"Yeah. Just a small one."

"You don't sleep much, do you, Travis?"

"Not really. I've always been one of those people who don't get enough sleep. Of course, I've hardly slept since all this went down." Travis ran his hand over his stubbly chin. "Or shaved. Or eaten. Or anything, really."

"Here. Have some cobbler. I shouldn't eat any more, anyway." Katie shoved her plate across to him.

Travis smiled slightly as he snagged a plastic spoon from a nearby cup filled with utensils. He dug in with relish.

"Jenni and I saw a few survivor holdouts on the way here, but nothing like this. It really is amazing how y'all got this up and running."

"We got lucky," Travis admitted. "Yesterday we were supposed to break ground. We were going to rebuild a historical building that burned down a few years ago. This whole area is about to undergo—was about to undergo—a serious reconstruction. A local developer, Steven Mann, was keen on turning downtown into a tourist attraction, complete with a rebuilt vaudeville theater and the hotel"—he gestured with his spoon in the general direction of the tall building—"as the focal points. Anyway, I was on my way to work when the reports started coming in."

"The race riot story?" Katie asked. "I heard those the night before."

"Yep." Travis sipped some of his cooling coffee, looking thoughtful. "It sounded weird to me. I couldn't figure out why there would be race riots breaking out all over the country. There'd been nothing on the news that would instigate that sort of violence. It was just so random."

"It made no sense to me either. None of the news did before the other morning," Katie admitted. She ran her finger down the outside of her water bottle, wiping away the condensation. "At least not until I realized it was zombies."

"It still doesn't seem real, does it?"

"But it is." Katie found herself drawing an *L* into the beads of water on her bottle and stopped herself. "What happened next?

"Well, by the time I got here, we were already hearing horror stories about what was going down in the cities. Peggy and the mayor had already established an emergency center at the city hall. Truckers were reporting all sorts of crazy stuff over the CB

and ham radio that was no better. The county's emergency co-ordinator told Reyes to hold tight and not pay attention to the chatter. FEMA would let the county know what the towns needed to do to stay safe. We were all on edge, not sure what to think. It sounded like an April Fool's joke, except it's still March. Juan kept saying it was zombies, but we all just blew him off." Travis shrugged. "I mean, it sounds crazy."

Katie sighed and ran a hand over her blond curls. "Yeah, it does. Completely."

"Anyway, the mayor decided that the best thing to do until we were sure what was going on was to get everyone in town out to the new high school. He told us we could go ahead and start to break ground, but he wanted the civvies safe." Travis leaned toward Katie. "The mayor is in the back pocket of the developer, you see."

"Ohhhhhh," Katie said.

"So we went to work, but kept getting distracted by all the stories pouring in on the radio. So, anyway, Curtis comes by and tells us that there was an attack at a service station down the road and the officer on the scene had to put down the at-tacker because he was so violent. They took the lady this freak attacked down to the clinic. He was real jittery and I didn't blame him. It all felt wrong, you know?"

"I think I know what you mean," Katie answered. Once the world had begun to unravel around her, it had been hard to ac-cept what was going on.

Travis shook his head. "It was just so fucked up. Anyway, we start to finally move the equipment into position to start dig-ging when we hear a big commotion down the block. Those cars out there come racing into the downtown area, careening like crazy, and crash. All hell is breaking loose in those cars, and we can see them rocking and hear screaming and what sounds like growling. Blood splats all over the car windows, and it sounds like a horror movie. Suddenly there are these . . . things . . . crawling out of the cars and they start running down the street

toward us. Now, it's not normal for a man to have his intestines tripping his feet and he still keeps running."

Katie winced at the thought and vividly remembered the first zombie to attack her. The grievous wounds on the man who nearly dragged her out of her car had been a clear indication that things weren't right. "I saw something very similar."

"It's unbelievable when you see it." Travis shoveled more cobbler into his mouth, chewing as he reflected back on what he had seen. "Four of the zombies ran straight for us, and Juan—he's a crazy son of a bitch—just swept them right off the road into a building with the arm of the excavator. The whole time he's yelling about zombies, and honestly, at that point, we believed him. Two of those things didn't get up. Their heads were bashed in. But the other two, despite having obviously broken arms and legs, were staggering toward us. So we grabbed some shovels and dented their heads in. About that time, Curtis comes back and says that some shit was going down at the clinic and that the dead were walking again. The mayor was freaking out because he saw us take out the four zombies from the cars, but we calmed him down long enough to listen. We told him that anyone bit needs to be tossed out on their ass. Because in zombie movies . . ." He shrugged his shoulders, the disbelief of that moment reflected in his expression.

"The bite is what makes them zombies," Katie said helpfully.

"Yeah. And so far . . . well, damn . . . so far, it's clear to me and I think everyone else who ever watched those movies that they got a lot right." Travis gazed steadily at Katie. "Even though I saw it, I found it hard to believe . . . but I couldn't afford not to believe."

Katie agreed silently, her eyes meeting his. Finally she said, "You have to believe, because you have to survive."

"Exactly. So we convinced the mayor to call the school and tell them to toss out anyone who has been bitten. There are only four other cops in the whole town, but none of them answer

Curtis's calls. Anyway, things are looking bad. The principal at the high school, who used to be the mayor here, tells Reyes to go fuck himself four different ways and upside down. Finally, he admits that they have bitten people in the high school and that the school nurse is taking care of them."

Katie winced. "When we went through Emorton, the school there was completely filled with zombies."

Travis leaned back in his chair with a weary exhalation. "Yeah. Within fifteen minutes, we lost all communication with the school. Then we knew we were in for a shitload of trouble. So we parked the construction trucks to block off any vulnerable areas and packed sandbags and cement bags around them. The hurricane fence could probably hold back a good number, but if the whole town decided to come visit . . ."

"It won't be pleasant," Katie agreed.

"So that is when we started building the wall. We recognized that we most likely would not be getting help from the outside. The mayor is still hoping, but the rest of us have realized that we're most likely on our own. And as Texans, we're okay with that." Travis shrugged and began to eat again.

"Strange, huh?" Katie slowly twisted the cap on her water bottle. "One moment, the world is normal. Pleasant. Everything you're used to. The next . . . you're building a wall."

"We just don't have a choice but to keep ourselves safe," Travis said wearily.

"The mayor doesn't make it easy, does he?"

"No. But . . . he's used to things being a particular way. We all have to adapt. He will, too." Travis finished eating and pushed the plate away. He returned his thoughtful gaze to Katie and she looked up at him. "We've met, haven't we? Somewhere. A ways back, maybe."

"Why do you ask?" Katie arched a brow then took a slow sip of water.

"Because I keep feeling like I know you. Your face seems so familiar. The second I saw you, I thought to myself that I knew

you, but I just couldn't remember your name." Travis laughed, looking a little embarrassed.

"I've never been to Ashley Oaks before, so probably not," Katie said at last.

"I wasn't always here. Originally, I'm from Houston. That's where I met Juan. We were working on a building together and became friends. He's from here and he got me to move out here when I decided I needed a life change. Of course, this was not the life change I was expecting."

"We went to Houston once in a while to visit Lydia's family. Maybe we met once, but I don't remember. Or maybe I just have one of those faces." She grinned, trying to push any awkwardness away. "You know we blondes all look the same."

Travis openly studied her face, then shook his head. "I don't know. But I do know I like your face. And my gut tells me you're good people."

Tossing back her head, Katie laughed. "You go by your gut, too, huh?"

"Always have. It hasn't led me astray yet."

Katie leaned her elbows on the table and rested her chin on her upturned palm. "It has led me astray a few times, but I'm sure that when it tells me that this is where I need to be, it's telling me the truth."

"I'm glad," Travis said honestly and earnestly. "You're smart and I like smart people."

Jack hit Katie like a two-ton truck, diving for the empty plate.

"Hey!" Katie struggled with the big dog, wrestling him away from the plate he was so ardently licking.

"Sorry! Bad, Jack. Come here!" Jason ordered as he entered the dining room with his mother.

Katie managed to get the German shepherd off the table and gave him a fierce look. "Be a good dog!"

Tucking his tail between his legs, Jack walked back to Jason, giving her plaintive looks as he went.

"And on that note, I think I'm off to bed," Katie said, sliding to her feet.

"I'm tired, too," Jason said with a long yawn.

"I'm wired! I want to do something!" Jenni said with enthusiasm. "Travis, what can I do?"

"I'm heading out on patrol soon. Want to come along?" He stood up and cleared the table.

"Yes!"

Katie couldn't help but laugh at Jenni's perky expression. "You two have fun. C'mon, Jason."

"Good night, Katie," Travis called out after her.

A few minutes later, exhaustion hit Katie like a sledgehammer. She almost felt drunk as she sat down on a cot in the small, empty storage room on the top floor of city hall. The old building's sloped roof made standing up straight a little difficult unless you were in the center of the room. She had a feeling Travis pulled some strings to get them a place inside the building and not camping out in portable buildings that were now dorms. Evidently, the basement of city hall had been designated as a bomb shelter during the commie scare and had still contained loads of cots and musty blankets that were now being used by those taking refuge in the fort.

Katie sat drooping on her cot, watching Jason fix a bed on the floor for Jack, using a blanket he had pinched when no one was watching the supplies.

She desperately wanted a shower, but the first opening on the shower's sign-in sheet wasn't until early the next morning. Everyone was using one shower, which was located in the city hall janitor's office.

Jason slid onto his bed under the small, narrow window. Jenni's cot was under the slant in the roof, forming an L with Katie's.

Jack, the zombie-hating dog, examined his bed, circled three times, fussed at the blanket with his paws, circled again, and lay down with a yawn.

"Uh, Katie?"

"Yeah?"

"Um . . . are you and Jenni gonna hook up?"

Katie double-blinked and said, "Huh?"

"My mom, after my dad divorced her for Jenni, hooked up with this girl for about two weeks. Mom was always going from guy to guy, and that was the only girl, but I was just wondering . . ." Jason trailed off, seeing Katie's expression. "Sorry."

"No, it's cool." Katie sighed and ran her hands over her hair, which fell free to her shoulders in soft curls. "Okay, just because I like girls does not mean I'm going to hook up with the nearest unattached girl. In fact, it is my own personal rule not to get involved with straight women. I value myself too much to be someone's experiment."

Jason considered this and said, "Yeah. I guess that's what my mom was doing since my dad was such a jerk to her. She made a big deal out of having a girlfriend and then it was over in weeks. Then she just went from boyfriend to boyfriend until she died in a car accident a few years ago. Some of them were cool, but most were jerks like Dad." His voice carried a hint of the emotional fallout of his broken home as it quavered slightly.

"Is that when you came to live with Jenni and your dad?"

"Yeah. I didn't really want to like her. Mom always called her 'that bitch,' but she's really sweet. Kinda goofy. She's more like an older sister than a mom. I'm really glad you saved her." Jason sighed and lay on the cot. "I just thought maybe because you're a lesbian, you two would end up together."

Katie shook her head. She didn't feel like hiding who she was anymore just to make someone comfortable. "I'm not a lesbian."

Jason sat up again and looked at her, shocked. "Huh? But you said—"

"I wanted you to pee." Katie winked at him. "But the truth is, I'm bisexual. Always have been. I dated guys and girls all through

high school and in college. It just happened that the person—" Katie's voice caught in her throat and she couldn't talk for a moment. "—I fell in love with and wanted to spend my life with was a woman. It was her: Lydia." She pulled out the phone and dared to waste a little bit of the battery, flashing the picture to Jason.

"She's hot," Jason announced. "Where is she?"

Katie stared at Lydia's beautiful smile, then snapped the phone shut. "Somewhere out there. One of them."

Jason winced. "Sorry, Katie."

"Me, too . . . me, too."

"So . . . uh . . . you like guys?"

Katie laughed and lay back on the bed. "I've had some boyfriends. I was even engaged to a guy."

"What happened?"

"To my engagement?"

"Yeah."

"I met Lydia. And that was that. I broke off the engagement. I just knew she was the one. Six years of heaven with someone who is . . . she was everything I needed."

"I bet your boyfriend was mad."

"Um . . . yeah. But we were together for all the wrong reasons. We worked together and shared ambitions. I think we took that to be more than it was."

"Oh."

"I often tell people I'm a lesbian so they're comfortable."

"I don't get it."

"Well, people like absolutes. And it blows most of their minds to try to think that I could find men and women equally attractive. It just freaks them out. They want me to be one or the other. So, since I was with Lydia, it was just easier to say I was a lesbian." Katie held the phone against her chest and tried not to cry.

"So you could end up with a guy or a girl?"

"Honestly, Jason, right now, I can't imagine being with any-one. I just . . ." She rolled onto her side and faced the wall. "I just miss her."

Jason was very quiet. Minutes ticked by while Katie's hot tears flowed. How could she imagine being with anyone ever again?

Lydia . . . oh . . . Lydia . . .

"I just thought if you and Jenni hooked up, you would take good care of her," Jason finally said softly.

Katie rolled over and gave him a soft smile. "That was a very sweet thing for you to say."

"Well, you know, if you change your mind—" Jason faltered. "—I mean . . ."

"I know." Katie tucked her phone under her pillow, then reached up and flicked off the light. Faintly, she could hear the few zombies moaning out beyond the perimeter. "But, Jason, honestly, right now I just . . . I loved her. The mere thought of being with anyone else just feels wrong."

Jason turned his head to look across the small, darkened room. "I know, Katie. I just thought it would be cool if you and Jenni hooked up. You take good care of her. Not like my ass-hole dad. He was so mean to her." Jason exhaled slowly. "And you make me feel safe, too. I feel like I've known you forever."

Katie smiled at him fondly. "I know. I feel the same way."

"Do you think it's safe here? For real?"

Katie looked toward the dark shape of the boy and chose her words carefully. "I think this is about as safe as we can get nowadays. We'll be okay."

"Promise?"

"I promise."

With a loud yawn, Jason nestled under the covers. "I hope so. I am so tired of being afraid."

"Me, too," Katie answered softly as she settled down to sleep. "Me, too."

3.
Dead Stars in Her Eyes

Jenni wandered along beside Travis, her hands tucked into her jacket pockets. It was cold now that the sun had settled below the horizon. She had finally let her long hair down from her ponytail to flow in the wind. It was a little bit of a ploy to get Travis to admire her, and it seemed to be working by the furtive looks he was casting in her direction. She really liked this tall, handsome, humble man. She was impressed that he warmly greeted everyone they came across. Their walk ended when they climbed on top of a truck to watch the zombies who had survived the slaughter. The undead kept trying to make their way closer to the living, but kept falling over their dead comrades. It was almost comical to see.

"I could shoot them," Jenni offered.

"No, they're not much of a threat down there, and we don't need to draw more of them to us until we are more secure." Stretching, Travis lifted his trowel-spear, freshly cleaned after the recent battle, over his head. Stirred up, a zombie woman tried to run toward them, fell over the dead bodies, and slammed headfirst into the asphalt.

"That had to hurt," Jenni said, almost laughing.

"I don't think they feel pain," Travis said sadly.

The woman tried to get up, but could not find stable purchase on the bodies around her and kept sliding around in the gore and muck.

"Seriously, I could shoot her," Jenni said again, somewhat hopefully.

Travis laughed. He rubbed his eyes and sat down in a chair that had been set up on the back of the truck. The truck's bed was full of earth, and the chair sank down a little under Travis's

weight. Jenni sat down next to him, crossing her legs, recognizing he needed the better view for his job.

"So. Zombies are holed up in the school?"

"Yeah, we think so. We considered having someone drive out there to check, but decided that might give them the incentive they need to break out. Juan noticed that when they can't see humans, they tend to just mill around. But when they spot living flesh, they go ape shit." Travis watched the zombie woman writhing around in the guts of her dead comrades. At one point, she tried to eat a bit of intestine, only to spit it out.

Jenni watched the zombified woman as well, with a small smile on her face. Her fingers were itching to draw her gun and blast a hole through the woman's skull. Something about this zombie's desperation to get to them—coupled with her bright, candy pink jogging suit and bouffant hairdo—annoyed the ever-loving fuck out of her.

"Most of the ones I've seen have been running to eat me. I never see them just standing around."

"Because we have these barricades, we've had a chance to see them kind of 'at rest,' just standing there, swaying or milling around, until they spot someone alive. But whenever a group figures out we're back here, they attack and just keep attacking until we kill them." He rubbed his chin contemplatively. "Sound sets them off, too. We used a radio to distract some of them once. When you and Katie arrived, we set off a car alarm from the roof of the city hall."

Jenni drew pictures in the earth with her fingers. "I was wondering how you did that. It seems that each time Katie and I encounter zombies, they are on us in a second. We just run."

"You and Katie had a rough time out there, didn't you?"

Jenni made a face as she nodded. "Yeah. Pretty much from yesterday morning on."

"It wasn't so bad here. Since most of the townspeople went to the school so early, we really have had limited interaction with the zombies. Honestly, we had completely secured the pe-

rimeter before pack of them showed up. I almost feel guilty that I didn't have to run for my life."

"Well, it's no fun, that's for damn sure. Just consider yourself lucky and don't feel guilty." Jenni looked down at what she had written in the earth next to some stick figures: *Benji*. She quickly rubbed out the word. She just couldn't think of those little fingers straining . . . straining . . .

"You okay?" Travis leaned forward and put a gentle hand on her shoulder.

Jenni looked up into his face and said simply, "No."

He pressed his lips together and inclined his head in understanding. "Of course you're not. Sorry."

She looked down, her brow furrowing. "Is anyone okay, really? I don't think I was okay before all this went down. I think I'm actually better now. That doesn't make sense, I know. My children are . . . but . . . something inside me feels stronger."

"Adversity brings out the best or the worst in people. Perhaps you are just finding strength you didn't know you had."

Jenni tilted her head, her dark hair falling softly around her pale face. She considered this, then shrugged. "I don't know. I'm not sure. I just know that when—" She faltered for a second. "—that when I saw what had happened to my children, the woman who I was just stopped existing. I think a piece of me died. And I came back to life in the truck with Katie. I'm weirdly comfortable in this world. Having Katie and Jason makes me feel solid. Safe. Being here makes me feel that way, too."

Travis gave her that smile that warmed her to the very depths of her soul. "I'm glad you and Katie and Jason made it here. I'm not sure what will happen next, but I know we're going to fight."

"I just want to kill them all. Kill them for killing . . ." She stopped and looked down at her dirty fingers.

The zombie woman finally reached the truck and banged on the side, moaning and screeching.

"I want to kill her."

"Then do it," Travis said, offering her the makeshift spear.

Walking to the edge of the truck, Jenni looked down at the zombie's bloodied, upturned face and all that damned hairsprayed blond hair. She felt Travis's fingers slip under her coat and grab her belt to hold her steady. She cast a grateful look over her shoulder at him and lifted the spear. Her gaze returned to the zombie and narrowed on the dead woman's face and her glassy, blank eyes. So much like Lloyd's when he had looked up at her as he stuffed more of Benji's tender baby flesh into his mouth.

Jenni let out a hiss and slammed the tip of the spear hard into the woman's eye socket. She felt the flesh giving way, the eye slicing apart like a boiled egg. Jenni shoved the trowel down as hard as she could. She felt things giving way, mashing and tearing. She lifted the weapon and thrust it down again. Almost growling, she stabbed the female zombie over and over again until the corpse slid down the side of the truck and lay still.

Jenni took great breaths of the rank, cool air.

Travis gently took the spear away from her and reached out to softly grasp her shoulder. "Better?"

"No. Not really. But it felt good." Jenni gave him an awkward smile.

"You're a strange, strange girl in a strange, strange world," Travis said, and gave her a soothing hug.

Jenni nestled into his arms. It felt delightful to be in the arms of someone kind and well meaning. She didn't even feel a little afraid of him; she already knew that he wouldn't try to take advantage of her or hurt her.

After a minute, she sat back down on the dirt and watched another zombie try to walk over his dead comrades. "Sure you don't want me to shoot him?"

Travis laughed. It was a wonderful sound to her ears.

4.
Breathing Space

When Jenni had finally come to bed, she leaned over and tenderly kissed Katie on the forehead. Katie sleepily opened her eyes to see Jenni lying down on her own cot and had reached out to take her hand. Soon she fell back to sleep, Jenni's fingers intertwined with hers.

In the morning, she awakened to find Jenni peacefully snoring and Jason sneaking out the door with Jack on his heels. She could smell hot, fresh coffee and pulled on her socks and boots immediately as her stomach let out a hungry growl. Groggily stumbling down the narrow staircase, Katie headed to the community dining room, where people were gathered for coffee and breakfast—probably the last of the leftovers from the fundraiser dinner.

After snagging a Danish, a breakfast taco, and a hot cup of coffee, Katie found a corner and sat down to enjoy her meal. The townspeople looked at her curiously, but seem locked in their own worlds. Of course, this was their town and it was now dead. They were probably in shock and in mourning and not sure what to think about any of this, including the blonde in the camouflage pants and black tank top.

Jason joined her at the table. Jack was close behind with his ears perked, looking at the boy anxiously for scraps. The teenager seemed a bit moody this morning and Katie didn't blame him. Being here, being safe, made her feel raw and more vulnerable emotionally. Being on the run, living on the edge of death, was numbing and comforting compared to the quiet when there was time to reflect on all they had endured and lost.

"Mom's still asleep?" Jason asked.

"Yeah, she seemed really tired."

"She was out late with that guy," Jason said darkly.

Katie opened her mouth and found that she didn't know what to say. Of course he was upset. Jason's dad was newly dead, and already his stepmom seemed to have her eyes on another man. She took a bite of the Danish; it was close to being stale.

Jason gave the dog a few bits of cold chicken. "Dad was a shithead, but . . ." He shrugged moodily.

"Yeah," Katie said, not sure really what she was agreeing to, but Jason nodded back at her and set about eating.

"It would be different if it was you," he said in a low voice, so no one else could hear. "At least you wouldn't be replacing Dad."

Katie reached across the table and touched his cheek. "Jason, I think Jenni is just dealing with things the best way she can. I don't think you have to worry about anyone replacing your father right now."

Turning his face away, he shrugged. "Whatever."

She sighed. They ate in silence. When she finished, Katie gave the boy a brief hug, patted Jack on the head, and headed downstairs.

When she stepped out into the fresh, cool air, she saw that the wall had been completed. Made of concrete, at least two feet thick and ten feet high, the wall stood sturdy and defiant, five feet inside the hurricane fence perimeter.

Hands on hips, she surveyed her surroundings. Above the wall, she could see the tops of the buildings that surrounded their little fort. From her glimpses of them yesterday, she thought most of them had been abandoned long before the zombies arrived, except for the Dollar Store across the street. Inside the little fort, a fairly clear path ran along the edges, except for where some of the bigger machinery was clustered in a corner. Katie remembered seeing the bulldozers and heavy equipment parked outside the wall.

Stretching, she felt the coffee giving her a nice little rush. She felt almost normal for a second. She started to jog at a nice, even pace along the path around the site, darting around the port-a-potties and the lunch wagon and behind the portable

office buildings. After a few minutes, she felt her energy increase and her endorphins kick in, and soon she was jogging at a fair clip despite her heavy Doc Martens.

She was on her third circuit around the fort when Travis joined her. He matched her pace easily and said, "Hey."

"Hey," she answered with a smile. Glancing at him, she saw that he looked a little groggy. "Late night?"

"Sentry duty until midnight kinda took it out of me. I really need coffee, but they were fresh out, so here I am," he replied.

"You jog?"

"Every morning," he admitted, and she noted the natural ease with which he carried himself.

"I used to run every evening with Lydia," she said, and was instantly tormented by the vision of Lydia attacking her. Her vision blurred with instant tears.

Travis jogged next to her, silent and watchful. He waited until she had control of herself, then said, "Ralph called in early this morning. He wanted to know if we'll be heading his way today."

Katie glanced toward Travis. "Are we?"

"I'm seriously worried about the school. They will eventually get out, and when they do, they'll come here."

Katie expertly dodged around a trio of construction workers who looked dirty, tired, and nervous. "How far away is the school?"

"Three blocks north."

"Three blocks!" She was so startled, Katie nearly ran into the wall. Travis grabbed her arm to steady her.

"Yeah. That's why I'm so nervous. They'll come straight here, and we'll be swamped. We will have to be able to better defend ourselves."

"Plus they don't sleep. . . ." Katie shook her head. "Yeah, we need to get the guns here soon. What about food?"

"We're okay for now, thanks to the fund-raiser and all the canned food from the food drive. Plus the truck that arrived yesterday was heading for a Walmart, and we managed to

unload a lot of it before a throng of zombies arrived. We've got a lot of canned and boxed food and other supplies. We won't run out of toilet paper any time soon." Travis grinned as they started on a fresh circuit of the complex.

"What a relief! I thought we were doomed," Katie said with mock seriousness.

Travis chuckled and she joined him. They sprinted around the lunch wagon and some people sitting in chairs enjoying the morning.

"But seriously, we have the wall up and food for a while, but we need a solid way to defend ourselves. I think our best shot is the truck you and Jenni came in. It looks tough and fast."

"We're out of gas," Katie reminded him.

"But we have some gasoline here in the fort," he said. "We just have to get it out to the truck and fill it up."

"How many zombies are out there now?"

"Six more showed up in the early morning. We're trying to lure them close enough to kill, but the dead ones keep tripping them up. We'll have to distract them. Probably with a car alarm like yesterday."

Katie lifted an eyebrow. "So that's how you did it?"

"We're clever that way." Travis grinned.

"So . . . someone runs over to the truck with gas canisters, fills the tank, and hauls ass to Ralph's?" Katie could hear her doubts in her voice.

"Yeah. You and me. The guys trick the zombies into heading for the other side of the fort and we run for it. There's a gas station ten miles down the road. We fill up the rest of the way there."

Katie laughed. "Sounds easy."

Travis's eyes cast a shy look at her. "Yeah, I'm easy."

That made Katie laugh even more. "Okay, so you and I run out there and risk our asses to get a load of guns and save the day, huh?"

"Gee, ma'am, when you say it that way, it sounds kinda romantic," Travis teased her.

Katie rolled her eyes. "Okay, I'm in. But I know Jenni will insist on coming with us."

"Yeah, she really does like to kill zombies, doesn't she?"

Katie remembered Jenni running out onto Ralph's balcony and shooting a zombie just because it looked like her father. "Um . . . yeah."

"Think she's okay, upstairs?" Travis asked meaningfully.

Katie pondered this, recalling Jenni's near catatonia, then her quick rebound into Linda Hamilton in *The Terminator*. "No. No, I don't think so. But I think Jenni had a lot of bad things happen to her in the old world, and I think she's dealing with what's happened as best she can. And better than many . . ."

They stopped outside the city hall, and Katie took time to stretch out her muscles. "I'm due for the shower."

"I'll go talk to Juan and Jenni."

"Juan?"

"Yeah, he's read the *Zombie Survival Handbook* a million times. I think he'll be a great backup."

"Okay."

His gaze intense, Travis shifted on his feet and crossed his arms over his chest. "If you don't want to go back out there—"

"I'm in. No worries," Katie said swiftly. "I'd rather be proactive than not."

"So we got a plan?"

"We got a plan," Katie assured him.

His gaze met hers in that way that made her avert her eyes. She felt a little flushed and shifted nervously on her feet.

Travis looked a little flushed, too. "Okay, rendezvous back here in twenty minutes."

Katie laughed. "I'm a woman. Make it forty." She turned and ran into the building.

Travis gazed after her with his expression showing all too clearly he knew she was a woman. Rubbing his chin, he exhaled slowly.

"She's gay, dude," Juan said in his thick West Texas accent from behind him.

"Shut up," Travis said gruffly, turning toward his best friend.

Juan grinned. "You have to pick the single, straight, available girls if you ever plan to get laid, man."

"Gimme a break, Juan. I'm not even thinking about getting laid," Travis protested.

"You're a guy. You expect me to believe that?" Juan flicked the brim of his hat, pushing it back on his head. "She's hot, but she's so not even playing the same ball game you are."

"Why don't we have a change of subject?" Travis cocked his eyebrow.

"How about your suicide run to get the guns?"

"About that . . ."

Juan narrowed his eyes. "Let me guess. You volunteered me."

Travis smiled broadly as he swung his arm around Juan's bronzed shoulders to lead him away. "You are our zombie expert. So, this zombie handbook you were telling me about—"

"Ah, shit," Juan muttered.

1.
Rush of the Dead

They were ready to go. Katie hugged Jason before leaning over to give Jack a kiss. Jenni stood nearby, her dark hair tied up in a high ponytail, a backpack slung over her shoulders. The sun was higher now, and Jenni looked pale but confident. When Katie released him, Jason went to Jenni and hugged her.

"We'll take good care of each other. I promise," Katie reassured him.

Jack whined at her, lifting a paw to scrabble at her knee.

"Jack, stay here and take care of Jason, okay?"

The dog looked from Katie to Jason, then walked sullenly to the boy's side.

It felt strange to leave the dog behind; after all, he had been a constant part of their life for the last two days, but Katie and Jenni agreed it was better to let Jason have the comfort of his company.

The diversion had started. Katie heard the car alarm going off on the other side of the complex. Standing on the roof of city hall were two men, one with binoculars, watching the zombies in the street below. They would not give the all clear signal until the road leading to the red pickup was devoid of the undead.

Katie stood quietly, hands on her hips, sunglasses covering her eyes to keep the morning glare from blinding her. She wore her customary tank top and pants, and Travis wore a T-shirt, jeans,

and heavy boots. If she had time, she decided, she'd get some new clothes at Ralph's. She slung her shotgun over her shoulder as Jenni tucked her revolver into her belt. Eyeing them jealously, Juan shifted his spear. "I cannot wait to have a decent gun."

Travis grinned. "You'll have one soon enough. Let's get moving."

Travis climbed up to the sentry platform and then shimmied down the ladder first. Katie followed, gripping the rungs tightly with sweaty palms before slipping over the top of the wall and scooting down a second ladder on the other side. The hurricane fence was their next obstacle.

Jenni and Juan joined them with Juan hauling a gas canister in one hand. Together, Katie and Travis moved the ladder to the chain-link fence, climbed up, and dropped down on the other side of the fence.

Katie took a deep breath as she looked back at the fence and the new wall. It had seemed so much safer on the other side. Knowing how close they were now to the undead, she felt her heartbeat speed up.

Jenni dropped down as Juan handed the gas canister over the fence to Travis. Noticing her expression, Jenni gave Katie's hand a reassuring squeeze.

"We'll kick their asses," Jenni said determinedly, obviously fighting back her fear.

"Of course." Katie forced a smile and looked at Travis. The tall man lifted a ladder that was lying on the ground nearby and leaned it against the truck barrier. Once it was steady, he gave them the thumbs-up.

Juan dropped over the fence as Mike, a construction worker, recovered the ladder. Mike was impressive in size. He stood a whole head taller than most people around him and his arms rippled with muscles under his dark skin. His shaved head glistened in the sunlight as he watched the proceedings with a worried expression on his face. Katie couldn't blame him. She was anxious, too.

"Remember, as soon as we get the signal, head for the truck. Just get in. We'll cover you," Travis said.

Jenni nodded. "I got it."

"No worries," Juan assured him.

Travis wiped his brow with his hand and looked at Katie. "You ready?"

"Oh, yeah. A little scared, but ready."

The men on top of city hall gave the all clear signal.

"Time to go," Travis muttered.

"Good luck," Juan said, shaking their hands.

Jenni gave them both hard hugs. "Run like the wind."

"Trust me. I'll set a new world's record today," Katie said with a wry grin.

"Let's hurry." Travis turned and headed up the ladder.

Katie followed, trying not to panic. She felt a little dizzy and sweat was trickling down between her shoulder blades. Maybe it was the sun, or the stress, or even both, but she felt light-headed and slightly unreal.

Reaching the top, she heaved herself onto the packed earth in the bed of the construction truck and looked around. The road looked clear. Juan passed the gasoline up to them, and Travis set the can near the edge. No one spoke; the tension lining their faces said it all. Travis dropped over the side of the truck and landed easily in the empty road. Katie handed him the gas can and spear.

Looking around one more time—no zombies in sight—Katie took a deep breath and swung herself over the side of the truck. As she dropped, she caught her forearm on the edge of the truck bed. There was an instant of pain, and Katie took a brief look at her brand-new, nasty scrape, but there was really no time to worry about it.

"Be careful," Jenni called out to her.

"We'll be right back with the truck," Katie promised before running after Travis.

They were halfway down the block, sprinting for the truck,

when Katie started to hear footsteps pounding on the brick road behind her.

Jenni screamed, "Katie, there's one behind you!"

Travis shouted, "Shit!"

Katie ran with her shotgun bouncing against her back and her arms pumping. Travis was a few feet in front of her. Katie started to panic as the stench of decay and death grew stronger and the footsteps got closer. The keening was louder, more hungry, more crazed.

"Duck!" Travis yelled, stopping and then whirling about.

Katie ducked and slipped around him as he lifted his spear. She heard a meaty *thwunk* and turned to see the spear jammed into the zombie's mouth. It fell back, twisting on the ground, trying to get up. Katie drew her shotgun as Travis reached for the spear.

"No time," she said, grabbing his arm. "More might come."

They both tuned and ran.

The truck loomed large and red before them. For the first time, Katie saw the gore and blood dried on its heavy deer guard. Despite her frantic thoughts, she looked closely to see that there was nothing undead lurking under the heavy truck. Scanning the street beyond their destination, she saw zilch stirring.

She reached the truck and whirled about, shotgun ready. She aimed down the street to cover Travis. She could see Juan and Jenni, still at the construction truck, watching them.

Katie heard a metallic pop as Travis opened the gas tank. Her eyes scanned the street and she reached out and opened the driver's-side door. Even in their haste, Jenni and Katie had shut the truck's doors when they fled the evening before. She thrust one hand into her pants pocket, and her fingers closed over the pickup's keys.

"More are coming!" Jenni shouted. She and Juan motioned frantically, urging their friends to hurry.

"Travis," Katie said in a strained voice.

"I heard them," Travis tersely answered.

The *glug glug glug* of the gas being poured into the tank was a welcome sound, but the howls and screeches of the approaching zombies were not. They rounded the corner, a torrent of battered, bloodied, ripe, dead bodies. Katie lifted her shotgun a little higher as she edged into the cab and put the keys in the ignition.

"Travis," she urged.

"Almost done," he retorted.

The zombies were closing fast. There were at least a dozen. They were running so fast, their limbs were popping, arms suddenly going limp, legs suddenly dragging. But a good number kept up a steady sprint.

"Travis," she implored again, "hurry!"

"Fuck it!" He threw away the gas container before it was empty, an arc of clear fluid splashing the brick road. He shoved the gas cap in place and darted around to the passenger side.

Katie yanked her door shut and gunned the engine. It didn't start.

Travis banged the passenger door shut. "Go! Go! Go!"

"It won't!"

"Keep trying! It was bone dry."

Katie kept turning the key and pumping the gas, her eyes on the zombies just a few yards away. The engine caught and roared to life. She shifted gears and floored the gas pedal; the pickup barreled through the zombies and toward the truck barrier, where Jenni and Juan were jumping up and down in excitement on top of the truck, waiting to be picked up.

"Drive fast so the zombies won't have a chance to catch up, then we get Juan and Jenni and go," Travis said breathlessly.

Katie nodded.

When they were a block away from the fort, the road ahead rapidly filled with zombies like water filling a basin. All sizes, all ages, rushing toward the truck, howling. The battered, torn bodies of men, women, and children stumbled, staggered, and even sprinted toward them.

Katie smashed her foot down on the brakes. "Oh, God."

Travis sat silently, watching the flood. "They're out."

Katie drew in a shuddering breath. "Yeah."

At least a hundred zombies were inundating the street between the truck and Jenni. Katie could see Juan pulling Jenni back toward the safety of the fort.

"Turn and go," Travis directed in a defeated voice.

Katie spun the wheel around as she pushed down on the accelerator. The truck plowed through the zombies that had originally been chasing them.

They were jostled around in the cab as the huge wheels churned over the dead. The truck broke free and raced up the long stretch of road out of town. Katie's gaze flicked to the rearview mirror. Some zombies were still in pursuit, but most of the others were beating their fists against the truck barricade.

Travis was very quiet alongside her, breathing hard, reeking of gasoline. Her shower was a moot point and she felt hot and sweaty. From the corner of her eye, Katie saw Travis run a hand slowly through his brown curls. Lifting his head, he said, "We just do what we planned."

Katie licked her very dry lips. "Yeah. Okay." Her throat felt tight and scratchy, and she forced herself to take a calming breath.

How they were going to get back into the fort would be dealt with later. For now, they had a job to do and they were determined to do it.

2.
Left Behind

Jenni was dimly aware of Juan pulling her back as she strained forward, reaching toward the red truck. She screamed loud and hard as the pickup spun around and retreated and the throng of the dead filled the street. Juan stumbled back with his arms locked around her as the dead began to bang on the side of the

construction truck, moaning and screeching. The heavy sand-
bags held the truck steady and the sides were too high and too
smooth for the undead to scale.

"They're not good climbers as far as we know, but let's not
give them any reason to try," Juan said in Jenni's ear as he half
carried, half dragged her down the ladder.

She struggled frantically. "Katie, no! She can't leave without
me!" Jenni felt like her head was going to explode. Juan dropped
her and they both fell behind the barricade. Safe but bruised,
they were hidden from the zombies.

Katie couldn't leave her. Katie was safety. Katie was her
friend. Her comrade. Her war buddy.

Jenni scrambled to her feet, drawing her gun and grabbing
the ladder.

Juan gripped her wrist tightly. "No. They are gone already!
They're safe!"

Jason was at the wall, waving and yelling at her. "Mom,
come back!"

She felt the world spinning around her and covered her face.
Mom? . . . Was she still a mom?

Those tiny fingers . . .

"Mom! Come back in!"

Benji . . . gone . . . Mikey . . . gone . . . Jason . . . Jason was
calling her.

She stumbled toward her son. Juan helped her scale the hur-
ricane fence. Jenni shoved her gun into her waistband and
dropped to the other side.

She turned back toward the outer perimeter, the morning
sun blinding her.

Katie . . .

Juan pushed her up onto the next ladder. "Come on, *loca*.
Get up there."

Jason reached down to her from the sentry post and she
crawled up the rungs to him. His arms went around her in a
tight hug. Jack was on the ground, whining.

"Katie left . . . ," Jenni whispered, her voice unsteady with fear.

"She'll be fine, Mom. She'll be fine." Jason held her tightly, supporting her as she walked.

"But we're a team. If I'm not with her, they'll get her. That's how it works. That's how it works."

"Travis is with her, Mom. She'll be okay."

Jenni felt numb, disoriented, and overwhelmed. Katie needed to be here with her, or she needed to be out there with Katie. That was how it worked. They had to be together or else the zombies would get them.

The world started spinning again. . . .

Jenni fainted.

3.
And Further Still

Katie looked at the gas gauge and frowned. The needle was hovering close to empty. The truck tore over the bumpy country road, jostling her about. Her hands gripped the steering wheel tightly to steady her nerves. She let out a slow sigh.

"It's up ahead. Soon," Travis assured her. He was peering at a map, much like Jenni had done the previous day.

Jenni . . .

Katie had a feeling Jenni was not taking their separation well. Actually, she wasn't either. They had bonded so quickly and strongly that to be separated felt more than a little odd. Travis's presence felt very different from Jenni's. It had her a little off balance. She wanted to reach out and take Jenni's hand and know that it was all going to be okay. Instead, she gripped the steering wheel tighter.

"I'm sorry," Travis said sympathetically .

"Why sorry?"

"It was my stupid idea to have us leave and now . . ." He

shook his head. "I'm sorry, Katie. I've never been a real leader before. I'm sure I'm fucking things up."

"No, no, you're doing your best. Hell, none of us have any idea what we are really doing."

"Except Juan with his zombie handbook. He assured me that the guns were important, though he mumbled something about blades," Travis uttered grimly.

"Guns are effective. They just draw a lot of attention because of the noise," Katie reminded him. "Still, I'd rather have a gun than a blade with some of the faster ones."

"Yeah, Juan is still bitching about that. He keeps complaining that they're supposed to be slow. But some of the ones that aren't as screwed up are really damn fast."

Katie let out a slight laugh. "Actually, Jenni spent a good deal of time bitching about the same thing."

"Gas station should be just around that bend." Travis looked at her with an unreadable expression. "I'm really sorry."

"It's okay. It's not like I haven't done this before." She smiled reassuringly at him as they pulled into the mom-and-pop gas station. "After two days of this, I'm an old pro."

The station was a very old building, with peeling white paint and heavy bars over the windows, but the pumps were new. An ancient, beat-up trailer was nestled behind the weathered building. Travis looked out his window. "It looks clear. I'll try to get inside and turn on the pumps. I can see that the readouts on the pumps are still working, so the electricity isn't out here."

Katie pulled her credit card out of her pants pocket. "We could just try this."

Travis looked at the card, then at her, and finally smiled. "I knew there was a reason I had you with me."

Katie slid out of the truck, her gun drawn and her gaze sweeping over the terrain. She was feeling a little hot and mushy-headed. Wiping her brow, she grimaced as her wound pulsed with pain. She watched Travis to see if the credit card worked.

He grabbed the nozzle and gave her a wink. "We're in business," he said.

"Just make it fast."

Her stomach gave a low growl, and a twinge ran through her intestines. Dammit, great time to have an upset stomach. Sliding around the front of the truck, she scrutinized the area, studying the shadows under the trees and the buildings in the distance.

"Do you have food and water, Travis?" It was a woman's voice. Young, perky.

Travis whirled around, as did Katie.

A young woman with red hair had opened what looked like a window for after-hour payments.

"A bottle or two of water would do us fine, Janet," Travis answered. "Glad to see you're okay."

"We got the family holed up in here. But nothing has come by since yesterday. Luthor shot it and we drug it out back."

Katie kept her gaze on her surroundings as she moved toward the building. She felt her stomach flutter. She hated being exposed in the openness of the parking lot. She took a long look down the side of the building to make sure nothing lurked there, then moved toward the window.

The girl waited for her, the window half-open, talking to someone hidden from view. That person handed Janet a bag and she pushed the window all the way open to pass it to Katie, who took it gratefully and peeked inside. Two bottles of water and some Danish. She was getting tired of Danish.

Janet looked at her, sizing her up. "You and Travis heading out of town together? Going to hide somewhere?"

"We're on a mission for city hall, actually."

"I heard on the CB that a lot of people were down there. We decided to wait it out here until the army comes," Janet answered. "We got food in here to last us and I'm sure the army will get here soon."

"What makes you think they'll come?"

"Because that's their job," Janet said briskly, and looked to-

ward Travis. "So, you and Travis are doing a mission? What kinda mission?"

Katie smiled slightly, realizing the woman was jealous. "Getting guns to blow the zombies to hell," she replied.

"Yeah? Hell, just go into any house around here and you'll find guns."

"And maybe zombies," Katie reminded her.

"Yeah, that's not good."

"Let's go, Katie!" Travis thumped the lid to the tank closed and waved to her.

"Thanks, Janet," Katie said, and quickly ran toward the bright red pickup.

She felt her intestines twisting again. Her head was throbbing, too. What the hell was wrong with her?

"You okay?" Travis looked at her with concern.

"Yeah," she assured him. She slid back into the driver's seat and put on her seat belt. Her hands felt clammy when she gripped the steering wheel, and for an instant, her eyesight swam.

Travis ran his hand over her hair gently. "Katie, you're burning up. I can feel it even through your hair."

She leaned her forehead against the steering wheel. "I don't feel well."

"Nothing got you?" Travis asked, his voice edged with fear.

"No, no. Nothing touched me even." She stared at him through a blond curl that had fallen over her eyes. "I just don't feel good."

"Let me drive," Travis said.

"Okay." Her strength was leaving her fast. She slid over into the passenger seat. The wound she had received when slipping down onto the road sent a sharp pain through her limb and she grimaced.

Travis came around and got into the driver's seat. He touched her forehead gently. "You feel feverish. You'd better rest. Here, drink some water."

Katie smiled at how sweet he was as he buckled her in and handed her the bottle of water. "Thanks."

His hands were rough, but very cool on her face and neck. "Katie, are you sure—?"

"Yes, yes. I wouldn't lie about that."

Katie took long sips of water and watched the road begin its never-ending crawl beneath the tires of the truck. The tank now full, the truck sped toward Ralph's tiny little town and his hunting store.

She was feeling worse and worse and closed her eyes. She must have dozed because she woke with a start. "Pull over!"

Travis slammed on the brakes and Katie flung open the door and threw up her breakfast. Heaving, she wiped her mouth with the back of her hand.

"It may not be safe here, Katie," Travis said, his hand on her back, a comforting gesture, yet she knew he was ready to yank her back inside.

"Okay," she said, and threw up all that remained in her stomach. She yanked the door shut and wiped her mouth with a kerchief Travis handed her.

Travis's face changed. Katie realized he had just noticed her wounded forearm. "Katie, what is this?"

"Scrape. I caught it on the truck when we jumped down."

Worriedly, he examined it. He poured water over it and found a napkin in the cup holder to cover it. "Just a scrape?"

"I would tell you. I don't want to be one of those things," she answered defensively.

Travis gazed at her solemnly and said, "I know. But you're scaring me."

Weakly, she took hold of his wrist and forced a smile onto her lips. "I'm sure it's nothing. Just something I ate."

Then she passed out onto his lap.

Dimly, she was aware of being carried. She heard Nerit's and Ralph's voices. Another voice—*the deputy,* she thought—was also talking.

"I'm afraid," Travis said at some point.

They put her into a very cold bath. Someone's hands kept her head above water. She tried to talk, but felt too weak.

"She wasn't bit. That's not a bite," Ralph's voice declared.

"But there was zombie blood and guts all over that truck," Travis said, and she heard a catch in his voice. "What if—?"

Katie's head swam. Her body felt so hot. . . .

"Katie," a voice insisted.

She opened her eyes to see Lydia kneeling next to the tub, her gaze very concerned.

"Lydia," she whispered.

"It'll be okay. I'm here. I'll be with you," Lydia said softly, reassuringly, kissing Katie's brow and holding her up in the cold bath.

Katie smiled at her feverishly. "Then it's all going to be okay." She sank back into unconsciousness.

· CHAPTER ELEVEN ·

1.
Other Voices

Juan sat slumped in a chair in the mayor's office, hands folded on his flat stomach, twiddling his thumbs and seriously considering smacking Jenni a few times. Yeah, she was hot. Way hotter than the blond chick, but she had been a fucking annoyance ever since Travis and the blonde had rode into the sunset together.

It had only gotten worse when Ralph radioed that Katie was very sick and that Travis was worried the zombie guts on the trucks lining the perimeter had contaminated her when she cut open her arm during their departure.

Jenni had become downright hysterical at that news. "I have to go to her! I have to! I'm her best friend, don't you see! We're sisters now!"

Juan had to pry Jenni's fingers off the mayor's shirt and helped Jason carry her out of the communication center so that they could actually hear what Travis was saying over the CB. Jenni had fallen apart completely as soon as they laid her down on her cot. As far as he knew, she was still there, in the storage room, with her son watching over her.

He studied his thumb for a moment. Years ago, he had accidentally chopped off the tip on another construction job. Every once in a while it would start throbbing. When he was nervous, he often found himself looking at its mutilated nail and gnarled

skin. Juan was a nail biter by nature, and that deformed, bizarre half nail called to him.

Just as he stuck the tip of his finger in his mouth, he received a deft slap across the back of his head.

"Don't do that. You look like a baby." His mother, Rosario—Rosie for short—stood in the doorway next to him. She was a very tiny woman with dark hair shot through with silver and pale amber eyes. They were very sad eyes, the eyes of a woman who had recently lost her husband to cancer.

"Sorry, Mom."

"Where's the mayor? I have that list for him."

"Not sure. He told me to wait here."

Juan had lived in Ashley Oaks all his life, except for the two years he lived in Houston with his big, black, beautiful wife, Candace. But that marriage had failed when he decided to move back home to be with his dad during his illness. Candace couldn't take the small-town living, and he couldn't blame her. They had parted friends and he still talked to her every other day.

At least he had, until . . . Not for the first time since the zombies arrived, Juan thought of Candace. . . . Where was she? Was she okay?

He took off his cowboy hat and ran a hand over his hair to smooth it. It was long and curly and, due to the heat, terribly frizzy.

"I made a list of all the people in the fort, just like the mayor asked," Rosie said, and sat down next to her son.

"Let me see." He took the clipboard and read the names. He knew just about everyone on the list. Forty-two people, including Travis and Katie. Fifteen construction workers, five city workers, twenty civilians—mostly family members of the local construction workers or the city workers. Plus Chuck the truck driver, Jenni, and Jason. And the dog.

He liked the dog.

"It's sad that we don't have more people here." He sighed and handed it back.

"Well, the way I see it, people went to where they thought it was safe and where they could stay with their families. My family was here at the site, so I came here."

Juan smiled at his mom, then leaned over and kissed her cheek. She gave him a pat on the back of his hand.

"It's a diverse group," Rosie said, "just like the town population. Sixty percent under the age of sixty-two, forty percent over sixty-two. Forty percent white, thirty percent Hispanic, twenty-five percent black, and five percent other."

"What the hell is other, anyway?" Juan snorted with a smirk.

"Raymond Gutierrez is Navajo Indian." Rosie gave him a wide smile. "Now, where do we put the dog? Other, because he is another species, or white, since he's German?" She winked. "The balance between men and women is really off. Women make up only thirty percent of those here."

"Guess I won't be dating anytime soon," he said with a grin.

His mother smacked him lightly. "It's just sad that we were so ill prepared. The city can only plan for things that seem plausible." She waved a hand contemptuously. "Zombies have never been a part of city planning."

"You were city secretary way too long, Mom," Juan said. Her head was full of facts and figures on the town population. "This isn't your fault. No one could have planned for this."

Peggy, the current city secretary, strolled in with her small six-year-old son pressed against one leg. Juan liked the late-in-life mother and her son, and he couldn't blame the kid for clinging to his mom. Lord knows he had wanted to cling to Rosie a few times.

Behind Peggy came Tobias, a tall black man in his late fifties and the city manager. His expression was grim under his scraggly eyebrows and his salt and pepper hair was a bit mussed. The mayor, Manny Reyes, filed in last. He looked tired and worn around the edges. His Spanish blood made him fair and very gringo-looking, but he loved tequila as much as Juan did. And while Juan knew what the hell was up, the mayor did not.

Manny was way too centered on being logical and finding exact answers. Juan knew that what was going on did not fit into a neat little box that Manny could understand.

Manny sat at his desk. The others took seats as well. Tobias's brow was furrowed, his gaze distant. Juan had seen his wife's name on the list, but not their children and grandchildren, who lived in Ashley Oaks.

Curtis, who also looked pale and tired, walked in and took a seat near the door. Juan felt bad for him. The rookie on the force was the last man standing. It couldn't be easy on him.

The mayor leaned back in his chair. He picked up a pen from his desktop and studied it for a second, then looked up. "Well, I called all of you in here to talk about the present situation. Peggy, are you sure you want Cody here?"

Peggy gently tried to pry her child off, but he only grabbed on tighter. "He won't budge."

The mayor nodded. "Okay. Travis says Katie has a fierce fever. He told me in no uncertain terms he plans to stay with her until she's better or, if she is infected, to make sure she is at peace."

"He has it bad for her. Too bad she's gay," Juan said grumpily. Travis was his best friend, and Juan had seen him fall for unattainable women more than once during their time in Houston.

His mother smacked him upside the head again, and he knew he deserved it.

The mayor blinked. "Oh, then Jenni . . ." He sat still for a moment, his fingers twisting the pen. "Oh, that makes sense now, how's she acting." He shrugged. "Anyway, we need to prepare for their return."

Tobias slapped the palms of his hands against his knees and leaned forward. "How do we do that? The infected are filling the street. Most of our fellow townspeople are out there. What we need to do is get ahold of the army and get them out here to treat those people!"

"They're dead. You can't treat them," Juan said. He couldn't believe they were still having this conversation. Some people took denial way too far.

"That is a ridiculous statement. The dead do not just get up, become rabid, and attack people. It has to be a virus, like the CDC said," Tobias said firmly.

"They can't be alive," Curtis said softly.

"Why do you say that?" Tobias turned a fierce look on him.

Curtis shrank under it, but replied, "Because some of them are dragging their innards on the road."

"Adrenaline does strange things to people. If they have large amounts coursing their system like the CDC said in the beginning—"

"Toby, the CDC took it back and called them the reanimated dead," the mayor pointed out.

"Which is a fancy term for *zombies*," Juan said. "We are dealing with zombies. You know, the living dead. They want to eat us. I thought we all knew that by now." Juan shook his head and folded his arms over his chest. People were so stupid.

"I do not believe we should give in to hysteria and superstition," Tobias responded.

Then Peggy's son started to cry, loud and desperate. She tried to shush him.

"Daddy tried to eat us! He kept banging on the window!" The boy was near hysteria. "His guts were hanging out!"

Tobias flinched and said, "Maybe he shouldn't be here."

"He's in this, too, Toby," Rosie said softly. "You can't shield a child from this."

Peggy pulled her son into her lap and kissed him on the forehead. He continued to cry softly, his tiny body shivering.

Curtis hunched in on himself, with his arms folded high on his chest. "Let's get back on topic. We need those guns. We can't keep killing them with spears."

"Yeah, blades aren't much help with these kinds of zombies if they get in," Juan said morosely. "The handbook did not have

running zombies in it. This is a whole other ball game, but the basics are the same. We need to make this place as safe as possible and think before we act. We missed out on the whole being-prepared thing, so we gotta do the best we can now."

"How do we get Travis back in? That's the question," the mayor said softly.

"Maybe someone on this list has the experience we need," Rosie suggested.

"Like someone has experience with zombies," Curtis muttered.

"The infected people out there deserve better than to be hunted down and murdered," Tobias declared. "We've been murderers for days now."

"They are not infected!" Curtis's voice almost sounded shrill. "They are eating people, Tobias!"

Tobias's eyes were swimming with tears, but he fought to keep his voice steady. "My family needs help, not to be butchered."

"They were already butchered! They are dead!" Curtis's face looked younger, now that he appeared close to cracking.

Juan stood up and tried to break some of the tension. "Look. We got construction equipment. We got that much. Now we need to get creative."

"Build a corral," the little boy said.

Juan looked at him. "What, kid?"

"His name is Cody," Peggy said softly.

"Build a corral. Like I do with my Legos. When Daddy and I—" He started to blubber, but pushed on. "—played with my cowboys and my Legos, we built corrals for the cows."

The mayor looked at Juan. "A corral?"

"Fuck me!" Juan exclaimed, and took a step back.

"Juan!"

"Sorry, Mom. I think we can actually do that . . . yeah . . . From the mouth of babes . . . from the mouth of babes!" Juan didn't wait to talk out the idea; he headed out the door.

Loca was standing just outside the room, spying. "I want to help," Jenni said, her big, dark eyes so beautiful and so nuts.

"No," he answered, blocking her way.

"I can help!" She faked trying to dive around him to the left, then darted to the right, slipping past him.

"Hey! You can't help. You're *loca*," he declared, snagging her around the waist.

"Maybe, but I can still help. I have to help!"

She grabbed his arm and they stared at each other for a long moment. She was nuts, yeah, but she looked determined.

"How?"

"I used to play with my kids with Legos all the time and build all sorts of—"

"We're not using Legos," Juan pointed out.

"Yeah, I know that!" Jenni stomped her foot. "I'm saying that I know how to make plans to make things work. My kids and I built entire cities with Legos."

"Me, too," Cody said.

The mayor was still twisting his pen in his hands. "Listen to what they have to say. It won't hurt."

Juan hesitated. Well, he actually wasn't sure how he would build this corral, was he?

"Okay, fine."

"I have some Legos!" Cody ran down the hall.

Juan looked at everyone gathered around him. They were all loco, he decided. Hell, the world was loco. And for some reason, this made him smile. "Fine, fine, the kid has a good idea."

An hour later, on a conference table, Jenni and Cody had constructed the basic outline of the fort, complete with the wall, the buildings, and the surrounding streets. Two Legos stacked together was the hotel, and a string of long narrow Legos created the perimeter. Jason had come in and started to help; his dog was lying down under the table. Juan sat nearby, flipping through a magazine and not really paying attention.

"So the zombies are all here," Jenni said, putting tiny little Lego men in the street in front of the wall.

Just back from a trip to the perimeter, Curtis said, "They're all in the front, spread across from here to here." He pointed, and Jenni rearranged the Lego men.

"It's like they feel that is our weakest point," the older kid said, and the dog whined.

Cody, now looking more like a little kid than like a scared rabbit, picked up a stack of several Legos and made a big noise as he dropped it between two buildings. He made very effective sounds of zombies being crushed. Now that he was playing, he was having as much fun as any little boy with his toys.

Juan and Curtis both leaned forward to watch Cody. Curtis lifted his eyebrows. Cody picked up another stack of Legos and smashed it down between two other buildings. Now all the fake zombies were trapped between the wall and two large barriers that hemmed them into a T-shaped area.

Jenni clapped her hands and high-fived the little boy as Juan and Curtis studied the configuration more closely.

Cody took a plastic Godzilla from his bag of toys and made it stomp the zombies into the ground, but the idea was already firm in Juan's mind.

Jenni looked up at the men. "We can do this, can't we?"

"We can have the zombies all penned in here," Curtis said, "and Travis can come in from over here, where there won't be any."

"But how do we get them into the fort?" Jenni frowned at the tiny, colorful town.

Cody laughed and picked up one of his Matchbox trucks. "Like this." He swung his arm like it was a crane and set the truck down in the fort.

Juan grabbed the kid and hugged him. "You've been watching us set up the site. Maybe we can't lift the truck in, but if Travis and Katie load everything onto a pallet, we can use the crane to lift the load—and them—over the wall to safety."

Jenni snuggled the little boy and kissed him. "You're a genius!"

"I just like big trucks," Cody answered, and plowed the zombies down with the toy truck.

Juan grabbed a piece of paper and started drawing. He felt Jenni's gaze on him and looked up.

"We're all in this together, you know," she said.

"You're still *loca,*" he told her.

She grinned at him, and much to his disgust, he smiled back.

2.
Threshold

Jenni sat at the edge of her cot, frowning. Jason was asleep, snoring slightly. Jack sat on the floor near her stepson's cot, staring at her quizzically.

Glancing over at Katie's empty cot, Jenni shivered in her nightgown. It was several sizes too big, but it was all she could find in the donation box for the needy. Pushing her dark hair out of her face, she rose and walked to the door.

Jack immediately got up and followed her. She rested her hand on his head and smiled down at the German shepherd. He was a good and loyal friend.

Slipping out quietly, she moved down the narrow stairwell, her bare feet not making a sound. Distantly, she could hear the zombies moaning. The living had kept well out of view of the dead all day, and now the zombies were just standing around, moaning. Juan had been right that staying out of sight kept the zombies calmer, but they hadn't gone away. And while most were just standing there, a few kept pounding on the trucks until their hands were a bloody pulp.

Jenni shivered as she thought of Katie looking like one of *them*—empty, lifeless, a mere husk with the spark gone from her eyes. Jenni had been all over the place emotionally today.

Juan had pissed her off by calling her *loca,* so later she had put on her best *I'm just a pretty girl* persona to get him to lay off her so she could watch him plan. She knew her initial reaction to the word that Katie was very sick and possibly infected had made her seem crazy in the eyes of some of the people, but she didn't really care.

Even now, the thought of Katie not being here was too much to bear. Katie had been the first good thing in Jenni's new life. Katie made her feel safe. Katie made her feel like she was okay. Normal, not a dysfunctional, battered housewife blundering through life. Katie was everything Jenni had ever wanted to be.

Katie had given her a second chance—a second chance at a new life in a very different world. Okay, all the rules had changed, but Jenni had found that she could actually function in this world. Maybe that made her *loca,* but she didn't care.

She brushed a tear away as she walked to the communication center. Curtis sat there, still in his uniform, looking worn out and shell-shocked. He had washed out his clothes and they clung damply to his skin, but he didn't seem to care.

"Avoid Houston at all costs," a voice was saying over one of the speakers. "Stay on the minor roads. I'll meet up with you near Texarkana."

"Come back again, good buddy," another voice said.

Curtis noticed her presence and looked up at her wearily.

"Who are they?"

"Truckers. Looking for a place to hole up."

"Did you tell them about us?"

"Too far out. Too little gas. A few may make it here in a day or two, but those things . . ." He shook his head. "We have to figure out how to make it safe for more people to come here."

Jenni stepped into the room, Jack pressing past her to go greet Curtis. The doggy love actually brought a smile to Curtis's face, and he leaned down to rub the German shepherd's ears.

"Anything new on Katie?"

Curtis sighed. "Still real sick. Real sick."

Jenni sat down on a cold metal folding chair and clasped her hands tightly together. "What do they think it is?"

"Travis is afraid it's the zombie sickness," Curtis answered, averting his gaze.

Jenni moaned. "But he's not sure."

Curtis agreed with a slight bob of his head. "Not sure."

Jenni looked at the little communications center, then said, "Can I sit here and wait? Maybe they'll call?"

Curtis returned his gaze to her and she gave him her best *little girl lost* look. He nodded. "Sure. You can stay."

Jenni smiled at him and pulled her knees up to her chin, her feet resting on the cold metal seat. "Turn up the CB. Maybe someone is out there that we can talk to."

Curtis gave her a shy smile. "Okay." He leaned over and turned it up. Jenni watched him, memorizing his actions.

The first chance she got, she would find out what was really happening to Katie.

3.

Beyond

Travis sat in darkness. The only illumination came from a small night-light on the far side of the room. Katie lay curled on the bed, her blond hair in disarray around her face. She looked waxen, pale, and frightfully drawn. On the dresser next to him was a revolver. Ralph had instructed him precisely on how to handle it. And Nerit had, intently, insisted that he could not falter, he could not flinch. If Katie rose from that bed as anything other than a living, breathing human being, he had to put her out of her misery.

Rubbing his hands together, he let out a low sigh. This was hard. Very hard. To sit here and wait for this woman to fade from the living world into the domain of the dead just so he

could put a bullet between her eyes seemed a cruel fate, considering the absolute joy he had felt in meeting her just two days earlier.

It had been one of the oddest moments of his life. He had just looked at her and known her. He'd felt that he should already know her name and that they shared a past. He had felt strongly if he opened his mouth, he'd say her name, even though he didn't know it. But somehow he knew *her*. Even when she had mentioned her wife—and that had kinda thrown him just a bit—in a way, he had known. He couldn't help but wonder if they had crossed paths long ago in Houston.

It was odd, considering that Jenni, with her long, flowing raven hair, pale skin, and luminous eyes, was everything he had ever found physically desirable about a woman. In fact, she looked startlingly similar to his ex-fiancée, Clair. But no, it had been the tall blonde with the long, lean body, intense features, and intelligent gaze who had instantly grabbed his attention. He had even noticed how her eyes turned up slightly at the ends, speaking of Nordic blood in her genes.

I know you, he wanted to say. And she had seemed to want to say it back to him.

Raised a good Protestant, he had never believed much in miracles or the mystical. But he did now. Zombies pretty much settled that argument. They weren't natural; he knew that much. But seeing Katie and knowing she was important to not only him, but also to all those in the fort—that surpassed anything his logical mind had ever grasped before. And now he sat in this dark room, listening to her breathe, waiting for the end.

At times she called out softly for Lydia. Sometimes for her father. Once or twice for Jenni.

"Please," she had begged Travis during a lucid moment. "Take care of Jenni."

He knew he would take care of Jenni, and Jason, and all the others. For Katie and her memory. She had endured more than

he had, seen things he could not imagine. His loss had been a Dear John letter left on his pillow. Hers had been seeing Lydia as one of those things.

There was a sharp intake of breath from the bed . . . then nothing.

Tears, hot and angry, filled his eyes and he picked up the gun. It was time.

Travis endured in the darkened bedroom, gazing down at the gun. His tears were fierce in his eyes, and his anger burned even hotter in his throat.

He heard the bed creak and, through his lashes, saw her sit up.

"I'm sorry," he said, and lifted the gun.

"Why?"

He blinked, and tears fell down his cheeks. "Katie?"

"Yeah?"

Travis flipped on the overhead light and she sat blinking in the sudden brightness. She still looked pale and feeble, but her eyes were bright. Clear. Alive.

"Oh, God, Katie! I thought—"

She kept blinking in the bright light, shielding her face with her hand. "I told you, nothing bit me."

"Katie, you've been so sick." Travis looked down at the gun and set it upon the dresser. As the heavy weight left his hand, a heavier weight lifted from his spirit. With great relief, he walked toward her.

For a crazed split second, he saw her with empty eyes, mouth opened in a scream, rushing toward him; then the vision was gone and Katie was giving him a look that said pretty much that she thought he was nuts.

"Sorry about the gun, but you were burning up and we couldn't get the fever down for the longest time. . . ."

"That's what I get for not getting the flu shot," Katie pushed a hand through her hair, wincing at the grubbiness of it. "Ugh, I must be a sight."

Travis laughed and impulsively leaned down to hug her. Af-

ter just two days of illness, she felt so tiny and frail. She was already slim, and the drain on her body resources had been powerful.

She awkwardly hugged him back, then tried to stand up, but was unable to get to her feet. "Okay, I guess I was really sick." She fell back onto the bed, looking a little woozy.

"Scary sick," Travis responded, and sat next to her. He took hold of her hand and looked at her arm. "We couldn't figure out if it was the zombie infection or not. Your scrape—I didn't know if the blood and guts from the zombies had infected you." Peeling back the bandage, he revealed a nicely healing wound. "We saw no signs of infection, but you were burning up and we couldn't keep anything in you."

Katie grimaced as she touched her hair again. "God, I'm so gross right now. None of you could have known that when I get the flu, I go down like an elephant. I always have, and that's why I usually get the flu shot. I skipped it this year because I had a big case and just never found the time. Who knows what diseases all those dead bodies have unleashed into the air?" She shivered at the thought. Looking down, she saw she was dressed in a nightgown that was probably Nerit's.

"The flu," Travis said with relief. "Thank God, just the fucking everyday flu." He leaned forward, elbows on his knees, and ran his hands over his face.

Katie draped one arm over his broad shoulders and gave him a little hug. "I'm a tough bitch. A little bug like that can't keep me down for long. I always bounce back."

He scrutinized her and said, "You're something else, you know that."

She gave him an impish smile. "I was called the Bitch Queen of the Prosecution. That has to say something about me."

"Tough as nails, eh?"

"Eat 'em for breakfast." Katie grinned.

She looked fragile, but her voice was strong. She had ridden out the worst of it and was on the mend. He could tell that by

the brightness in her eyes. Now that she was sitting next to him, smiling at him, he couldn't imagine why he had thought she would leave the world so easily.

"I was really worried about you." He took hold of her hand. It felt a little cold, the bones under her skin so very delicate. "I thought you were gone. And we need you. You're smart, resourceful, and . . . and . . ."

"Bitchy."

"No, very real. I feel like what I see is what you are. I like that about you. That's why I wanted to know you better the second I met you. I knew in my heart that you were the type of person who could help all of us survive and keep us human. Not just keep us from becoming zombies, but keep us compassionate."

"You give me way too much credit," Katie said swiftly.

"You rode into town with a kid, a dog, and a woman who doesn't have all her marbles, and you were all alive and not bitten. That is an amazing feat all unto itself. When Jenni told me about everything else you've done . . ." He shook his head. "To have lost you would have cost all of us."

Katie frowned at him and said, "Stop it. I'm going to cry. And I don't cry! Well, not until all of this went down."

Travis laughed and his eyes sparkled with tears. "Well, I'm much more butch than you, and I cry."

Katie rolled her eyes, then laughed, running a hand over her hair. "Ugh, my hair!" She staggered to her feet and went to the mirror on the wall. "I need a bath. Fast."

"I would insist on you lying back down, but I don't think that will work."

"Absolutely not." Katie fussed with her greasy, matted hair and threw up her hands. "Ugh!"

"Okay, you can take a shower, but I'm staying right here and you're leaving that door open in case you fall."

"Fine . . . fine . . ."

She stumbled a bit as she moved, and he considered helping her, but figured she wouldn't appreciate it. Grabbing a fresh

pair of jeans and a white tank top, she managed to get herself into the bathroom.

There was a gentle knock on the door and Travis opened it. Nerit stood there, with her yellowish hair falling over one shoulder and one hand holding her flannel robe shut.

"How is she?" Her voice was concerned. She saw the empty bed and heard the shower. "She's up?"

"And lucid. And feisty. Weak as hell, but she's okay."

Nerit clasped her hands together. "Oh, thank goodness! I woke up fearing the worst."

"Honestly, I almost put one between her eyes. But, luckily, she spoke. I was so convinced she was gone."

Nerit hugged Travis and cast a look toward the open bathroom door. "I must tell Ralph!" She scurried off and Travis hesitantly walked toward the bathroom.

Maybe I'm dreaming and she died and I shot her and I'm dreaming, he thought. He saw her outline behind the shower curtain, and the tension between his shoulders lessened.

Again, for a moment, he saw a flash of Katie sitting up, eyes dead, screaming, and rushing toward him. . . .

But that hadn't happened.

He felt like his emotions were seesawing back and forth and he tried to regain some balance as he waited. He stood with his back to the bathroom and hands in his pockets. He was still afraid. Afraid of what had nearly happened.

Katie finally emerged with her wet hair up on top of her head in a tiny ponytail. Damp little curls spilled over her brow. Her shoulders, poking out of the tank top, looked a little bonier than before. The men's jeans she was wearing hung a little low on her hips and showed that she had lost weight. But despite her fragile appearance, Travis knew she was going to be okay.

"I need to talk to Jenni," she said, ignoring his obvious examination of her appearance.

Feeling a little embarrassed and awkward, he nodded.

Taking her arm, he helped her down the hall. He knew she

was feeling weak because she did not protest. They entered the small room where the CB radio was set up and a man in his forties with a wide, pleasant face looked up. He had sandy colored hair, wide shoulders and a good size beer gut.

"Hey, you made it!" He gave her an enormous grin that lit up his rather plain face.

"You're Bill, right?"

"Yep, that's me."

"Good to meet you, Bill."

"Happy to see you alive, Katie. I take it you want to call your friends?"

"Please," Katie sat down heavily in a chair and Travis steadied her with one hand. "Then I want to eat something really bad."

"Sure thing, give me a moment." Bill adjusted the dials and started talking.

Katie looked up at Travis and laid her hand over his. "Thank you. For watching over me. For making sure I was okay."

Travis flushed. "No problem."

". . . she's up and talking," Bill said into the microphone.

It sounded like there was a brief struggle of some kind on the other end. Then a woman's voice said, "Katie! Katie! It's me!"

Bill handed the mic to Katie. Travis couldn't help but laugh a little, imagining Jenni climbing over Curtis to get to the microphone.

"And it's me, Jenni. I'm okay. It was just the flu."

"Oh, thank God!" Jenni broke down; her sobs were loud over the speakers. "I was so scared! We're going to find a way to get you back in and you'll be safe here!"

"I know, Jenni, I know. And I know you were looking after me in your own way. I felt it. We'll come home. I promise. Soon."

Travis could see tears in Katie's eyes and turned away. He felt emotional and unsteady on his feet. Nerit and Ralph appeared in the doorway. Katie reached out to them, and they all held hands.

The most radiant smile he had ever seen on any woman's face lit up Katie's features, and he felt almost as if he were basking in it.

For the first time since the world had slid sideways into hell, he felt a moment of happiness, and it felt delicious.

· CHAPTER TWELVE ·

1.
Dancing for the Dead

Two days later, the excitement in the fort was a tangible, electric force sweeping through all the survivors. It seemed as if everyone was drawn out into the morning sunlight to watch what had been dubbed Operation Little Doggy.

Even Old Man Watson came and sat in a plastic chair in the sun. He was their oldest survivor at ninety-three, and he had been saved only because he was at city hall, paying his water bill, when the zombies had arrived. His arms were covered in tattoos from his navy days and he mostly sat around smiling at everyone. It took Jenni a while to realize he couldn't hear hardly anything said to him. Then she'd gone out of her way to explain the plan to him, talking very loudly.

When she'd finished, he patted her on the head and said, "You give 'em hell, kid."

Jenni had been the first person to sign the volunteer sheet for Operation Little Doggy. Jason was the second. They were both determined to help in the project that would bring Katie and Travis home safely with their load of guns and supplies. Everyone else in the fort was more concerned about Travis returning with the guns than they were about Katie. That annoyed Jenni, even though she understood that these people didn't know Katie like she did. Also, the more she listened to the townsfolk talk about Travis, the more evident it was that when he moved to

Ashley Oaks to work on the reconstruction of the downtown area six months before, he had caused an immediate stir. He had been part of the crew that finished the renovation of city hall.

"Movie star looks, nice as can be, volunteering down at the senior center," Peggy said to Jenni as they washed dishes the night before—it was their turn, according to the chore list. "All the ladies, old and young, had mad crushes on him. And honestly, I don't think he noticed. He's nursing a broken heart. He told me his fiancée left him when he gave up his high-paying job as an architect in Houston and went back to construction."

Jenni had absorbed that, considered it, and tucked it away for later. She had seen Travis's subtle charisma in action and she was very much affected by it. Weirdly, she thought Katie was, too. But she had seen something in his eyes when he gazed at her, and she felt pretty confident. Time would tell, of course.

Now she stood next to Jason, clad in the same outfit she had been wearing since they left Ralph's. It had been washed every day since her arrival and now had a softness to it that she found comforting. Jason had told Jack to stay with Old Man Watson so he wouldn't get in the volunteers' way, and now the German shepherd sat faithfully next to the old man, getting his ears scratched.

"Okay, the cement is mixed," Juan said, approaching the groups of volunteers. "Just do what we told you and make it quick. We don't want to give these zombies any ideas. Try to keep low and out of view."

Jenni and Jason quickly scaled the ladder over the cement wall and down the other side. The hurricane fence was easy to climb over and she dropped down on the other side effortlessly, with Jason right beside her. The other members of their team, six in all, formed a bucket brigade to pass long, wicked five-foot spikes over the wall and fence.

The day before, a group of construction workers had spent hours with sledgehammers and shovels, creating deep gouges in

the sidewalk that separated the fence from the line of trucks. Now, Mike helped lower the base of one of the spikes into the ground. Jenni and Jason held it in position while freshly made cement was poured into the deep hole around the bottom of the spike.

It seemed simple enough at first, but as the morning wore on, Jenni grew tired. The spikes were bits of the old wrought iron fence the construction crew had torn down. They were heavy, and after a while, her muscles ached and she was covered with sweat. But if, as Juan feared, the zombies became capable of climbing, something had to be waiting for them when they tried to drop down. The spikes were set at a slant and staggered in such a way that you had duck low and around them to get safely through. Jenni's little team moved quickly, but work was exhausting. What made it harder was the nasty stench and sounds of the dead on the other side of the ring of trucks. Their increasingly loud moans and screeches indicated that they were stirred up, sensing warm flesh nearby.

Jason's hair hung in wet, long strands in his eyes and he peered at her as he blew them up and out of the way. "Eh, maybe I do need a haircut."

She giggled. They helped maneuver another spike into place.

Soon the forest of spikes was ready; all of them angled at a deadly slant to capture anyone attempting to jump down.

Finally, the volunteers clambered back into the fortress, where they were greeted with a round of applause. Juan walked toward Jenni and the rest of the crew and said, "Okay—so far, so good."

Jenni pulled off her heavy gloves and snapped her fingers. "Piece of cake."

"So far, Loca, but we have more to do." He walked past her and climbed the stairs that led to a sentry post in one corner of their makeshift fortress to join Mike. He looked out over the crowd of zombies and then turned around to motion to the crane operator.

Time for phase two.

The forty-foot long metal storage containers near the back of the fort had been rigged with chains so that they could be lifted. With a whine, the huge crane snagged the first of the units and lifted it high into the air. The container, which stood almost ten feet tall, had originally been filled with materials that were to be used during the renovation of downtown Ashley Oaks. Now it would serve another purpose. The crane arm slowly swung the now empty unit over the construction site as Mike took over directing the operator. Juan hurried to another location, to keep an eye on the shifting zombie crowd and communicate with Mike using hand signals.

Jenni joined some other people standing on a pile of cement bags to watch. Slowly, the arm swung into position and the container was carefully aligned with the road below. Juan motioned again and the container lowered slowly over the heads of the zombies reaching for it. Finally, it descended, smashing them beneath its weight. It fit almost perfectly across the road, reaching from the truck barrier to the side of the building on the other side.

The crane arm swung back as Jenni ran across the site to where Juan was. She had to get closer, to see what was going on. As she ran up the steps, the sea of zombies came into view, and she gasped.

Some were beating on the storage container that now almost completely cut off the street to the right. Most were reaching toward the people who were visible on the platform, screeching, howling, and pushing hard against the large trucks in front of them.

The crane arm swung overhead again, this time dropping large bags full of earth between the end of the storage container and the storefront it had settled in front of.

Now the road was completely blocked.

Juan turned to Jenni. "Not bad, huh?"

She grinned at him.

Tobias stood nearby, shaking his head. "We slaughter them instead of helping them."

"What do you suggest we do, huh? Give them some vitamin C and aspirin and tell them to get some rest?" Juan gestured toward the zombies. "You really think that would work?"

Jenni noticed that the crowd was shifting slightly, almost as if they knew they were about to be trapped in a narrow space with nowhere to go. "Shit!" She watched some moving toward the area that Juan said they needed to keep clear for the second container to be lowered. Since the plan was to contain the zombies, he did not want any slipping past the perimeter. Some were looking up at the container that now dangled above them.

Jenni took off running, down the stairs, across the site, toward city hall. Rushing up the back stairs, she wasn't sure just what she was doing until she saw the staircase to the second floor. She ran up the steps, taking two at a time, then turned down another hallway. The third floor had a small, narrow balcony that was forbidden to everyone, since it both overlooked the street and had yet to be renovated. It was probably unstable and unsafe. She ripped down the DO NOT ENTER sign, pushed open the door, and stumbled out onto the balcony.

It gave a warning creak, but held her weight.

"Hey, dead fuckers! Up here!"

The ones that were moving toward the forbidden area turned and looked straight up at her. Immediately, they screeched and reach for her. They pushed up against the truck barrier.

Jenni noticed that a few that were not paying attention so she danced along the balcony, screaming, "Over here, stupid fuckers! Hey, dead ass! Up here! Fine quality human flesh up here!"

Jenni waved her hands over her head and flipped off the zombies when they looked up. Seeing she had an audience, she showed them her ass, wiggled it, and made the most annoying faces she could think of. The zombies howled as she whipped them up into a frenzy.

The container was on its way down, so she ran to the end of

the balcony and leaned over, getting as many zombies as she could to move directly under her.

"Hey, freaks, hey, guess what? I'm not for dinner!"

The container was dropped. There was a mighty *thunk* as it settled onto the road and a gush of blood and gore came from beneath it. Jenni had managed to get almost ten zombies taken out with one blow.

Laughing almost maniacally, she grabbed hold of the balcony rail and taunted the nearly completely trapped zombies to follow her away from the slight gap between the storage container and the wall of the store across the street from her. She kept taunting them until the crane arm delivered the bags of dirt that completely cut off the left-hand side of the street. The zombies were now trapped between the two barriers and the wall, leaving only the main road from the fort open. Dancing back across the balcony, Jenni laughed her ass off. The balcony gave a loud moan, and Jenni realized the show was over.

"Oh, shit!" She dived back into the building. The balcony shuddered, but stayed in place.

Jenni grinned, turned, and held her hands over her head like Nixon flashing the victory sign at the zombies and retreated into the city hall.

Behind her, the zombies moaned and groaned.

2.
Family Ties That Bind

Jason trudged across the construction site, Jack at his heels, one hand wiping the sweat off his brow. He was exhausted. He had been helping with defenses all day and his body hurt with every movement. His long bangs were soaked with sweat and he had finally borrowed a rubber band and managed to get most of his hair into a stubby ponytail. Now a few wisps fell around his face and he flicked his hand at them with annoyance.

Jenni was sitting at a table with several of the townspeople. He was proud of her. He knew how hard it was for her to socialize with more than one or two people at a time. But she seemed to be changing, getting bolder. Hell, that dance on the balcony had proved that.

His dad had been a shithead. Pure and simple. It had taken years for Jason to realize that. His mom told him horror stories of her marriage to his dad, but he hadn't believed her. Even when numerous family members told him that the reason his mom had custody of him was because his dad sent her to the hospital too many times for the judge to ignore, he hadn't believed it. When his dad had come for his supervised visits, he was always charming and kind and brought Jason the coolest new gadgets for a kid his age. There was no way his dad was an abuser.

It wasn't until his mother died that he was finally been able to meet his half brothers, Benji and Mikey. For a long time, he had refused to meet them or his stepmother out of loyalty to his mother. He was all his mother had, after all. Then, when she died, he had been packed up and shipped off to his dad's house, a state away. Jenni sent him a very sweet e-mail asking about his likes and dislikes, and he had hated her for it. When he arrived at the house, he had been shocked to see how much Jenni looked like his mom. More shocked when he had been shown his new bedroom and everything he had told Jenni he liked (some of it bullshit) was in the room. She had decorated it in his favorite colors with his favorite band posters on the walls. He hated her more for that. He went down to dinner to find his favorite dish on the table. He had fiercely hated her.

And then that fateful day came. His perfect father became irate at something Jason had done, and his face had contorted with a terrifying rage. He had lifted his hand to strike Jason, but Jenni threw herself in front of him and took the blow. Jason had watched in horror as his dad beat her without mercy for interrupting his "discipline of my son."

Mikey, who everyone said was growing up to be a football player, had launched himself across the room and onto his father. And then all hell had broken loose upon their household.

When Jenni came into his room several hours later to put a glass of water on his bed stand, her lips puffy and cracked, one eye swollen shut, limping slightly, Jason had flung his arms around her bruised body and wept uncontrollably. It was then that he realized that all those years, his mother had been telling the truth. He wept tears of guilt over his doubt.

After that, he didn't hate Jenni at all. He had come to love her very much. And he had loved his siblings. In some weird way, he even loved his dad, but their home had been violent. He and Jenni had worn bruises. Sometimes, even Mikey. There were times all of them, even Benji, were in the brawl. That their home life had ended in violence was not surprising.

In city hall, Jason saw several older people carefully cataloging all the remaining food. It had been moved into one room for storage. Up the stairs, he headed for the dining room. Tobias stood near the windows overlooking the street. Curtains covered the windows to keep the zombies from seeing the humans, but they still knew that living flesh was just out of their reach.

"When he looks up at me, I know he knows who I am," Tobias said in a tormented voice.

"What?" Jason stopped in midstride, not sure if the man was speaking to him.

"My son." Tobias drew back the curtain and pointed.

It was hard for Jason to determine which zombie he was indicating. The hot Texas sun was slow-cooking all the zombies, and their skin had crisped to a dark color and was splitting. It was hard to tell anyone's ethnicity.

"He looks up at me and I know, I know, he wants me to help him and the children," Tobias said softly. His voice sounded very distant.

"Look, dude, I think maybe we should go find your wife."

"I don't want to speak to her. She's given up on them. But I won't. I can't." Tobias looked at Jason, but Jason wasn't sure the man was actually seeing him. "How can I?"

Jack whined a little and Jason moved to close the curtains. "You shouldn't let them see us."

"How can I give up?" Tobias persisted.

"You can because they're dead," Jason answered. As he closed the curtain, he said, "My brothers, my dad, my friends are all dead. And now they're just like that. Undead. You have to let them go or else they will kill you and make you what they are."

"But this isn't how the world works. They have to be sick. In need of medical care, but we slaughter them." Tears slipped from Tobias's eyes.

Jason shifted on his feet uncomfortably. "Look, dude, I think we should find someone to talk to you."

Tobias shook his head adamantly. "There is no talking. They need us and we deny them. We need to go out there and tend their wounds. I don't believe these lies about those poor, sick people eating us. It's a lie."

"No, I swear, it is not. I've seen it!"

Tobias glared at him, then turned abruptly and started down the hall.

Jack whined. Jason took a breath and ran a hand over his hair before following Tobias. This was definitely not going to be a good situation. He could feel it.

There were construction workers coming into the building, and Jason had to push through a bit of a crowd to get down the stairs and outside. He looked around for the older man. The site was messy, considering all the work they were doing, and he couldn't see Tobias right away. Easing his way past large piles of equipment and living areas set up under tarps, Jason finally saw Tobias standing on the sentry platform above the zombies. Juan had told everyone to stay off it until they could put up a screen to shield the guards from the zombies' view. Tobias was waving at the crowd beyond the truck perimeter.

"Hey, dude, get down from there!" Jason started to jog toward the older man. Jack immediately fell in beside him, excited by all the commotion.

Tobias hesitated at the sound of Jason's voice but then pushed one of the longer ladders over the wall, over the fence, and toward the top of the trucks. The ladder seemed precariously balanced by the wall, but the older man didn't test its sturdiness. When it formed a wobbly bridge to the trucks, he started to crawl over it.

Jason reached the platform and fell to his knees to grip the end of the ladder to hold it in place. The crowd of zombies was going nuts. The sight made Jason feel sick.

"Come back, dude! Come back!"

When the ladder seesawed, Tobias stopped for a second, and then continued heading for the zombies.

"Mom!" Jason shouted. "Mom! Somebody! Anybody! Help!"

Jenni looked up from her far corner, saw him holding the ladder, and came running.

Tobias reached the fence and crept over the line of spikes between the fence and the trucks.

Nearby, a woman cried out; Jason was sure it was Tobias's wife.

Jenni reached the steps just as Juan did. They jostled each other as they moved up the stairs and reached the platform at the same time. Jason noticed that his mom was holding her gun.

"What the hell is he doing?" Juan took off his cowboy hat and slapped it against his thigh. "Dammit!"

"He was talking about his family. About how they needed help. He said he didn't believe the stories about them eating people!" Jason answered breathlessly. His hands were aching from trying to keep the ladder secure.

Jack started barking crazily at the zombies, and Jenni gave him a stern look and ordered him down the stairs. Jack responded with a mournful look but obeyed.

Tobias reached the top of the truck and got to his feet. He maneuvered over the dirt trucks, the cargo trucks, and the heavy sandbags, his arms held out to keep his balance.

"Tobias, come back!" A woman had joined them, and her expression was desperate.

Tobias hesitated and glanced back at them. "I will not abandon our family. I will not give in to superstition." He walked on until he reached the edge of the truck perimeter. Kneeling, he held out his hand toward the throng below. He started calling names, and Jason could see the crowd getting more and more riled.

"Come back!" the woman kept screaming.

Jason looked at his mom just as Jenni showed Juan her gun. Juan nodded, and Jason looked back toward Tobias in disbelief.

The older man was now lying on his stomach. He reached down over the crowd, probably toward one particular zombie, but it was hard to tell. And then it happened: One of the taller zombies managed to snag his arm and started to pull Tobias down into the crowd. Since the man's back was to them, Jason did not know if Tobias had finally realized the error of his ways or not. Jenni's gun let out a sharp bark and Tobias's head split open. Limp, he was dragged down into the crowd.

Jenni turned away, but Jason couldn't help but watch as gouts of blood exploded over the heads of the zombies and a battle for flesh began among them.

"Don't look," she said in a sad voice.

"You killed him!"

"I saved him," Jenni replied defensively.

Jason looked at her finally, horrified at what she had done. "But you killed him." She was so sweet, so kind, so nice, he couldn't fathom it.

"I saved him. He won't have to know what it feels like to be torn apart. He won't have to know what it is to be living dead. I saved him."

Jason looked down the stairs to where Jack was waiting for

him. Pressing his lips together, he gave her a curt nod. "I get it. But, Mom, you're a mom. You're nice. You shouldn't kill."

Jenni put her arm around him and they descended the stairs, Juan at their backs, guiding Tobias's sobbing widow. "In this world, Jason, we all have to kill."

They reached the bottom, and Jenni turned to the other woman. "I'm sorry."

"No, no, thank you," the widow said softly. "You did the right thing. He just couldn't accept what is happening."

Peggy came and led the woman away. Juan followed, shaking his head.

Jason studied Jenni's face, then said, "I'm glad you're my mom."

She kissed his cheek, then made a face and stuck out her tongue. "Ewwww . . . go take a shower!"

Jason gave her his best sullen look. "Fine. You're so bossy." He trudged away, glancing back at her a few times. She stared down at the gun, running her other hand over it gently, her expression distant.

"This is one fucked-up world," Jason told Jack.

The dog woofed in agreement and they walked on.

1.

A Taste of Hell

Katie sat at the kitchen table taking a long sip of very hot, slightly bitter coffee. It almost scalded her tongue, but it felt deliciously good going down. Nearby, Nerit was finishing up the breakfast dishes. Katie had offered to help her, but Nerit gently rebuffed her. It was fairly obvious that Nerit had enjoyed nursing Katie back to health these last few days, fussing and fretting after her and making sure she rested.

She was still weak. Dizziness, nausea, and the occasional fever had haunted her up to thirty-six hours ago. Now, at last, she felt stronger, felt that the sickness was finally behind her.

The old hunting dog strolled in, slow and steady on his stiff legs, and went up to his water bowl to get a drink. Katie let her fingers brush over his back as he passed her by and wondered how Jack was doing. She had talked to Jenni for twenty minutes the night before, but she couldn't remember if Jenni had mentioned the dog. Jenni had mostly talked about how they had corralled the zombies and how someone had been stupid enough to try to "save" his family from the mass of living dead. She also told Katie how they had fixed up the fort, roping off some sections as "living" areas, while others were security or construction related.

Katie had seen Travis making all sorts of drawings and writ-

ing down odd equations. She knew that he and Juan spoke a lot late at night.

Once Katie was standing up, holding her cup tightly in her slim fingers, she strolled over to the counter and leaned her hip against it. "Nerit?"

"Yes, Katie?"

"Why won't you and Ralph come to the fort?"

Nerit finished drying a plate before she looked at Katie. "This is our home."

"But once we leave, you'll be here alone."

Nerit slowly put the plate in the cupboard, her expression thoughtful. Picking up a glass, she started to dry it. "Katie, Ralph has three sons. I have two sons. We have grandchildren. We do not know where they are. If they are safe, alive, on the run, or . . . They will come here if they can. At least, Ralph's sons will. Mine are in Israel. I have very little hope of hearing from them."

Katie looked down as her vision blurred a bit from tears. "I see."

"This is all we have left now. If we leave, we leave behind all of it. We are old, and all we have is this shop. This little town. The hope that our children may still be alive with their children somewhere out there."

Katie pressed her lips together. She couldn't blame Nerit. If she could have holed up somewhere with Lydia, safe and secure, and ridden this out, she would have. "I understand."

"Besides, we have our truck back and if we have to flee, we will."

"That's an awesome truck. I creamed a lot of zombies with it," Katie said, grinning.

"That old white truck is pretty bloodstained, too," Nerit pointed out with a wink.

"It's kinda nice to have the old truck back. It did get me and Jenni to safety."

"And it will get you back to your fort safe and sound, I'm sure."

Travis leaned in the doorway. "Katie, how are you feeling?"

"Good. Good."

"I could use your help," he said. "If Nerit doesn't mind you abandoning her."

Nerit laughed and shooed them away. "Go, go, do what you need to."

Katie walked out into the hall and scrutinized Travis. He appeared surprisingly sheepish.

"Okay, Ralph and I have packed up all the guns, ammo, and clothes from the shop that we think the fort needs. Now we're heading over to the grocery store." Travis blushed deeply. "Uh, there are . . . um . . . things." He was looking everywhere but at her face. "Uh . . . women things."

Katie rolled her eyes. "Oh, my god, Travis. Didn't you ever buy tampons for a girlfriend?"

Travis winced. "I try to block that memory."

Katie brushed past him, laughing, and headed down the stairs. Bill and Ralph were in the store, both dressed in hunting outfits, rifles slung casually over their arms. Katie looked out the window at her old white truck. She felt a pang of sorrow for the old man who had died saving her, but also a flash of nostalgia when she remembered being on the road with Jenni. Travis had constructed a sturdy pallet on the truck bed to carry their haul back to the fort, and Katie was grateful for his resourcefulness.

"I hear we're going shopping?" Katie said to Ralph.

"Yep, next door. Put on a jacket and grab a gun," Ralph answered.

"I thought you cleared out the town?"

"Can't take a chance," Ralph reminded her.

"There are probably more out there wandering around," Bill added. He pulled on a cowboy hat. "There are lots of farms and trailer parks out in those hills. We can't let down our guard."

"Makes sense," Katie admitted.

Travis handed her a hunting jacket and she shrugged it on.

Picking up a gun, she looked over her shoulder at the men. "So, basically, I'm risking my life because you pansies don't want to pick up tampons," she said, arching her eyebrow critically.

All three nodded.

"Yep."

"Pretty much."

"Uh-huh."

Katie shook her head as she looked out the front door at the grocery store across the way. It was very small and old fashioned. The road was clear except for the truck. When she'd first awakened and noticed the lack of the smell of decay, she'd asked about the corpses. Ralph and Bill had piled the bodies into the back of a truck and driven a ways out of town before dumping them into a ditch. This was not a time for proper burial.

Ralph and Bill were first out the door, followed by Katie, then Travis. Travis walked stiffly, the gun in his hands obviously making him uncomfortable, but he'd told Katie that Ralph had been working with him.

"There aren't any zombies left in there?" Katie wondered.

"Once they got the door rotating, they all came spilling out," Ralph answered. "Nerit and I cleared out the two left crawling around inside. None left now."

Ralph swept his gaze over the few buildings that made up his town and motioned to the others that the coast was clear. One by one, they passed into the small grocery store through the revolving door. Inside, it was in shambles. Dark brown blood was smeared everywhere. Bits of flesh were rotting on the floor.

The stench made Katie cough and she covered her mouth with one hand. Travis pulled a bandanna from a nearby stand and tied it around her head, making sure it covered her mouth and nose. He did the same for himself. Bill and Ralph just seemed to deal with the smell. With the impromptu mask in place, Katie found that the scent of rotting flesh was blunted by the fresh, starchy smell of brand-new cloth.

Grabbing a cart, she started to walk down one of the store's four narrow aisles. There were lots of cans and boxes on the floor, but there was still plenty of stuff crammed onto the shelves. She found the health section and started to load up. Vitamins, cold and flu remedies, allergy medicine, pain relievers, and cough medication all went into her cart. The men busied themselves sorting through the food items.

It was cold in the store; the air conditioner was still whirring away. How long the power would stay on was anyone's guess. Katie started shoving shampoo, deodorant, and all sorts of hygiene items into the cart. It filled up pretty quickly. She returned to the front of the door, trying not to look at a small gray hand not attached to a body tucked under the edge of the front counter. She took another cart and went back to work filling it.

About ten minutes later, she heard a noise coming from the back office. She fearfully gestured to Travis and he crept up beside her. She pointed at the door and took a stance that showed she was ready to shoot. Ralph had said the store was clear, but they couldn't take a chance.

Travis leaned forward, turned the knob, and shoved the door open, revealing the manager's office. There were two little black and white TV sets on the desk. Both were on. The office looked empty. Katie and Travis both looked at each other and shrugged.

Then they head the whispering. "Not fast . . . enough . . . not fast . . . enough . . . not fast . . . enough . . ."

Travis and Katie slid into the office, nearly filling the narrow space. Drawing close to the desk, they looked over and saw the tip of a woman's pink shoe.

"Hello?" Katie's voice cracked slightly.

"Not fast . . . enough . . . not fast . . . enough . . ."

A woman's pale face appeared out of the shadows. She gazed up at them for an instant, then retreated back under the desk.

"Not fast . . . enough . . . not fast . . . enough . . ."

Katie leaned forward enough to see the woman's eyes glinting in the light from the twin TVs. Katie looked at the monitors.

The security videotape was playing, showing what had happened on that horrible first day. A man was lying on the floor, having a violent fit. People were gathered all around him. Then he stilled. Even though she knew it was coming, when he sat up and grabbed the nearest person and attacked, Katie jumped. Some people ran. Others just stood and gaped. The man stood up after wresting a huge chunk of flesh from his first victim.

A woman spun around and ran, with a little boy following. They were almost to the back of the store and out of the camera's view when the first zombie grabbed the boy.

The VCR rewound. Katie peered under the desk and saw that the woman was clutching a remote control.

". . . not fast . . . enough . . . ," the voice whispered.

Travis glanced at Katie and then returned his gaze to the screen. "Oh, God."

Katie took a deep breath. "Ralph! We found a survivor!"

The minute the words were out of her mouth, she wondered if it was true. For from beneath the desk came a voice devoid of life whispering, "Not . . . fast . . . enough. . . ."

2.
The Abyss

". . . not fast . . . enough . . . not fast . . . enough . . ."

Katie wedged herself past Travis so she could kneel down and really see the woman hunkered under the desk.

The woman flinched when she saw Katie and turned her head to one side, her body quivering. She kept one eye firmly on the TV sets as she tried to draw her legs under the desk.

"C'mon," Katie said. "Let's get you out of here."

". . . not fast . . . enough . . . ," she said again.

One of the refugee's hands was curled around the remote control. The other hand was braced against the side of the desk. She was a young woman who was so haggard she looked old. It

was difficult to determine the color of her hair it was so filthy and her dirty skin was stretched taut over her facial features, her arms and legs emaciated. She reeked of urine and shit. Katie could see that she was sitting in a nest of her own filth.

Katie pulled the bandanna away from her nose and mouth so it hung loose around her neck. The smell was awful, but she needed the woman to look at her and not at the TV.

"My name is Katie. This is Travis. Our friends Ralph and Bill are here, too. We're going to take you somewhere safe."

The woman shook her head violently, but her eyes never left the TV. ". . . not fast . . . enough . . ."

Katie looked over at Travis. "This isn't going to be easy."

He looked perplexed and out of his depth. "Just tell me what to do."

Katie edged forward and reached out to the woman. "We're going to take you away from here. Please, give me your hand. You can take a shower and eat some food."

The woman again shook her head; one bright blue eye fastened determinedly on the TV.

Katie looked at the image replaying once more on the grainy black-and-white set. Sighing, she said to Travis, "Get ready."

He blinked, confused.

Katie twisted around and ejected the tape from the VCR.

With a hoarse scream, the woman was on her immediately. Her bony, desperate hands clawed at Katie's, trying to wrest the tape from her fingers. Travis grabbed the bone-thin woman about the waist and lifted her up into the air and over the desk.

Kicking and screaming, the woman thrashed in his arms. Her body twisted into odd angles, and dried bits of excrement fell from her dress and legs. Katie gagged but managed to get to her feet despite the woman's flailing legs. The woman's eyes were wide, terrified, and uncomprehending. Katie handed her the tape.

The woman instantly went limp, clutching the tape and the remote control against her heaving chest. Her staring eyes saw

nothing; Katie guessed that the black-and-white images were still replaying in her mind's eye when she once again murmured, ". . . not fast . . . enough."

Now that she was still, Travis set her on her feet. The woman swayed but stood, staring blankly. Katie took hold of her arm. Ralph and Bill stood in the doorway, both wearing looks of utter shock and revulsion.

Finally, Bill said, "It's Laura Matthews."

"I opened the door when I first checked the store a few days ago, and nothing ran at me or answered when I called out. I didn't think to look under the desk," Ralph said remorsefully. "I'm sorry, Laura, hon. I didn't know you were hiding."

Laura Matthews didn't move. She showed no recognition of her name.

"She had a son?" Katie questioned.

"Younger brother. She basically raised him after their mom died." Ralph shook his head sadly. "We dumped his body with the rest of them a few days back."

"How did she survive?" Bill looked amazed.

Ralph pointed toward a water dispenser tucked near the desk. "Probably drank water. Don't need food as long as you got water. At least for a while."

"I'll take her to Nerit," Katie volunteered.

"Travis, go with her to keep watch. Bill and I will finish up," Ralph decided.

Katie gently pulled on her arm, and Laura stumbled but managed to walk. Katie carefully led her through the store, trying not to breathe deeply or look into the young woman's vacant eyes. Once outside, the girl shuddered and grabbed tighter to the tape and the remote. Katie looked at Travis to see that he was quite ashen. She tried to smile reassuringly at him as they walked across the road.

A shriek made her jump and drop the girl's arm. A flash of movement had her twirling around, gun raised.

"Shit!" Travis fumbled with the safety on his gun.

Katie saw something streaking toward her, a flash of red, black, and white. She raised the rifle effortlessly and fired. Fine red spray splattered her and Laura as the zombie sprawled onto the ground a few feet from them.

"Yep. Still not safe," Ralph said as he stepped into the road behind them, drawn out of the store by the gunfire.

Katie took hold of the young woman's arm again. Laura was staring at the zombie, blood splatter decorating her drawn features and scrawny body.

". . . not . . . fast . . . enough . . . ," she said.

Katie sighed. "Yes, we were. We were fast enough. We're safe. You're safe."

She pulled the girl along toward safety. But as they walked, Katie realized that the young woman so desperately clutching the videotape of her brother's death would never truly be safe again.

3.
Down the Rabbit Hole

Katie pulled Laura into the hunting store, then turned toward the men. "I have her. You guys can finish up."

Travis looked into her eyes. "Katie . . ." He faltered, as if he wanted to say something but wasn't sure what.

"Nerit and I will take care of her."

He nodded and left the store. The door shut behind him with a loud click.

Laura was shivering violently, her teeth chattering. Katie gently led her along, trying not to be aware of the sweaty, greasy feel of the woman's skin.

"Nerit!"

The older woman appeared at the top of the stairs, exclaimed, "Laura!" and rushed down.

"She was in the grocery store. Hiding under the manager's

desk," Katie explained as she helped Nerit guide the catatonic girl up the stairs.

"But Ralph looked . . ."

"She's in shock. She wouldn't have responded to Ralph. She just kept watching the security tape of her brother dying over and over again."

". . . not fast . . . enough . . . ," Laura whispered.

Nerit said softly, "It's okay, Laura. You're safe now."

Laura did not even glance in her direction.

Together, Katie and Nerit got the girl up the stairs and into the shower—fully clothed. Her dress was plastered to her skin with her own urine and excrement, so it would have been hard to remove without hurting her. The water soon ran hot and cleansing over the young woman's emaciated form, but she barely blinked, barely acknowledged what was happening. She just clung to the VCR tape and the remote control and stared straight ahead, whispering, ". . . not fast . . . enough . . ."

Once the water ran clear, Katie and Nerit undressed the girl with some difficulty. They had to make sure Laura always had a grip on the tape as they maneuvered her arms out of her sleeves. Both winced at the sight of her wizened body. Laura's ribs and pelvis stood out sharply beneath her pale skin. Nerit and Katie didn't speak as they bathed the girl. Cleaning her up with clinical aloofness seemed the only way to avoid feeling the sheer horror of this woman's mental and physical condition.

Finally, when they were done, they dressed her in one of Nerit's nightgowns and gently guided her to the kitchen. The entire time, the girl did not release the tape or the remote control.

"Sit down, Laura," Nerit said gently.

The young woman obeyed. Her black hair fell to her chin framing a face with blue eyes, a strong nose, and a wide mouth. She looked like she might be of Eastern European descent and Katie wondered if her ancestors were some of the original Czech settlers in this area of Texas.

Katie sat down across from the girl and finally let herself feel

the brutal reality of it all. The girl had been starving to death slowly since this had all begun. While she and Jenni had taken refuge with Nerit and Ralph, this young woman had been in that office, with zombies on the other side of the door. It must have been awful, and Katie felt guilty at her relief that she was not in her shoes.

Nerit sat down with a small container of pudding in her hand. She opened it and spooned a little out. "Laura, it's time to eat."

Laura turned toward Nerit and opened her mouth.

Katie guessed hunger had finally made Nerit's voice register with the girl. She watched Nerit tenderly place the spoon in the girl's mouth. Laura slowly closed her lips, and her jaw worked slightly. For some reason, it was too much to bear.

"I need a breather." Katie stood.

Nerit nodded, accepting. "Go. I will stay with her."

Katie walked out of the kitchen and onto the balcony. She stood there, gripping the railing and taking deep breaths. She felt like a bitch abandoning Nerit, but she couldn't deal with this right now. She just couldn't. At the same time, she couldn't just do nothing at all.

Moving, she snagged her rifle as she went through the living room, and went downstairs to help the men load the truck. They were surprised to see her, but she simply said, "I need to help," and immediately went to work, packing boxes with supplies while Ralph stood watch over the street.

Everything was boxed, labeled, and taped shut. There were two piles—one for the supplies Nerit and Ralph would keep, and the other for what would go to the fort. Once the pallet was packed, they began securing the load, using ropes, a large hunting net, nails, and wire. By the time they were done, Katie was certain nothing would be tumbling off the thick pallet. Four thick towing chains were attached to the four corners of the pallet. The chains connected to a large metal loop that rested on top of the supplies. Katie knew that the plan was to attach

the pallet to the crane's hook back at the fortress and use it to lift them all over the wall. She had felt leery about this plan at first, but now, seeing what Travis had concocted, she felt a bit more secure.

As they walked inside, Travis rested his hand on her shoulder and drew her aside. "Are you okay?"

"Yeah, sure. . . ." Katie started to pull away, but Travis tugged her back.

"I don't think you are."

Pressing her lips into a firm line, she struggled to control her emotions. "That girl . . . Jenni was like her in the beginning. Staring ahead, not talking, just blank. But she snapped out of it."

Travis flinched. "Oh."

"I see what Jenni could have been in that girl."

"Oh." Travis rubbed her arm lightly and kissed her forehead very tenderly. "But Jenni's okay."

Katie closed her eyes. "It's sheer luck, Travis. You, me, Jenni, all of us . . . being alive. Being okay. We were just lucky to get to safety. We all could have been Laura."

His fingers were very gentle as he stroked her hair. "Yes, but that reverend saved you and you saved Jenni."

"And you saved us," Katie added. She fastened her gaze on him. "This world is fragile. I can't bear to think too much, of what it would be like to lose . . ." Her voice broke.

"Jenni."

"Or Jason. Or Jack," she hesitated. "Or you . . . Nerit . . . Ralph."

He smoothed her hair and gave her a little hug. "I have waking nightmares. I see people—the people around me—transformed into those things. Juan, the mayor, Peggy . . . When you were sick, I kept seeing you like that. Just for a split second. A waking nightmare of my—"

"—fear," she finished for him.

"Yes."

Katie looked up at him, her eyes full of tears. "I think we all have those fears."

"We'll take Laura home with us. We'll help her find her way back to the land of the living. We'll keep each other alive." Travis's voice was full of determination.

Katie draped her arms around his waist and hugged him. "Help each other be strong and not afraid."

Travis held her as he nodded. "Yes. We'll go home tomorrow. To Jenni and Jason and the dog and all the others."

Katie let herself relax into Travis's warm embrace. His strength reminded her of her father. His arms felt so safe and comforting.

"We'll be okay," Travis promised.

"Of course. We have no other choice."

"Besides, I promised Jenni I'd build her a gazebo so she wouldn't get sunburned."

"Oh, you did?" Katie giggled at the thought of Jenni relaxing in the shade of a fancy gazebo.

"Yeah. I have a soft spot for beautiful women," Travis said with a grin.

"That's something we have in common," she quipped.

Travis slung his arm around Katie's neck and guided her toward the steps. "You're the prettiest competition I ever had," he teased her.

Katie smirked at him as they climbed the stairs to join the others.

4.

In the Heart of the Abyss

Nerit helped Laura lie down on a couch in the living room and covered her with a light blanket. She sat with her and stroked her clean hair until the girl finally slept. Even in her sleep, Laura still clutched the VCR remote and the VHS tape.

Dinner was a low-key affair. Though Nerit made a delicious meal of baked chicken, sweet potatoes, and green beans and Ralph opened a bottle of wine, the conversation was muted and there was a great sense of sorrow at the table.

Since the day things had changed with the arrival of the zombies, Katie had found refuge in working hard, planning, just keeping herself and her friends alive. Laura had brought the reality of this new world starkly into view. It was hard to deny the horror that existed in the world beyond their tiny conclaves of safety. Finding Laura had reminded Katie that Laura's fate was the norm, not theirs. She, Jenni, Jason, Ralph and Nerit, Travis and the others at Ashley Oaks—they were lucky. For one reason or another, they had escaped the initial bloodbath. Laura was also alive, but not nearly so lucky. How many, like her, had survived the initial outbreak only to slowly starve to death as the dead grew to dominate the earth? How many, like her, were shells of their former selves, their minds broken by the horrors they had seen? How many of the lucky ones would one day see something too terrible to endure and slip into that twilight world . . . or become one of the walking dead?

All this remained unsaid. They spoke instead of their plans to keep themselves safe, alive, and healthy. They had the luxury of being in a remote area, far from the cities that were surely overrun with the dead. And they knew it. It was a blessing and a burden.

After dinner, Katie walked onto the rooftop patio and sat in a chair next to Ralph. She didn't speak, just looked up at the brilliance of the stars above as the fragrant smoke from Ralph's pipe trailed up to the heavens.

"It's not the end, Katie. Just the next step," Ralph finally said.

"We are all acting like we're at a funeral," Katie decided with a sigh.

"I think we are. The funeral of the world. And we're the mourners, the survivors, picking up the pieces and finding a

way to move on," Ralph said in one of the longest sentences she had ever heard him utter.

"I feel so guilty," she confessed.

Ralph dipped his chin in agreement. "It's called survivor's guilt, and I betcha we all got it."

"I see Laura and know that I could easily have been her. Or a zombie. I don't understand why I'm here."

"To live. Keep going. Rebuild." Ralph gazed at her steadily, eyes never wavering from her face.

"Sounds so easy," Katie breathed.

"But it's not. This is a new and dangerous world. Got a map downstairs with circles around pockets of survivors. I talk to them online or on the CB. Each day, fewer people respond. Maybe the grid in their area has gone down or the Internet has failed. Or maybe they're dead. It's a tough world. Every day, I talk to a trucker stuck out in the hills somewhere. He ran out of gas. He's low on food. I can't go get him because he doesn't know where he is. He's going to die out there. And I'm his only friend."

Katie shivered and slumped back in the chair, holding herself. "I hate leaving you both here."

"It's where we belong. Same as you going back to the fort. It's where you belong." Ralph took her hand in his and gave it a firm squeeze. "You help Travis and the others keep safe. You keep strong."

Katie smiled. "And you do the same."

Ralph nodded as Nerit appeared at the door. "It's time to sleep, you two. We have an early morning."

Ralph unfolded his body from the chair with a little grunt. He walked over and kissed Nerit on the cheek. She smiled softly at him and held out her hand to Katie.

Katie went to her, and Nerit clasped her hand, drawing her inside.

Laura was still asleep on the sofa, curled up tightly, still clutching the tape. Bill was lying on a cot nearby, snoring a little.

"You and Travis need to share the guest room now, since we gave Laura the sofa. Is that okay?" Nerit asked.

Ralph turned to protest, but was silenced by Nerit's expression.

"I don't care. It's not like he's a jerk who'll try to feel me up," Katie joked.

"It ain't proper—," Ralph started, but Nerit kissed him firmly on the mouth, shutting him up.

"Good night, you old codger," Nerit said, patting his cheek.

"Good night, honey," Ralph answered lovingly. "I'll be up soon, but I don't think—"

"Shush, you." Nerit cut him off as she followed Katie.

"Night, Ralph."

"Night, Katie."

Ralph gave Nerit a look as they left the room, and she just waved her hand at him. Katie was amused by Ralph's old-fashioned sensibilities, but mostly she was tired and wanted to sleep.

Travis was already in the guest room, lying on his back on the bed, on top of the covers, with his eyes closed. Katie almost laughed at the sight.

Nerit caught Katie's hand, drew her aside, and kissed her cheek before whispering, "I'm going to miss you."

Katie smiled at her. "I'm going to miss you, too. I hope that one day I can be as strong as you are."

Nerit looked flattered, yet a little sad. "Just remember to always be true to your heart and do your best. That will make you strong."

Katie kissed Nerit's cheek gently and hugged her. "Good advice."

Nerit yawned, moving toward the door to her bedroom. "I'll see you in the morning. Sleep well."

"You, too, Nerit."

Katie slipped into the darkened bedroom and lay down on the bed.

"Don't try anything," Travis said sleepily. "I'd hate to punch a woman."

"I can barely contain myself, but I'll keep my hands off," Katie assured him with a little laugh.

Travis opened one eye to look at her. "I've turned gay women before."

"Suuure."

"Yep, turned their stomachs and sent them screaming," Travis teased groggily.

"That sounds more plausible. I can barely keep from gagging." Katie rolled onto her side and tucked her hand under her cheek, facing him. "But seriously . . ."

Travis rolled over to face her. "Yeah?"

"Tomorrow . . ."

"Yeah?"

"If I don't make it—"

"You will make it."

"But if I don't, take care of Jenni and Jason."

Travis sighed. "Okay. But you are going to make it, Katie."

Katie wasn't so sure anymore. Today had made her feel vulnerable.

Travis reached out and took her free hand. "We both will."

"Okay, but don't let go."

"I won't," Travis promised, and held her hand until she slept.

1.
Falling into the Abyss

"Don't let go!" Katie swung over the zombies, feet kicking as she tried to get back onto the pallet.

Travis's hand, slick with sweat from the heat and nerves, had an iron-tight grip on her wrist. "I won't! Grab on to my arm with your other hand!"

Katie's body was jolted as the pallet swung about, and she screamed. The moans and growls of the zombies below made her shiver with fear. People in the fort were shouting, yet over all of them, she could hear Jenni screaming her name.

Travis was holding firm to the heavy chain that connected the pallet to the crane's hook. Bill was clutching the net secured over the supplies for dear life, struggling not to fall off.

The pallet was swinging crazily from the crane.

This is it, Katie thought. *This is how it ends for me.*

Katie kicked hard, trying to somehow swim through the air and get a better grip on Travis. Her free hand finally managed to grip his strong, thick wrist. Her fingers barely fit around it. She gagged on the stench of the dead below; her terror felt as if it was choking her. Travis's grip on her felt tenuous, but he gazed down at her with grim determination.

The pallet that made up their makeshift elevator swung in long loops over the heads of the undead, making them shriek all the more at the sight of the humans dangling teasingly from it.

How had it come to this?

The journey back to Ashley Oaks had been uneventful. Travis drove the old white truck with Katie squeezed in between him and Bill. Laura sat hunched on Bill's lap, staring straight ahead. Nerit had given her a crocheted purse and put the VCR tape and remote control into it. Laura found this acceptable. Her fingers stroked the purse endlessly during the trip.

Travis had avoided the main street into the heart of Ashley Oaks, taking a series of side roads until they came up to the outside of the enormous hotel that backed onto the fort. No zombies had appeared as they parked the vehicle. The enormous crane, perched over the fort, had already been moving, its long arm extending toward them. Travis moved to the pickup's bed while Bill and Katie covered him, guns drawn. Bill kept one hand on Laura's shoulder.

". . . not fast . . . enough . . . ," Laura had begun to murmur.

She had been silent since they left the hunting store, so it startled them to hear her speak.

"She's starting up," Bill had whispered.

They worked as quietly as possible, trying not to draw too much attention. The cries and moans behind the barrier let them know that the zombies were well aware of their presence. Travis had climbed onto the pallet and connected the metal ring to the crane's hook.

"Okay, remember where I told you to stand. It's all about weight distribution to keep us from tipping over," Travis had said.

Laura whispered, ". . . not . . . fast . . . enough . . ."

Katie helped Bill get Laura up onto the pallet. Katie pressed Laura's hands onto the handholds Travis had made out of rope, and Laura had gripped them firmly despite her blank stare. Katie had taken up her position, slinging her rifle over one shoulder, while Bill and Travis took theirs.

"Nervous?" Travis had asked.

"Not at all," Katie had lied.

The pallet lifted smoothly. When they were high enough to be safe, the crane had begun to swing them over the zombies, toward the fort. The stink of dead had filled their nostrils with an almost burning sensation, and the screams from below were hellish and chilling. Katie had tried not to look down. She checked on Laura, who stood near her, holding the ropes tightly. Her lips had been moving, and Katie had barely heard her whisper, ". . . not fast . . . enough."

Bill had looked down and let out a whistle. "Damn. There's a lot of zombies."

Katie couldn't help herself then; she looked down, too. It made her gasp to see how many were beneath her, jumping and swinging their arms, trying in vain to reach the living swinging overhead.

Laura had looked down as well. Her voice had risen in volume and speed. ". . . not fast . . . enough . . . not fast enough-notfastenoughnotfastenough . . ."

"Laura, calm down. Look away," Travis had urged the frightened young woman.

"Laura, don't look," Katie had insisted.

Laura stopped muttering and looked at each of them one by one. "We can never be fast enough," she had said clearly.

And then she let go.

"No!" Katie made a mad grab for the girl and had caught her hair for just an instant before gravity dragged the young woman into the hands of the zombies below.

Unfortunately, Katie wasn't the only one who had lunged for Laura. Bill and Travis reflexively reached out as well, and Bill, who was heavier than all of them, shifted his weight too much, and the pallet had tilted to one side, swinging wildly.

Katie, holding on by just one hand, had fallen. She clung desperately to the rope handhold, but her unbalanced weight made the pallet swing ever more dangerously.

"Katie!" Travis grabbed for her as she dangled over the zombies.

Bill had almost fallen off, trying to regain his footing, and sprawled over the top of the supplies, gripping the netting fiercely. Katie hung, suspended; the feeding frenzy below made her feel like throwing up. The slurping noises, the harsh crunching of bones, made her even more desperate to get up onto the pallet.

"Don't move," Travis ordered. "I have you. Just hang there."

Katie stared into his eyes and trusted him.

Slowly, the pallet stopped its crazy swinging and came to a halt above the zombies, slightly listing to one side. Finally, the crane started to move again.

"I'm slipping," Katie whispered.

"No, you're not," Travis responded firmly. "I have you."

Her fingers clutched his wrist. His hand had such a tight hold on her that she felt as if he were crushing her wrist and hand.

Bill didn't dare move. He whispered, "Oh shit . . . oh . . . shit . . . she jumped."

Katie dared to look down and saw the dirt-filled trucks beneath her along with some very evil-looking black spikes. Then they were above the fence and finally, last of all, the concrete wall.

The pallet began to descend, and Katie sobbed with relief.

"Katie! Katie! Katie!" Jenni's voice wafted up to her.

Abruptly, hands were all over her and for a moment, she had one of Travis's waking nightmares and thought *they* had her. But when Travis let go, she fell into Juan's arms.

Jenni was next to him, tears on her cheeks, and she grabbed Katie's bruised hands.

"You made it!"

Katie felt wetness flowing down her own face as she pulled Jenni into an embrace. Jason threw his arms around both of them while Jack barked for attention. Katie kissed both Jenni and Jason on the cheek firmly, then hugged them again. It felt delicious to be alive and with them once more.

Travis swooped down and seized them all in a big bear hug. Jenni threw her arms around his neck and kissed him.

"You saved Katie!" Her expression was one of absolute joy.

Travis shook his head. "Nah, she saved herself. She held on so tight, I think she broke my wrist."

Jason didn't smile at Travis, but he hugged Katie again and whispered, "I'm so glad you're back."

Katie grinned and kissed his cheek again. She was amused when he blushed.

Juan walked up to them and looked at the pallet. "Okay, I gotta ask. Did you get any smokes?"

After a pause, Katie burst into laughter. She felt overwhelmed with emotion. Happiness, sadness, fear, relief, remorse, guilt, all mingled together. But relief overrode all of them and she flung her arms around Juan and kissed his cheek.

"What? What? Why are all of you women crazy? I just want my smokes," Juan protested.

Travis just shook his head, one arm slung around Jenni's shoulders. "One-track mind . . . one-track mind."

Katie slipped her arm around Travis's waist and gave him a sideways hug. "Thanks, by the way."

Travis kissed the top of her head. "I promised Jenni I wouldn't let you die."

"Yes," Jenni said happily. "And he kept his promise!"

"Seriously," Juan said again. "Did anyone grab some smokes?"

2.
Dead of Night

Night finally descended, pushing back the heat and letting the cool evening breeze waft into the fort. The wind would have been even more welcome if it hadn't carried the stench of the dead with it.

Travis stood in the middle of the construction site, drinking a soda and surveying the property with Juan. His best friend had done a good job of getting the site a bit more organized, even designating one corner specifically as a living area. The lunch wagon, two portable office buildings, and a variety of chairs and tables had been arranged on what remained of the old building's foundation. Blue tarps had been made into makeshift tents. Building materials, tools, machinery, anything at all that could be used to defend the fort was neatly organized in another corner. It was all about imagination and making do at this point.

Travis had been damn impressed with the spiked perimeter. He had never thought of breaking down the wrought iron fence for something like that.

Juan said, "We got people out there still alive. Curtis has been talking to them every day on the CB. If we could actually make a safe, not crazy-ass, way to get into the fort, we could bring more people in here."

"Yeah, but do we have the resources?"

Juan shrugged. "Who knows? We just gotta figure it out as we go. This is the new Eden, dude, whether we like it or not."

Travis looked around glumly. "Yeah, dammit. Just how the hell are we supposed to save the world?"

Juan tipped his cowboy hat back on his head and shrugged again. "Not the whole world. Just what little we can carve out of it for ourselves."

Travis waved toward the hotel. "I want to get in there. There's plenty of room for everyone, and it would be helluva lot more comfortable than trailers and cots."

Juan whistled. "That will be a big undertaking. At least they hadn't officially opened, and there was only training staff there— maybe twenty people? But now that we have guns, we can clear them out easier."

Travis sighed. "I'd like to avoid guns at all costs. It will probably draw more of the zombies' attention. Katie grabbed some

crossbows and archery stuff back at Ralph's, but we'll need to practice a lot with those before we use them."

"You know, it's really sissy of you not to like guns."

Travis gave Juan a look. "Yeah, well, I had staunch Democratic parents who were former hippies. They even moved to England for a while to live in a commune. I don't always agree with them, but I'll admit guns do scare me. I always believed there was a peaceful solution to everything."

"Well, 'give peace a chance' will get your ass kicked nowadays. Well, more like eaten," Juan reminded him.

"Yeah." Travis rubbed his forehead. "Yeah. The rules are all different."

"Except the lesbian rule. Lesbians are still hot," Juan stated. "Especially those two."

Travis looked where Juan was pointing to see Katie and Jenni standing on the back steps of city hall. Katie wore a tank top and shorts, and Jenni was in an oversized man's shirt that went down to her knees. They were animatedly talking and laughing. It was very late, so they probably couldn't sleep. The day had been tiring but invigorating at the same time. Travis and Katie returning with Bill had been seen as a victory in the fort.

"Katie is a lesbian, but I don't think—"

"No, no, dude, they're together. Everyone knows it." Juan grinned and nudged him with his elbow. "Too bad they don't like guys. Maybe they'd invite one of us to have fun, you know, if they liked the ol' man meat."

Travis gave Juan a long look. "Man meat? Really?"

"But I wouldn't mind watching, even if I couldn't touch."

"You're really something, you know that?"

Folding his arms across his chest, Juan grinned at him.

Travis shook his head, laughing slightly. "I think you're wrong, anyway. I'm pretty sure that Jenni—"

"Nope, she likes the *chicas*. I heard it on good authority."

"Well, damn," Travis said, his voice edged with disappointment.

"Yeah," Juan drawled, obviously daydreaming about something highly pornographic.

Katie and Jenni walked toward them, both barefoot, Travis noted. Katie looked better than she had in days, which made him feel good. He really liked her. She was a hot lesbian buddy, he thought. And Jenni, well, she was just crazy and precious all rolled into one.

"Hey, guys, what's up?" Katie asked.

"Figuring out our next move," Travis answered. He couldn't help but study both of them rather suspiciously.

Jenni gave him her sweetest smile. Her long black hair flowed around her face, and occasionally she would wrinkle her nose at the stench.

Juan said, "Talking about the archery stuff. I don't know if anyone is going to remember their camp days good enough to figure out how to use it."

"Oh, yeah, but if we could use bows and arrows instead of guns unless in high-pressure situations, it could cut down on how much attention we attract," Katie said.

"Attracting attention," Juan said in a way that let Travis know he wasn't talking about zombies.

"Um, yeah." Katie scrutinized Juan intensely.

Jenni was still smiling at Travis. "What do you think, Travis?"

"That we're fucked," Travis answered truthfully. "But we can do our best to get unfucked."

Katie gave him a long look. "Sounding a little bitter there, Travis."

"Well—" Before Travis could complete his sentence, one of the construction workers called his name and ran over to them. It was Mike.

"We have a situation," Mike said.

Travis saw that Mike was holding one of the new rifles. That made him nervous even though he knew Mike was former army. "What is it?"

"You better come see," Mike answered. Shaking his bald head, he muttered, "It ain't good, that's for damn sure."

Following the tall man, they ended up at the far end of the complex, where a new platform had been erected for the sentries to keep watch. They had created a blind to keep the zombies from seeing the guards, but it also limited what the guards could see. Mike had taken down the blind and he pointed down, over the wall and past the hurricane fence.

Four zombies were twisting on the metal spikes, groaning and pumping their arms and legs as if they were trying to swim away. A fifth had landed headfirst on a spike and was finally really dead. The four impaled zombies saw the living staring at them and went nuts trying to get free.

"Fucking shit, they're climbers now." Juan cursed in Spanish.

Travis swallowed hard at Juan's words. "Some of them, at least. Wake up some more people, Juan. We need to triple the guards and get them armed. We don't need those things swarming us in the middle of the night."

"We better check the entire exposed perimeter," Katie suggested.

Travis saw she and Jenni were holding hands. "Yeah, dammit. Just when this place was feeling a little safe."

"I knew those fuckers were smarter than they appeared. Dammit, first they're runners, now they're climbers. They're breaking all the fucking zombie rules!" Juan looked personally insulted by this development.

Travis turned to the two women and laid his hands gently on their shoulders. "Both of you get some rest. We'll watch the perimeter."

"Fuck that! I've slept enough. I'm gearing up," Katie argued.

Jenni nodded, agreeing. "I'm with Katie. If there are zombies coming over our walls, I'm going to be there to shoot them."

"You're both crazy, you know that?"

"Yeah, Travis, but that's why you like us," Jenni said flirtatiously.

Katie flashed her brightest smile. "We'll be right back, Rambo."

Travis watched them hurry away and turned back to Mike and Juan. He could tell how dire the situation was. Juan hadn't even glanced at the departing women.

"This isn't good," Juan said grimly.

"We'll deal," Travis answered. "We have no other option than to deal with it and not let them in."

Mike picked up one of the makeshift spears. "I'll take care of them."

"Make it quick," Travis answered. "We don't need to give the rest of them ideas."

"Climbing zombies. That's definitely breaking the rules," Juan complained.

Travis ran his hand over his holstered gun. "Yeah, well, the rules are shit now. Let's get to work."

3.
Not Fast Enough

Katie couldn't get dressed fast enough. Shoving her feet into her boots, she glanced over at Jenni, who nearly toppled over as she hopped into her jeans. Jason was fast asleep and snoring; Jack was snuggled into the boy's side and watching the two women suspiciously. After zipping up her camouflage pants, Katie leaned over and quickly tied her boots. Her arms and hands hurt from dangling off that damned "elevator over hell," as Juan had put it.

"Think they'll all come over?" Jenni asked worriedly.

"No, or they would have already, but we need to move fast, before enough figure it out to cause us real trouble." Katie grabbed her rifle and headed out the door. "Meet you down there."

"Okay! I'm almost ready!" Jenni flopped onto her cot and started in on her boots.

Dashing down the stairs, Katie ran into a few other people,

all men, who were also on their way out to help fortify the guards. She had been surprised by the lack of women in the fort, though it took her a while to notice it. All this made her feel that she needed to prove herself and pull her own weight.

Juan stood near the back door, instructing everyone where to go. One by one, the defenders spread out. At last, Juan turned to Katie and said, "Travis wants us to meet him up on the balcony." He looked very tense.

"Why?"

"I don't know. Hey, Loca, we're wanted upstairs," Juan said to Jenni as she came up to them. There was an evil glint in his eye.

"Bite me, redneck," Jenni retorted, making a face at him.

Juan made chomping noises at her.

"I'm so out of this," Katie said. She turned to head back into the building and up the stairs. She could hear Juan and Jenni still arguing as they followed her.

"Redneck."

"*Loca.*"

"Redneck."

"*Muy loca.*"

"Redneck," Jenni said again as they followed Katie up the stairs.

"Are you calling me a hick spic?" Juan asked in his thick West Texas twang.

"No! I'm calling you a plain ol' hick!"

Juan laughed and Jenni smacked him.

Katie decided not to pay attention to their antics. It has been clear since she had returned that Jenni and Juan were locked in a bizarre battle of words.

Stepping carefully onto the rickety balcony, she found Travis looking over the zombie horde. Because all the guards were visible to the crowd, the zombies were fairly evenly dispersed inside the corral.

"I don't see a weak spot," Travis decided.

Katie looked over the perimeter slowly, studying it. "Me neither."

"I'm telling you, they've gotten smarter," Juan said, his tone serious as he lingered just inside the doorway. "Just like in Romero's *Day of the Dead*. Remember Bub?"

Jenni timidly stepped out and surveyed the crowd below. "They're just doing what they always do."

"Yeah, but somehow five managed to get over the trucks." Travis rubbed his chin nervously. "I don't see how."

Katie's gaze swept slowly over the mass of the living dead. Something was amiss. She scanned the crowd again before she registered what it was. All the zombies were going crazy trying to get to the guards, but one zombie, toward the back, was standing still, studying the trucks and the barriers that kept it from its meal of warm flesh. It kept swinging its head back and forth.

"Some are thinking." She pointed and the others looked.

"Shit, she's right," Travis grunted with disgust.

The zombie moved slowly to one side to let a small crowd of zombie children through to pound on one of the trucks. The "thinker" was one of the more stripped-down zombies; not much flesh was left on its bones. Its skull-like head turned once more to look at the perimeter.

Kate slipped the safety off her rifle.

The zombie moved resolutely toward a large truck that was full of dirt with cement bags packed under it and between the cab of the truck and the load. It forced its way through the crowd, reached up, and started trying to open the door.

"Dammit!" Juan's voice was an almost feral growl. "Fucking shit! These things are breaking all the gawddamn rules!"

Katie slung her rifle off her shoulder and raised it.

"Katie?" Travis looked at her curiously.

"Can't afford for a smart one to survive," Katie answered.

Her finger started to close on the trigger; then she hesitated. "Travis . . ."

The zombie, its broken body barely able to stand, gave up on the door. It staggered to one side and clawed at the sandbags, as if to get purchase to lift itself up. Around its neck hung a crocheted purse.

"I think that's Laura," Katie whispered.

"Shit." Travis said.

"Who's Laura?" Jenni asked.

Katie took aim again, sighting the remains of the girl carefully. The zombie that had been Laura managed to get a good grip and started to heave itself up. Katie shot it through the head and it fell back.

The other zombies ignored the shot and continued to bang on the trucks.

"They're getting smarter," Katie muttered.

Travis, looking ill, agreed. "Yeah. I think so."

"We have the ammo. It's time to kill them all," Katie declared.

Jenni vigorously bobbed her head. "Yeah! They're all corralled! Easy pickings!"

"We can't—," Travis started, but stopped himself. "Okay. In the morning."

"We shouldn't waste all that ammo," Juan muttered. "Even if it is like shooting fish in a barrel, we gotta be careful."

Jenni had one of the biggest grins on her face Katie had ever seen. "Yeah, it'll be fun. Like shooting fish."

"You are so *loca*," Juan scoffed. "You don't even get a vote on this."

"Oh, yeah, hick spic?"

"I am so not a part of this," Katie declared, and slipped past them into the hall. She felt Travis following her, and when they were far enough from the arguing two, she turned toward him. His face was a mask of pain and uncertainty. "We have to do this."

"Once we start firing those guns, we may bring more down on us, Katie."

"Do you want to risk more of those things figuring out how to get past the trucks?"

Travis exhaled with exasperation. "Yeah, I know. In theory, the spikes could slow a lot of them down. The hurricane fence would probably stand for a little while, but then they'd be up against the wall."

Katie's expression was tense. "We cannot afford to lose ground to them." She felt it in her bones that if the zombies ever breached the first perimeter, things would not go well for the living, despite the security of the wall. They needed to gain ground, not lose it.

Travis looked back at Jenni and Juan, who were now cursing each other out in Spanish.

Katie glanced back down the hall, then grinned. "Kinda like kindergarten flirting, huh?"

"Uh, you're not jealous?"

Katie snorted. "Yeah, right. Like I'd be jealous of Juan." Despite her joking, her stomach was coiled into knots. She was horribly afraid. Would there never be time for peace?

Travis said, "Let's start planning what we're doing. I guess I'll wake the mayor."

She reached out and touched his arm. "Travis, it's a war. We have to fight."

Travis's expression was heavy with worry as he answered, "The thing about war is that there are always causalities."

Katie felt a chill flow down her spine, and glanced toward Jenni. She felt her stomach tighten, then returned her gaze to Travis. "We have no choice."

"Yeah, I know," he answered miserably.

They stood in silence.

At last, Travis said, "We better get the mayor. . . ."

· CHAPTER FIFTEEN ·

1.
The Killing Grounds

Jenni flipped Juan off discreetly behind Katie's back, then found a place to sit down in the mayor's office. The mayor looked weary and overwhelmed by the news that the zombies were climbing over the trucks. Tobias's death had weighed heavily on him, and he looked haggard. Curtis, on the other hand, looked a little better than he had a few days earlier. It was as if he was finding his role in this world and growing comfortable with it. Jenni thought he was cute in a little boy sort of way. Jason and Curtis often hung out, talking and just being guys. It made Jenni happy. Jason needed a friend, considering all he had lost.

Jenni was glowing with happiness. Katie was back. And, of course, Travis was back, too. That fact made her girlishly giggly with delight. She couldn't help it.

During the meeting, Jenni paid attention only when they talked about killing the zombies. She was surprised that anyone opposed the plan, but Juan was worried about running out of ammunition if they used so much right off the bat. The mayor was concerned about riling up the zombies even more. Jenni rolled her eyes at some points, and Katie leaned over and took her hand. Jenni knew it was the *behave* signal, so she tried not to give any more snarky looks—which wasn't easy.

The debate went back and forth. Katie was adamant about

wiping out the zombie horde before it got any bigger or they got any smarter. Jenni thought that made the most sense. Travis was conflicted about the whole gun issue, but agreed with Katie. Juan argued that maybe they should try to find an alternative way to wipe out the zombies. Jenni mentioned smacking him upside the head.

Juan was sitting near her and kept muttering in Spanish. Jenni muttered right back at him. Soon they were discreetly swearing at each other. The crux of the argument was that Jenni was a bloodthirsty psycho and would waste all the ammo while Juan was too stupid to understand guns were made to be fired.

"Where did you learn Spanish?" Katie whispered at one point.

"My mom was Mexican," Jenni whispered back. "But my dad was Irish."

"So you're a lazy drunk," Juan quipped, wagging his eyebrows at her.

"I am so going to kick your ass," Jenni said with a surly pout. Part of her was sure she hated Juan's guts, but another part of her really got off on their arguments. It was too much fun. And she had to admit, fighting was a stress reliever. Neither one of them really took the insults seriously.

"Look, I'm all for killing the zombies, but if we use all our ammo now, we're fucked. I say we thin them out with spears and then use the guns for the ones we can't reach," Juan suggested.

"What if they rush us? Guns are so much faster!" Jenni protested.

"We can't take any risks right now," Travis added. "I don't like the idea of using the guns and bringing more zombies down on us. Trust me. This isn't easy."

"We have to think about the people we're protecting," the mayor reminded them. "We have to do the right thing."

"But if we use all our ammo, we're screwing ourselves," Juan reiterated.

"Don't we have people who are good shots? Use them. I always used to go to the range with my dad. I can hit a target. I can kill those zombies." Katie looked at the faces around her and tried to fight back her agitation. "If they're coming over the barricade, how do we have a choice?"

"I'm all for killing them!" Juan snapped. "But what if—?"

Mike ducked in through the doorway, and the mayor looked up. "What is it?"

"Two more. They climbed over the back of one of the trucks. One of them fell right onto a spike and took his head clean off. The other one tried to jump past the spikes and ended up impaled at the pelvis. This isn't good," Mike insisted. "I'm worried a whole slew of them will be heading over onto our side soon."

Juan threw up his hands. "We're screwed."

Katie turned to the mayor. "What do we do?"

The mayor set down his pen and appeared to make up his mind. "When the sun rises, we'll kill them all using the guns and ammo we have. Agreed?"

Jenni looked toward Travis, who nodded. "Yeah, agreed."

Juan stood up slowly and said, "Okay, so we have no more time and no choices. But we can't do it this way again. We won't always have guns or ammunition. We need to be able to defend ourselves in other ways."

"Absolutely," Katie concurred .

Travis obviously agreed wholeheartedly by the adamant nodding of his head. "The guns make us safer for now, but, yeah, you're right."

Jenni stood up and stretched. "Just tell me where to go and I'm so ready."

Juan laughed. "Big surprise there."

Jenni gave him her snarkiest look.

2.
Tinker Bell of Death

"I don't like this," Katie said as she stood beside Jenni.

Jenni shrugged. "We have to be able to hit the ones that are out of view."

Katie sighed. "Yeah, but why you?"

" 'Cause I volunteered. Besides, I get to be harnessed up and fly." Jenni grinned. "Kinda like a lethal Tinker Bell of death!"

Katie laughed despite her worries while she watched Juan securing Jenni's harness. Mike had also volunteered for the front line and he was already strapped up. They would be positioned on the dirt trucks directly in front of the fort. If there were any zombies in that area, they were not visible from the sentries' positions. If Nerit had been at the fort, she probably could have taken them out from the top of city hall, but no one else had her sniperlike skills.

Jenni kissed Katie's cheek, then swatted at Juan's hands. "Hey, stop feeling me up!"

Juan gave her a look. "Aw, am I turning you on?"

"Ewww," Jenni responded. She felt giddy and excited. It always felt good to be doing something and she enjoyed killing the enemy. Each time she dispatched one, it was delicious revenge for her dead children.

Katie hugged her, then headed for her post. She and Travis were going to be on one of the platforms. Since only people who had experience firing a gun had been recruited for this task, the freshly built sentry posts along the newly constructed wall were now staffed mostly by hunters of both sexes and a few former military men.

"Be careful, Mom," Jason admonished, and hugged Jenni tightly.

Holding him close, she closed her eyes and relished the feeling of being a mother. "I will be. I promise."

Jack was giving her a quizzical look, probably not sure what to make of her harness. The dog probably thought it was a weird leash.

Jenni bent to kiss the top of his head. "I'll be okay. I promise."

"Ready?" Juan asked.

Mike and Jenni both gave him thumbs up. Juan signaled the two crews handling the wires.

They were hoisted up into the air. Quickly, the horde of zombies sprang into view.

"Kinda wished they didn't smell so bad," Mike complained.

"Yeah," Jenni said, and wrinkled her nose.

They had reached a good height and were slowly moved forward. Jenni enjoyed being swung over toward the dirt truck. It felt like flying, so she struck a Superman pose that made Mike laugh. But her joy died away as the zombies grew more agitated and the enormity of what they were doing was made clear. They were carefully lowered onto the truck, and both immediately knelt down so they were less visible to the zombies below.

"You know," Mike said after a beat, "the black man always gets it in these scenarios."

"Well, in the zombie movies, the black guy is usually the hero," Jenni said in an attempt to console him.

Mike laughed. "Yeah, but that cracker shot him at the end of the first movie."

"Oh, yeah," Jenni said, and winced. "But Peter survived in *Dawn of the Dead* with Fran."

"Good point. So, we'll just keep steady and we'll both be okay, right?" Mike said, obviously trying to convince himself this was true.

Jenni grinned. "And at least my name isn't Barbara."

That made Mike burst out laughing and they high-fived each other. "You're crazy, girl, just like Juan says."

"We're all in position. Starting the countdown," Travis said over the walkie-talkie attached to Mike's belt.

Mike winked at Jenni. "Keep cool, girl."

Jenni winked back. "Keep cool, dude."

"You got it."

"Five, four, three, two, one . . . ," Travis intoned.

The crack of rifles filled the early morning air.

Jenni and Mike stood up, aimed and fired. Her first target was an old man, and she split his head nicely in two. Barely moving the rifle, Jenni sighted the next zombie, a young woman with her face torn away, and fired.

Aim . . .

Fire . . .

Aim . . .

Fire . . .

She reloaded as quickly as possible and kept shooting. The zombies were pushing hard against the truck and she could feel the massive vehicle shaking slightly under her feet. Mike fired with precision and swiftness. Jenni tried to match him the best she could. With every successful shot, she was glad of the Sunday afternoons she'd spent with her grandpa when she was a kid, shooting old tires and soda cans.

Each mangled, screaming, distorted face that dissolved into bloody mist beneath their assault made the knots in her stomach ease just a bit. They were thinning the crowd, making them pay for what they had become. She hated them. She fiercely, passionately hated them, and each time a head burst beneath the hail of bullets, she felt her smile grow.

Ten minutes in, with the killing in full swing, Jenni paused to reload once again. Just then a male zombie came up over the sandbags and charged her. She was so startled by his abrupt appearance that she was surprised when she instinctively drew her revolver and shot a nice little hole into his head.

"Wow! I'm more of a badass than I thought," she exclaimed with surprise.

"Fuck," Mike swore. "More coming!"

Another was scrambling easily onto the truck.

Mike took this one down, firing over Jenni's head.

Jenni stood up and Mike quickly went back to firing into the area that he was assigned. Jenni stepped cautiously toward the edge and blinked, then blinked again in horror. "Juan, get us the fuck off of here!" she screamed.

By killing the zombies toward the front of the crowd, they had inadvertently made a nice little ramp of bodies right up to the top of the truck.

Two more zombies appeared at the far end of the truck and started to race for them. Jenni shot both of them.

"Fuck!" Mike grabbed the walkie-talkie. "Get us the hell off this thing!"

More zombies were beginning to charge now. At least four. Jenni kept firing, but more were coming.

Her body was jerked up so hard that the revolver fell from her hand. She gripped the rifle tightly through the pain that erupted through her back and arms as she was dragged upward. The zombies kept coming. She swiftly curled her legs up to her chest, out of the reach of the undead. They swung their arms fruitlessly under her, trying to catch her. Being far taller, Mike was much longer, and therefore had trouble pulling his legs out of the way. One zombie gripped his leg. Mike shouted in anger and fear as he fired point-blank into the zombie's face. Another zombie had grabbed his booted foot and was lifted with him. Mike kicked his leg hard, but the creature was tenacious, trying to pull itself up for a bite.

Jenni tried to take aim with her rifle, but they were swinging wildly due to being hoisted so quickly. "I can't get him."

"Muthafucka," Mike snarled, and kicked as hard as he could. The zombie fell and landed face-first on a spike.

At least a dozen zombies had clambered up onto the truck now.

"Why aren't they swinging us back?" Jenni screamed.

They had been lifted high enough that no zombie could grab hold of them.

"We're bait," Mike answered in a grim tone. "We're fucking bait."

Sure enough, Jenni saw that all the zombies climbing up onto the trucks were gathering directly under the two humans.

"They can't move us back to the fort or those things will follow," Mike explained. "And that will compromise everyone."

"Do we shoot?" Jenni held tight to her rifle.

"Praying sounds better to me. Told you, the black man always gets it," Mike grumbled.

Twenty of the undead were now crowded onto the truck.

"We're not dead yet," Jenni said.

"Yeah," Mike said. "Yet."

3.
Close Encounters

Things were going to hell. Katie felt as if the world were toppling around her. The guards were all shouting at each other. Jenni was screaming and Mike's voice was blasting out of the walkie-talkie. Juan was arguing with the mayor. Jason was yelling, "Get my mom down!" And the zombies were clustered on top of a truck, trying to get to Jenni and Mike.

"Cease fire!" Juan shouted, the command being relayed down the line. "We don't want to hit Jenni and Mike!"

"Fuck me," Travis whispered.

"Who's a crack shot?" Katie demanded, looking around at the men and women with the rifles lined up along the wall near her.

"I am. Through the eye every time," one man said. He was older and had a weather-beaten face.

"Take out the zombies on the left end of the truck," Katie ordered.

Travis looked sharply at her. "Are you sure? They're so close to falling into the spiked area."

"As the zombies fall back, they'll block that ramp of dead bodies, and the other zombies won't be able to scramble over them." Katie pointed. "We might be able to eliminate that slope in the pile and make it harder for them to get up."

Travis studied the situation. "Yeah. I see that. And if they try to climb, they'll pull the dead ones down on them. Go for it, Ed." He signaled to the volunteer.

"They're as good as dead." Ed began to target the zombies.

Katie watched as the zombies tumbled backwards into the corral.

"Shoot the fucking ones under us!" Mike shouted into the walkie-talkie.

"They can't reach you," Juan's voice answered over the cackling static.

Katie gripped her rifle tightly in one hand, watching the zombies falling under Ed's sharpshooting. Jason came running toward the sentry post. "Katie, get her down!"

"Jason, we're doing our best without compromising everyone's safety," Katie answered, resting one hand on his shoulders. Her gaze returned to where Jenni dangled and the zombies that clawed hungrily at the air, desperate to reach her. Swallowing hard, she fought down her own fear.

Jack was barking hysterically at the zombies that were still intent on getting hold of Jenni and Mike.

"Why don't we have grenades? Or flamethrowers or something like that!" Jason's voice was high and strained.

"Because we're not soldiers, Jason. We're just trying to survive." After glancing back one more time in the direction of Jenni and Mike, she ran down the steps from the sentry post toward where Juan was directing his men from another platform. A scan of the zombies revealed that Ed, the hunter, had significantly reduced the population atop the dirt-filled truck.

But there were still maybe ten or so under Jenni and Mike. "Juan, what are we going to do?"

Juan intently studied the situation. He lifted his walkie-talkie to his mouth. "Travis, status?"

There was a burst of static, then, "We've slowed them down. They can't just walk up onto the truck anymore; they're struggling to try to get up now. Katie had a good idea, but it may not last. The more they claw at the dead, the more slide down. They'll be able to get back up soon if we don't hurry."

Juan looked at Katie, then at the zombies on the truck. "I think we should pull Jenni and Mike back until they're above the spikes and let the rest of the zombies try to reach them and fall."

Katie winced. "I hate using them as bait."

"We don't have a choice, Katie." Juan shrugged, his expression somber.

"We need better weapons," Jason said furiously .

"Yeah, we do. Know where to get any or how to make them?" Juan's voice was sharp. He turned and began talking into the walkie-talkie, instructing the pulley operators. Jason threw up his hands and stalked away angrily.

Katie glanced toward Jenni and Mike. They seemed so vulnerable up there. The operators on the pulleys began to tug them back and the zombies leaped for them. Four tumbled into the no-man's-land where the spikes were. Two were impaled, but two more glanced off the spikes and landed on the ground.

Juan cursed loudly in Spanish as he motioned to the operators to stop hauling. Another zombie made a flying leap at Jenni; his fingers glanced off her shoe before he fell hard against the hurricane fence. Three more tumbled onto spikes while the rest reached the hurricane fence and rattled it.

"Gawd, this keeps getting worse!" Shaking her head with disbelief, it was difficult for Katie to fathom how everything had gone so terribly wrong.

Travis's voice crackled through the walkie-talkies again. "We have a breach." He sounded overwhelmed.

"And now it's even worse." Juan threw his hands. "Fuck!"

Katie looked up to see more zombies flowing onto the trucks. Because they had pulled Jenni and Mike back, when the zombies tried to reach their prey, they were hurtling into the spiked area. Many were impaled, but more and more were falling to the ground as they glanced off their undead companions' skewered bodies.

"Juan, we're fucked if we don't hold that line," Katie screamed, and headed for the stairs that led up to the sentry post where Travis was. Juan followed her as the mayor shouted at them to do something fast.

"Keep the guns thinning the herd at the back of the corral," Travis instructed Ed and the other men.

"We need to go in with spears," Katie said, almost over him.

"We need to keep someone shooting the ones trying to get over the truck," Juan added.

"Sounds like a three-pronged plan," Travis said. He grabbed Katie's arm as she turned to pick up a spear off a pile of them near the wall. "You don't have to."

"Yeah, I do," Katie answered. She slung her rifle off her shoulder and set it aside before double-checking her revolver. The rifle would get too easily in the way in such close quarters.

Jenni and Mike were now dangling over the spikes, screaming to be pulled to safety, but Juan barked at them that it wasn't going to happen. Katie understood why. At this point, Jenni and Mike were the main focus of the undead cannibals. Drawing them into the fort would just turn the zombies' attention to all of them.

Unable to hear Juan, Jenni and Mike kept shouting to be pulled back.

"Where is the fucking bullhorn?" Juan shouted.

Travis darted down the row, grabbing men off the firing line. He quickly explained the new plan as shots rang out in an attempt to keep the zombies at bay.

"This is crazy!" Jason's voice drew Katie's attention. "We need better weapons. We need grenades and . . . and . . ."

"Jason, we'll take care of it." She saw Travis and his men rushing toward the guard post. "We've got a plan."

Jason threw up his hands in frustration, his terrified gaze resting on his mother.

Juan and several others lowered ladders from the sentry posts into the area between the wall and the hurricane fence.

"We get down there and deal with them as fast as we can," Travis ordered as the men grabbed spears off the pile.

"This was a bullshit plan from the beginning," snapped a man with blond hair and a cowboy hat.

"Let's just kill the damn things," another man with a bushy mustache growled.

Katie scrambled up onto the sentry platform first and felt her heart pound even harder at the sight of the ravenous undead below.

Travis joined her, taking in the view, the color draining from his face. "Shit."

Juan looked down, sweat beading on his face, and took a deep breath. "You gotta kill them or we're going to be in a whole heap of it."

Peggy darted up the stairs and thrust the bullhorn into Juan's hands before rushing back down to her screaming child. For the first time, Katie became aware of the fort's inhabitants who were bystanders in this battle. They were clustered around the living quarters, holding on to one another, fear etched into their features.

A few zombies had seen them and begun rattling the fence. Katie muttered "fuck" a few times before starting down the ladder. Her hands were shaking so badly, it was hard to hold on. All that separated her from a gruesome death was a wire fence.

Travis climbed down behind her, followed by several construction workers. Katie pressed herself back against the wall and stared at the crazed, rabid faces of the zombies just on the other side of the fence. She gripped her spear tightly, her body shivering.

"Katie?" Travis whispered, obviously concerned.

"Yeah," she answered, struggling to get her terror under control. She could hardly take a breath, she was so afraid. "I'm good." She peeled herself off the wall and took a step forward, determination settling into her features.

Beside her, a short Hispanic man drove his spear through one of the holes in the fence and into the eye of a zombie. And with that simple act of violence, the world turned bloody and surreal. The rest of the construction workers thrust the screwdriver-tipped spears hard through the fence, trying to drive the sharp blades through the eyes or mouths of the screeching zombies.

Katie took a deep breath. She gazed into the face of a female zombie who was screaming and growling on the other side of the fence. The woman's fingers, stripped of most their skin, clutched the fence as she wrenched at the metal, trying to rip down the barrier keeping her away from a meal—Katie. Katie lifted the spear and aimed at the woman's eye. As hard as she could, she thrust the spear forward and felt the sickening squish of the zombie's eyeball. Shoving harder, Katie pressed the spear deep into the screaming woman's head and finally into her brain.

"Scramble it!" Travis voice was jagged with exertion as he struggled to impale an enormous zombie on the other side of the fence.

Katie jiggled the spear around and felt the woman go limp with one harsh cry. Shifting her weight back, she drew the spear out of the now dead zombie's flesh. Blood splattered her clothes. "Shit."

"On a stick," Travis said.

More zombies were leaping off the trucks, eager to reach the living, but due to Travis's and Juan's foresight, the truck perimeter was a good distance from the fence. The undead kept landing on the spikes or tumbling to the ground.

Katie felt sweat dripping off her as she thrust the spear into the eye of another zombie. Then another. Over and over again.

It was hard work—gory work—and the screaming faces made her quake. But she kept going.

Juan's voice sounded over the bullhorn. "Travis, the corral is nearly empty. Most of the zombies are now up against the truck or down in the trenches with you."

"Then this fucking battle is almost over," Travis grunted.

"Let go! Let go!" someone shouted, followed by a harsh scream.

Katie snapped her head around. A construction worker had been foolish enough to brace his foot against the fence while he drew his spear out of his victim, and two zombies had managed to grab on to his boot, throwing him off balance. As Katie watched in horror, he fell sideways against the fence, and his hair and clothes were snagged by frantic bloodied fingers. Where he had grabbed on to the fence to try to keep himself from falling, a zombie had bitten off his fingers. Now the zombies were tearing away bits of his flesh with their fingers and teeth.

Katie dropped her spear and walked over to the man. Another construction worker, Shane, was trying to wrestle the fallen man away from the zombies. She drew her gun.

"No, no, just save me," the bitten man pleaded.

"I am," she answered. She fired four shots, point-blank, through the fence, killing the zombies who had attacked the man. Despite her quivering stomach and tattered nerves, her aim was sure.

"Thank you, thank you," he whispered.

Katie said softly, "No problem," and shot him square between the eyes.

"Bitch!" She was tackled from the side and knocked to the ground. Shane, who had been trying to save his colleague, punched her so hard that her vision swam. "Stupid fuckin' lesbo bitch!"

He hit her again and her sight darkened. Dimly, she heard Jenni screaming, "Get off her! Get off her!"

Someone shoved the man off her.

Katie tried to roll over and tasted blood in her mouth. She spit it out and managed to flip onto her knees and palms. Men were shouting and arguing. She heard the impact of a fist against flesh. There were more screams. She crawled to the wall and used it as support while she slowly drew herself up. Her body was shaking and she felt like vomiting. The world swam around her. To her surprise, she realized she was still clutching her gun.

Swinging around, she took in the scene in a flash. Shane had Travis in a stranglehold. Two other construction workers were trying to get him off Travis, nearly tearing Shane's shirt off in the process. The zombies were almost all dead; just two were left to jangle the fence and screech.

"Let him go," she rasped, aiming her revolver at the man who had struck her. No one paid any attention. The men continued to fight. "Let him go!"

Shane glared at her when she shouted, his blue eyes bright with fierce anger. He released Travis abruptly and lunged at her. The gun slid up his slick skin to his neck as he tackled her to the ground.

"I'm going to feed you to those things," he spat in her face. "You killed my brother, you bitch."

"He was already dead," Katie managed to say as his weight slowly pressed the air out of her lungs. Her finger tightened on the trigger. Shane put his hands around her throat and started to squeeze.

Something fell on him from above, smashing into the back of his head. Katie gasped as the added weight knocked the air out of her lungs. Breathless, she tried to stay awake and to hold on to the gun. Her assailant's eyes rolled up into his head as he slid into unconsciousness.

Then Jenni was bending over her, smoothing back her hair and whispering, "It's okay."

Travis pulled Jenni away and pushed the limp attacker off

Katie. He leaned over Katie and took the gun from her hand. "Katie, try to breathe, okay?"

Behind Travis, Jenni kicked Shane a few times in the side.

"Stop it!" Travis ordered as two other men pulled Jenni away.

"He hurt her!" Jenni protested, pulling free.

Katie struggled for breath as her hand grasped his arm.

"He's not important right now. Katie is," Travis snapped.

"Oh, Katie!" Jenni exclaimed, her anger dying in her eyes. She fell to her knees and stroked Katie's hair gently.

Finally, Katie managed to say, "sonofabitch."

Both Travis and Jenni smiled with relief.

Travis lifted Katie into his arms and carried her toward the ladder. She could see that the no-man's-land between the truck barrier and the fence was littered with dead bodies. There were no moving zombies left.

"We . . . did . . . it," she whispered hoarsely.

"Yeah," Travis assured her, and hoisted her up.

Juan and Mike lifted her over the wall and laid her down on the platform.

"Dropping from the harness is real loco, Loca," Juan informed Jenni as she climbed up behind Travis. "What if you had missed and hit the spikes?"

"Um, you would miss me?"

Juan snorted. "Yeah, right."

Travis leaned down and gingerly touched the side of Katie's face where the attacker's punch had landed. It was throbbing and hurt like hell. "Katie, Katie . . ."

She passed out cold.

· CHAPTER SIXTEEN ·

1.
Voices

Katie swam to the surface of consciousness slowly. The darkness was deep and stifling. She clawed at it, trying to break free.

"... defending all of us ..." She recognized Travis's voice.

"... shot a man in cold blood ..." The mayor.

"... no cure for a bite ..." Juan sounded pissed.

"... we would have had to shoot him anyway ..." Curtis was defending her. Wow.

She struggled to push up through the thick membrane of the darkness and strained to speak.

"Don't be an idiot ...," Peggy, the city secretary.

"Yeah, this world has all new rules. Katie did that guy a favor." Jenni, safe and sound.

"Who is in charge around here?" The mayor again, sounding shrill.

"Well, I would say Travis," Juan said.

There were murmurs of agreement.

"I'm an elected official!"

"Well, new elections were just held and you lost," Juan answered.

"Take the handcuffs off," Travis ordered.

Handcuffs?

As feeling swept back, Katie abruptly realized the coldness around her wrists was metal. She tried to open her eyes and failed. Something cold and wet was resting on her forehead and eye. An ice pack.

"Curtis, I am your boss!"

"Not anymore," Curtis replied.

"Give me the keys," Travis ordered.

Again, she tried to open her eyes.

"Hey, you awake?" Travis's voice, warm and strong. So much like her father.

Her eyes fluttered, and light broke through the darkness. She felt him fumbling with the handcuffs.

"Kinky," she moaned.

Travis laughed and his features swam before her eyes and slowly solidified. More figures pushed into her vision and she saw Jenni's large eyes.

"Not dead . . . ," she managed.

"And not arrested," Juan assured her.

"You can't let her go," the mayor protested.

"Watch us," Travis answered, gathering her into his arms.

The ice pack tumbled off her head and onto the cot.

Wrapping her arms loosely around Travis's neck, Katie whispered, ". . . need . . . to . . . stop . . . playing . . . romantic hero . . ."

"Yeah, I keep telling you that, but you just don't listen," Travis chided her playfully.

"She's bullheaded that way," Jenni agreed, following him as he carried Katie out of the room.

"Head hurts," Katie said.

Then she slipped away again.

2.
Movement

In the city council meeting room, Jenni elbowed her way past the many people gathered there. Everyone in the fort—except for those on sentry duty—seemed pressed into the room.

At the council table sat Travis, Juan, the mayor, Peggy, and Curtis.

The meeting was already in an uproar.

"We should have a say . . ."

". . . who says what we should do . . ."

Jenni was relieved to see that Katie seemed alert despite her swollen face and blackened eye. She sat next to Bill in the first row. Her cracked and bloodied lip didn't take away from the fierce look on her face.

Jason was saving a seat for his mother near the front of the room. When she sat down, Jack rested his chin on her knee so she could scratch him behind his ears. He gave her a doggy grin of satisfaction.

Curtis stood up slowly. "Okay, okay, let's be civil about this. A lot has happened since yesterday. We need to stay calm."

The room quieted down a bit.

Curtis sat down and Travis stood up. "I'm not real good at leadership stuff, but we need to do something to make sure that what happened yesterday doesn't happen again. Now, my strong point is building, and I can design new fortifications for this . . . uh . . . fort. Juan also has a lot of ideas and we are working together to expand the fort and make it safer. Safer to live in. Safer to get in and out of. We're going to need a lot of volunteers to help with that.

"Now, the mayor here, he can run a city and he will be dealing with the logistics of food distribution, water consumption,

living quarters, all that. Peggy is going to take over the communication center and maintain the inventory of supplies."

The mayor slowly raised his head and Jenni could see that he was a defeated man who had grabbed on to whatever was left of his power base.

"What about the lesbo?" The voice came from the back of the room.

Travis's face darkened, but he kept his temper. "Katie, Bill, and Curtis have experience in law enforcement—"

"She killed Patrick in cold blood!"

"Patrick was bitten," Travis said softly. "A bite is deadly in this new world. He was dead already. If you get bit, you are going to be delivered out of this life fast and quick to keep the rest of us safe."

"That's murder!"

Jenni strained to see who was talking.

"No, it's being humane. Now, Bill and Curtis are going to work together to make sure that everyone understands the new rules around here."

"Who gave you the right?" An older man now.

"No one. We'll need everyone to work hard to keep this place safe." Travis looked grim. "We need to work together, or we will all die."

Katie said in a low voice, "Tell them the plans."

Travis took a deep breath, then continued. "First off, we seem to have cleared out the zombies, at least for now. None have been seen since yesterday. Tomorrow, we'll dispose of all the bodies and remove the corral. . . ." He next outlined Juan's plan to devise a new entry point using the street to the east by rigging up what he called the "Panama Canal," a simple series of walls with gates.

Anyone entering by vehicle would have to drive through two locks, which would give the guards time to shoot any zombies who slipped in as well. Then the vehicle would enter a walled-off area behind the construction site and pull into the garage of

the building that had once housed the newspaper office and distribution center.

The survivors would have to go into the hotel and the old newspaper building and clear it out, then brick up every entrance that faced the outside world. Once that was done, everyone could move into the hotel. Other teams would take trucks into the surrounding streets of Ashley Oaks and bring back supplies.

Still other teams would look for survivors. All the teams would be armed, of course, and Mike would train those volunteers, since he was former army.

Juan added, "I'm heading to the library. We need books on farming, medicine, weapons, warfare. . . ."

"We have a window of opportunity before another batch of those bastards shows up." Travis said. "We don't know how long it will be, so we have to do as much as we can as fast as we can."

"What about the army coming to rescue us?" Ed called out.

Curtis shook his head. "There's no news out there anymore. No one is coming."

"We have to rescue ourselves," Katie declared .

Jenni looked at the people in the room and saw that they understood. There was seriousness in their features and a firm determination that gave her hope.

"What about the lesbo bitch? Shane is locked up because of her." The speaker was a tall man with dark brown hair and a heavy mustache. He was the same man who had spoken up before.

Curtis stood up slowly. "Philip, if Shane agrees to act like a civilized man, we'll let him out to help us out. But the rule remains: You get bit, you will be given the gift of a quick death."

After a moment of silence, Rosie, Juan's mother, said, "That is fair. And right. A decent death."

There were murmurs of agreement.

Travis motioned to those at the table. "Come talk to us. Volunteer. We all need to work hard to get this done."

Jenni raised her hand as high as she could. Travis acknowledged her.

"I just want to say that in every zombie movie, internal fighting is what finally lets the zombies in to win," she said, and gave Travis a big smile.

Juan nodded. "She's right. We keep it together or we die."

Philip snorted, then shrugged. "Fine."

Jenni gave him a long look and leaned over to whisper to Jason. "He'll be trouble."

Jason agreed. "Yeah, I know."

The meeting finally broke up. Most of the people actually seemed relieved to know that there was some sort of plan. Katie stood slowly, one hand rising to her battered face. Travis turned to her to make sure she was okay. Jenni hesitated, feeling a little jealous. Katie was her best friend, not Travis's. She sighed and fought the emotion. It was hard to share at times. Katie gave Travis a little smile, then gave Jenni an even bigger one. Jenni grinned happily.

As Juan moved away from the table, Jenni said, "Hey, I'm going with you to the library. I want to help."

He stared at her for a moment, studying her doubtfully, then shrugged. "Fine, Loca. But you'll do as I say."

Jenni smirked. "Of course I will."

Katie looked amused. "I wish I could go along just to enjoy the banter."

"We don't banter," Juan said with a sniff.

"We argue," Jenni agreed.

"We hate each other," Juan added.

"Viciously," Jenni said with a solemn nod.

Travis looked at both of them, then at Katie. "I think they're secretly dating."

Juan sputtered and Jenni made a face.

"Definitely," Katie agreed playfully as she took a seat.

Juan and Jenni eyed each other, then shook their heads vehemently.

"I'd rather date you, Travis," Juan asserted.

"Oh, how cute!" Katie laughed and wagged her finger at both the men. "It would be a match made in heaven."

Jenni flung her arms lightheartedly around Katie's neck as she sat on her lap. "And I have a partner."

Katie giggled.

Travis and Juan slipped away. Travis thrust his hands into his jean pockets, his expression dour. He wasn't sure which he felt grumpier about: taking on a leadership role or Jenni and Katie's affectionate banter.

"Told you," Juan said simply.

"Yeah," Travis said glumly. "You did. I still don't believe you."

"I recognize the expression of a man going down in flames. I've been there many times before. My ex-wife, my childhood sweetheart . . ."

"Belinda, right?"

"Yep. The girl of my dreams since I was a little kid. So I can recognize your desperation as you go sailing headfirst into the abyss, amigo."

Travis arched an eyebrow at Juan. "Why are we pals again?"

"We bonded over broken hearts with a big bottle of tequila."

"Two bottles, if I remember correctly. I remember the hangover from hell the next two days."

Juan laughed. "I don't remember much about that night other than you said you wanted a change from Houston and I suggested you come here."

"You're really good at fucking up my life, huh?" Travis folded his arms over his chest as they walked.

"It's not my fault you are all *Chasing Amy* with Katie."

Chuckling, Travis stopped near the back door of city hall and shook his head. "I guess I really do suck at the whole dating thing."

"Wanna hold my hand?" Juan held out his heavily callused hand and winked.

Travis snorted. "Ha, ha."

"What? I'm a sexy bitch!"

Travis shoved open the door and headed out onto the construction site. "You're also a pain in my ass."

"It's a sign of a good friendship," Juan assured him, and followed.

3.
What Have I Become?

Katie felt trapped within the fort, now that others were venturing out into the town. It was three days since the great battle and she was a walking bruise. Her jaw ached and her eye looked worse than ever. She was healing, but her bruises were still rising to the surface and revealing themselves in all their colorful glory.

The first group had returned with truckloads of food from the local grocery and survivors from the convenience store where she and Travis had stopped on the way to Nerit and Ralph's. Unfortunately, they had been too confident, and two zombies had dragged down one of the fort's men in the grocery store. It was a sobering event that reminded everyone vividly that danger still existed even though zombies were not crowded outside their walls. It was a bitter irony to add ten new people to their company while losing another.

Travis canceled all outside missions and got Mike to once more go over gun safety and procedure. Curtis helped with the demonstrations. They couldn't afford to lose anyone else.

As her body slowly healed, Katie sat in on planning sessions for the new entrance and the assault on the hotel. It quickly became apparent that Juan and Travis were clever and resourceful. If she were well enough, she would be joining the team that was going to clear out the hotel. Jenni had volunteered to go to the library with Juan and to stand guard at night.

Katie suspected Jenni was interested in night duty because Travis was also taking the late shift. It was pretty clear to her that Jenni had a crush on Travis. Whether the attraction went both ways, she wasn't sure.

Unable to sleep with Jack and Jason snoring loudly on the nearby cot, Katie slid off her bed and wandered up to the roof. The soft wind was cool on her skin and she hugged herself to keep warm. Sitting down on a plastic chair, she looked up at the bright stars.

It was hard to feel at peace when you knew you could kill without remorse. In her mind, she replayed the image of that man, torn and bleeding. He had not even realized her finger was pulling back the trigger. He was so relieved that she had saved him. And then she truly *had* saved him.

Rubbing her hands together, she leaned forward and sighed. Staring at the rooftop between her feet, she took a deep breath of cool, fresh air. With the zombies' bodies gone, the air was clean once more.

"We do what we have to do," Lydia's voice whispered.

She looked up to see Lydia sitting in a chair next to her. "Baby?"

Lydia smiled and reached out to run her fingers lightly down Katie's cheek. "I'm here, sweetie."

Katie lurched out of her seat, fell to her knees, and wrapped her arms around Lydia's waist, clinging to her. Her cheek pressed to Lydia's lap, she started to weep. "I'm dreaming."

"It's okay, though, isn't it?" Lydia's long cool fingers stroked her hair gently.

"Yes, oh, yes. I was afraid I wouldn't dream of you anymore. Not after what I did."

Lydia lifted Katie's chin to gaze down at her. "And what did you do?"

"I killed that man. I just killed him."

"But you killed Jason's friend and his friend's father at the camp."

"They wanted me to. They knew they were infected!" Katie face was wet with tears.

Lydia lovingly traced the contours of her face with the tips of her fingers. "And how is this different?"

"I just . . . did . . . it." Katie's voice caught and she shivered. "And I don't . . . feel bad."

"I know, darling. And you shouldn't. You shouldn't feel bad. You saved him from my fate. You liberated him from hell. You did what you had to."

"I don't feel bad, Lydia, because I hate them. I want them all to die. I don't care what they are or once were. And when I knew he would be one of those things, he stopped being human to me and I killed him. And I don't fucking feel bad!"

Lydia leaned down and gently kissed Katie's forehead. "I know, Katie. I know. But there is more, isn't there?"

Katie drew back. "I don't want to talk about it."

"Katie, tell me."

"I can't!" Katie stood up and wiped at her face with unsteady fingers.

Lydia slowly stood up, too, and took Katie's face between her hands. With infinite tenderness and love, she kissed Katie on the lips. Katie clung to her and kissed her back.

"I love you, Lydia. I should have . . ."

Lydia lightly kissed her again. "Tell me."

Katie shivered and whispered against Lydia's soft lips, "Oh, God . . ."

"Tell me."

"I should have killed you!"

Lydia drew back. Her figure altered before Katie's eyes. A huge hole opened in her chest, and her emptiness was revealed. Raising milky eyes, Lydia whispered, "You should have."

And then she rushed at Katie, screaming.

Katie woke, tumbled off the plastic chair, and landed hard on the roof. Travis was there in an instant, helping her up. He had been standing guard nearby when she must have fallen asleep.

"Geezus, you're shaking," he said with concern.

Katie looked around, terrified. Her fingers gripped his shirt tightly as she searched desperately for the ghoul from her nightmare. But the rooftop was empty except for them.

"Travis," she sobbed.

"I'm here," he answered.

"I let her down," Katie choked out the words, then collapsed against him, weeping.

Travis wrapped his arms around her and held her tight, feeling her shivering violently against him. Tenderly, he stood stroking her hair as she cried, not understanding her rambling words. But he knew her heart was shattered, and his broke for her.

When her sobs subsided to mere tears, he helped her down the stairs and back to her room. She walked slowly and leaned heavily against him. When he entered, Jenni was just lying down. Seeing Katie, she immediately sprang to her feet and rushed to Katie's side.

"Katie, honey, what is it?"

Travis released Katie reluctantly and watched Jenni help her lie down. He stood awkwardly as Katie and Jenni clasped hands.

"Lydia," Katie said, her voice clear at last. "She's still out there—one of them."

"I know, Katie." She pushed her cot up to Katie's and lay down. Katie seemed to relax as Jenni curled up next to her and held her hand.

Travis backed out of the room slowly and shut the door.

Juan was coming up the stairs, smoking despite all the THANK YOU FOR NOT SMOKING signs all over city hall. The recovery team had brought back beer and cigarettes from the grocery store, and Juan was a happy man. When he saw Travis, he stopped and studied his friend's face

"Want to talk about it?" Juan asked after a beat.

"No," Travis answered.

"Eh, yer fucked," Juan decided.

"Yeah." Travis looked at the storeroom door.

"Well, I'm off to get shut-eye. Loca and I are heading out tomorrow around noon."

"Take it easy out there," Travis responded automatically.

"As long as Loca doesn't shoot me in the ass, it should be just fine." Juan grinned and walked on.

Travis looked back at the closed door and thought of Jenni's expression when she had seen Katie. The compassion in her eyes had touched him deeply. Yeah, he shared something with Katie, but it didn't seem to compare to the bond the women had.

That made him feel very alone.

He walked on slowly, deep in thought.

4.
Not Always as It Seems

"Coast is clear!" Mike shouted.

Juan signaled to Jenni and she quickly let herself down the ladder and onto the main street, with Juan close behind. The street was empty of bodies and covered in about half a foot of rich fresh earth to stifle the reek of the dead. She walked quickly and confidently to the city truck Juan had chosen for their expedition to the library. He had once worked in maintenance for the city and was sure the vehicle was reliable and ready to go.

"Almost seems like a normal day," Juan said, strolling along beside her with his rifle in his hands. His long, curly hair flowed crazily from beneath his cowboy hat. His lean but muscled form was clad in tight blue jeans, a T-shirt, and denim jacket. Jenni glanced briefly at his ass. For a jerk, he wasn't that bad looking.

"Want to go by McDonald's for a McGriddle?"

"Do not torture me, Loca. I loved those fuckers."

The truck perimeter had been moved outward and a new wall was being erected directly inside it. The storage containers

had been moved to their new location, where the first of the "locks" was built. Everyone was working hard, except for Old Man Watson, the oldest person in the fort. He sat around, smiling and nodding as he observed the new construction. Jenni loved his old faded tattoos and his big hugs.

As they neared the truck, Jenni ducked down to make sure there was nothing under the vehicle. Satisfied, she peered into the cab, then opened the door and slid in. Juan followed suit and slammed his door.

"Okay, we are taking the shortest route there. We don't do anything fancy unless we have to. Okay?"

"Okay."

"Promise me."

Jenni gave him a petulant look. "I promise."

Juan rolled his eyes and started the truck.

Jenni settled back in her seat and rested her rifle across her knees. Before they left, Mike had briefed them on procedures. They were to stick together at all times. At the first sign of more than one or two zombies, they were to run for safety. If possible, they were to get to a safe position and take out the zombies. Juan and Jenni had done well together during their training and felt confident.

Jenni watched the buildings gliding by her window. Many of the businesses were shut down, their fronts boarded up.

"The town was dying," she said.

"Pretty much dead," Juan agreed. "A local developer came in and sold the city council on a big plan to revive it. In the old days, the hotel was actually a prime spot for the Hollywood stars to come and relax and go hunting out in the hills. We're talking early 1920s—not even talkies, but silent films. The developer was going to tap into that and raise up a little bit of old Hollywood here. Even had others interested in buying up stores and making them into retro-style diners and stuff. The big clincher was that the guy was lobbying to get gambling legalized in the county. It was a crazy idea, but the guy has . . .

had . . . money." Juan shrugged. "I thought it sounded like a load of shit, but it gave a lot of us jobs."

The truck turned down a residential road and they both tensed. There was more of a chance of finding the undead in this area than in the mostly shuttered downtown. Juan swerved around a bike in the middle of the road, dried blood and guts clinging to its frame.

"Fucked-up world," he said.

"Yeah."

Jenni glanced into the large picture window of a house as they passed. A woman and little boy stood inside, beating on the window. Neither one was alive. "There are some trapped in these houses."

"And wandering outside," Juan said. The truck bounced as they ran over a legless zombie, smashing in its skull and killing it.

Jenni snickered. "Pop goes the weasel."

"Yer a sick *chica*," Juan said, but his voice seemed to be tinged with appreciation.

"Yep. Pretty much." She flashed her biggest smile at him.

"Too bad yer gay. I might actually ask your sick ass out."

Jenni rolled her eyes. "Oh, please. I'm so not gay."

"Ah, c'mon. Everyone knows about you and Katie." Juan made a really obscene action.

Jenni flipped him off. "Not gay."

"Yep."

"Nope."

"Yep."

"Nope."

"Yep."

"Love the penis, I assure you," Jenni asserted, and wagged an eyebrow.

Juan nearly drove into a car. "Shit, girl!"

"I do! I was a married woman! I love men."

"So you and Katie aren't—?" Juan made another obscene gesture, and Jenni smacked him.

"No!"

"Oh." He sounded rather disappointed.

"I kinda like Travis, honestly."

Juan blinked. "Yeah?"

"Yeah."

"Oh, I think he's got a hard-on for your former girlfriend."

Jenni blinked. "Huh?"

"Yeah. Though I'm sure he thinks you arc a fine piece of ass. *Loca,* but fine."

Jenni frowned a little. "Katie is gay. She's the gay one."

Juan shrugged. "Travis just . . . he's always confused about women. You should go for him. He'd enjoy your *loca*ness."

Jenni smacked Juan again. "Get out! Really?" She smiled at the thought of being even a little alluring to Travis.

"Yeah. Stop hitting me, I'm driving."

"Oh, yeah." Jenni was beaming now. "Well, Katie is gay, so maybe he'll look my way. I need makeup. And a cute top." Jenni glanced down a side street as they passed by. "Think we'll get to kill zombies?"

"Your mind just goes all over the place, doesn't it?"

"Pretty much."

Juan pulled into the nearly empty parking lot of what had probably been a very modern building in the '70s, but could now be safely classified as an atrocity of architecture. Across the street was a nice park. There were no houses nearby, so it was easy to look around and see that the area was pretty clear of danger. There were only two cars in the lot and both seemed empty.

"Just keep smart, Loca."

Jenni rolled her eyes as she slid out of the truck. She flicked the safety off her rifle and walked slowly toward the library's main entrance.

Their first obstacle was soon in plain view. The library had a

set of glass double doors with a small foyer between them. Trapped in the entryway was an old man, dead, hungry, and beating on the interior door. It was kind of funny that he still clung to his library book.

"He wants in," Jenni observed.

"Possible survivors?"

"That's what I'm thinking."

Juan strode over and peered past the old man. "Can't see anything but a card catalog up against the door."

"Survivors, then."

"Maybe. If they had food."

The old man became aware of them and instantly started banging on the door to the outside. Surprisingly, it wasn't locked and slowly opened under his weight.

"Shit," Juan gasped.

"Fuck." Jenni raised her rifle.

"Shoot it, Loca."

Jenni waited until the zombie managed to stagger outside before firing, neatly taking off the top of his head and shattering the glass door behind him. "Got him!"

Juan looked down at the zombie's book. "*Better Sex after Sixty*," he read.

"No!"

"Yeah."

Jenni checked out the title of the book and broke into wild laughter. "Oh, shit. That is funny. He probably got here early to turn it in before his buddies saw him."

They became aware of three anxious faces looking at them over the top of the card catalog. They were a little drawn and pinched, but alive. The heavy piece of library furniture was pushed out of the way, and a woman unlocked the inner door.

"Oh, thank God! Juan!"

"Belinda!"

Juan hugged the woman tightly and slipped into the library. "Everyone okay?"

Jenni sized up Belinda. She had long black hair, amber eyes, and a tiny frame. She was obviously Hispanic and very pretty. The other woman was older, blond, and very short and stout. The third person was a young teenage girl with red hair and a spray of freckles across her nose.

"Thank God someone came for us!" the blond woman cried.

"Gretchen, good to see you alive," Juan said.

"Same here, Juan," she replied.

Belinda locked the door behind them. "We've been here since it started."

"We were almost out of food," the teenager said.

"We're here now," Jenni said with a smile. "We'll get you somewhere safe."

"Thank Jesus. We've been eating snacks out of the vending machines. We're almost out," said Gretchen.

"Mr. Marsters showed up with a bad bite. He said someone bit him as he was stopped at a stoplight. We tried to help him, but he died," Belinda explained.

"We had already heard about them coming back and so we were carrying him outside when . . . ," Gretchen continued.

"We almost didn't get away from him. He tripped and fell and we managed to lock the door," Belinda finished.

Jenni studied her a bit longer. She was fairly sure that librarians were not supposed to be attractive or sexy. She felt uneasy around her, but wasn't sure why.

Juan quickly described the fort and all they had endured. Gretchen kept clasping and unclasping her hands and saying, "Dear sweet Jesus." The teenager just seemed dazed. Belinda kept hugging Juan, which really annoyed Jenni, much to her surprise.

Jenni wasn't sure she liked any of them. But then again, Jenni had never really had any real relationships with any women other than members of her family and, now, Katie. It annoyed her to feel her past insecurity returning. She had often felt awkward around women who seemed prettier or more intelligent

than she was. Belinda reminded her of all the girls she had envied growing up, and she struggled to get a rein on her feelings.

Juan finished his account by clarifying why they had come to the library. Belinda straightened, wiped the tears from her eyes, and said, "Okay. Give us the list."

Juan rummaged around in the pocket of his worn jeans and pulled it out.

Belinda took it and quickly scanned it. "Okay, we'll divide it up, load up the book carts, and get out of here."

Jenni tried not to frown at her. Who had put her in charge? She knew it! Belinda was just like those popular girls who always bossed everyone around. Struggling to contain her growing dislike, Jenni listened to her new assignment. She trudged along behind Gretchen, pushing a book cart that was soon loaded with what looked like a lot of really boring books. Juan went with Belinda while the teenager, Darcy, collected all the remaining candy from the vending machine.

Jenni was almost disappointed when they went back to the truck and there were no zombies in sight. She was feeling edgy and irritable and wanted to shoot something. Somehow, they all squeezed into the truck. Belinda sat next to Juan with the teenager on her lap. Gretchen squeezed in next, and Jenni ended up crammed in almost on top of Gretchen.

The trip back was even more boring than the trip out. She saw more zombies trapped in houses, but none broke out. She thought of Mikey, sighed, and felt even more like shooting stuff.

Back at the fort, the newcomers were helped into the construction site while Juan loaded the pallet Travis had built with books, and Jenni and others stood watch.

Finally, she went over the wall, Juan behind her.

"Well, Loca, we're safe and sound."

"Big fucking deal."

Juan looked at her and frowned. "What?"

Jenni wrinkled her nose at him.

"What?" he repeated.

"I didn't get to kill anything on the way back!"

Juan started to laugh. "Yeah, but you're back and okay. So you can go flirt with Travis."

Jenni considered this option, but it didn't seem quite as alluring as before. "Oh, yeah. I guess I could."

"Time to come out of the straight closet, *chica*." Juan mussed her hair with one hand and strode off to join Belinda.

Jenni scowled after him.

1.
The Terrible World

Jenni walked out through the new gate cautiously, her rifle in her hands, safety off. Bill walked with her, sweeping his gaze over the abandoned street. Curtis was right behind them, looking very edgy. This was his first time out of the fort, and he was sweating profusely.

Jenni had been asked to accompany the former cops on a search and rescue expedition. Either Juan had talked up her skills and craziness to grandiose proportions or her actions in the fort had made her seem crazy yet competent. Maybe both. It amused her that they wanted her to tag along, probably because they knew she had no issue about killing zombies. Unfortunately, there were those who were reluctant to kill their former friends and neighbors. On one rescue mission already, someone's aversion to killing his zombified grandmother had resulted in a death.

The construction workers attempted to shut the gate behind them. There were a lot of teeth-jarring screeches and a lot of swearing. Juan had told Jenni that there were some issues with the gate, and obviously this was true. Hopefully, they would have it fixed by the time the three rescuers got back.

Despite her efforts not to be perturbed, Jenni was having trouble dealing with Juan. It was all about Belinda, and she hated that the woman bothered her so much. She suspected that Juan's real reason for the library excursion was to save Belinda.

Of course, she had no proof of this. Since Belinda arrived, Juan had been acting like a total idiot, trying to be all smooth and sophisticated. If Jenni even tried to pop a joke in his direction, he'd get annoyed. Though she was utterly loath to admit it, she missed their banter. She tried flirting with Travis to make herself feel better, but that had fallen flat. She wasn't sure what was wrong with her, but she always felt better when she was working on something useful.

She strode quickly toward the minibus they had collected from the school to use for rescue missions over the past few weeks. The fort's population was growing, and the ratio of men to women was slowly evening out. There were at least a half dozen children in the fort now, and Peggy's son had plenty of other kids to play with. At times, Jenni felt upset by their presence. It was hard to see other children alive and well when hers had died so quickly.

Fate was a bitch. It had been cruel to so many and spared others for no apparent reason.

"Keep it short and sweet," Bill instructed.

"We're going to stir up the captive ones again," Curtis groaned.

"Let them bust out. If we shoot them, we won't have to deal with them later," Jenni said with a grin.

Bill shook his head. "Such a bloodthirsty woman. You PMSing again, Jenni?"

Pushing open the door to the minibus, Jenni turned to the two men. "Yeah. Be afraid, be very afraid."

Curtis legitimately looked a little afraid, but Bill just laughed and lugged his girth into the driver's seat. Warily, Curtis slid past Jenni and sat in the front passenger seat. "Juan tells stories about you."

Jenni shut the door and smiled back at Curtis. "Really? I didn't know he still talked about me since his girlfriend showed up."

Curtis shifted in his chair uncomfortably. "Uh . . . well. He calls you Loca."

Jenni wagged an eyebrow and held on, staying on the top step near the driver's seat as the vehicle rolled forward.

Bill just chuckled good-naturedly. "Well, I think Jenni is a little girl who's a killer shot, and if she's *loca,* I can deal with that."

Jenni smiled. "Thanks, Bill."

Bill was always nice to her. Ever since he arrived with Katie and Travis, he had been somewhat low-key. Like Jenni and Katie, he had been an outsider to the townsfolk; it had been hard to find their niche. Only now were they starting to feel as if they were actually part of the community. Sometimes, she missed Nerit and Ralph, but she was able to talk to them every few days. She kept hoping they would come to the fort, but the Toombses were intent on staying in their own small haven.

The minibus slowly crawled down the street toward one of the residential neighborhoods bordering the downtown area. It drove past a burned-out gas station, abandoned restaurants, an old cinema that had closed its doors long ago, and a car lot that stood empty of cars. It turned at the first block of the neighborhood of small early-twentieth-century homes. Most were in good repair, but a few had fallen to the elements and leaned dangerously to one side or had collapsed altogether.

Bill drove very slowly, giving anyone who was alive enough time to come to a window or doorway. Of course, this meant the undead were hearing the steady hum of the engine as well. A few appeared at windows. Sometimes the zombies escaped; sometimes they didn't. If they did break out, a bullet to the head settled the situation. The bus had never been swarmed.

"No one alive on this street, it looks like," Curtis decided.

"Yeah," Bill answered sadly. He turned a corner and they started down another block.

Jenni watched the shrubbery and the houses with equal interest. Once she had seen half a man stuck in a hedge. She'd wondered if he had tried to hide and been pulled out and eaten. So far today, she hadn't seen any zombies outside the houses,

which was a relief. There was a great fear in the fort that more swarms of zombies would converge on them. Maybe a lot of zombies would just start moving in the same direction and happen upon the town. Maybe there was a real danger of them migrating toward the living. Did it really matter? In the end, they just had to be prepared.

"That looks like a situation," Curtis said suddenly, pointing ahead.

Two zombies were rushing across the street toward a house where four others were banging on ground-floor windows, trying to break into the structure. The front door was shattered, and it looked like a piece of furniture had been shoved up against it from inside. The second-floor window was open and a teenage girl was waving her arms at the minibus.

Bill slowed to a stop and they all stared at the scene. The zombies had not yet noticed them. They continued to assault the house, screeching at the girl who was desperately signaling the bus.

"Kill 'em all," Jenni said after a beat.

"No choice if we're going to rescue her," Bill agreed.

"Take the ones on the left," Jenni told Curtis. "I'll get the ones on the right."

"I'll cover you both," Bill added.

Curtis took a deep breath. "Okay." He nervously fingered his service revolver, then nodded grimly and stood up. "Okay."

Jenni opened the door and stepped out cautiously. She and Curtis took up positions near the bus so they could retreat quickly. She looked out at Bill, who had the driver's-side window open and his gun drawn.

"Ready?"

"Sure," Curtis said softly.

Jenni lifted her rifle and sighted the most dangerous-looking zombie, a fully intact male. She fired and he went down. Immediately, she swung toward the next target; she heard Curtis firing. A faceless woman was turning toward them. The bullet

Jenni fired slammed through the woman's forehead and sheared off the top of her head. Next to her, Curtis's shots went a little wild as his nerves got the best of him. One of the zombies he shot fell down, one leg useless, but continued to crawl toward them.

"Shoot 'em in the head!" Jenni's finger closed on the trigger again and another zombie fell, bits of its brain flopping out onto the sidewalk.

Curtis took a deep breath, steadied his hands, and fired quickly. This time his aim was more accurate. Jenni was relieved when his shots found their proper targets and the zombies dropped.

"Watch out! Behind you!"

Jenni whirled around to see an old woman staggering toward her. She looked like she had died recently and was not as mangled as the other zombies. To her amusement and horror, the woman had a stranglehold on a living cat. The cat had been systematically eating the woman's arm, probably since she had died. It looked skinny and bedraggled. Jenni almost burst out laughing, but instead aimed carefully and took out the dead cat lady. The zombie's corpse dropped to the street, still twitching, the cat squealing and trying to get free. Jenni walked over and pried the old woman's dead and decaying fingers off the cat. The animal gave her a few swats with its claws, but only snagged her jacket. The dead fingers finally released the angry feline and it rushed off with a little house cat roar. The cat lady was the last of the zombie attackers.

"Now, that was fucked up," Jenni said to Curtis with a grin. Her expression grew grim as she saw what emerged from the house.

The teenage girl was first, followed by a man who was probably her father. He was carrying a little girl who was almost completely wrapped in a heavy blanket. A young boy followed, along with a woman who was undoubtedly his mother. The woman was pale, gray, and sickly looking.

"Thank God! Thank God," the man cried out. "We were hoping someone would find us. We ran out of food two days ago!"

The mother stumbled a little, and the little boy steadied her.

"My wife and daughter need immediate medical attention," the man continued.

Curtis looked at Jenni and they both sighed.

"When were they bitten?" Jenni asked.

"What?" The man didn't register her words. "What?"

"When were they bitten?" Curtis repeated. "They aren't well. We can tell they were bitten."

"Yesterday the front door was broke and two got into the house," said the older daughter. "Daddy killed them, but they got Mom and Angie. But it's just small bites. It was a little kid who jumped on them. Just little teeth marks."

Curtis exhaled slowly, and Jenni looked down at her boots for a moment.

"Well, that was enough," she said finally. "They are both as good as dead. We can't take them with us."

"What do you mean? You can't leave them here!" The man's face flushed, red and fierce. "They need a doctor!"

"There are no doctors in town," Curtis answered in a composed tone. "And there is no cure for the bite. We can't take them with us. It's too dangerous."

The little boy began to cry and cling to his mother. She looked down at him sadly. Her pale blue eyes were sunken and her cheeks hollow. Her color was very bad, and Jenni was sure she didn't have much time left. The father backed away from the minibus, clutching his ailing youngster in his arms.

"We can't leave them behind," he protested.

"You have to if you want to come with us. We have a safe place where many survivors are staying. If you want to be with us, you have to leave without them," Curtis said in his best police officer *everyone stay calm* voice.

Jenni considered just killing the mother outright, but it seemed too cruel. But they couldn't waste time arguing.

"Let's go," she said simply.

Curtis hesitated, then nodded. "Okay."

The teenager looked at her father desperately. "Daddy? We can't stay here."

The father was holding tightly to his youngest and backing toward his wife. "We're not leaving."

"Yes, you are," the woman said decisively. "I can feel it burning inside of me. Cold and hot. I'm going to die and be one of those things. Give me our daughter, Douglas."

Douglas looked at his wife with a desperate expression on his face. "Catherine, I'm not leaving you here."

"Give me Angie and take our kids to a safe place."

He shook his head and looked down at his daughter. Her breathing was ragged, and she looked worse than Catherine.

"Give me Angie, Douglas!" Catherine held out her arms for her child. "Take Michelle and Ricky and go!"

The teenage girl grabbed her brother and pulled him away from their parents.

"Mom . . . Mom . . . ," he cried.

"Ricky, go with your sister," she ordered. "Douglas, give me Angie."

Reluctantly, he offered his wife the small, precious bundle.

"Now, go with our other kids to safety. Go!" Catherine held her daughter tightly to her, cradling her head against her shoulder. "Go!"

Jenni motioned to the kids to get on the bus, and they obeyed. They looked shell-shocked and terrified, but they moved. Curtis took Douglas's arm and guided him to the bus. The man could not take his eyes off his wife and child.

"If we can get them to a doctor . . . ," he mumbled.

Curtis shoved him into the bus and climbed in after him.

Catherine stared at Jenni sadly and her grip increased on her daughter as the small form started to thrash and growl. Blood splattered across her cheek and lips as she clutched the child closer. Jenni raised the rifle, and the woman looked down at her

undead daughter tearing away at her breast. She nodded, tears on her cheeks.

Jenni could hear the woman's husband and children screaming.

"Catherine! Catherine!"

Jenni fired.

The first shot stilled the child and tore a hole through Catherine's chest. The woman was still falling when the second bullet finished her life.

Jenni got onto the bus. The family had fallen silent. The father was clutching his children and whimpering. The two kids were near hysterics. Curtis was pale and had tears in his eyes. Bill looked calm and resigned.

Jenni closed the door and leaned against it. Tears slid down her cheeks as she thought of her dead children and once more felt the sting of their deaths. She hated the world. Hated how it stole children from parents and parents from children. She wanted never again to see a family torn apart by this plague of living death. But she knew that she would, and it made her angry.

"When we get back, I'm going to hug Jason so tight," Jenni said softly to Bill.

He put the bus in gear for the return trip to the fort.

2.
The Quiet Before the Storm

Katie walked up the stairs to one of the platforms overlooking the new entry point. The sun was setting, but the construction crew would work hard until the last shards of light faded.

Crews had been working long hours. It was rough going and stressful. There had been a few attacks by zombies, but the guards handled them with no loss of life. As the days had passed, small raiding parties went out into the town to salvage what

they could, and a trickle of survivors arrived. They were usually pale shadows of the people they had been, near starvation and severely dehydrated.

Belinda hunkered down with a stack of medical books and tried hard to make do with the supplies that had been gathered from the local drugstore and convenience store as well as the supplies they had brought in from Nerit and Ralph's town. She urged them to raid the clinic, but Juan had explained that the clinic was packed to the gills with zombies. If they went into the clinic, it would have to be carefully planned out, and loss of life would have to be expected.

Katie rubbed the tip of her nose. Her face was healing, and now there was just a pale swath of green and purple bruising. Her lip had healed and the soreness was fading. But she still felt battered and bruised emotionally from that huge battle. The terror she had felt plus the raw energy of the kills, and shooting that man and just not giving a damn.

That still haunted her. She had killed him and not cared. At first, she wasn't certain why she had found it so easy to pull the trigger, then but after her dream, she fully understood.

Once someone was bitten, the end result was inevitable. To put them out of their misery quickly and efficiently was not only humane, but also necessary for the safety of all.

Looking over what had been accomplished so far, Katie couldn't help feel proud. The outline of the lock system was up. A sturdy, high wall, three feet thick, extended the length of a block and a half. They had blocked both ends of the stretch of street with the storage containers and other heavy equipment during construction. They had gone into each building to make sure it was clear. The abandoned businesses had not been incorporated into the fort due to their dilapidated condition, but the wall had been built right up against them.

Travis had explained that they planned to use the rooftops for sentry duty. Any entrances to the roofs from the buildings had been cemented over. Fire escapes had been dismantled and

the parts moved into the fort. Everything that could be used was being salvaged. And now nothing and no one could get up on top of the buildings or scale the wall.

The new gates were being tested. They were heavy metal doors from an old warehouse. They had been giving the workers some trouble. A second set of gates would be going up soon inside the long, narrow entry point. Already a fence was being constructed to keep guards safe and slow down the zombies in case of infiltration.

Travis joined her and smiled. "Looking good, isn't it?"

"Awesome, actually. It almost looks like a castle."

"Yeah, I can see that," Travis responded with satisfaction.

"It almost feels like we're on top of this," she said.

"Yeah, almost." He glanced back at the hotel and the many windows shimmering with the fading sunlight. "That's gonna be the big victory."

"When are we going in?"

"As soon as the entrance is done. See where they bricked up a back entrance? We'll go in there. But if there are more zombies than we think in there, they could flood the fort as soon as we break open that wall."

"So what are you planning?" Katie tilted her head and looked at the back end of the hotel. Her blond hair billowed around her face in the cool breeze.

"Build a small wall around the entrance area and use the old wrought iron gate as the door. When we go in, we'll have the gate locked behind us and guards standing post," Travis answered solemnly.

Katie sighed. "Everything we do comes with such a great risk."

Travis leaned back against the railing. "We have a great opportunity right now to get ourselves secure before we get slammed with a fresh bunch of those things. I feel them coming, don't you?"

"Every day," Katie answered truthfully.

"Once the gate is fully operational, we'll extend the search area out a few more blocks."

"We may just lure more back here," Katie warned him.

"I know, but I have a feeling any survivors out there are quickly running out of time."

Katie turned her gaze toward the reinforced truck perimeter. It had been built up higher, and spikes had been planted in front of them. If there was a push to get to the trucks, the zombies in the back would end up impaling their comrades in front of them.

"We need to get into the hotel soon. Things are getting cramped in here. We're up to a hundred survivors."

Travis made a face. "We don't have enough experienced construction workers, Katie."

"Then teach the rest of us how to do it. I can probably help build that entrance to the hotel you are talking about."

Travis studied her and laughed. "Yeah, probably."

"Jenni is going out on rescue missions. Jason and Curtis are trying to figure out how to make new weapons. Belinda is working hard to become a self-taught doctor. Peggy runs inventory like a general. Give me something to do, Travis." She gave him an intense look. "Stop protecting me."

He looked startled at her comment. "You got hurt."

"Yeah, but I'm pretty much healed."

"I just thought . . ."

Katie raised an eyebrow.

Travis just stared at her. "Okay, okay, I'm trying to protect you."

"Why?"

Rubbing his face, the tall man sighed. "Um . . . because . . . look, I need you to help me figure all this out. I can't risk you getting . . . You've been hurt twice. . . . You . . ."

Katie held up her hand. "Okay, you're being a total wimp right now. Out with it, Travis."

"I don't want to lose you to those things. Or to some dumbass who goes after you because you're gay. Sorry if I shouldn't be so protective, but I might as well tell you—"

Katie didn't want to hear his next words. She quickly hugged him tightly and kissed him on the cheek. "Okay, okay. But I don't need a big brother. I need to work. To keep busy."

Travis blushed a little. "Yeah, well." He seemed to consider going on, telling her the truth they were both avoiding.

"Uh-huh. No worries," Katie said briskly, deftly avoiding looking at him. Instead she directed her attention toward the new entrance and watched the gates open and close in short jerks. "Things are getting better, but more complicated."

"It's the way of life," Travis decided. He put an arm around her shoulders and gave her a little squeeze. "Let's get some dinner."

"Sounds oh so exciting," Katie joked.

"Yeah, I hear it's Dinty Moore beef stew night!"

"Yummy. Ah, filet mignon, I miss you so."

"Hamburgers . . . God . . . I miss those," Travis confessed.

They walked down to join the others for dinner.

3.
Promises

Katie glanced up from her meal—Dinty Moore beef stew and freshly baked corn bread—as a very pale and pensive Jenni sat down across from her. Travis had been called away just before he was going to sit down, so she was alone at her table.

"What's wrong?"

Jenni shrugged and used her spoon to poke apart the bits of beef in her stew.

"Jenni?"

"It's just not fair, you know? It's not fair that this thing splits up families. It's not fair that my kids are dead. It's not fair that your wife is dead. Why can't families survive together? Why is that so fucking hard?" Jenni shoved a spoonful of stew in her mouth and chewed furiously.

Katie blinked, then slid her hand over to gently pat Jenni's free hand, which rested on the table in a tight fist. "What happened?"

Jenni spooned more food into her mouth and shrugged again. Her eyes were angry and not focused on anything or anyone in particular.

Katie looked toward the entrance to the dining room and saw Peggy talking to a distraught-looking man who had his arms draped across the shoulders of a teenage girl and a young boy.

"You rescued a family," Katie said, understanding filling her eyes.

"Half a family. The mom and the little girl were nearly zombies when we got there." Jenni stabbed a potato with her spoon until it was mush. "They were bit two days ago. If we hadn't gotten there in time, the whole family would be dead by now."

"But you did save some of them, and that is something good," Katie said softly.

"Is it? Really?" Jenni covered her face with one hand. "Katie, the only thing I even feel a little good about is that I killed the mother and kid so they aren't out there running around. How fucked up is that?"

"Honestly, I understand. I wish . . . I wish I had had the strength to kill the thing that was Lydia so she wouldn't be out there right now. I wish it with all my heart. So be glad you gave that family at least that much," Katie responded in a low, tortured voice.

Jenni lowered her head. "I wish we had put Mikey and Benji to rest. Lloyd . . . fuck him . . . but the kids . . ." She sighed wearily.

Katie ran her fingertips over her brow, then leaned forward to look at Jenni straight on. "Jenni. It's ripping me apart knowing that Lydia is out there. Lately, it's almost unbearable."

"I'm sorry, Katie. I didn't realize."

Katie leaned her chin on one hand. "Promise me, if I am ever bitten, that you will give me an out."

Jenni nodded vehemently. "I will. I promise. And you will do the same for me."

Katie held Jenni's slim hand in hers, smiling sorrowfully. "Strange, isn't it? The vow to kill each other has suddenly become sacred."

"I'm telling you it's a fucked-up world!" Jenni crammed more food into her mouth.

Katie let go of Jenni's hand slowly. Her gaze traveled to Travis, who finally had grabbed a plate and was sitting across the room eating with Mike and Juan. "Yeah, it is."

After finishing, Katie got to her feet and carried her plate and glass over to the big plastic bins set up for the dirty dishes. It was looking pretty messy tonight, and she was glad her kitchen detail had been the night before, when they had just served sandwiches and chips.

Moving down the hallway, she sought out the former record room, where all the library books had been set up. As she suspected, Jason was seated at the table, his food congealing beside him, Jack dozing at his feet, as he flipped through a book on chemical warfare.

She was relieved to see that he was alone except for the dog.

Sliding into the chair across from the boy, she rested her elbows on the table and regarded him thoughtfully. "Jason?"

"Yeah?" He didn't even look up.

"I have a favor to ask," Katie informed him.

"Yeah?" He looked up, obviously trying to shift gears in his head. "Huh?"

"Remember our talk a while back about my sexuality?"

"Yeah?"

"You didn't tell anyone, did you?"

Jason kind of smiled. "No. I let them all think you and my mom are doing it. Keeps the guys away from both of you."

"Oh?" Katie thought about that, then laughed. "Okay."

"Yeah." He shrugged. "It works out better that way. I thought

for a while Juan was gonna try to hook up with Mom, but he's all about Belinda."

"Yeah, he seems to be," Katie agreed. "But anyway, I don't want you to tell anyone I'm bi, okay?"

"Why?"

"Well, for the reason you stated. I don't really want to deal with guys hitting on me."

Jason blinked, thinking, then blinked again. "Um, okay, but . . . wait . . ." He frowned a little. "Why is this important all of a sudden?"

Katie hesitated, then said, "A guy likes me and I don't want him to get his hopes up."

"Because you're not over Lydia?"

"That's one of the reasons."

"Is this about Travis?" Jason's eyes narrowed suspiciously. "You're not clearing the way for my mom, are you?"

Katie flinched. "Sort of."

Jason frowned even more and sat back in his chair.

"Jason, your mom likes him and he's such a great guy—"

"Then you go for it! You like guys!"

Katie shushed him, making a face. "I don't want to. I can't. Lydia—"

"Lydia is dead."

Katie felt her jaw set with anger, but reminded herself sternly that she was dealing with a teenage boy. "Yes, she is. But I am nowhere near being ready to be with anyone else, male or female."

Jason looked at her angrily. "So why is my mom ready? Why is she ready, Katie?"

Looking down, she sighed. "Because, by the time it all went to hell, your mom already wanted to move on. You know what your dad did. She wanted to be free."

Jason furiously wiped a tear away. "I know. But why does she want to move on from my brothers? Why isn't it good enough to be my mom?"

Startled by his outburst, she thoughtfully considered her words before answering. "She wants to be your mom, Jason. You mean the world to her. But she has a right to find happiness beyond that one role. The way you find happiness beyond just being her son."

Jason scowled even more. "Yeah, but . . ."

Katie lifted an eyebrow.

"I'm not replacing anyone."

"Neither is she, Jason. Who did she replace with me?"

Jason lowered his head and then slowly looked up at her. "No one." He sighed. "Okay, fine. I won't tell Travis or anyone else that you like guys, too." He did his best pouty teenager look. "I wasn't going to, anyway."

Katie smiled at him softly. "Thank you."

"Yeah . . . yeah . . . ," Jason said moodily.

She went in search of Travis.

1.

When Truths Are Revealed, No One Is Safe

The low hum of the gate opening was joined in harmony by a steady squeal. Huge lights had been rigged up over the new area of the fort, and a team was diligently working into the night on resolving the issues with the gate. The new area was still cut off from the rest of the fort and accessible only by long ladders and a single small platform that bridged the two walls.

As Katie walked across the site, she could hear Juan's voice rising over the din. She knew he was working long hours to get the first gate working properly before the second gate went up. It was dangerous work, and stress levels were high. Occasionally, a zombie would try to attack the construction workers. The sharp-eyed former hunters on sentry duty would take them down.

Travis was on watch at the far side of the fort, far away from the construction of the gate in the corner where the wall met the old hotel He was gazing out at the now empty main street, where so many zombies had met brutal deaths in the town's first real victory against the undead. Since that first big battle with the zombie horde, the main street had been eerily empty. The moans were fast becoming a distant memory, and a thick layer of dirt covered the smell of death and decay. As spring took a firmer hold, grass and wildflowers had taken root, and Katie suspected the street would soon look like a little field in the country.

But the terror of that crowd of zombies moaning and screeching in their desperation to reach the living had burned deeply into the psyche of those who had been in the fort since the beginning. It had been decided that they had to keep the zombies from gathering in a horde outside the wall again. Many suggestions had been made on how to keep this from happening, but after the almost-disaster of the mass slaughter when the zombies breached the perimeter, every idea was being heavily scrutinized.

Katie strode up the stairs to Travis's side, and he glanced her way.

Spring was in the air, and in Texas, that meant cold nights and warm days. Katie was wearing the reverend's jacket tonight. Its fragrant tobacco smell and comforting warmth were a gentle reminder of the man who had died for her.

The sheer luck of the draw that enabled so many in the fort to survive that first hellish day still wore on Katie. Her fingers lightly traced over the now dead cell phone in her pocket. It was difficult to let go of her last connection with Lydia, even if she couldn't see her lovely picture anymore. Call it survivor's guilt, but it was not easy to deal with. She knew that Travis was dealing with it as well. Maybe all the survivors suffered from it. At times, it was hard to talk of their life before the zombocalypse and the people they had lost. At other times, there was relief in their conversations as they spoke of their future plans. It was like being caught between heaven and hell: both happy and sad to be alive.

"I think I saw a few flashes down the side road," Travis said after a beat. "They looked almost like headlights."

"Think other survivors are coming this way?"

"Maybe. Though at times, I'm afraid those things have learned to drive. Or remembered how to," Travis answered, his brow furrowing.

Katie shivered at the thought. "Well, since that time when Laura's remains tried to open that truck door, we haven't seen

any more of them appearing to exhibit any signs of actual deductive reasoning."

"Yeah, I know. I keep hoping that what she did was due to some sort of memory, not any real thought process." Travis continued to stare down the street intently. "The last thing we need is thinking zombies."

Katie leaned against the railing, rubbing her hands together. She and Travis were ill at ease with each other, which was not the norm for them.

"About earlier," Katie started.

Travis sighed but didn't look at her. He double-checked the spotlight—presently turned off—to make sure it was properly hooked up. "Probably just my imagination. It probably wasn't headlights."

Katie rested her hand on his shoulder. "No, not about that."

Travis straightened and looked down at her. "It's okay. I shouldn't have tried to say anything. I realized that during supper."

"No, no, it's okay. I'm partially to blame. I was pushy about it and then chickened out."

Travis gave her a sheepish look. "I've been kinda obvious, huh?"

Katie smiled warmly. "Yeah, kinda."

Travis flushed and shook his head. "Juan says I'm a sucker for the unattainable girl."

Katie laughed. "Yeah, me, too. For a long time. Then I found Lydia."

Travis sighed. "You're so lucky to have had her. My ex-fiancée and I never had what you did. I was always trying to please her and make her happy and in the end, I guess I failed. I'm not good at this whole girl thing."

"Travis . . ."

"I know, I know, Katie. I know how this goes down. Yeah, I've tried to pretend, but I knew even during moments of hope it was not going to happen." Travis looked down at the rifle in his

hands, then at the street. "You've been one of the few good things in this new world. Everything has changed and gone to hell, but you help make it tolerable."

She couldn't help but smile at his words, and she hugged him gently. "You and Jenni and Jason are very special to me. My new family. I want you to understand that."

Travis looked down into her eyes, sad and resigned. "But?"

Katie rested her hand on his cheek and found the words harder to say than she had imagined. She opened her mouth to speak, reconsidered, and closed it. What was there to say? Instead, she kissed his cheek softly. It was rough and slightly scraggly against her lips. He clung to her, and in that comforting moment between them, the world felt far away.

Travis shifted slightly and pressed a quick kiss to her lips. "Friends?"

Katie nodded mutely.

Travis nodded as well, then kissed her lightly again. Forgetting all her reservations, Katie kissed him back, softly and sweetly. The kiss turned into something neither of them had expected, and energy pulsated between them. Wrapped in each other's embrace, their kiss became real and intense.

Sharply, overwhelmingly, Lydia filled Katie's mind. Images of her lovely face, sweet kisses, gentle hugs . . . and then her screaming, reanimated corpse.

Pulling away abruptly but reluctantly, Katie said in a quivering voice, "I can't."

"I know," Travis said with a sigh. "I know."

"Jenni adores you," Katie began lamely.

"Let's not go there," Travis answered almost bitterly.

"Okay," she said, helpless. She wanted to comfort him, but the energy of their kiss still tingled over her skin, and she couldn't risk it. She had to stay true to Lydia. To what they had shared. She had to mourn her and remember her. How could she let herself care for someone else when Lydia was still out there?

"I'm sorry, Katie. I really am. But you can't just deflect my

emotions onto Jenni. Don't get me wrong. She's gorgeous and makes me laugh. I really like her a lot, but please, just don't do that."

A bright light suddenly blinded them both. The roar of an engine broke through the sounds of the construction at the other end of the fort.

"What the hell?"

"It's a motorbike!" Travis flipped on the searchlight and aimed it down the main street.

An old, battered motorbike wobbled into the light. A scraggly-looking young man and his equally scruffy girlfriend looked up at them with desperate, terrified expressions.

"Let us in! They're right behind us!"

Travis flashed the light up the road to reveal a crowd of zombies running toward the fort, obviously following the motorbike. Katie saw that a few wore doctors' coats or nurses' uniforms.

"The clinic. They went to the clinic!" she exclaimed in disbelief. "How could they be so stupid?"

"Shit!"

"Let us in!" The boy yelled loudly, stirring up the pursuing zombies even more.

"There's a gate around the corner, but it's not working right. I need you to swing back around two blocks west and lead the zombies away, then head for the gate when you've lost them," Travis ordered.

"Fuck that, man. I'm almost out of gas! I'm heading for the gate!" the kid answered, and gunned the engine.

"That moron! He'll lead them straight in!" Katie declared angrily.

"Shit! Shit!" Travis grabbed the walkie-talkie. "Juan! Close the gate! Close the gate!"

There was a cackling noise, then, "We're working on it, dude. Chill out."

"Zombies coming, Juan!"

"What? Shit? From where?" Juan's voice demanded over the static.

"The clinic. There is a kid on a motorbike heading around the block to get into the gate."

"Gawddammit!" From the sound of his voice, it was obvious that Juan was terrified.

Katie headed down the stairs, running as fast as she could. Even from across the great distance between Travis's post and the new entrance, Katie could hear Juan shouting, "Shut the gate! Shut the gate!"

Travis caught up with Katie, and they both sprinted to the far side of the construction site. More people came running, carrying guns and spears. The squeal of the gears as the gate started to close filled the night air. Some of the construction workers clambered up the ladders out of the new area to safety. Travis and Katie scrambled to the sentry platform overlooking the gate.

"What's going on?" Jenni caught up to them at the platform and looked down the road.

The guard at this post had aimed his spotlight down the road already, illuminating the two teenagers on the sputtering motorbike. It was near to stalling. The zombies trailed close behind. The bike was dangerously weaving from side to side, zombies snatching at the girl holding tight to the driver.

"That idiot's leading them right toward the gate," Travis growled.

Katie saw the gate was still closing. Juan and two other men were trying to oil the gears.

"We didn't have enough fucking time,!" Juan shouted. "Not enough fucking time!"

More of the construction workers made it over into the fort, breathing heavily, terrified.

The loud screeching of the gate ripped at her ears as Katie lifted her rifle to try to get a clear shot of the zombies. It was hard to get a bead on any of them with the kids on the sputtering

motorbike swerving back and forth in the foreground, both obviously panicking. The bike stalled and died just before the gate. The two scraggly teens slid off the motorcycle mere seconds before the zombies grabbed it. Together, they ran the few last feet toward the opening.

The gate seemed to be taking forever to close. The kids sprinted through the now narrow gap in the gates, and a few people cheered. The zombies hit the gate and tried to push through the breach that was now wide enough for only one body to squeeze through at a time. Shots filled the air as people on the walls opened fire on the zombies still rushing down the road.

"Juan!" Jenni ran across the bridge between the two walls.

Katie followed, dodging some of the men scrambling into the fort.

Jenni reached the top of the other wall and knelt. The first zombie was pushing through the gate. The last two men with Juan were now climbing the ladders. Jenni aimed and fired and the zombie's head split open. The body fell and became lodged in the gates, keeping them from closing completely.

Juan ran toward the opening, a shovel in one hand.

Meanwhile, the two newcomers were trying to climb up a single ladder, jostling each other in their haste. Katie ignored them and moved along the top of the wall to a better position to fire at anything coming through the gate. Jenni almost slid down the empty ladder in her desperation to help Juan.

Juan used the shovel to force the corpse out from between the gates. The desperate hands of the zombies blocked by the dead body tried to grab him. Katie watched in horror as Jenni ran straight up to Juan.

"Loca, what are you doing here?"

"Saving your ass," Jenni answered. She stood right next to Juan and started firing through the narrow gap in the gates.

"Jenni is fucking nuts," Travis said from beside Katie, then started down the ladder.

Juan was slowly losing his battle with the zombies. The corpse was slowly being pushed forward, and soon the "living" zombies would be able to try to squeeze through into the "lock." Travis hit the ground and ran to help. Katie stood ready to fire, Behind her, she could hear the shots of those trying to thin out the zombies at the back at the pack.

The dead zombie body shuddered and to Katie's horror, a hand burst through his rib cage. A grotesquely gnawed face shoved itself past the other zombie's ruined head. It was literally ripping apart the corpse to get to the living.

"Fuck you," Jenni said, and blew its head off.

But the damage was done. The first zombie's body crumpled, and more of the animated ones pushed forward, trampling the dead ones beneath their feet.

Travis grabbed another shovel and joined Juan in shoving them back as the gate managed to close another inch or two. The whine of the mechanism filled their ears. Jenni kept shooting at the zombies through the narrow gap, trying not to get in the men's way and not to hit them accidentally.

Katie felt helpless. She didn't dare look away or blink. Butterflies were gnawing at her stomach as she tried not to think about how vulnerable Travis and Jenni were.

Mike appeared beside her and climbed down into the lock as fast as he could. Running to join the others, he grabbed a wood plank from a pile of lumber. Avoiding the grasping hands of the dead, he shoved the board against the zombies, who grabbed it, probably to push it away.

"Good idea," Juan said. He and Travis put the tips of their shovels against the wood. Instead of soft bodies that gave way, the plank gave the men adequate leverage for their pushing. Mike and Jenni joined them, and using the board as a shield, they shoved the zombies back through the gap. The gate shuddered and closed, leaving a small gap where the zombie limbs were caught. The men barely got their shovels out of the way in time.

Katie sighed with relief and lowered her rifle. A few arms,

hands, and feet were sticking out from between the closed gates. Some were even moving.

Jenni picked up a shovel and began hacking at the limbs, severing them, blood flying, until Juan pulled her back. Jenni flung her arms around him and they both staggered backwards, then fell into a heap. Travis and Mike high-fived before Travis smiled up at Katie. "See, Katie? Easy."

Katie laughed and ran a hand over her forehead, feeling the thick sweat slick on her fingers.

"You're fucking crazy, Loca," Juan teased Jenni as he helped her to her feet.

"I kept your ass alive!"

"Yeah, so, what, I owe you?"

"Yep!"

Juan pulled out his wallet and thumbed through the now obsolete bills. "How about a buck?"

"I'm so worth more than that!"

"Two dollars?"

Jenni smacked him and they ended up in a shoving war.

It was then that Belinda made her appearance, climbing down the ladder, tears streaming down her face. Katie saw Jenni quickly back away from Juan, and Juan looked up expectantly.

But Belinda ran to Mike, flung her arms around him, and they clung to each other. Travis even looked surprised. Juan's expression was beyond words.

Katie watched as Jenni walked up to Juan and put her hand lightly on his shoulder.

But there was no time to really understand what was going on, because the fort was victorious once more and cheers were going up. People came swarming over the bridge to climb down the ladders to greet their heroes. Travis accepted their hugs and handshakes, smacks on the back, and even a kiss on the cheek or two, before managing to make it up to Katie on the wall.

Grabbing her close, he kissed her lips lightly. "I'm not giving up, okay? I'm going to wait."

Katie was in tears as she nodded. "It may be a long time. Maybe not ever."

Travis laughed and smiled down at her. "I can wait. . . ."

The image of Lydia flickered in her mind's eye, and Katie closed her eyes and hugged Travis tight.

"I can wait, Katie," a voice said. She wasn't sure if it was Lydia's voice or Travis's but she knew she was afraid.

1.
Twists and Turns

Jenni tailed Juan through the throng of celebrants and up, out of the new entryway. Mike and a few other workers were busy finishing the job Jenni had begun, hacking off the limbs of the zombies who had managed to push an arm or a leg through the gate as it closed. Juan wasn't talking and Jenni knew why: Belinda. The unhappy expression on his face and his tightly clenched fists said it all. Jenni felt terrible that his heart was broken. Early in her marriage, she had come to love Lloyd. When she realized he was not her true love, it had devastated her. Losing the dream of love everlasting had been one of the worst experiences of her life.

"Juan?" She wasn't certain why she wanted to console him. Maybe it was because it seemed odd for him not to be jovial or making sarcastic comments.

"Loca, I'm not in the mood," Juan answered briskly.

"I was just going to say how sorry—"

Juan turned and pointed at her with a fierce look on his face. "Don't."

Jenni lowered her gaze. "Okay."

"Ed, did you see where the punk-ass kids went?" Juan inquired as the grizzled old farmer passed him.

Ed pointed over toward city hall. "Curtis has them over there."

"Thanks, man." Juan turned on the muddy, gory heels of his cowboy boots and headed straight for city hall.

"What are you going to do?" Jenni hurried after him, worried about his state of mind. He seemed so hurt and furious.

"Deal with business," Juan responded tersely.

Peggy and Curtis were near the back of city hall, talking to the two newcomers. Things already looked strained and heated when Juan marched right up to the young man and punched him square in his greasy face, knocking him down.

"Whoa, Juan!" Curtis grabbed Juan as Jenni quickly stepped forward, just in case the spaced-out-looking girl did anything. But she just stood there, looking mildly bemused, swaying back and forth.

The boy slowly rose up, glaring at Juan, and shouted, "That hurt!"

"You went into the fucking clinic!"

"Hey, we were in need of . . . medical treatment," the teenager said in a defiant tone. His eyes were so red, they looked as if their blood vessels had ruptured, and his skin looked clammy. Jenni grasped that she was looking at two very strung out young people who had probably gone to the clinic looking for their next high.

"Meth is not medicine, fucker," Juan spat furiously, trying to break Curtis's hold on him.

Peggy observed as she explained to Jenni, "You're looking at the local crystal meth dealer."

Jenni recognized that the situation was tense and that Curtis did not have it completely under control. "I think we need Bill, too."

Peggy assessed the scene unfolding before her, the flesh between her eyebrows puckering as she scowled. Curtis was nervous and close to his breaking point. "You're right," she said, and rushed off to find the older officer.

"Where's the rest of your posse, huh? Where are they?" Juan's voice was close to fury.

"Dead, dude. It was bad. Real bad," the boy answered.

The girl giggled.

Curtis pushed Juan behind him. "Ritchie, you went to the clinic for drugs, and your friends got eaten, huh?"

Ritchie shrugged. "Nah. It's not like that, man. We needed medicine. Carrie got bit and we needed medicine."

Everyone looked at the girl. She was staring at the outdoor lightbulb hanging over Curtis's head.

"Those things kept trying to get into the 7-Eleven we were shacking up in. It got real crazy."

"Which 7-Eleven?" Curtis raised an eyebrow.

"You know, the one over by the McGee place. There was a lot of those things there."

The girl giggled again, swaying on her feet, and covered her mouth with her fingers. Jenni saw the distinct bite visible on the girl's hand. It was swollen and pus-filled.

Jenni put her hand on Juan's arm, trying to calm him. "I think that girl is Carrie. We have a situation."

Juan shrugged free from her and was practically snarling when he said, "So, Ritchie, how did you get out? Where's Sergio?"

Ritchie rolled his eyes, laughing. "Well, we drew straws and someone lost and that someone had to run out the side door to draw them away. Luckily, it wasn't me being bait."

Juan looked ready to punch him again. "Was it Sergio? Did you make my cousin do it?"

Jenni kept an eye on the girl, her fingers stroking the butt of the revolver tucked into her belt even though she was out of bullets. She wondered if she could get to the ammo stores before the girl went zombie on them.

Ritchie squinted his eyes and appeared confused before answering, "No, no. It was . . . um . . . that Freddie guy."

Curtis was looking more pissed off than Jenni had ever seen him. "So you made one of your guys run out there so the rest of you could escape?"

"Yeah, pretty much. Then we got to the clinic, walked in, and things were fucked up there, too. That's where Sergio got it. That was fucking sick, dude. They just grabbed him and went at it!"

Jenni seized Juan's arm as his fist went sailing forward. The momentum of the thrust sent her tumbling into Ritchie. Jenni was grossed out by the sheer reek of the boy and scrambled quickly away as he fell flat on his ass. Juan lunged toward him, shouting angrily in Spanish. Jenni flung herself at Juan and he clutched her, probably so he could shove her aside.

"Loca, out of my way!" Juan yelled.

"It's not worth it!" Jenni shouted back.

"I'm gonna kill that sonofabitch!"

Curtis motioned to the boy to stay on the ground and away from Juan. "You need to calm down now, Juan," he said, not sounding all that calm himself.

"He killed my cousin! We all knew he was a good-for-nothing lowlife, corrupting the kids of this town with his homemade shit! Now he's gotten Sergio killed and you want me to fucking calm down?"

Jenni kept her hands pressed firmly to Juan's chest. "Juan, Juan, please."

"No, Jenni, he's a fucking murderer and we're letting him get away with it."

The girl threw up all over Jenni, then staggered back and fell against the wall.

Jenni cried out in disgust.

"Shit, that's gross," Ritchie decided.

Jenni was beyond grossed out. She yanked her blouse off and threw it away before it soaked through to her tank top. "Oh, shit! Gawd! Gross! Ugh!"

Juan's anger seemed to vanish in that instant. He yanked off his T-shirt and started to wipe the muck off her hair and face. "Man, Loca . . ."

Curtis looked down at the girl, who was now convulsing on the ground. "Shit." He drew his gun slowly. "Shit."

Jenni turned around just as the girl's eyes rolled back into her head. "I tried to tell you!"

Ritchie was on the ground, too, wasted and laughing. He reached out for his girlfriend.

"If she bites him . . . ," Curtis started.

"Fucking shoot her!" Jenni screamed at Curtis.

The girl's pupils abruptly came back into view, now glassy and dead. She opened her mouth and let out a growl that sent chills down Jenni's back.

"Shoot her!" she repeated.

Curtis hesitated.

Juan didn't. He took his good ol' boy shitkickers to the girl's head, heel first, and slammed her skull into the brick wall beside her. He kept kicking until her head was mush.

Curtis looked stunned. Jenni just lifted an eyebrow. Juan looked down at his bloodied boots and gore-splattered jeans before returning his gaze to Jenni. "C'mon, Loca. We need a shower."

Curtis finally moved and grabbed Ritchie. "I'm locking him up."

"Check him for bites, man," Juan said. He reached for Jenni and she took his hand.

Bill walked toward them, looking very cop-ish. "I'll help."

"I'm so sick of this shit," Juan grumbled.

Jenni walked after Juan, casting a look back at the two officers trying to deal with the stoned moron. The drug dealer was still giggling, his now very dead girlfriend slumped beside him.

"If we had let her bite him, we wouldn't have to deal with him," Curtis said to Bill.

Bill just shrugged. "Not for us to decide, Curtis."

"Yeah," Curtis reluctantly agreed. "Yeah. You're right."

Juan drew Jenni through the doorway into the narrow hall that led to the janitor's shower everyone in the fort used. It was in the back of the janitor's office. A clipboard hung from a rusty nail with a sign-in sheet attached to it. Billie Jo, an older woman

who had been rescued a few days before, was just exiting, wearing a bright blue bathrobe. Seeing them, she blushed deeply and hurried past. Waiting to go next was a man Jenni didn't know, but he saw their condition and didn't complain when Juan pushed past him and pulled Jenni into the janitor's office.

"I'm really sorry about your cousin," she said in a gentle, sympathetic tone.

Juan walked into the bathroom and turned on the shower. "It doesn't matter now."

"But he was your family."

"Yeah, and he's dead and that fucker Ritchie is still alive. There really isn't much justice in this world." He shoved her, completely clothed, under the water and got in with her.

Jenni tilted her head back to let the lukewarm water flow over her and rinse off all the disgusting vomit. The smell was making her eyes water and she just wanted to be clean. Juan took off his hat and tossed it to the floor. He leaned forward until his hands rested on the ugly green-tiled wall on either side of her and their foreheads touched.

"Loca, I'm losing it."

"No, you're not."

"Yes, I am. I can't do this."

"Do what?"

"Make it safe for all of us and keep my head together." Juan's voice was ragged, overwhelmed.

"You're doing a good job. The gate closed tonight when it needed to."

"But too slow. They almost got in. We can't afford fuck-ups. And all because of that fucker that got my cousin and his drugged-out buddies killed."

Jenni's clothes were soaked and the water was going cold. "We could throw him to the zombies."

"Don't tempt me. I might." Juan watched the blood and gore rinsing off his very beat-up boots. "Help me, Loca, okay?"

"Okay. But I'm not sure how."

"Let's get a bottle of tequila from storage and go up to the roof. I want to get fucking drunk. You were looking out for me out there, and I trust you to watch my back."

"Okay." Jenni ran a hand over her hair and found it to be muck free. She grabbed the almost empty bottle of shampoo, dumped some on her head, and scrubbed. "But I need clean hair first."

Juan pushed her hands away and lathered up her hair, making horns at one point, amusing himself.

Pleased, she smiled up at him. It felt good to have him back after his puppy-dog antics with Belinda. The librarian had annoyed her from day one, and Jenni was sure she wasn't good enough for Juan.

Rinsing off her hair, Juan covered her face with it. "You look better this way, Loca."

"I'm so gonna kick your ass."

Juan stepped out of the shower, rinsed off and looking a little better. The well-defined muscles beneath his undershirt rippled as he dried off his curly hair with a clean towel from a stack near the sink. Jenni swallowed hard as she finally embraced the truth about her feelings for him. Her hand shook at her side as she resisted the urge to reach out and touch his well-toned back. Glancing down at herself, she saw that her tank top was very wet, and not much was left to the imagination. She felt the sexual tension in the room explode, and nervously averted her gaze from Juan's admirable physique. Pushing her hair back from her face, she dared to look him in the face. He was staring at her.

Just like that, everything was very different between them. She could see it in his eyes as he slowly lowered the towel. He appeared as stunned as she felt. Crossing her arms over her breasts to hide her erect nipples, Jenni struggled to think of what to do or say. Licking her lips, she angled her hip to one side and took a deep breath.

"Wanna fuck?" Jenni asked flippantly, looking him straight in the eye.

"Later. After the tequila." Juan's gaze was appreciative, but he looked dazed.

"Okay. Meet you up there in twenty." Jenni flashed a smile, brushed past him, and escaped out of the room. She felt Juan watching her leave. Her body was singing with arousal and she took a deep breath, feeling something wonderful filling her. She hurried down the hall, casting an awkward look at the guy waiting for the shower.

As she walked, she heard him say to Juan, "If I had been in there with her, we wouldn't be out already."

"Was she always that hot?" Juan asked, bewildered.

"Pretty sure she was," was the answer.

Jenni grinned and ran up to her room.

· CHAPTER TWENTY ·

1.
Dead Man's Party

Jenni changed into a pale green tank top and jeans and ran up the stairs to the roof. To her surprise, there were quite a few people up there enjoying the evening, including her son, who sat in a small circle of preteens and teenagers. There were only five of them, two boys and three girls. For the first time in a long while, Jason was smiling. The ever-faithful Jack was at his side, smiling a doggy grin. The kids were drinking cola and listening to a CD player someone must have snagged on a supply run.

"Hey, Mom!" Jason scrabbled to his feet to give her a hug. "Is it cool if I camp out with the rest of the kids tonight?"

"Yeah, sure," she answered, and eyed the pretty brunette she had saved earlier that day. The girl's haunted eyes were less swollen and red. Jenni was glad to see she seemed comforted by the companionship of the other teens.

"We're trying to cheer up Michelle. Her mom and little sis got killed today," Jason explained.

"I totally get it," Jenni assured him. She was slowly starting to panic. What if Juan arrived while Jason was still standing there, beaming. Her son looked so happy; she didn't want his smile to disappear. Though Jason had never spoken to her about her being interested in someone new, she had seen the tightness around his lips and the narrowing of his eyes when she had been crushing on Travis. And now, much to her surprise, she was

about to try to move on with Juan. She knew Jason would not take it well.

Abruptly, Jason frowned and Jenni turned around, worriedly wondering how to make Juan recognize the need to be low-key.

Instead she saw it was Travis and Katie walking onto the roof. They were talking animately and not touching, but somehow looked intertwined. Jenni felt a pang of jealousy and pouted. She didn't care if Travis was in love with Katie, but Katie had to be close to her, not Travis.

Katie smiled at Jenni as she walked over to embrace her and kissed her cheek. Jenni clung to her and felt better. The world was so cruel right now; she did not want to lose anyone else dear to her.

"I heard what happened with those kids. Glad you're okay," Katie said, touching Jenni's damp hair.

"Juan took care of it. Kicked the shit out of her head."

"He's a good guy. Glad he had your back." Katie hooked her thumbs into her jeans pockets and let out a long breath. "Glad this day is over."

"Tell me about it." Jenni watched Jason rejoin his group of new friends and tried not to freak herself out. She had already made up her mind that she was going to get laid tonight, and she couldn't let herself be afraid of what Jason thought.

Travis set a huge pack of beer down on the roof as Mike and a few other workers emerged from the stairwell. Curtis came up last, holding candles in one arm and some bags of chips in the other.

"It's turning into a party." Jenni tried not to look uneasy. Her time alone with Juan and a bottle of tequila had evolved into something completely different.

"We need one after this day." Travis handed a beer to Katie and offered one to Jenni.

"No, thanks. I'm waiting for tequila." She tried to look nonchalant as she checked the arriving group of partygoers for Juan.

There was a flurry of activity as folding chairs and tables were

brought up. More people spilled onto the roof, conversing excitedly, shaking off the fear of the earlier attack. In the distance, the moans of the zombies still clawing at the gate could be heard.

Soon, candles were burning in little jars set up along the edges of the roof, and people were milling around, drinking beer and soda, talking, and relaxing. There was a sense of relief among them. Once more, disaster had been averted.

Jenni and Katie linked arms as they chatted, while Travis made the social rounds.

"You look sad," Jenni said after a few minutes.

"Overwhelmed, that's all. Tomorrow we're going to get ready to go into the hotel." Katie was very obviously trying not to look at Travis as she sipped her warming beer.

Jenni watched Travis try to engage Jason and his friends in conversation. Jason watched him with the scrutiny only a teenager could achieve.

"Uh-huh." Jenni instinctively knew more was going on. "Is your mood about him?"

Katie shrugged dismissively. "He's a friend."

"And?"

"Jenni, you know." Katie arched an eyebrow, her tone slightly disapproving.

Jenni rolled her eyes. "Look, I know you're into chicks, but maybe you could . . ." Jenni felt the full weight of Katie's objection to her train of thought bear down on her. "Okay, that was just dumb of me."

Katie forced a small smile and shrugged her shoulders slightly. "I just need time. Even if he were the hottest woman in the world, I wouldn't pursue. I need to deal in my own way. It's only been a few weeks, and though I was once nefarious in hopping from relationship to relationship, I need time."

"You miss her terribly, don't you?"

Katie let out a puff of breath as she looked down at her wedding ring. "More than I can bear at times."

Over Katie's shoulder, Jenni witnessed Juan literally trip

onto the rooftop. His boot had snagged on one of the electric cords being run up to power the stereo. Confusion in his gaze, he sought out Jenni. After spotting her, he wandered toward her, trying far too hard to look casual. In one hand, he held one of the biggest bottles of tequila Jenni had ever seen. In his other hand were two shot glasses.

Casting a wary glance at Jason, she saw him speaking to the new girl and not gazing in her direction. Tonight she just wanted to embrace life. She could talk to Jason about her need to move on once she knew for sure what was going on with her and Juan. Looking toward the well-built, fine-looking Mexican-American, she couldn't help but smile at the thought of what might happen.

Katie studied Jenni's suddenly flushed face and nervous body language, lifted both eyebrows, and said, "I thought you had a thing for Travis?"

Jenni flipped her drying hair back from her face and flashed a brilliant smile. "A girl can change her mind."

Katie chuckled. "God, I've been a fool."

"What do you mean?" Jenni looked at Juan coyly over one shoulder, signaling him with one finger to hold on.

"Nothing. Go have fun." Katie winked at Juan and playfully poked Jenni. "I won't wait up for you."

Jenni pulled Katie close and kissed her hard on the cheek. Letting free all her feminine wiles, Jenni tucked her hands into her jeans pockets and sauntered toward Juan. Jenni knew she was turning it on sufficiently when several guys turned to watch her strut by. Juan still looked a bit dazed, but he smiled when she drew near.

There are times in life when pretense is just bullshit and a waste of time. Juan and Jenni spent about ten minutes at the party before disappearing downstairs. Holding Juan's roughened hand in her own, Jenni dragged him down to the janitor's room. Grabbing the shower sign-in clipboard, she scribbled, OUT OF ORDER on it.

"Loca," Juan chuckled. "What are you up to?"

"Shut up," she ordered, shoving him into the room.

He barely managed to put the still closed bottle of tequila on the sink before Jenni was on him. She had already made up her mind that he was hers, at least for tonight, and she claimed him with burning kisses as she seductively wrapped herself around him.

"You're *loca,* Loca," he said with a satisfied grin as she pulled his clothes from his muscled body.

"Yeah, you keep saying that. It's about time you experienced it," she countered flirtatiously.

Fire and water, heat and passion, desperation, and perhaps something more fueled their lovemaking. Jenni felt no fear as only the second man she had ever been with lifted her into his arms, pressed her naked back against the cool shower tiles, and slid himself into her. She tangled her hands in his wet hair and kissed him deeply as the nightmare world they lived in faded to the dim edges of her reality. Only she and Juan existed. It was perfect.

Nudging Travis in the ribs, Katie watched Juan and Jenni exit the roof. They were sitting side by side at the edge of the roof, their legs dangling. Travis glanced at their departing friends and raised his eyebrows as he turned his attention to Katie.

"I've been really oblivious to some things, evidently," she confessed.

"Well, at least now I won't have to worry about you fixing me up with her." Taking a long swig of his beer, he smirked at her.

Katie elbowed him lightly and took another draft of her beer. The mood on the roof was surprisingly relaxed, considering that a small crowd of zombies was gathered outside of the gate. No one really wanted to deal with the undead tonight. People were tired of the zombies and tired of the siege. For a few weeks, they had been able to go out scrounging supplies

and rescuing survivors. During that time, they almost recaptured a sense of normality. Now the zombies were back, but the survivors still wanted to forget how trapped they truly were.

Katie observed Jason talking intently with the other teenagers and a few preteens. They were drinking soda and eating chips, and once in a while, Jason would laugh or smile. It was great to witness. It reassured Katie that he had not seen his stepmother disappear with Juan.

Travis rubbed the back of her neck with one hand and she looked over at him. He gave her that sad-eyed smile that made her heart ache for him. So she did the only thing she could think of—she crossed her eyes and stuck out her tongue.

Laughing, he drew his hand away and leaned toward her. "You know, it's little things like that which make me think there is so much more to you than meets the eye," Travis asserted.

"Oh, there is," she admitted, feeling a pang of guilt at her determination to make him think she was an unattainable lesbian. That she was drawn to him felt like an utter betrayal of Lydia. Trying to keep the mood light, she said, "I have all sorts of deep dark secrets."

"Ah, I see," he said, squinting at her. "You know, I don't believe you."

Katie giggled. "Seriously. I have secrets that would scandalize you. But that's okay. My life as a super-spy should be kept secret. I made James Bond look like a wuss."

"Well, then, I won't tell you that I'm a space alien," Travis said somberly, but with his eyes twinkling.

Katie smirked and clicked her bottle of beer against his. "You got a deal."

Curtis wandered over and looked at them uncomfortably. "Did you get an update on our newest addition?"

"Yeah, Bill said you had him locked up," Travis answered.

"Look, I know I'm not one to say what does or does not happen, but I think we should just put him out of his misery and dump him over the wall. Seriously, he's nothing but a piece of

white trash." Curtis looked more upset than Katie had ever seen him.

Travis stood, took Curtis's arm, leaned toward him, and said, "Curtis, this is something that we'll all have to discuss together. Seriously, in this world, I feel everyone has a chance, even the local crack dealer."

"Meth dealer," Curtis corrected.

Katie stood up as well. "But, Travis, at the same time, we need to make sure our safety isn't compromised by people who have no idea of how to work within a community."

Travis looked startled. "Talking like a prosecutor there, Katie?"

"Yeah, I am."

"A human being is a human being, Katie."

"Yes, but at the same time, what will this human being add to our community? If he sacrificed his friends to save his own life, then how do we know he won't do the same to us?" Katie lifted her eyebrows.

"That's bullshit, Katie. I'm sorry. They were all strung out and not in their right minds. Now he has a chance to do better. To be better." Travis put his hands on his hips and returned her gaze.

Curtis threw up his hands in disbelief. "Look, Travis, I have some serious concerns and I'm sure others do as well."

"Then we handle it as a group," Travis retorted immediately.

"Don't get defensive if we don't agree with your opinion, Travis." Katie set her hands on her hips and glowered at him.

"I just don't understand how you cannot see that everyone has a right to life," Travis protested.

Katie looked away from him, annoyed with his argument. Her gaze settled on the new lock area. There were at least four men up on the wall. From their gestures, they seemed to be shouting at the zombies. Katie noticed that one was even peeing on them.

"Travis, I think we may have other troubles," she said, and pointed.

"Ah, shit."

Katie watched as another man flung a beer bottle at the zombies. Maybe it was because she was now aware of the situation, but she could swear the zombies were getting louder.

"I'll get Bill. We'll take care of them," Curtis said gruffly, walking off.

Travis said, "I'm going to go get them down before one of them takes a header into the crowd."

"I'll come with you," Katie said, setting down her half-empty beer.

Travis headed for the stairs with Katie in his wake, her hands in her jacket pockets. As they passed the closed door to the tiny room she shared with Jenni and Jason, she smiled, realizing she and the boy were probably going to have to find somewhere else to sleep.

Out in the courtyard, there was more commotion. Ed was talking loudly to Mike, demanding that he shut up the men on the wall.

"They're going to bring the zombies down on us," Ed complained. "We won't even be able to get out of the gate once it's fixed if there's a whole lotta them out there!"

"We'll take care of it," Mike assured him. "We'll take care of it right now."

"Never ends, huh, Mike?" Travis said as Mike fell into step beside him.

"Nope. Never does. The older folks were already complaining about the party when those morons got up there and started whooping it up." Mike was obviously exasperated. "Damn fools."

A few more men, drunk and rowdy, had climbed onto the wall next to the gate, jostling each other, trying to get into position to either throw things down at the zombies or urinate on them.

"Let's get them," Travis said to Mike.

Curtis and Bill emerged from city hall and hurried toward the commotion.

"You guys need to get down." Travis was standing at the

bottom of the platform that served as the entrance to the lock area.

Shane, the redneck who had punched Katie, turned and laughed. "Ah, c'mon, they just stand there with their mouths open."

"You need to get down now, Shane," Mike said forcibly as he stood behind Travis, looking up at the rabble-rousers .

"Haven't you caused enough trouble?" Travis added.

"Look, Travis, I promised to behave if you let me out, and I ain't doing nothing wrong," Shane responded belligerently.

Next to him was his best buddy, Phil. "Yeah, Travis, they're just a bunch of dead dumb fucks."

The pounding on the wall was frantic.

"You're stirring them up. Come on down," Travis repeated.

Several of the obviously very drunk men laughed. Shane said, "C'mon, Travis. Stop being pussy-whipped by your lesbo girlfriend. Lighten up." He whipped out his cock and waggled it at Katie before turning, drinking a slug of beer, and urinating onto the zombies.

Katie turned away in disgust.

"Enough of that," Mike barked. "Do not make me go out there and get you!"

"C'mon, boys. Bring it back in," Bill said in a firm, authoritative voice. He was walking up with Curtis in tow.

"You ain't a cop no more. Back off," Phil snarled.

"Acutally, I am. Sworn in and everything." Showing his badge, Bill gestured for Mike to move aside and took a step onto the stairs.

Shane sneered at the badge. "Looks like a toy."

"This is going to turn dirty," Katie whispered to Travis.

"Shut up, lesbo bitch! Who asked you to fucking open your mouth?" Phil's voice was full of hate, and his gaze was hostile.

"Nah, Phil. Let her open her mouth. I got something right here for it," Shane stated, thrusting his cock at her.

"God." Katie averted her gaze, revolted.

Bill patted her shoulder. "We'll take care of this, Katie. Curtis and I are the law now. You go back to the party."

With a slight nod, Katie started walking slowly toward city hall. Hoping no one would notice, after a few steps she stopped and turned back to watch the confrontation unfold.

Curtis stepped around Travis and gestured, indicating he should step back. "Now, Shane and Philip, you need to stop being assholes and start obeying the laws of the fort. Shane, you agreed to abide by the rules when we let you out."

"I ain't done nothing but show that woman what's she's missing out on," Shane slurred.

"Get down right now. This has gone far enough," Bill said in a calm, deadly tone.

"She just needs to be shown a good time with a good man," Philip chortled.

Travis angrily took a step forward, but Bill caught his arm. "We got this, Travis. You go on back to the party."

Recognizing he needed to support the police officers' authority, Travis headed after Katie.

"She ain't gonna give you any, Travis. She's a waste of ass," Shane said mockingly.

"Fuck off, Shane," Travis snapped over his shoulder. He saw Katie in the shadows and shifted direction to join her. Unfortunately, that drew the attention of the men on the wall.

Shane continued to dance around, exposing himself. "She don't know what she's missin'!"

Travis swiveled on his heel, looking ready to go out onto the wall and punch Shane's lights out.

Katie grabbed his arm. "Let it go."

"Yeah, Travis, let it go. She don't want you. Maybe we should just bend her over and turn her back to the man side of the force," Phil said nastily. He began fumbling drunkenly with his zipper. He wobbled and went tumbling forward. He hit the

top of the wall sideways and started to roll off. Shane grabbed him.

"Oh, God," Katie murmured as Bill and Curtis rushed onto the narrow top of the wall to rescue Phil.

The zombie moans and screams grew louder and the banging on the gate was more energetic.

Bill and Curtis managed to get a grip on Phil. With the help of Shane and a few others, they succeeded in pulling Phil to safety. Mike stepped out onto the wall to herd the rest of the men back to the platform.

"Waiting for me, baby?" Shane sneered at her.

Katie had had enough. She turned and walked away. Without looking behind her, she knew Travis was following. He caught up to her and slid his arm around her shoulders. Looking up, she could see he was more upset than she was.

"Travis, I'm used to it."

"I'm not, and it was bullshit," Travis answered darkly.

"Let it go. It's not worth it. Lydia and I sometimes got comments like that. It's not uncommon. Some men are very intimidated by lesbians."

Travis turned her toward him, his hands on her shoulders. "Yeah, but I don't like it."

Katie tilted her head. "But they have a right to live here, too. And to be a part of this community."

"Don't twist my words back in on me," Travis growled.

"Look, we just have to deal, that's all," Katie answered, then yawned. "God, I'm tired. And I have a feeling I don't have a place to sleep. Maybe Peggy can put me up."

"No, come with me. Sleep with me."

"Travis?" She blinked in disbelief.

"I said sleep. I didn't say have sex, okay?"

Katie hesitated. "Okay."

Travis led her toward the beat-up portable building that was being used as a dorm. Having entered quietly, they walked past recently constructed doors and walls that formed tiny rooms.

Travis's office was at the end of the hall. It was crowded with a desk, light table, and file cabinets. Up against one wall was a sofa bed. The bedding was still rumpled from the night before, but Katie was too tired to care if it was freshly turned down or not. Sliding off her jacket, she flopped onto the thin mattress, boots and all, and stared up at the ceiling.

She felt exhausted, physically and emotionally. Shane and Phil had reminded her of all that she and Lydia had gone through together. Now she was dealing with it alone, and the ache inside her was intense.

Travis shed his own jacket and lay down next to her. "I'm sorry those guys are such shits."

"Not your fault. Just part of life." She closed her eyes and rolled onto her side.

She could sense Travis beside her and his great need to reach out and touch her. She ignored it and squeezed her eyes shut. Curling up, she felt the ache pulsating inside, eating at her.

"Fuck this," Travis whispered. Suddenly his arms were around her, dragging her deep into his embrace. He held her tenderly and she clutched his wrists with her hands. "I can't stand to see you in pain."

Turning her head, she opened her eyes and gazed at him gratefully. She knew she was a bullheaded Norsewoman, prone to moodiness and solitude, but he bulldozed her defenses and she needed that.

"You're a very good friend, you know that?"

"I'm trying," he answered, and snuggled against her.

She closed her eyes again and enjoyed his closeness. Her pain was fading, but she was too tired and stressed to think too deeply about what that meant. For once, she didn't want to think. She wanted to relax, to not care, just for a little bit.

Rolling over in his arms, she kissed his lips very softly. "Just for a moment," she whispered, her gaze searching out his.

Travis kissed her slowly and deeply. His hand rested tenderly on hers. Somehow knowing when the kiss had grown to be too

much for her to bear, he drew away and pressed his lips to her forehead. "Just for a moment," he said, closing his eyes.

Katie fell into a peaceful slumber.

2.
Dead Man's Party Ends

At last the party ended and people crept off to their beds, some so drunk, they barely found their way. Peggy hustled the kids down into the dining room to camp out after a few sprinkles of rain had fallen toward the end of the party. Silence descended except for the ceaseless moaning of the zombies.

A few hours later, a steady rain started and many of the guards rushed to get ponchos.

During the brief chaos, a heavily laden figure made its way to the roof of the city hall. Without a pause, it dropped its burden—a human body—over the edge. In utter silence, the person tumbled, arms and legs flailing, then landed with a painful thump.

Shambling zombies wandering along the walls soon found it, and a feast erupted in the street.

When the guard returned to his place, he noticed a heavily ravaged body standing in the street, swaying back and forth, its head turned upward.

Its mouth was taped shut.

It was Ritchie.

1.

Skin Against Skin

Skin against skin . . . breath consuming breath . . . limbs inter-twined . . . soft moans . . . gentle whispers . . . pleasure build-ing steadily . . .

Katie's hands slid over the broad shoulders of the man above her . . . her head tilted back . . . she sighed softly, rapturously.

"Travis . . ."

His mouth slid over hers in a soft kiss, and her fingers tangled in his hair.

Suddenly, something gripped her leg painfully. She opened her eyes to see Lydia, mangled, bloodied, and dead, leaning over them.

"How could you?" Lydia demanded in a raspy voice.

Then she lunged forward, bloodied teeth desperate for flesh.

Katie awoke and nearly fell off the bed in her haste to defend herself and Travis. Her heart was thundering in her chest and she pressed the flat of her hand against her breast, feeling the harsh beat beneath her fingers. Looking around, she realized the sun must be up, for a yellowish light was seeping in around the miniblinds.

Travis was nowhere to be seen. Katie felt panic billowing up in her.

Resting her feet against the floor, she sat up and leaned for-ward, taking deep breaths. Nothing had happened between

her and Travis except for their good night kiss, but she still felt agonizing guilt. Rubbing her face with her hands, she tried to scrub away the vision of Lydia lunging forward to bite into Travis.

Feeling like crying, she shakily stood up and grabbed the reverend's jacket. She slid it on and ran her hands over her hair. It felt tangled and crazed, so she pulled out the rubber band to let the curls fall around her face.

Travis entered, his expression grim and his gaze haunted. He saw her face, and his concern clearly showed as he moved toward her. "Katie . . ."

She took a deep breath. "I had a nightmare."

"Evidently. You look pale as a ghost." He touched her cheek sympathetically.

She had trouble looking him in the eye and he gently turned her face toward him.

When he saw the pain in her eyes, he gently lowered his hand. "Lydia?"

Nodding mutely, she fussed with her hair again, lowering her head so she wouldn't have to look at him.

"Katie, I know what is going on is confusing," he started.

"You're not the one betraying your wife. Your entire life. You're not living with the knowledge that your wife is one of those things now!"

Travis drew back, his expression tormented and sorrowful.

"I spent most of the last decade with an incredible woman who did nothing but love me unconditionally and believe in me. I loved—love—her with all my heart and it kills me that she is gone."

"I understand."

Katie tried hard not to cry, and vehemently shook her head. "No, you don't. You don't know what it is like to share your life with someone you love more than life itself and have people treat you like shit because of it. How you don't hold hands or kiss in public out of fear. Or the way it feels when you do finally

come out to a society that swings back and forth between wanting to see you fuck your wife or drive you out of the neighborhood. You don't understand. You can't."

Travis took hold of her wrist and drew her near. His voice was raw with emotion. "Don't tell me that I don't know what it's like to love someone. If you haven't figured it out, I love you. Maybe I'm a fool to believe you could love me back, but your kiss last night gave me hope. Lydia may have been your life before, but now she is your tormentor."

"Fuck you!" She jerked away from him.

"Katie, our old world is dead. Everything we were is dead. This is the new world. It's only been a few weeks, but it feels like that world was a lifetime ago, doesn't it? Who you are now is not who you were before."

Tears streamed down her face as she nodded mutely. That first day did seem like an eternity ago. Time seemed odd and cruel. Everyone seemed to be living at an accelerated pace.

"I feel lost without her. I miss her! Every day I miss her, and the only way I can deal with it is not to think about her." She gasped at her own words and covered her mouth with her fingers.

Travis's gaze warmed as he reached for her. "Katie, you're not doing anything wrong. Lydia loved you and you loved her. But you can't let that stop you from living."

She blinked the tears from her lashes and took a slow, stuttering breath. She shuddered at the impact of his words as he slipped his arms around her and held her gently. Laying her hands on his chest, she sighed. "I can't forget her."

"And you shouldn't," he assured her. He kissed her forehead and let her go.

She rubbed her face and smoothed her T-shirt as she tried to regain her composure. What Travis said had hit a harsh chord within her.

"You didn't come in here just to calm me down," she said after a beat.

"Yeah." He sighed. "We have a situation. It's not going to be pleasant. Someone threw Ritchie over the wall, bound and gagged."

Katie dropped her hands in shock. "What?"

"He's out there in the street, staring up at city hall. He's pretty much eaten away, but you can tell it's him."

"Oh, God, that's awful," Katie gasped.

"Yeah. I have to go find Juan. He's suspect number one, followed by Curtis."

Katie shook her head. "No, no, I don't believe either one of them would do that."

"Yeah, but Bill is investigating, so we need to find Juan." Travis's expression was grim.

"He's with Jenni," Katie said.

"That's why I thought you should come with me."

It was early morning and most people were having breakfast or still asleep. The sun was barely up and a thick mist, two feet deep, drifted over the ground. As they walked, Katie saw absolute devastation written on Travis's features. He was taking a lot of hard knocks, and she knew she was part of that situation.

She was struggling hard against her internal turmoil. Never had she felt so conflicted. Well, actually, she had, back in high school when she came out as a staunch lesbian and endured much vilification at the hands of her former friends. Cheerleaders were not gay. Then, in her senior year, she and her girlfriend had broken up and Katie had unexpectedly fallen in love with a boy. It was a huge relief to her parents and friends, but it had thrown her a little.

Still, she embraced her boyfriend with the same love and passion she had given her girlfriend. When he started pushing her to have sex with another girl and let him watch, she had ended their relationship. He had been pleasant enough, but she despised him for trying to use her sexuality for his pleasure.

With both a boyfriend and a girlfriend behind her, Katie had

felt secure in the knowledge that she could love a person for who they were. The series of girlfriends and boyfriends that followed had thrown her family and upset her mother. Some in the lesbian community thought she was a lesbian in denial or just confused. The straight community often wanted to portray her as promiscuous. More than one guy she had dated expressed delight at the thought of threesomes, only to have her apartment door shut on him for good. There were good boyfriends who had not worked out. There were good girlfriends who had not worked out.

And then there was Lydia.

Katie was jarred out of her thoughts by Travis suddenly jolting to one side as someone passed them. He looked shaken and took a breath.

"Waking nightmare?"

"Yeah. I wish they would go away. I'm afraid one day I'm going to shoot someone, thinking they are one of those things or not shoot a zombie, thinking I'm imagining it."

Katie rested her hand on his shoulder. "We're both pretty screwed up, huh?"

Travis laughed bitterly. "Who isn't?"

Upon entering city hall, they hurried up to Katie and Jenni's room. The door was closed. Katie tapped lightly on it.

"Uh . . ." Jenni's voice, sounding wide awake.

"Jenni, it's me."

"Okay, come in."

Katie opened the door. Jenni was sitting on her cot in a red tank top and shorts. Juan was lying down behind her with his hands behind his neck. Jenni was eating a small fruit cup and looked flushed and rather happy. Juan was wearing only his jeans and looking equally happy.

"Hi," Jenni said with a giggle.

Juan noticed Travis's expression and sat up quickly, his smile gone. "What's wrong?"

"Someone gagged Ritchie and tossed him over the wall."

"Who?"

"No one knows, but you're a suspect. So is Curtis."

"I was with Jenni," Juan said.

"Obviously," Katie said with a slight smile.

"He was. All night. We barely slept," Jenni said, spooning up more fruit.

Travis blushed slightly. "Okay, so he has an alibi, but Bill will want to talk to you both, anyway."

Jenni stood up and waved her plastic spoon at Travis. "How could anyone think that Juan would do something like that?"

"Because he tried his best to take Ritchie out last night," Travis answered pointedly.

Jenni sighed. "True."

Juan pulled on his boots and reached for his shirt. "Fine, I'll go defend myself. But this is bullshit. What's Bill going to do to whoever got rid of that piece of shit?"

Travis lifted his shoulders in a shrug. "I have no clue. Hell, how do we handle a murder? Or any crime?"

"Shane got off with a promise to behave," Jenni groused. "He should have gone over the wall right away."

"I almost agree with you," Travis mumbled, flicking his gaze toward Katie.

Juan tugged on his shirt. "Travis, you know I would not do this."

"I know that. And I know you were here with Jenni. I don't think anything will come of it."

"Yeah, well, you try to be a Hispanic male in a white society and see if you feel comfortable with that answer," Juan said. He pushed past Travis and Katie, his face set and eyes blazing. "Where is Bill?"

"On the roof," Travis answered.

Jenni grabbed Katie's hand as they moved up the stairs and leaned toward her. "Are you okay?"

Katie smiled at her slightly. "Nightmares."

"Lydia?"

Katie nodded.

Jenni sighed and rubbed Katie's back with one hand as they walked. "I really didn't sleep."

"Yeah, I figured that out," Katie said smirk.

Jenni giggled, then grew serious as they heard Curtis's voice from above.

"Yeah, I said to put him out of his misery and chuck him over!" Curtis was shouting at Bill.

"So you wanted Ritchie dead."

"Because he's a threat, Bill. Or he was." Curtis looked fiercely upset as they walked onto the roof.

Nearby, Jimmy, one of the construction workers, was keeping watch on the street below. He said, "I was gone for maybe ten minutes. I helped the kids move their stuff downstairs, then grabbed a poncho and headed back up here. Whoever it was moved fast."

"The door to Ritchie's cell is easily unlocked from outside. It's just a dead bolt. Anyone could have done it," Juan said as he joined Bill and Curtis.

"Juan was with me last night," Jenni said quickly, her hand grabbing his. "All night."

Bill blinked and looked back and forth between them. "Okay, but I still need to question you."

Katie strolled over to look down at the lone figure standing in the street staring up at them. The duct tape had survived the feeding, as had part of the teenager's T-shirt. Much of him had been stripped almost to the bone, but some of his long pony-tail, with its skull and crossbones clasp, remained. He moaned when he saw Katie and reached one skeletal hand out to her, staggering forward slightly.

The questions continued behind her. Katie wondered why Ritchie stood there, alone, while the rest of the zombies banged away on the gate.

With a squeal of tires, a big red Ram 1500 4x4 came roaring around the corner and slammed into Ritchie. The boy's head

splattered against the grille, and his body flew across the street as the truck came to a screeching stop. There was a moment of hesitation; then the truck charged forward.

"Ralph and Nerit are here!" Katie called to Travis, who ran forward to see.

They both watched the truck speed down the street and slam into another wandering, slow-moving zombie. The truck swung around and came to a stop.

Jimmy lifted his binoculars and peered through them. "I only see a woman, and she looks pissed."

"Nerit," Katie whispered.

The truck turned and made a run for the gate.

2.
Death by Red Truck

The truck vanished as it raced around the block toward the gate and the mob of zombies desperate to gain entry to the fort.

Katie ran along the rooftop, finding a better position to watch from just as the red truck slammed into the outer fringe of zombies, wiping out a slew of them in one fell swoop. The truck came to a hard stop right before the entrance, then backed up, drawing the surviving zombies away from the gate. Nerit drove slowly backward, allowing the zombies to nearly catch up before she hit the accelerator and the truck lurched out of their grasp. The truck reversed up the road quite some distance, and Katie had a good idea of what would come next.

As she expected, the red pickup charged forward and slammed into crowd of the dead. Zombies flew in every direction, bodies bursting apart, pieces of bodies flying across the street.

"Shit," was all Travis could manage.

The truck backed up slowly again. The few still-staggering zombies tried to follow. Nerit waited until they were within a few feet, then sent the truck surging forward and knocked them

flat. Then she reversed and ran over the bodies. Then she drove forward again. The zombies were crushed beneath the tires. The red truck drove slowly up the carnage-covered road and idled outside the gate.

Travis drew his walkie-talkie from where he kept it on his belt. "Open the gate. It's clear now."

Juan stared at the dead bodies and the gore-splattered pickup. "Wow."

Katie and Jenni headed for the stairs. They both knew something was horribly wrong.

Juan looked at Travis and said again, "Wow."

Travis smiled slightly. "Tough women are sexy, huh?"

"Shit. I think I want to marry her."

3.
Nerit's Story

Travis ran behind Jenni and Katie, who were hurrying at top speed down the stairs, out the back door, across the site, up onto the platform, across the bridge, and down the ladder into the new entry: it was a mad dash the whole way.

The gates opened and the red truck slowly slipped through. Armed guards stood ready to make sure no zombies got in, but Nerit had cleared the street. The truck's deer guard was slathered in blood and gore, and the tires left grimy reddish black smears on the pavement.

As they waited for Nerit, Travis studied Katie. Her expression was desperate, sad, fearful, and wary. Though he could see her outward strength, Travis feared that her internal fortitude was failing. What was happening or not happening between them seemed minor compared to the haunted look in her eyes.

Jenni clung to Katie's hand, appearing scared. Her long black hair caught the morning breeze and streamed behind her. She really was lovely and he was glad Juan had found comfort with

her. Belinda was just bad news for him. She had been his eternal crush, and Travis watched Juan be lured in only to get spurned yet again.

Travis was mad for Katie. Never had he been in love with any woman as he was with her. He did not want to cause her any more pain than she was in, but he'd had to tell her how he felt.

Now, looking at Nerit's expression as she climbed out of her truck, followed by her dog and clutching her sniper rifle in one hand, Travis could see just how devastating love could be. Nerit looked pale; her eyes were red and swollen. She held out her arms to the young women, who rushed immediately to her comfort her. Safe in their embrace, she let out a soft whimper and Travis' heart broke.

Nerit didn't have to say a word. Ralph was gone.

"This isn't good, is it?" Juan asked from behind Travis.

"No, it's not."

Thirty minutes later, Nerit sat in the council room, a hot cup of coffee in one hand and a freshly lit cigarette smoldering in the other. Juan had given her a pack from his sacred stash.

Travis sat across from her while Jenni and Katie flanked her. Nerit looked calm, yet her hands were shaking.

"It happened yesterday," she started, then took a long drag on her smoke. "I was bored. I had read all the books in our home, so I went across the street to the grocery store. I thought I'd grab some paperbacks and magazines." She rubbed her weary eyes. "Ralph was on the roof, working on our new garden. It felt safe, but I still had my rifle, you know?"

Katie nodded. "I know. We can't take chances."

"No, no, we can't." Nerit tilted her head, concentrating on some point in the past. "So, I'm looking through the paperback rack and I hear a noise outside. There's a van with four men getting out of it in front of the store. One of the men told Ralph to open the door. Ralph says not until he knows that none of them has been bitten. So one of these men . . ." Nerit

faltered, her eyes lowering as she took a deep breath. "One of them shot Ralph."

"Shit," Juan hissed.

Jenni bowed her head, and Katie took Nerit's hand.

Nerit gripped Katie's hand so tightly, Travis could see that her knuckles were white. "Then they started trying to break in. They broke the windows but couldn't get past the bars. That building is old and strong. I went up to the roof of the grocery store. . . ." Nerit fell silent as she gathered her strength.

Travis shifted in his chair, picturing the scene clearly in his mind. Nerit, the former Israeli sniper, calmly getting into position; the men below, oblivious.

"I could see Ralph slumped over, and there was so much blood. I . . . was going to shoot . . . make the bastards pay . . . when another man came out of the back of the van, dragging a naked woman by her hair. She was bound and gagged. She was struggling, and the man was laughing. It was horrible. Horrible." Taking a long drag on her cigarette, Nerit paused, clearly trying to keep control of her emotions.

Travis stood up and moved to the window. He had a feeling the story was only going to get worse, and the pain emanating out of Nerit reminded him far too much of the pain he felt flowing out of Katie at times.

Juan sat down next to Jenni and put an arm around her shoulders. She leaned into him, weeping, overwhelmed by grief.

"He kept kicking the girl, and I was going to start with him when I saw the girl's face. It was . . . wild . . . dead . . . hungry. He said, 'I told you she was bit,' and kept kicking her. Her thighs were raw and covered in blood. Her breasts bruised and cut. To me, it looked like they raped her until she was dead. But she was alive again, as alive as those things are.

"So I knew then what to do." Nerit took a long slow pull off her cigarette, and her eyes became cool, calm, and dangerous. "I shot off her bonds. I took some flesh with them, but she was already dead. Those idiots were making so much noise, they

never heard. I watched her get up. I watched her get her revenge on the one who had been kicking her. The other men panicked, and some shot at her." Nerit paused and smiled. "I shot the weapons out of their hands and let her have them. All of them. And when they rose, I put them down, one by one. And at the end, I gave that poor girl her peace."

They were speechless. What could they say? Travis was at an utter loss. What Nerit had seen and experienced was beyond anything he had encountered. He felt sick to his stomach.

"I went home. Ralph was alive, just barely. He was shot in the gut. I got him downstairs and laid him on the bed and gave him morphine. I sat with him and held his hand until the end." Tears streamed down her face, but her expression was stoic. "I sat with my revolver against his temple and waited. But after his last breath, he didn't stir again. I covered his body with a blanket and closed the door."

"Why didn't you call us?" Katie asked.

"What if those men had friends out there listening? I didn't dare. I just packed up as much as I could and the dog and I started out this morning once I was sure there were no more bandits lurking around my town." Nerit stubbed out her cigarette and sighed. "I did not want to lead them here."

"We need to double the guards," Travis said urgently.

"We need to finish the gates," Juan said, standing up. "We can't take any risks if we have more to worry about than just zombies."

Jenni peered up at them, tears streaming down her face. "If they'd just shoot an old man without a second thought, what would they do to us?"

Katie had her arms around Nerit, comforting her. "We need to make sure we are ready for them if they do show up."

Travis laid a gentle hand on Nerit's shoulder. "I'm sorry, Nerit. I liked Ralph."

Nerit smiled at him slightly. "And he liked you. But he did teach us one final important lesson."

"What's that?"

"It's the bite that brings them back. We have nothing to fear from those who die naturally." Nerit rubbed the bridge of her nose with her fingers. "And for that, I am grateful."

· EPILOGUE ·

The reality of the new world, in all its brutal and violent glory, had enveloped the fort. A murder had been committed by one of their own, and despite Bill's rigorous investigation, the murderer had not been found.

There was some relief when it was announced that a normal death did not bring about a zombie birth, since there was a small aged population in the fort, and no one wanted to have to kill Old Man Watson or any of the others if they rose again.

Juan and Travis worked tirelessly on the gates, taking only brief breaks to sleep or eat. Travis redesigned the gate system, and the construction crews not only fixed the first gate but soon erected the second gate in addition. Incorporating the old newspaper building into the fort, they soon had a working garage. Unfortunately, the building had sat derelict for a long time. To clean it out and make it habitable would take weeks, maybe months.

They needed the hotel.

Nerit found a place for herself in the fort relatively quickly. She, Katie, Jenni, and other volunteers built a gated entrance that would open to the hotel. Nerit seemed energized by the work. Her dog, Tucker, had bonded with Jack, and the two animals could often be seen near the womens' worksite, watching everything with great interest.

Jason gave up his bed to Nerit and moved into a room with another teenage boy. Jack went with him.

Katie knew that Jenni regularly sneaked out of their room to be with Juan and was happy that her friend had found some happiness in this dead and rotting world. She continued to struggle with the ghost of Lydia, feeling guilt for any ounce of happiness she found. The only way to stop the guilt was to limit her time with Travis, which hurt both of them. But what else could she do?

The winds shifted, and April gave birth to May. The world grew hotter and fiercer. The bluebonnets faded away to tall grasses, and the spring showers gave way to long hot days. Despite all they had endured, they all sensed the one unavoidable truth none wanted to speak of.

The worst was yet to come. . . .

AUTHOR'S NOTE

The First Days was inspired by a brief image that flashed in my mind one day when I was at work. I saw a young woman with black hair clad in a pink bathrobe standing on the front steps of her home, staring downward. I wondered what she was looking at with such a horrified expression. Then suddenly I saw those tiny fingers pressed under the door.

It was a terrifying image, and I couldn't wait to write about the woman and her zombified child. When I had my break, I immediately wrote down what I thought was a short story and posted it online. The response from the readers was quite overwhelming. In fact, quite a few contacted me to ask, "Where is the rest of it?"

I considered the question and realized there was so much more to the story. So I began to write. . . .

The First Days: As the World Dies was written in bits and pieces as I traveled far and wide across the Great State of Texas for my job as a governmental consultant. The people and the towns I visited inspired me as I wrote about the fort tucked away in the Texas Hill Country. Writers are often advised to write about what they know and love. Well, I know Texans and I love the zombie genre.

At night, I sat in my hotel room and wrote out the mini-chapters for the nearly daily installments online. Typing away

on the laptop, I never imagined how popular this story would become. Even though the online version was very rough and not edited, the readership grew. Many fans took the time to write and let me know how much they were enjoying the story.

As both minor and major characters fell to the zombie hordes, I found out just how beloved the fort inhabitants had become as mournful messages poured into my inbox from emotional readers. A few lobbied to keep their favorites alive. Of course, I couldn't pay attention. This is a zombie story, after all. Some people live. Some people die. That's the way it has to be.

When the story was done, the outpouring of support and affection for it was almost overwhelming. There was an almost unanimous cry of "This needs to be published!"

At that time, the zombie genre was in its infancy and had yet to take full hold of the public imagination. After a year of dead ends at attempting to find an agent and publisher, my husband urged me to self-publish the story. Day after day, fans were sending me e-mails asking when the published version would be available. Encouraged by the fan base and my husband, I decided to self-publish. Utilizing the amazing skills of our friends, we worked to release a revised version of the story that had appeared online.

My mother, Connie Frater, and a friend, Michelle Downey, both worked to make the story flow better, while Detra created the original cover for *The First Days*. Hoping for the best, I released the first version in August 2008.

Within a year's time, I had two offers from publishers to reissue *The First Days* and its two sequels and an offer to option the story for film. At the urging of other authors and my entertainment lawyer (who would negotiate the TV and film rights), I started to look again for an agent.

Happily, I was blessed that Hannah Brown Gordon of the Foundry Literary + Media agency loved my story and believed that she could find the best publisher for it.

And she was right!

In March 2010, I got "the call" every author dreams about. I could barely talk when Hannah told me that Tor wanted to publish my zombie novels. It would take weeks for the shock to wear off and the reality to settle in that my zombie story about two women fleeing into the Texas Hill Country would be published by Tor.

If not for the encouragement of all the original readers, I would not have the pleasure of seeing my work published by my dream publisher. I am eternally grateful to those first die-hard fans who pushed me and believed in me.

Thank you. . . .